SPANIA

PAULA CONSTANT

FEHU PRESS

For Dr Som Ling Leung
My dearest friend

NOTE FROM THE AUTHOR

Spain in the late 7th and early 8th centuries had been united under the Visigothic crown for almost a full hundred years, a fact I have come to realise is not widely known. The term "Mater Spania", or 'mother Spain', was a colloquial expression during Visigothic rule that referred not only to the physical country, but to the idea of nationhood.

I refer to the Imperial armies often as 'the Greeks', despite the fact that they were part of the Eastern Roman Empire. This is to reflect the language used by Spaniards themselves in primary sources at the time.

Paula Constant

LÆLIA

FEBRUARY, AD 693

Illiberis, Spania
Granada, Spain

During the years Theo had been absent from her life, Lælia had, many times, imagined the manner of their reunion. Sometimes she had dared envision herself, fresh from the bathhouse and scented with rose and almond, wearing a fine gown, her hair unbound. She had imagined what she might say, and Theo's surprise at learning she could speak, when he had only ever known her silent and gesturing her words. Such imaginings had been rare pleasures she had offered herself only sparingly. There had been no certainty he would return. She had not dared overindulge in such dreams for fear they might somehow curse the future.

Nonetheless, Lælia had dreamed.

Never once, however, had she dreamed that her powers of speech would abruptly desert her. Nor that rather than taking Theo's proffered hand, she would scramble inelegantly to her feet and simply stare at him. And certainly not that, having barely managed to give the order to free Oppa and watched him ride, dark faced and furious, from the Illiberis courtyard, she would simply turn and walk away from Theo and the group of men surrounding him, feeling the brilliant green eyes that had haunted her for the past five years sear her back as she went.

She stood in the dim light of the stables, her head bent against the comforting warmth of the black horse. She had brought the twin animals, black horse and white mare, down from the low pasture by the mountains long before the battle for Illiberis began. Having them close was her way of having Theo beside her as she faced battle. The black horse had long been her link to Theo. From the day they had sat together in this stable and pulled forth the twin foals from her mother's mare, Lælia knew a part of both her and Theo had lived inside the two animals, the black colt and white filly. Many nights she had whispered her secrets to the colt and imagined it was Theo's soul she saw in its bottomless topaz eyes, his ears that heard her confessions.

Lælia stroked a trembling hand along the horse's back. Now Theo was here, in Illiberis. She could tell him anything she wished. But she was not out in the courtyard in command of her men, as she had so assuredly been these months past. She was not standing boldly at the head of an army, nor, conversely, was she dressed in a fine gown. Theo had come across her bloodied and dishevelled, covered in dirt from Oppa throwing her to the ground.

But she had not required Theo to save her.

For that, at least, Lælia thought fiercely, she was grateful. Even if she had fled barely moments after Oppa himself had.

Even if she hadn't heard his footsteps, the horse's tension would have told her who it was that approached. The colt quivered under her hand, snorting softly, turning to look through the door where the last of the daylight glowed umber over the mountains. A large shadow fell upon the straw, and Lælia felt Theo behind her.

"You're riding Titus." She was proud her voice was steady,

even as she silently berated herself for such an inane beginning. Her hands gripped the horse's mane so tightly the wiry strands cut into the skin.

"*Ja*." His low voice sent a shiver of reminiscence down her spine. "Titus has saved my life more than once since I left Illiberis. I promised him once that I would one day bring him home. When I encountered him again, in Septem, it seemed right that we should return together."

"I am glad."

Don't be a coward. Lælia forced her hands to release their grip on the black mane. *You must face him eventually.* Her limbs feeling thick and clumsy, she turned slowly around.

Theo was silhouetted in the doorway. *He is big,* Lælia thought. Broader and harder than the young man who had once stood in exactly the place he did now. His face was indiscernible against the dying light behind him, so Lælia did not know how to interpret his sharp intake of breath as she turned and a final ray of sunlight lit her own.

"I named them," she said, her voice slightly unsteady. "The foals. I named the colt Ares." She touched the white mare on her other side. "The filly I called Pallas."

"They are fine names." Theo stepped forward tentatively then stopped, as if unsure of his reception.

"I thought naming him for the god of war might lend you Ares's strength in your battles." She felt her face burn and shrugged one shoulder. "I know it is fanciful."

"No." Theo's response came swift and clear. He stepped forward again, his hand touching Ares's shoulder behind her, so Lælia had the warm strength of the horse at her back and the broad wall of Theo before her, so close she could smell the leather and sea salt of his travels. "I dreamed of them." His voice was slightly rough, his eyes roaming over her face in the fading light. "The foals. I saw them, sometimes. In my dreams."

"They, too." More than anything, Lælia wanted to touch him. To know, after the long day of blood and death, that he was truly here. He was barely a forearm distant and yet she could not force her own hand to rise and breach the gulf. Lælia swallowed. She had been speaking of the horses, she remembered, her thoughts seeming to have scattered on the growing chill air. "There were times I knew you were… in pain. I could see it, in Ares. He knew them, your struggles." She forced herself to meet his eyes and felt a shock go through her at the depth and intensity she saw there. "We fought for you," she whispered.

His mouth twisted at the edge in the half smile that had haunted her dreams for so long. "Mane magic," he murmured. "Your grandmother's old ways."

Mention of Acantha broke through the rich spell as painfully as a sword cut. Abruptly Lælia spun away from him, her hand going out to the wall to steady herself. There was so much to be done. Her grandmother – and Theo's brother, Alaric. She winced. How was it that she had fled from Theo without so much as telling him of his brother's death? Shame and pain tumbled into the stables in equal measure, and they were no longer alone but surrounded by the burden of the day's death, the myriad of things that must be attended to.

"Your brother." When Lælia turned, she was no longer a girl quivering at the proximity of a man. She was the Lady of Illiberis, who barely hours earlier had commanded men to their deaths.

The same Lady who had put an arrow through her own grandmother and watched her fall.

She pushed the memory of Acantha's face from her mind. "Alaric is dead." Lælia forced her voice to remain steady, her eyes to hold Theo's as she said the words. He flinched slightly at his brother's name, his eyes narrowing. For the first time since his arrival, Lælia truly saw the deep, savage scars that crossed his face, polished ravines that whorled and distorted his skin. "Alaric rode here after Toletum fell. He came to take me away, to Septem. But we had already mounted our defence – and then he learned that Rekiberga, his betrothed, had not yet arrived, despite the men he had sent to find her." She paused but Theo did not speak, just watched her silently, waiting. "We were atop the hillfort when Alaric saw Rekiberga coming across the valley, barely ahead of Giscila's army. Alaric rode out to meet her. To see her safely inside the gates."

"And did he?" Theo's words rasped like an old key in the lock. "Is Rekiberga safe?"

"He saved her, yes. But then Oppa's men took her. Rekiberga is alive, but she is miles distant by now. And in Oppa's custody."

"I will get her back." Theo's hand clenched in the horse's mane just as Lælia's had earlier. The horse nudged his shoulder, but Theo, Lælia knew, did not feel it. He was staring over Lælia's shoulder, into the past he had shared with his brother, and to the reunion he had missed by less than a day. "Where is he?" Theo's eyes settled back onto her face. "Where is my brother's body?"

"I sent men of the tribes to recover him, and the others of ours who fell." Lælia swallowed hard, pushing the memory of her grandmother from her mind. Acantha was one, amongst many. "I am going to ride there now," she said quietly. "We could ride together, if you wish it."

"I do." Theo stepped away from the black horse, his mouth a hard line. "I do wish it." He nodded at the horses. "I will help you saddle them."

"No." Lælia shook her head. "They are not yet broken to rein." She didn't want to admit that she had secretly hoped that breaking the horses would be something they would one day do together, that doing it alone had felt in some strange way like a betrayal of the bond they shared. But in the uncanny manner he had always possessed, of understanding what Lælia did not say, Theo nodded.

"I'm glad," he said simply. Lælia began to walk past him and he caught her arm. She found herself barely able to breathe. Jadis, the mountain cat she had raised from a kitten, growled low in her throat beside Lælia. Theo glanced curiously at the cat but didn't comment. Lælia put a hand on Jadis's head, and Jadis calmed under her touch, her golden eyes watching Theo warily. "Acantha," he said quietly. "She, too, died in the battle?"

Pain twisted her voice to a hard, rough rasp. "I killed her myself." Lælia met his eyes. "Acantha rode to take Giscila's life, but her act of revenge also saved a life: Rekiberga's. She knew she rode to her death. I did what she would have done for me."

A strange expression passed Theo's eyes, like a shadow over water, and Lælia felt as if he were standing beside her on the hillfort as she drew the bow and let the arrow fly, that he stood with her as she watched Acantha fall. "So it is done, then," Theo said. "Our revenge. Giscila paid, in the end. For the lives he took from us both."

Lælia nodded, somehow not surprised that he knew of Giscila's role in the Summer of Blood that had taken her parents, and his mother, and too tired to wonder how he had learned of it.

"Then they both died well." Theo nodded slowly. "My blood, and yours."

"Yes." He released her arm, and Lælia felt oddly bereft. "They died well." She moved past him, and they stepped into the dusk, walking slowly toward the villa, where men milled about in the edgy, uncertain aftermath of what they all knew was a temporary victory.

Theo turned to her as they approached the horses. "Would you like to ride Titus?"

"No." Lælia scratched the big bay gelding's nose affectionately and he whickered in recognition. "He is yours now. I'm riding Hermes." She nodded at the stallion that was usually reserved for breeding only. "It seemed fitting."

A very large, heavily bearded man with hands like meat hooks snorted audibly from close by. "Horses, they speak of. Five years the *schnecke* waits to see his bride, and now it is horses." He shook his head and rolled his eyes at the even larger, pitch-black man beside him. "For this, we cross a sea?"

The black man grinned widely, his white teeth gleaming in the gathering dusk. "You crossed a sea because we promised you a chance to wet your steel on Oppa's blood, *wenkai.*"

"A promise that once again you do not keep, *brudder minus.*" The bearded man glared at Theo. "Why did we let the bastard go, *schnecke*? Finally we have a chance to put steel through the swine, and you let him ride away. So far, I am not liking this country of yours, Spaniard."

"Lælia." Theo nodded at the two men. "These are my friends. Leofric" – he nodded at the bearded man – "and Silas." The black man bore wicked scars along each side of his face, and he wore two lethal, curved swords at either side. But his smile was wide and open, and his tone was deep and resonant when he returned Lælia's greeting. The other man, Leofric, gave Lælia a smile almost hidden by his beard, with a gruff nod that she suspected might well be the limit of his emotional expression.

"We are riding to the hillfort." Theo mounted his horse and turned to the men, so Lælia did not see his face when he said quietly, "My brother fell in the battle. He lies on the ground there."

Neither of his companions answered that, but as Lælia mounted Hermes she saw Silas grasp Theo's shoulder in one large hand, so firmly Theo's whole body swayed in the saddle, and Leofric wordlessly pass him a silver flask. When Theo took a deep swallow of whatever was inside it and handed the flask back, Leofric raised it in salute and drank deeply, then passed it to Silas, who did the same. For Lælia, who had lived so much of her life in silence, their conversation was as eloquent as any spoken words. Briefly she felt a stab of something almost like envy. Theo may have lost a brother, but he had these men at either side, as close to him as any blood would ever be. The thought made her feel oddly lonely. Part of her wanted to turn to Theo and his companions for advice, counsel. To ask the questions that haunted her in the after-math of battle. Questions about whether Theo intended to help her fight for Illiberis. If he thought she *should* fight, even though such a question would have been unthinkable to her even days ago. The truth was, Lælia didn't know how best to save Illiberis, nor what course of action she should take. And watching Theo with his men was a heartbreaking reminder of how very alone she was, now that there was neither Acantha nor Paulus left to consult.

But Illiberis was her responsibility. Whatever might lie between her and Theo, it was as yet far too unknown to burden with such questions. A brief memory of Dahiya's face crossed her mind. Dahiya, she knew, would never allow another to carry the burden of her decisions. It was a reminder to Lælia that she, and she alone, was mistress of both her own destiny, and that of Illiberis.

She pushed her momentary weakness aside with hard discipline.

It was grief, she knew.

Turning her horse, she led the way from the courtyard, riding into the blood-soaked night.

* * *

TORCHES BURNED at the gates of the hillfort, and men lay moaning on the ground before them. Most were men of Giscila's army who had not been able to flee with their comrades. Barely a handful of Dahiya's desert Riders, who had made up the bulk of Lælia's army, had been killed, the others bearing only superficial wounds. Giscila had led Oppa's army into an ambush that had killed most and seen the few survivors flee into the mountains. Most would never emerge from those passes. The mountain tribesmen did not take kindly to strangers invading their lands. They favoured death by stealth and would even now be stalking those who thought to escape.

8

Lælia watched Theo slowly dismount beside Alaric's prone body. Teudolfo, Alaric's longtime companion, had laid his corpse on linen away from the others. He sat beside it, head bowed in grief, looking up as Theo came slowly to stand at his brother's side. For a moment Teudolfo stared at him blankly, without recognition; then he leaped to his feet and pulled Theo into a hard, wordless embrace that made Lælia's throat catch.

"*Dauhter.*" Tosius, the small tribesman who was never far from Lælia's side, emerged from the darkness. "I have your grandmother." He tilted his head behind him, to a figure on the ground around which several tribeswomen stood. Lælia glanced at Theo, standing with his men over his brother's body. *He must grieve,* she thought. *As must I.*

She walked through the men of Illiberis, murmuring instructions to Gratimo, the head of her grandfather's *thiufa,* comforting a wife here, a mother there. She paused when she came to Zdan, the chief of the desert Riders. He greeted her with a hand over his heart and formal words, in the manner of desert men. She returned his greeting. "Your men fought as Imazighen," she said. "They honoured Dahiya and the Jerawa."

Zdan shrugged off the compliment in the manner of his people. "Those we fought were not men." He bared his teeth in a grim smile. "We barely tasted blood." His eyes travelled to Acantha's body, behind Lælia. "You go, now, to be with your dead?"

"Yes." Lælia nodded. "I will take her to the caves, as you do your own." Zdan tilted his head in approval, and Lælia went to her grandmother's body.

Tosius helped her fix Acantha to her grandmother's horse, who stood patiently and bore the lifeless weight with stoic acceptance, as if knowing the gravity of its cargo. "I must go alone," Lælia said quietly, and Tosius nodded.

"We will stay close, *dauhter.*" He touched his lips and brow as he bowed to Acantha's still form. As Lælia rode away, she heard the tribespeople begin to sing their song for the dead, a song she knew they sang for Acantha as much as their own. Lælia rode into the night, Jadis running silently at her side. The cat had disappeared in the moments after Theo's arrival, slinking off and watching warily from a distance. She had prowled into the stables when he dared approach her mistress, watching Theo with gleaming, suspicious eyes. Now, as they rode into the mountains along the familiar paths, the cat's tension was gone for the first time since his arrival. It was not Theo himself, Lælia knew, that Jadis reacted to, but Lælia's own emotions. The cat sensed her jittery tension and had rapidly deduced that it existed in relation to the tall, white-haired stranger. Jadis had yet to decide if Theo was friend or foe.

Lælia was aware of Tosius close by. He would no sooner allow her to ride unaccompanied into the mountains so soon after the battle than he would take a knife to her himself. But he knew her too well to interfere or force his presence upon her. Laying Acantha to her rest was something Lælia had to do herself, and alone. Tosius, she knew, respected that.

The cave was near the abbey in which Acantha had spent much of her life, high on a ridge. A flat table of rock jutted out from the cliff. As they looked up it, Jadis's nostrils flared in warning. The cat stopped, low to the ground, her tail straight out behind her, growling a warning.

"Yes." Lælia rode on, speaking aloud to the cat. "It is the place I found you, when you were a kitten. The place your mother led me to. Acantha found me here, that night. Beneath the waning moon of the scorpion. She understood this place, and the sacrifice your mother made that you might live. Now Acantha herself is dead in sacrifice. It is fitting she should lie here, in what was once the den of a warrior she respected."

By the running stream beneath the ridge, Lælia unwrapped her grandmother's body and washed it in the manner of the tribes, singing softly as she worked. From nearby the women of the tribes joined her song, honouring the woman they had looked to as their own, as they did her successor's right to perform the burial ritual alone. The moon bathed her grandmother's body in a pale, pearlescent glow that felt to Lælia as if the great Mother herself wended into Acantha's shroud, wrapping the long limbs in an eternal moonlit embrace. The thought gave Lælia comfort. She placed flowers over Acantha's heart, and river pebbles over her eyes to ensure they stayed closed to this mortal world and opened again in the afterlife. Then she closed the linen over the body, raised it to the horse once again, and walked up the trail to the cliff.

On the rock ledge beyond the entrance, she laid the body down and sang as the moon reached its zenith. Lælia sang the songs of the tribes, of the women who had walked Illiberis before she or Acantha were born, and whose blood ran still in Lælia's veins as it had in her grandmother's before her. She sang in honour of the stern, austere woman who had lost all her children to the sword, and who had then been teacher, mentor, parent, and guide for the only grandchild that remained to her. She sang for the Lady of Illiberis who had defied a world of men to carve her own path, honouring the traditions of her ancestors in defiance of the priests in their brown cloth and the superstitious fear of their followers. Her song came back to her from the wilderness around, carried by the tribeswomen who remained close by and echoed by the rocks and earth of the land Acantha had nourished.

As she sang, it seemed that the land beat beneath her with a steady pulse, drawing her into it even as the last of her grandmother's spirit flew into the next world. As she sang Acantha into the wind and the stars above, Lælia knew she also sang herself into the earth in her place, binding herself to root and stream even as she freed her grandmother from those same earthly responsibilities.

Lælia sang until the moon began to sink behind the trees, and then she gently carried her grandmother deep into the fissure of the rock, past the tiny bones of the kittens that had died the night Jadis was found, to the cavern beyond. Here a slight depression in the rock made a natural cavity, just long and tall enough for her to lay her grandmother's body. From high above, a sliver of moonlight shone through a tiny opening in the rock, lighting the old ochre paintings on the wall. One of them was of a horse, barely more than a shadow of colour on the rock.

Lælia bowed to it. She took a last look at Acantha's shrouded figure. Here her grandmother would lie for eternity, her bones at rest inside the earth to which her spirit had remained loyal to the end. When Lælia turned from this place, that loyalty would be hers to carry, and to honour. No longer could she look to others to shoulder the weight of her heritage, nor to guide her path. She drew a deep breath and stepped away.

Outside, she rolled a heavy rock in place, sealing the cave closed. From the many nights long ago when she had tracked Jadis's mother, she knew the cave was almost impossible to find. Now none would see it, even if they did come this way.

Lælia touched her fingers to her lips, and then to the cold stone, closing the door upon her childhood.

Then the Lady of Illiberis turned and walked away, toward the land that was now hers, and the uncertain path of her future.

2

OPPA

FEBRUARY, AD 693

Illiberis - Corduba
Road between Granada and Cordoba

Oppa rode ahead of his men. None had dared approach him since his humiliating defeat at the hands of Lælia of Illiberis, barely fifty miles behind them. Oppa had ridden hard to put distance between himself and the recollection of her rapt expression when she had seen Theudemir of Aurariola atop his horse before her. The years apart, it seemed, had served only to increase their bond. *Savour it whilst you may,* Oppa thought savagely, spurring his horse hard along the road at the memory of the glittering triumph in Theo's eyes. The Illiberis victory, Oppa consoled himself, would be short-lived. Spania was once again held by Oppa's father, King Egica. Retribution against those who had defied Egica in this rebellion, Oppa knew, would be swift and merciless. He smiled grimly and touched the leather-wrapped parchment he had carried from the wreckage of Sebastopolis. It bore Theo's own signature and was both the key to his and

Lælia's salvation, and the instrument that Oppa would use to destroy their seemingly unbreakable bond.

After Theo's father had joined Sunifred's doomed rebellion, their family lands in Aurariola were forfeit to the Crown. If Theo's father and brother were not already dead, they soon would be. The fact that Theo himself had been abroad serving in the imperial fleet, the *Karabisianoi*, throughout the entirety of Spania's civil war would not, Oppa knew, prevent Egica holding him to ruthless account for his family's treason.

Yes, thought Oppa, *it is well indeed that I planned beyond the steaming morass of Sebastopolis and foresaw precisely this scenario.* Oppa had known that if Theo escaped the imperial defeat at the hands of the Arabs, he would run to Illiberis and Lælia at the first opportunity. Oppa had hurried back at speed, and now here they were, both returned to Spania – but the balance of the scales in which their respective fortunes had been held these past five years was irrevocably changed. Theo was no longer the son of an honoured nobleman, with the might of the imperial fleet at his command. He was the son of a condemned traitor, betrothed to the daughter of another, returning from a bitter defeat at Arabic hands to face a hostile king. And Oppa was no longer a powerless king's bastard but a man of considerable fortune, with an army of his own and influence that extended into the darkest corners of Church and court. He had already taken over his mother's riverside brothel and sent his own people to make it into the kind of exclusive debauch he had become adept at managing in foreign lands. Oppa had become wise in the acquisition of secrets. And after seeing the might of the Arabic army first-hand at Sebastopolis, Oppa knew Spania itself would soon face a reckoning it was entirely unprepared for. Now was the time for building secrets into networks, and the networks into a power base that would see him at the forefront of whatever future Spania faced. Oppa did not intend to take a petty revenge on Theudemir of Aurariola. His ambitions reached far beyond that.

No. Oppa's hands clenched reflexively on the reins and his horse tossed its head, snorting at the sudden tension. What Oppa intended was at once far darker and more practical. He intended to put Theo in a harness no less restrictive than the bit between his horse's teeth. One that would bind Theo to him forever, whilst also making the best use of the man's undeniable talents. For no matter how he might loathe Theudemir of Aurariola, Oppa was also too astute to ignore the man's value. Theo was a man other men followed. He was a skilled warrior and diplomat. He had close ties to the highest levels of the Greek military. Most importantly, he knew how to run a fleet. And whatever the future brought to Spania's shores, Oppa was certain of one thing: it would come across the seas. Which meant he needed to control them.

Far better than destroying Theo would be to save him, and in doing so, bind him so tight the man had barely room to breathe. It was a bind that would have the added satisfaction of driving an ugly and irreversible knife into the hearts of both Theo and Lælia of Illiberis. One that could not be removed, a weeping sore that would slowly corrode from within, ultimately destroying the one thing that had sustained them both through the long, hard years of separation: their loyalty to one another.

Oppa again touched the parchment tucked inside his tunic.

It was an agreement that, after the fact of Theo's marriage to Lælia, traded his portion of Illiberis for Aurariola. A document witnessed by priests and signed by Theudemir himself, done when Theo had thought Oppa his ally. A document every bit as powerful as the army of barbarians Lælia of Illiberis had wielded, with devastating effect, against Oppa's own. It did not grant Oppa Illiberis in entirety – that would take the goodwill of the king and an official agreement. Its true power was mental and emotional. Theo's willingness to trade his wife's inheritance without her consent was a weapon. One that Oppa intended to use.

The fact that Oppa had just ridden from the humiliation of Illiberis with his life was a demonstration of the power inherent in that secret signature. Even now, after all that had gone between them, Theo understood that he might well need Oppa as his ally. Else he would never have allowed that Illiberis witch to set him free.

His horse, sensing Oppa's sudden surge of fury, tossed its head again. Oppa forced his anger under control with the discipline of long practice. He would not dwell on Illiberis. He had learned long ago to see the victory where other men saw defeat, to find gold where others saw only ruin. Oppa had learned at an early age that the destruction of most men lay in their hopes and expectations. Take those away, and men of honour were lost, tossing their dice in the air in a search for either divine explanation for their sorrows, or a savage and immediate revenge. But those who sought power rather than honour did not allow themselves to be governed by emotional impulse, nor the toss of the dice. The gaining of power was, rather, a long, strategic game of Tabula, in which each person was merely a chequer to be moved, each conflict a gambit. In the game of power, Oppa had long learned, there existed no such thing as defeat. One merely wiped the board clean, reassembled the chequers, and devised a new strategy. To many, the Spania to which Oppa had returned, in the aftermath of a bloody civil war and surrounded by covetous enemies, could be perceived as a smoking ruin.

Oppa, however, saw only chequers and a fresh board.

He had taken great pains in the alliances he had forged with Arabic forces. It was a delicate process. An ally placed too close was a dangerous play; one too distant, a powerless one. Oppa had chosen his man carefully. One close to the caliph, but far enough from the action at Sebastopolis that their association could not easily be discovered. Abd al Aziz was the uncle of the current caliph, Abd al Malik. Far more importantly, in Oppa's eyes, Abd al Aziz was the governor of Egypt. For now, that mattered little. In time, however, Oppa knew, it might well matter a great deal. Abd al Aziz would be the key player in any potential march upon Spania's shores. Thus it was to Abd al Aziz whom Oppa's spies had whispered snippets of information that helped shape the caliph's own plans, granting Abd al Aziz even higher esteem with the caliph; in turn, it was the governor's ships and men that had carried Oppa to safety in Carthage. With a little trade thrown in, it had been a profitable alliance for both parties thus far, and the governor, Oppa felt, would prove an important, if long-term, piece on the board.

Several of the other, closer pieces were even now due to be recalled to Toletum. As soon as he had finished tightening his hold on Theudemir of Aurariola, Oppa intended to make the acquaintance of Wittiza, his younger brother and Egica's legitimate heir. The fact that Theo's sister Egilona was even now at Tui with Wittiza was an added bonus, one that would only serve to increase Oppa's power. Roderic, the son of Theodofred, Duke of Corduba, was with them also, along with his cousin, Pelayo. All three children were now the descendants of traitors. They were also intimately related to either Theo or Lælia. They had been Wittiza's closest companions for some years now. Hidden away in the back-water of Tui, high on the north-western coast of Spania, was the future court of the country itself. Those particular chequers were ones Oppa intended to make his own. His father would not live forever. The sooner Wittiza's succession was publicly affirmed, the more secure Oppa's future would be. And when Wittiza came into his crown, it was Oppa who would stand behind it. Older brother, trusted friend, wise counsellor – and holder of a purse Wittiza would not be in any position to disdain. Whether Wittiza ruled Spania as an entirety or was forced to part with some of it to Arabic forces, Oppa intended to ensure it was he who made his brother's decisions.

No, Oppa's time as a powerless bastard was certainly over. And any resentment he might once have held about his birth was long gone. Oppa did not aspire to sit beneath the votive crown. Crowns, his family history had taught him, could easily be taken, the heads beneath them gone with their shining surface. Oppa liked his head firmly fixed upon his shoulders, able to turn in the direction of the most favourable wind. His father's ambitions, once so lofty to his boyish eyes, seemed now inconsequential to the man returned from imperial wars. Oppa no longer thought only of Spania's future. He thought of continents and national alliances, of emperors and caliphs – and of how best he might position himself to serve either, or indeed both.

He no longer sought to humiliate Theudemir of Aurariola simply for his own enjoyment – or rather, he mentally amended, not *solely* for that purpose. If Oppa had read the game right, and he rather thought he had, Spania would soon have a new regime. Whether the head beneath the crown was Arabic or Visigothic, Oppa intended to be not only the power inside that head, but in possession of as many pieces of the game as possible. That meant controlling both land and the men who might be considered leaders of that land.

Theudemir of Aurariola was a valuable piece.

Betrothed to another valuable piece.

Oppa's hands clenched involuntarily on the reins. His idea of conquering Theo and his betrothed by force had failed. Now, the game would change. He would own them in his own way: by pulling the strings of their existence. With secrets, games, coin, and paper. It had been stupid, Oppa could admit, privately at least, to resort to the crudity of battle. Such things were the provenance of stupider men. It had been a moment of weakness, a shadow from the boyhood during which he had still thought prestige came at the end of a sword. The man he had become favoured more elegant solutions – and more permanent ones.

A memory scratched at the edges of his mind, a voice that, despite his best efforts, still sent a chill down his spine with the memory it brought, of being helpless and facing his own imminent death. A voice that no amount of whores or wine had managed to drown. The calm, cultured voice of Yosef, the exiled Jew, saying: *You know nothing of the wisdom before your own time. Know nothing of learning, or knowledge, or beauty; value nothing more than the petty strength of your own arm...*

Shivering, Oppa collected the reins and spurred his horse onward. Time had taught him that revenge was, indeed, a dish best served cold. He had learned how to wait. The Jew would pay, and when he did, his payment would be a hundredfold the weight of his insult.

Oppa Egicason, king's bastard, rode the back roads toward the recently humbled city of Corduba, planning his long game.

Theudemir of Aurariola would come north eventually, Lælia and the Jew with him.

He, Oppa, would be waiting when they did – and the game would begin anew.

3

THEO

FEBRUARY, AD 693

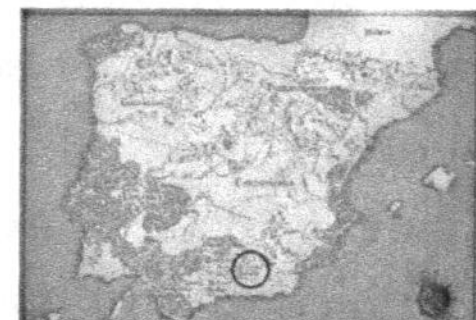

Illiberal, Spania
Granada, Spain

Theo stood vigil over his brother's body in the stone church at Illiberis for the duration of the long, cold night.

Teudolfo had helped wrap Alaric's battered remains and bear them down the steep hill and over the rushing water to the church. As they rode, he had told Theo the brief, hard news of Toletum's fall.

His father, Theo knew, was dead. Had he survived there would have been word to Illiberis, a messenger. After so many years apart, to have arrived so soon after the deaths of both his father and brother seemed to Theo the cruellest of ironies. The vigil he stood in the church was not for God, his brother's soul, nor any sense of duty.

Theo stood with his eyes hard open throughout the long night to honour the boys they had been, and the father who had raised them to men. He stood to remember a world he had thought worth fighting for, the nation of his ancestor

Geila and the sons of Chindasuinth, a world of honourable men who had dreamed of a nation of laws and prosperity. In the torn, bloodstained body of his brother, now cleaned and wrapped in a linen shroud, Theo saw not only the end of the fiery young man who had fought fiercely for that same dream, but the end of the dream itself. Alaric, he thought bitterly, in many ways had been the best of Suinthila's sons. He had loved Spania, and all that the Goths had made there. He was born to walk alongside their ancestors and wield steel as they had done, for their women, their land, and what was right. He had fought tyranny to the last – and lost.

Athanagild, Theo's other brother, still lived. Teudolfo said he had risen high in the Church. There was something in the way he said it, a certain respect, that gave Theo the impression Athanagild had grown into a man of considerable presence. *I still have a brother,* Theo reminded himself. Not for the first time, he felt deeply grateful their father had raised them to be such, even though they were brothers by marriage rather than blood. *And a sister,* Theo thought, thinking of the tiny blonde child he had left so long ago. Teudolfo knew only that Egilona had been taken hostage during the rebellion. She had been sent away with the king's own son Wittiza, Roderic, the son of the disgraced Duke of Corduba, and another rebel lord's son, Pelayo. Teudolfo didn't know where they had gone. Nor did he have word of Elsuith, Theo's stepmother. Given that it seemed Oppa's army had landed on the coast somewhere near Aurariola, Theo privately doubted his stepmother still lived. Or if she did, she was in Oppa's power now.

The parchment Oppa carried haunted Theo's thoughts as much as Lælia's face. He was still uncertain he had done the right thing in allowing Oppa to live. Not that it had been entirely his choice.

"Let him go," Lælia had said scornfully when Theo had looked to her for a decision. "Illiberis defended itself against a barbarian attack. I will not win today only to be condemned for the treasonous murder of the king's son."

Under any other circumstances, Theo would have argued for taking him captive. Without Oppa, he knew, they had no leverage at court. Killing him might indeed be unwise. Exposing his treachery, however, would have at least given them something with which to negotiate.

But he had not argued.

Instead, he had stood silently by and watched Oppa ride away, carrying the one document that would now, Theo knew, decide both his and Lælia's future.

What could I have done? he thought, for the hundredth time since he had watched Oppa go. Was he to meet Lælia again after so many years, only to lose her in the same moment by telling her of the deal he had once made with Oppa to trade her inheritance for his own? Perhaps she would have listened. But the truth, Theo knew in his own heart, was that he was not prepared to risk the other outcome: that she would turn away from him forever. Nor, if he was honest, could he bear to share the delicate stage of their reunion with Oppa's insidious presence.

For it mattered not, Theo knew, if he bitterly regretted the moment of weakness in which he had stooped to signing his name to that parchment; nor if Oppa had manipulated him into doing so. Signing away Illiberis was the one act, he felt, that Lælia could never truly forgive – and particularly not today, of all days. She had just lost her last living relative and good men of her own household to defend Illiberis. She had done it knowing she might die, had mounted a sophisticated and well-thought-out defence, in which she had fought at the forefront. His own brother, Theo thought bitterly, had died in that defence, and for the woman he loved.

Whilst he, Theo, had signed a paper betraying all that for which Alaric had so bravely died, and had then arrived too late to do anything but bury his brother's body.

Theo's hand tightened on the hilt of his sword, his teeth so tightly clenched his jaw ached. Silas and Leofric were outside the churchyard. Teudolfo had remained. He stood as silently as Theo himself, no more than a few feet away, his grief a palpable force. He had been as much a brother to Alaric as Theo himself. More, perhaps, for they had been brothers in war, and Theo knew well the bonds such experiences made in a man.

Despite the melancholy of his vigil, part of Theo wished the night might never end. When dawn came, he knew, he would have to face conversations and decisions he had no idea how to manage. The Riders were already restless. They had fought the battle they came for. They waited now for the order to sail home, back to the sands and their beloved Dahiya. Once gone, Illiberis would be largely undefended. The military strategist in Theo wondered if Lælia had truly considered what might come after the battle to save her home. Her disdainful dismissal of Oppa suggested she thought she might yet have a voice at court, rather than understanding what Theo saw as the truth: that her grandfather's actions had already condemned her as a traitor. Illiberis was lost, whether she had won the battle or not. Somehow Theo suspected Lælia had yet to face that reality, though he knew she soon must.

Lælia.

Theo's every muscle tensed, a rush of heat followed by a chill of shock at the recollection of her nearness. At times over the years, Theo had wondered if time would have changed her, altered the deep bond between them that had sustained him through the hard years of slavery and war. It had taken less than one glimpse of her to know not only was the bond still there, but it was also deeper and more fascinating than he had remembered in even his most private dreams. Theo wanted Lælia with a fierce, visceral ache. A force licked between them, an intangible pull that he found as disturbing as he did fascinating. He was aware of her every movement, alert to the slightest shift of her eyes. Nothing of what she had become surprised him. That she could contrive such a plan for Illiberis's defence, and command men as she had, seemed to him no less than he had always known her capable of. Her speech, too – somehow her voice sounded just as it had in his dreams. Her spoken words were as natural to him as her gestures had been, and just as sparing. Lælia's speech revealed no more of her inner heart than her gestures ever had. She was as hidden and unknown to him as she had ever been, and yet an even more magnetic force than he recalled. Theo had no more idea how to broach the topic of their future with her than he did how to manage the implications of his return.

After so long dreaming of his homecoming, now that it was here, Theo was as lost as he had ever been on a foreign shore.

He stood over his brother's body and prayed to the God who had seen him safe in chains and on battlefields. He prayed for Alaric and for his fallen father, wishing bitterly that he had been granted a chance to ask, one last time, for their counsel. He prayed for Athanagild and for Egilona, feeling the responsibility for their futures settle upon his own, inadequate shoulders.

As the silent darkness grew to a grainy pale dawn, Theudemir of Aurariola stared at the iron cross over the altar and asked in vain the question he knew God would never answer: what should he do now?

* * *

THEY BURIED Alaric in the graveyard on the edge of Illiberis, face to the east that he might see the second coming of Xristus. Into the crude wooden coffin Alaric was laid with his sword and a coin of Geila at his neck, that his ancestor might lie with him. "It was your father's final gift to him," Teudolfo told Theo soberly. "Alaric gave his own coin to Rekiberga, as his promise."

Just as I once sent mine to Lælia. Theo hoped his promise would have a happier ending.

Only men were buried in coffins, to separate them from

24

the earth. Women returned to the ground, that they might nurture it. Theo found himself oddly comforted by the thought that Alaric's body was contained, even if only by thin wooden walls. Seeing him safely into the earth was one thing Theo could control.

When he turned to walk from the graveyard, he found Silas's reassuring figure standing at the gate.

"Your brother fights now on the field of his ancestors," Silas said by way of greeting.

Theo nodded, accepting his condolences. "Do we have news of Garnata?"

"It held." Silas met his eyes. "But it will not do so for long, I suspect. Leofric rode last night to meet with your Jew and discover how it stands." He glanced sideways at Theo. "What of Lælia? What does she plan?"

"I don't know." Theo stopped by the low stone wall overlooking the road and leaned on it, staring down at the people milling about below, carrying the dead and wounded to rest, clearing away the chaos of war. "She let Oppa go." He kicked the stone wall. "And before you say it, Silas, I know I should have stopped her and kept that bastard here, where I could watch him."

Silas maintained a diplomatic silence that nonetheless spoke volumes.

"Oppa is evil," Theo went on slowly. "If we held him, I would have had no choice but to tell her of the deal I made with him, and the parchment he holds. He would have found a way to do it if I did not. And Xristus knows I cannot bear to admit to either." His mouth hardened. "But I will have to tell her, and soon. Else whatever we may have will be built upon a lie."

"What you *may* have?" Silas looked at him quizzically. "Are you not certain of her heart, then, *wenkai*?"

"She has been in the desert with Dahiya. She designed and mounted the defence of Illiberis. And if I understand matters correctly, she has more than once defied both Oppa and his father, the king, in the Toletum court." Theo clasped his hands tightly on the stone wall and stared grimly beyond it, seeing nothing of the people there. "She has no need for me, Silas, and when she knows what passed between Oppa and me she is likely to have no wish for me, either."

Silas lifted one shoulder. "Then perhaps now is not the time for such discussions, *wenkai*."

"What?" Theo twisted his head to frown at his companion. "You are ever an advocate for truth. Now you would have me lie to her?"

"Not lie." Silas's white teeth gleamed as his lips parted in a slow smile. "But perhaps, *wenkai*, you might like to discover what lies between you before you take a hammer to it, no?"

"What is it you are taking a hammer to, African?" They both turned to where Leofric was approaching. "Since landing in your country, we have yet to so much as draw steel," Leofric went on. "You promised us a war, *schnecke*. But instead we come to find your bride has fought it already."

He guffawed, and even Silas grinned, though his eyes on Theo were kindly.

"I would not so quickly assume Lælia is still my bride," said Theo dryly. "She certainly needs no help from me to hold her lands."

"Not your bride?" Leofric rolled his eyes. "Are you blind as well as stupid, *schnecke*? Do you not see the way the girl looks at you?" He snorted. "The only question you should be asking is how quickly you might find yourself a priest. *Not your bride!* Pah!" He shook his head and elbowed Silas. "Speak sense to this one. Five years the only thing he talks about is this girl, and now we are here he is green as a new recruit."

Silas opened his mouth to reply then closed it as Zdan, Gratimo, and Teudolfo came toward them.

"Theo." Teudolfo was pale and strained, the grief of Alaric's death still written on his face. "We wished to speak before Lælia's return."

Theo was about to say that he did not speak for Lælia,

then he caught sight of Silas's warning eyes and thought better of it, switching instead to his natural role of commander. "What are your concerns?"

It was Gratimo who answered. "Lælia contrived a strategic defence. None here would say otherwise. Illiberis would have been lost had it not been for her planning. I am the first to say I did not think she could do it, and the first to admit I was wrong." There was a quiet murmur of agreement amongst the others present. "But a battle is not a war," Gratimo went on. "And Egica will not long allow a prize such as Illiberis to remain in the hands of traitors – or the descendants of traitors." Gratimo paused. His words, Theo knew, were a warning intended not only for Lælia, but for himself, also. "Zdan and his men need to return to the desert. If they linger long enough for Egica's forces to reach us, their lives will be spent in chains. And there is not enough left of the Illiberis thiufa to hold against the most meagre attack – even with you, and your men, to aid us." Gratimo nodded respectfully at Leofric and Silas, who didn't argue.

"You want me to tell her she is beaten," Theo said flatly. Gratimo lifted his shoulders silently. Theo looked around at the other faces watching him expectantly, waiting for his judgement. He felt once again the weight of new responsibilities falling upon his shoulders. It was different, he thought, to commanding men in the emperor's fleet, where his responsibility was to the man beside him and the commander he followed. Here, in his homeland, it was his lands, his heritage, and those of the people he loved, that were at stake. Theo knew that until this moment, faced by men who instinctively placed their fates in his hands, he had not known the meaning of true command. It felt heavy indeed.

"We can take the girl and turn back across the seas, *wenkai*." Silas spoke directly to him. "Regroup, return with greater forces."

Gratimo's face darkened. "If he flees, they will both be considered exiled traitors."

"And what of the Jew?" Leofric spat on the ground and eyed Theo. "I left him in Garnata, talking to that rabble of merchants who fancy themselves a Jewish army." His rolled eyes left nobody in any doubt of his opinion of Garnata's defenders. "Does he, too, plan to ride to Toletum and meet this king of yours?"

"I imagine he will stay for a time, at least. Discover how far along the Jewish rebellion is, here."

"Rebels! Ha!" Leofric snorted. "Fools, the both of you. Ilyan's court has good wine and beautiful women. But always you will ride away from such things, *schnecke*."

"You said you wanted a war." Theo smiled grimly. "If we ride north, we will find one, one way or another."

Leofric snorted, but he didn't argue.

Theo saw Lælia's slender form on the mountain track behind the church and instinctively tensed. "I will talk with Lælia." He cast a warning look over the group. "Until I do, mind your own counsel. We will talk again, soon enough."

They nodded and dispersed, all except Silas, who stood at Theo's side as the lone rider approached. He found himself reluctant to hasten the conversation he knew must be had. "She will be keen to meet Yosef," he said to Silas. "I will find him, and give them a chance to talk, before I speak with her."

"Wait." Silas looked at him in surprise. "You don't want to speak with her now?"

"No." Theo spoke slowly, his eyes not leaving Lælia as she came toward them up the road. "No, Silas. Let her have this, the moment of triumph amongst her people and of welcoming Yosef home, before I must say words that will cast her victory into the dust."

4

YOSEF

FEBRUARY, AD 693

Garnata, Illiberis, Spania
Granada, Spain

"We must build on this victory." Hasdai's family had once owned many of the flax fields that now belonged to the Illiberis *latifundium*. Despite his reduced circumstances, Hasdai's manner of address retained a certain natural authority. He was an impressive man, standing nearly six feet tall, with strong, hawkish features and deep brown eyes currently gleaming with purpose. "With Illiberis and Garnata standing firm, others will follow. And Ilyan will send aid."

"If Ilyan plans to help us," said another voice, this one older and more weary, "then why has he not done so already?"

"What do you call the desert Riders, if not support?" countered Hasdai.

"The Riders came for the Lady of Illiberis," said the old man tiredly. "Not for us." He shook his head. "And we never spoke of outright rebellion, Hasdai. We fight for our right to practise our faith, and to trade, not for power itself. Conquest has never been our way."

Hasdai's chin jutted forth stubbornly. "Perhaps it is time we changed that."

The old man made a dismissive noise. His pale-blue eyes, red-rimmed and rheumy with age and exhaustion, slid to where Yosef stood quietly to one side, in the corner of what had once been his father's study. "What say you, Yosef ben Arun?"

As all eyes swivelled to him, Yosef felt the unwelcome weight of their collective expectation settle across his shoulders. "I think," he said slowly, "that any decisions must wait until we have spoken with the Lady of Illiberis and gained a full understanding of our position."

"And I say that our position is clear, and our time is now!" Hasdai pounded Arun's desk. Yosef suppressed an involuntary wince at such brute force in what had always been a peaceful, studious space. He supposed he should be grateful the house had been left empty. It was a mark of respect, he knew, for the man his father had been, rather than any consideration for Yosef's possible return. Nonetheless, now that he was here, the Jews of Garnata seemed certain Yosef had returned for good – and with promises for their future.

"What of the trade you went to the East to establish?" This speaker was a shrewd-faced merchant whom Yosef's father had laughingly referred to by so many disparaging names that Yosef could not for the life of him remember the man's real one. "Do you return with the coin we need to mount a proper defence of Illiberis, for long enough, at least, to force Egica and the Church to hear our demands?"

Yosef resisted the urge to pass a hand over his face. He had barely slept in more than three days, and the shock of homecoming had yet to fade. Even here, in the house he had once known as home, he felt oddly disjointed and out of place. It bore traces of his old existence, in the dusty pots on the shelf, the furniture of his childhood. But whatever it was that lived inside a house and made it home was long gone. The garden at the rear was overgrown with weeds, the citrus trees so carefully tended by his mother shrivelled in their pots. His father's treasures, of course, had long been removed, packed carefully away in the cave high in the hills where Yosef himself had once hidden to escape Oppa's wrath. No; the house now was no more than a crumbling reminder of a life that was no longer his, and Yosef had no desire to inhabit either that life, or this house, again.

"The fruits of the mission east will take time to bloom," he said, unconsciously invoking the flowery language of diplomacy. The merchant – *Haym!* Yosef recalled his name with relief – scowled at this.

"Such language is the talk of rabbis and mystics, not businessmen," he said bluntly. Yosef felt the unfamiliar jolt he had felt many times in the day and night that had passed since he returned to Garnata, the reminder that he was no longer an exotic stranger with what he now realised was the advantage of an air of mystery. Here, he was Yosef ben Arun, the son of a man who had been respected, but also considered something of an eccentric amongst his own people; and Yosef himself was, after all, an exile who had been on a mysterious voyage of which few of them knew even the most basic details. The merchants of Garnata had not travelled further than their own valley in generations. Their world was the fields and rivers of this place, the laws by which they must live, and the local authorities who administered those laws. Yosef's journey meant little to them beyond what profit it might represent to their own affairs.

"We need to know if there is coin enough to buy the men and swords to hold Garnata against any who might come for it – and to pay authorities to look the other way until our position is secure. That was the purpose of your journey in the first place, after all. Was it not?" he finished amidst a murmured chorus of agreement and yet more expectant eyes.

Yosef stifled the impulse to sigh. Perhaps he had known

this moment awaited him upon his return; but part of him, he had not realised until now, had somehow hoped to avoid it. He had become so accustomed to living in the shadows that finding himself suddenly thrust into the spotlight was a strange, disorienting experience. Nonetheless, now that he was here, he must find a way of managing their expectations, without alienating them.

"I was sent to the East to establish new routes of trade. This I have done. Some of you have already seen profits from the agreements I have established." He waited until there were a few reluctant nods and grunts of agreement, smiling to himself at the familiar game of watching men try to hide their wealth from others. "We planned to fund a rebellion, it is true," he said, "and replace the existing regime with one more sympathetic to those of our faith. But we were pre-empted by Sunifred's failed efforts, and so we must now look to different methods to achieve our ends. What you were not told," he went on without waiting for a response, lowering his voice for dramatic effect, "was the true purpose of my journey east: to establish a silk industry of our own."

"There is nothing new in this," Hasdai interrupted rudely. "My family have traded in silk for decades –"

"I do not refer to trade, Hasdai." The slightest hint of disdain shaded Yosef's tone, not enough to insult, but rather sufficient to highlight Hasdai's own crudity. "I refer to the production of silk itself." His words, and their elegant delivery, had the desired effect. Hasdai coloured and subsided. It was, Yosef thought, almost too easy, like wielding a master-crafted sword against a pitchfork.

"And did you?" It was Haym who asked the question, his eyes both wide and, disconcertingly, shrewd. It was an almost comical combination. "Discover how silk is made?"

"I did." Yosef let the words fall into the room, not above enjoying the splash they made, and the resulting silence. He waited until he felt the ripples had created full effect before continuing. "I have made all arrangements to ensure we will have an industry of our own. But the creation of silk is a complex process, one that will take time and your full attention to understand. What is more pertinent to this conversation is that the profits we might expect from it will also take time." He shrugged, holding out his hands. "To spend coin that is not yet in our hand is to risk the wrath of God himself, my friends. This, I think you will agree, is not wise."

This immutable truth brought forth a rumble of agreement. Yosef did not wait for the inevitable counter-arguments before going on. "This does not mean coin is not available to us, but we must think carefully of how best that coin is to be used. At this stage, it is Illiberis who has defied the Crown's forces. Not Garnata. Until we are in possession of the profits from silk, it may be best to talk with our allies across the water, bide our time, and wait to discover how matters in Illiberis will stand with the Crown."

After that, it was simple. Distracted by the shiny promise of a silk trade of their own, absorbed in speculation about how such a miracle might take place, and still eager to discuss their own victorious moment, the men were quickly dispersed.

Yosef rode slowly back to Illiberis along the familiar road he had taken so often throughout his youth that he had once known every divot on the path like his own body. Now it was a bittersweet ride of old and new, the shape of the road the same, yet the stones upon it undeniably different. *It is in those small details,* he thought as he rode, *that familiarity lies. I know this place. I will always know this place. But when I don't know the stones upon the road and where the holes are, it is no longer* mine. *It is just another road.*

He tucked the thought away to ponder for another time and rode up to the tall stone gates that led to the Illiberis villa, passing through them when the guard told him Lælia was still in the town. It was at the casual mention of her name that the excitement began to build, the road once again to take on meaning. *That is the other time the road has meaning: when it leads to someone who means home.* And even after all these years, Lælia, the sister of his heart, was the only remnant left to him of what he had once called "home".

As he neared the familiar walls, Yosef's heart skipped almost as much as it had when he had first realised it was Sarah standing in Ilyan's chamber. More, perhaps, for if he had kept Sarah like a secret in his heart during the long years of his journey, Lælia he had kept like an oath.

Yosef and Lælia met as they both reached the crest of the rise into town, she riding out of it, he in. A golden animal that looked like some kind of great cat stalked with lethal grace at her side. Yosef saw the moment that the expression in Lælia's eyes shifted from wariness into surprise, and then to slow, dawning wonder. As she drew rein and stared at him, Yosef found himself frozen in place, his hard-won self-control fled as if it had never been. Yosef was once again a Jewish boy from Garnata, and Lælia his only friend, the fierce, silent heiress to Illiberis, who shot her arrows at the local Gothic boys who dared bully him.

"Yosef." He saw her mouth move but the word travelled to him from a distance, and when he answered, his own was little more than a croak.

"Lælia." He forced himself to smile. "You can speak." He had heard she'd found her voice, but the shock of hearing it was profound. Yosef found himself gesturing as he spoke, his hands unconsciously falling into the patterns of their youthful conversations. She inclined her head gravely, but her own hands remained still as she said, "Yes. I can speak, now, Yosef." Her eyes took in the slender dagger at his waist. "And you, it seems, can fight with more than a slingshot."

"I no longer need your arrows, it is true." He watched as she dismounted with the same fluid grace he remembered. The movement was unbearably familiar, recalling sunlit days and the stern, wise faces of her grandfather Paulus and Yosef's father Arun. The pain was swift and unexpected, leaving him momentarily breathless. He saw her eyes flicker past him to where Theo stood, surrounded by men, his back to Yosef and Lælia, allowing them privacy for this first greeting. Seeing the shadow cross Lælia's face, however, he suspected she was still uncertain of Theo's attention to her.

"He thought only of you," Yosef said quietly. "Theo." Lælia's hand dropped to the head of the cat beside her as he spoke, the pair staring at Yosef with the same unblinking topaz gaze. "When I met him during our time away," Yosef went on, "he spoke only of returning to you. All this time. It was what sustained him – over there." He waved a hand clumsily. No gesture could encapsulate all that "over there" had been, for both him and Theo. From chains to blood to the endless days and nights on strange soil, in worlds not their own. Back here in Spania those nights and days seemed insubstantial, no more than a dream. Standing on the ground of his childhood, Yosef's grown body felt almost strange, as if the two paths existed at once – that of the life he had lived when last here, and the one he walked now, on his return. He half expected to turn and find his father coming up the road, ordering him and Lælia back to the study for lessons.

"And you?" He realised Lælia was addressing him a full moment after she had spoken. "What sustained you, Yosef? Over... there?" Her hesitancy mirrored his own, and Yosef remembered that she, also, had ridden through the sands at Dahiya's side, had known nights in a place not her own. The thought was comforting. At least they shared that understanding.

"At first it was the task my father had left me. Then, it was the memory of Sarah, though I felt unworthy of her." He stepped toward her. "Sarah told me that Acantha helped her escape to Septem. Rode with her to the coast and saw her safely aboard a *dromon*, with a tribesman to protect her on the journey."

"I did not know of that." The cat twined between Lælia's legs, purring softly. Lælia's mouth twisted. "It would be like Acantha, to do such a thing," she said quietly. "She told me only that Sarah was safe."

"She was with child." Yosef saw Lælia's eyes widen. "Sarah. She had a son. After… what happened." He held Lælia's eyes and saw the memory of that ugly day, when Sarah had been raped before his very eyes as Oppa stood by and watched.

"That was no fault of hers." Lælia returned his gaze without flinching, her own hard and fierce.

"No." Yosef spoke in quiet agreement. "Sarah is brave, and stronger than any man I know. She named the boy after my father." Yosef smiled crookedly. "He is my son, now. They are both safe in Septem."

"You will return there, to them?"

"Eventually." Yosef nodded toward the road that led north. "I will stay for a time. To understand the situation here."

"The situation is that we won a victory." Lælia's chin tilted proudly, her eyes flashing. "Oppa's army, led by the exile Giscila, was defeated. It will take time for Egica to regroup. Time enough to gather what is left of the south and mount the defence we need."

Yosef tensed inwardly. Just as quickly as he had lost his composure a moment earlier, it came back, enabling him to voice his next words with the same care he had back in Garnata.

"You know that the Jerawa men do not belong here, Lælia. They will wish to return to their homes and families."

"I made a deal with Dahiya."

"For horses in exchange for men, yes. She told me." He gestured at the hillfort beyond the river. "The Riders fought well for you, Lælia. But I believe Dahiya would feel that her – and their – duty to you is done."

Lælia drew a sharp breath, her eyes narrowing, but she did not contradict him. Eventually, she said, "Well… Theo is returned, now." Her eyes stared at something over his shoulder, and when Yosef followed their gaze he found Theo's eyes trained on Lælia. Even from a distance Yosef could see the tension in his figure, feel the air between them crackling. He turned back to see the colour mounting in Lælia's cheeks. When she looked back at him, her eyes were glittering with edgy excitement. "The men of the south will listen to Theo more easily than to me. Together, we will defend Illiberis, and Garnata, for as long as they may be held." She paused and then, as if sensing Yosef's reserve at her words, said, "That is why he came back, is it not, Yosef? Why you both returned? Was it not the dream of all our forefathers that we fight for what is ours?" There was a note beneath her challenge he could not quite make out. Long accustomed to reading what men did not say, he yet found it almost impossible to discern Lælia's heart. Perhaps, he thought, it was the past they shared. He could not separate his emotions from hers, place logic between them. Yosef realised he was unsure if she was asking his opinion or daring him to deny the truth of her words.

Worse, her questions tugged on old emotions he had thought long ago put to rest.

Yosef found it hard to meet her eyes, and the diplomacy that had been so hard won had never felt so disingenuous as when he answered her: "There are many ways to fight, Lælia. And Theo has seen them all. If it is a fight you wish for, you could have no better counsel."

The sound of hooves clattering on the road made them both turn back toward Theo and the men. It was a messenger on a sweating horse. Yosef was not unhappy at the interruption. He knew neither he nor Theo could give Lælia the answers she looked for. Yosef felt the tremulous hope in her voice, knew with pained certainty that the future she envisioned, of her and Theo leading a united southern defence against the power of Toletum, was not one any soldier of Theo's experience would easily commit to, just as he himself could not reassure the Garnata Jews that their small, poorly trained band could form the crux of a proper army. He thought of the parchment Oppa carried and the choices Theo must soon face, and he feared for Lælia and Theo both, for the future of the almost uncanny bond they shared.

As Lælia made to move toward the group of men, Yosef stepped forward with a sudden urgency. "He loves you," he said, the intensity of his words taking him by surprise. "Theo. He loves you more than his own life. Remember that, Lælia. He crossed seas to return to you. Whatever comes next, never doubt that."

Her face coloured at his words, her eyes rich topaz fire, but she did not speak, just gripped his hand and stared at him for a long moment. In the familiar silence that had characterised their childhood, Yosef saw inside her, to the dark nights she had feared for Theo's life, and the terrible hope and fear that had haunted her dreams.

She let him go and moved toward the men. Yosef walked slowly after her, wondering what would become of that emotional turbulence, now that the goal so long wished for had happened. She had successfully saved Illiberis from Oppa, and Theo had returned to her – but Yosef wondered if Lælia understood that both were the beginning of a much longer journey, rather than some kind of fairytale ending.

"I am the Lady of Illiberis," Lælia called out as she approached the messenger. "What news do you bring me?"

The messenger, though, did not answer her but rather stared straight past her, to Theo. "You are Theudemir of Aurariola, are you not? I recall seeing you with your father in Toletum, years ago."

"I am." Theo inclined his head, unsmiling.

"Then I bear sad news, Fráuja." The messenger's eyes were grave. "Your father died on the battlefield at Toletum. As did your own grandfather, my lady." He nodded respectfully at Lælia, who absorbed the news with the stoic resignation of one who had expected it. The messenger turned back to Theo. "The Lady Riccilo of Corduba sent me here, Fráuja." Yosef saw Lælia step forward and open her mouth, then close it, frowning, as the messenger carried on, addressing his comments to Theo rather than her. "My lady says that Theodofred, Duke of Corduba, has been taken to Toletum, held in custody awaiting trial for treason. The day following the battle at Toletum, the king announced there would be a council at Toletum, to be held on the twenty-fifth of April, at which the fate of the traitors will be decided. He has sent word that all must attend – my lady included." He nodded again at Lælia but his eyes did not leave Theo's face. Yosef saw Lælia stiffen. Her eyes travelled slowly over the group of men, all looking to Theo for his reaction, even Gratimo and Zdan. Not one of them, Yosef noticed, looked toward Lælia. They turned as instinctively to Theo for command as did his own men, and Theo, accustomed to assuming it, frowned at the messenger and said, "What news of my stepmother, Elsuith? Of my sister Egilona? Or of Aurariola itself?"

"We have had no word from Aurariola. Your stepmother was with child and had remained there – but it is rumoured that the king's bastard landed forces near Cartago Nova. If that be the case, then she is in Oppa's custody now. Your sister remains hostage with Lady Riccilo's son, Roderic. They are safe, so far as we know, for the messenger from Toletum said Lady Riccilo would see her son when she comes to Toletum for the council." The messenger glanced at Lælia but addressed his next comments again to Theo: "My Lady Riccilo bids the Lady of Illiberis to ride with haste to Corduba, immediately. She would talk with her before she leaves for Toletum." The messenger paused, waiting, his eyes on Theo.

"Very well." It was Lælia who spoke. "You will ride back to my aunt and tell her to expect us in no more than three days." The messenger shifted awkwardly, his eyes swivelling to Theo, clearly uncertain from whom he was to take direction.

"You heard the Lady of Illiberis." Theo's voice held the unmistakable ring of authority. "You might like to add that I and my men will, with your permission, Lady" – he inclined his head toward Lælia – "ride north in her company, to Corduba."

There was a faint softening in Lælia's features as she nodded, but Yosef, seeing the wariness in her face, sensed that she had discerned the subtle shift in power just as he had. It did not, Yosef suspected, bode well for what they would soon face.

"If we are to fight," said Lælia as the messenger led his horse away to change it for another, "we must take my aunt's counsel. We must know what she plans, and what news there is of the remnants of the army that rode north." If she saw the sceptical looks exchanged by the men nearby, she gave no sign of it. She turned back to her horse and mounted. "Gratimo, you will remain here until my return. Ensure the defences are rebuilt on the hillfort, and that no man goes hungry. I will ride for the villa now, and we will leave before the day is out. Tosius will ride with me."

Gratimo lowered his head and murmured his agreement, but his lone eye flickered uneasily to Theo, whose own face was the impenetrable bland mask of a man long accustomed to concealing his plans from those in his command. "I will join you at the villa as soon as my own men are reassembled," Theo said politely to Lælia as she rode by. She gave him no more than a nod of acknowledgement, but Yosef saw Theo's hand brush her leg as she passed, the heightened colour in her face as she briefly met his eyes, the dark heat in Theo's own. It was no more than a moment, but it was enough for Yosef to understand that two entirely different games were at play between them – both as volatile as the other.

Theo gave a couple of curt commands to his men, who went to fetch his horse and the others of their band, but his eyes remained firmly trained on Lælia's proud form as she rode away.

"I will ride to Corduba with you."

Theo turned at Yosef's words as he came alongside. He nodded, almost smiling. "Good." The hint of humour faded as he looked back at Lælia, worry clouding his eyes like a shadow over a high mountain lake.

"You haven't told her," Yosef said. It wasn't a question.

Theo shook his head slowly.

"That is probably wise."

"It is wrong, Yosef." Theo spat the words harshly under his breath. "I lie to her with my every word."

"It will be even more wrong if you break what is between you before it has so much as breathed," said Yosef calmly.

"That is what Silas said." Theo met Yosef's eyes. "What happened in Garnata?"

Yosef tilted his head, staring into the middle distance. "The Jews of Garnata are unified under a man named Hasdai. They are flush with victory and convinced that Illiberis will be the cornerstone of a wider rebellion, or at the very least, the wedge they need to negotiate with the Crown regarding laws against the Jews. They see this battle as the beginning of their rebellion, not the end of the last one."

"And you, Yosef? What do you believe?"

Yosef brought his eyes back. "They are merchants, weavers, and farmers of flax. Not warriors, or politicians. They cannot begin to imagine what they will face in a true battle, and neither are they equipped to fight Egica and the Church."

Theo leaned against Yosef's horse, stroking its shoulder unconsciously. "I thought as much. There is no real form to the rebellion they speak of, is there?" Yosef's silence was answer enough. Theo was uncomfortably aware that after so long facing the immense threat posed by an Arab army, the ambitions of a small party of rebels seemed to him insignificant, at best. He wondered if Yosef felt the same. "You know as well as I that Lælia cannot hold Illiberis, Yosef." Theo's hand tightened on the horse's mane but he left unspoken the second part of his thoughts: that there was little point in holding Illiberis, when Spania itself would soon enough face a foe far greater than anything Egica might field. "We will go to

Corduba, then we will face the court – and Oppa – in Toletum at the council. There is no sudden reprieve, no surprise defenders coming to our rescue, and nothing with which to negotiate. Egica has Riccilo's husband, and her son. Her invitation is not a kindly word from an aunt to her niece. It is a summons by the king given to her to deliver to Lælia. But it *is* a summons, and when Lælia rides to Corduba, it will be to the king's custody."

"And if that is the case, you will find a way to trade with Oppa, if you must, for her freedom. But, for what it is worth, Theo, I think you did the right thing in not telling her of the deal you made." Yosef met Theo's eyes, feeling a rush of sympathy for the anguish he read in them. "Do not underestimate Lælia's passion for Illiberis. She has just risked her own life to defend it. Now, perhaps, is not the time to tell her you have already signed the means by which she might lose it. You know as well as I how fast war can shift, Theo. Do not leap before you must. There may yet be another way."

"There may." Theo stared after Lælia's retreating figure, his mouth working grimly. "But I don't like it, Yosef. I don't like it at all."

5

LETTER FROM SAFIA TO COUNT ILYAN
FEBRUARY, AD 693

Tuy, Spania, to Septem, Mauretania
Tuy, Portugal, to Ceuta, Morocco

M*y honoured father,*
       Your messenger reached me and, God willing, will return with this reply.

I am servant now to the Lady Egilona, sister to Theudemir of Aurariola. Despite her precarious status at court following her family's involvement in the recent rebellion, Egilona insists on the household staff here in Tuy using her formal title. All bow to her request. Though only nine years old, Egilona of Aurariola is devastating both in beauty and command. I know you like to see what I do, so I will describe her for you.

She has the white-blonde hair and porcelain complexion prized amongst the Goths, and blue eyes so startling that little more than a glance is required to reduce any male in her vicinity to quivering submission. The males in question may be but children themselves, but we both know, Father, that children do not long remain innocent in such times.

Egilona is the lone female in a small court of three. Roderic, son of the recently humbled Duke of Corduba, and Pelayo, son of the conquered and now dead Duke of Gallæcea, are her companions, a small party of hostages who dance attendance upon Wittiza, King Egica's legitimate heir. At thirteen years of age, Wittiza is the eldest of the group, and by far the most capricious. Wittiza has been indulged since birth. Though good-hearted enough — soft-hearted, even — he is plump and lazy, far more committed to pleasure than learning. His three companions cater to his every whim, of which there are many, but it is Egilona who truly rules here.

Before the rebellion, it seems their parents had planned a betrothal between Roderic and Egilona. They have been playmates since infancy, and though Roderic is two years Egilona's senior, he is slavish in his desire to please her, and he clearly still regards her as his own, at some distant point in the future. Egilona, however, is rather more of a realist. She is also ambitious, and astute. She has struck up a written correspondence with the old queen, Liuvgoto, who despite advanced years, the king's hostility, and several attempts on her life, remains very much alive, even if she is cloistered in a monastery. She is a formidable mentor to Egilona in games of state and a woman's power at court. Egilona believes her correspondence with Liuvgoto a secret kept even from me, whom she trusts only slightly more than the household staff, who are all clearly handpicked by Egica himself and report to him. Of course, I know what she writes. Egilona may have found a messenger she believes her own, but you taught me long ago the power of coin and how to use it; Egilona's spies all report to me. In time this will be part of the way she will learn to trust me. Egilona neither trusts nor respects anyone she considers inferior in intelligence to herself. Given she is surrounded by fawning boys on the threshold of adolescence, it is unsurprising that she has an over-inflated opinion of her own abilities.

Roderic himself is much as one might expect of a boy raised to be heir to Spania's most powerful seat outside of the Toletum palace itself. Corduba is a rich and powerful jewel, one Roderic still believes himself heir to. He has not yet grasped the reality: that his father, Duke Theodofred, languishes in the Toletum dungeons awaiting trial for treason, whilst his mother, Riccilo, stays in Corduba, watched closely by Egica's spies. Roderic is cheerful and carefree, trusting entirely to the privilege of his birth. He does not comprehend that with a stroke of a bishop's pen, all he takes for granted might easily be taken from him. Egilona, by contrast, is entirely aware of how precarious their positions are, and she has shifted her allegiance accordingly. It is upon Wittiza that she practises her native charm. He goes nowhere that she does not accompany him, makes no decision without first consulting her. But she is careful, too, never to become either dictatorial or maternal. Egilona is ever slightly elusive. Like mercury, she cannot long be contained, slipping away to form a new, fascinating shape all three boys seek to hold. She has the natural ability to know exactly how to tug at their strings, so that much of their time is spent in trying to find new and more interesting ways to capture her fleeting attentions, whilst she affords each just enough reward to keep them slavishly devoted. Wittiza, as their undisputed lord and future king, she handles with a dexterity that perhaps only I, as the daughter of a truly great concubine, can appreciate. Wittiza worships her. I do not think he will take kindly to his father ordering his betrothal to any but Egilona — an outcome Egilona herself, of course, has long planned, and of which it seems the old queen is an enthusiastic supporter. Liuvgoto, of course, wishes for a return to court. She sees Egilona and Wittiza as the opportunity by which that end might be achieved.

Pelayo should by all rights be the least amongst the group. His father, Favila, was Duke of Gallæcea on Spania's northern border and paid only nominal homage to the Crown in Toletum even before the rebellion. Favila was one of the first to turn on Egica and was killed early in the rebellion. Word came to us not a month hence of his brutal death. It is said he was dragged behind Egica's horse along the road south in a gruesome message to those who would defy the king, his torn remains marking the road until there were none left to drag. Pelayo did not by so much as a twitch show a reaction to this news when it came. Favila's son has been raised in a much different environment to the rarefied atmosphere of the Toletum court to which the others are accustomed. He is no stranger to death, or violence.

Pelayo has a self-possessed manner that is not dissimilar in power to Egilona's own, though lacking entirely her conscious manipulation and ambition. The same age as Roderic (their fathers were both sons of Chindasuinth, though I am certain you know this already), he is utterly devoted to his cousin. It is a quiet devotion, but a friendship I suspect will endure. Pelayo told me once that when Favila sent him south to the then relative safety of Corduba, it was with only one instruction: that the grandsons of

Chindasuinth remain loyal to one another, whatever future Spania faces. This advice, I believe, is Pelayo's only true dogma. Though he pays polite homage to Wittiza, his unspoken but steadfast loyalty to Roderic is evident in his every watchful movement. Both Wittiza and Egilona sense this and, I suspect, like it little. Roderic, in his careless, carefree manner, is the only one oblivious to such undercurrents. He is happy being Wittiza's partner in any manner of indulgent pastimes, and just as content to have Pelayo's steady presence at his right arm. Of them all, it is Pelayo who has the stuff of which true men are made, perhaps because he was forged in a place and world that relied upon honour and loyalty for its existence. He has already seen much of death and knows first-hand the depravity of kings. He does not bow quite so easily to Wittiza as do the others, nor worship quite so adoringly at Egilona's altar. This has the effect of causing Wittiza to unconsciously seek Pelayo's approval, and Egilona to aim her most acidic barbs his way.

Ours may be a small court, but it is nonetheless rich with intrigue. And I, trained by you and like my mother before me, am attuned to every nuance.

The same messenger who brought word of Egica's victory over the usurper Sunifred told us also that the Sixteenth Council of Toletum will be convened in April of this year, barely two months away. The king, it seems, intends to waste no time in publicly denouncing those who rose against him. He has summoned us back to Toletum for the spectacle, no doubt to parade all three of his hostages as proof of his power. What their fates will be following the council none of us can yet know. Egilona, at least, is doing her best to ensure her own position at Wittiza's side is unassailable. Pelayo, I fear by the shadow behind his eyes, knows he has little choice now but to bind himself to Wittiza and hope for the spoiled princeling's favour to save him. Such fawning does not come easily to one of Pelayo's clear integrity. If he survives at all, it will be because Roderic, for all his carefree ways, truly loves Pelayo — and Wittiza loves Roderic.

Before we ride for Toletum, we are expecting a visitor of rather more interest to you: Oppa, the royal bastard.

Oppa has sent word that he has arrived in Spania and will soon come to visit Wittiza, his half-brother. There are rumours that he landed an army somewhere on the eastern coast — though where, and to what purpose, I do not yet have word. I had hoped to send you more on this, but I cannot risk waiting for another of your messengers. I will send more as I know it. I am working on a messenger of my own, but I must be cautious. Egilona is no fool and, as I said, we are not yet entirely in one another's confidence. She suspects me of being a spy for Roderic's mother, Riccilo. I am, of course; but I tell Riccilo only enough to satisfy her. Riccilo's future is not yet certain. Egilona, however, I would stake a kingdom upon. She will find a way, I suspect, to prevail, no matter what fortunes life brings her. If Pelayo has the stuff of which true men are made, Egilona is forged of that from which the greatest queens emerge. Never have I met a girl so clearly destined for a crown. Egilona will have one, no matter what she must do to gain it. I believe she was scheming to rule in the womb, and Liuvgoto will undoubtedly guide her path to greatness.

I shall walk it beside her, confidante and witness, as you, my dear father, schooled me to be. Soon, I shall be at the heart of the Toletum court, and your eyes there, as we planned.

I am, as ever, your most loyal and obedient servant,
Safia

6

LÆLIA

MARCH, AD 693

Illiberis–Corduba
Road between Granada and Cordoba

They left Illiberis behind on a frigid March morning, when mist lay across the valley like a shroud and the air smelled of smoke and old blood.

Lælia had spoken little to Theo the previous night. She had excused herself with the organisation of Illiberis in her absence, the necessity to return the herd to the care of the mountain tribes and give instruction to her household servants. She was uncomfortably aware that all the above were excuses she sought to avoid both the harsh reality that she was leaving her home, for who knew how long, and the uncomfortable realisation that despite her victory, her men were looking to Theo for their instruction. No matter his pretence of deference to her wishes, Lælia felt the shift, and her own inadequacy in the face of Theo's experience. Of course men such as Gratimo and Zdan would look to him. He had led men in countless battles, was the son of one of Spania's most famed military leaders and the grandson of the mighty Geila, who had once been king. She, by contrast, was no more than a young girl who had pulled off one unlikely victory.

She had left Zdan and his men with Gratimo at Illiberis, despite the questioning expressions from both her own and Theo's men. Theo himself had not questioned her decision. He had, in fact, made no more attempt to be in Lælia's company than she had to be in his. She did not know whether she felt hurt or relieved by his distance.

Part of her ached to ask his counsel. No, she thought, her hands gripping the reins with unnecessary force, not just part of her. It was taking more discipline than she could have imagined to keep her own counsel, the pretence that she knew what to do next.

She didn't.

Part of her — the girl who had learned of Giscila's murder of her parents, the one who had long ago faced down Oppa at court — wanted to fight on. Wanted to turn back to Illiberis this moment and plunge headlong into strategy and alliance, use everything at her disposal to build a small kingdom around Illiberis and lock herself and Theo inside it. Riding away from the land she had fought so hard to defend felt like a betrayal at the very core of her.

If only she knew the truth of what Theo wanted, what he foresaw. Not just between them, but for their future. The future of Spania itself. But there had been no time for questions, and Lælia was not in the habit of asking such things. Instead, she had given her orders, trying not to notice the sceptical looks of the men who had, until Theo's arrival, looked only to her for guidance.

Lælia knew Zdan could not stay forever. But nor was she ready to leave Illiberis undefended. "I will not ask you to stay," she had said to Zdan the previous night. "It must be your decision. I do not yet know what we will face."

Zdan had responded with a simple hand over his heart. "We came to defend Illiberis for you. Until your return, that is what we will do."

Lælia had heard the carefully phrased answer. "If I do not return within a turn of the moon, I will send word. I know you cannot linger long on foreign soil, Zdan. You have families of your own and war coming. I know you must return home before the heat is too great for you to go into the sands."

He had put his hand over his heart again in silent acknowledgement and they had said no more. Lælia knew Yosef thought she should have sent them home immediately, and she suspected he was not the only one. Gratimo had spat to one side and frowned when she had told him Zdan would stay, and not, Lælia knew, because the grizzled old commander didn't like the man from the desert. They had, in fact, formed a strong understanding during the weeks leading up to the battle at Illiberis. No, Gratimo, Lælia knew, shared the view of most men surrounding her – that Illiberis was already as good as lost.

Do they think I do not understand? she thought fiercely as she spurred her horse into the silent dawn. *That I do not know Riccilo's summons comes from Egica rather than her, that I am expected to ride to Toletum, and prostrate myself before the king, seeking his mercy? Do they think I have learned nothing from a lifetime under my grandfather's tutelage?* Lælia knew what Egica expected. She knew what Riccilo would want.

Lælia was not naïve enough to believe her fragile force could hold Illiberis indefinitely, despite the words she had thrown at Yosef the day he had arrived. And she knew her questions to him had been unfair. The dreams of their fathers had died with those men. Whatever future they built now would inevitably be different. But was it so wrong of her, Lælia thought, to hope that they could still, the three of them, build something together?

With the right men – her eyes slid of their own accord to the tall, strong figure of Theo to her side – and enough of them, Illiberis could yet hold. It wasn't an impossible dream. Had Ilyan himself not set Yosef's mission into play to gain a foothold in Spania, in preparation for the Arabic forces he foresaw as a threat? Was he not still prepared to invest in Spania's future, and thus his own prosperity and defence? She had heard the Jews of Garnata talk of fighting. She knew they were in touch with exiles in Septem, Jews that had money enough to have influence.

Holding Illiberis into the future would not be simple, Lælia knew. But nor was it impossible.

"I heard you speak to Zdan in the language of the desert."

Not having heard Theo approach, she turned in surprise. They were riding across the valley floor, where the road was wide enough for them to ride side by side but beyond the immediate earshot of others. The lingering mist made their conversation seem even more private. Jadis was running off to the side, a low yellow shadow slipping through the mist.

"Yes." She found herself choosing her words carefully, every nerve aware of his knee close to her own, his arm within touching distance. "I learned during the months I spent with the Jerawa." She glanced at him. "I understand that you, also, know Dahiya."

"A little." His mouth curled in the same smile that had lived so long in her memory, though now the movement twisted the gleaming scars on his face, an effect Lælia imagined men might find fearsome, but which to her seemed thrilling, and oddly touching. "You learned something of the Arabic armies she has fought, then."

"Yes. Though I have not seen them, as you have." She cast him a sideways glance. "Are they as fearsome as we are told?"

Theo looked straight ahead. "They are a formidable fighting force, it is true." It was a calm enough response, but there was a certain care to his words, combined with a barely discernible pause before he spoke, that let Lælia know he was censoring what he said, for fear of upsetting her. She did not push for more; war, after all, was something few men liked to speak of, in her experience.

"It was Apsimar I knew well, rather than Dahiya." Lælia accepted the change of topic without comment. "He

commanded the fleet that fought on those shores, and he was
my commander after that, also." His eyes met hers briefly. "It
was Apsimar who took Silas, Leofric, and me from the market
in Carthage where we were captive. It was Titus, here, who
brought him to me." He clapped the horse's dark bay neck,
grinning at Lælia's surprise. As they rode, he told her about
recognising Titus when he was a slave in the market. "Yosef
had already found me," Theo explained. "I told him to bring
Dahiya and Apsimar to the market, and to make sure
Apsimar purchased Titus. I waited until after the deal was
made, then I used the skills I learned when I was with you."
He told her how he used the Illiberis signals to command the
horse, first to attack the man who held him, then to draw him
to the place where Theo and his men were held. "When
Apsimar came to retrieve Titus, we showed him the scars
where the slavers had cut the totem of the imperial fleet from
our hands. Apsimar bought our freedom immediately."

"He does not tell the full story." It was Leofric who rode
up on Lælia's other side, his eyes gleaming with dark mischief.
"Us, we could have been sold to a great man, gone to an easy
life carrying wine. But no. Instead, the *schnecke* here, he makes
Apsimar take the whole crew into the Karabisianoi. Even
though most had never held a sword in their lives." He rolled
his eyes in exaggerated annoyance. "After this, the African and
I" – he nodded his head at the mountainous black man on
Theo's right side – "must not only teach the *schnecke* here to
fight, but a whole crew of peasants also. It is a long summer,
this one, I tell you."

Lælia found herself laughing aloud. She could not recall
the last time she had done that. "What is he like? Apsimar?"
she asked, turning between the men. "Dahiya never spoke of
him, except to say he was the father of her sons. But I never
met her sons, so it meant little."

Theo nodded at the figure ahead of them. "You can ask
Yosef about her sons." Yosef turned at the sound of his name
and reined in his horse to join their conversation. "He rode

with them all the way to Jerusalem," Theo went on. "And then they helped us escape Sebastopolis, by sea."

"Really?" Lælia was fascinated.

"As for Apsimar," interrupted Silas, in his deep, resonant voice, "it is Theo who can tell you the most of him. Apsimar showed him rare favour."

"Yes, well, they do say that Apsimar's brain is addled with age," interjected Leofric. Lælia went into another fit of laughter and the men were off, bantering with the ease of long familiarity, talking over one another as they filled in the blanks of the missing years. Lælia knew the stories glossed over the hard facts that she could nonetheless discern beneath their careful telling – the long, grim months as slaves, the years of tension in Sebastopolis, the ceaseless ventures into foreign territory. Amongst those were interspersed Yosef's stories, much less detailed and usually no more than a brief observation or recollection, but still enough to leave her with an impression of the breathtaking scope of his travels. *They have all travelled so far,* she thought, not without longing. Lived lives she could hardly begin to imagine. Lives not permitted for a woman of Spania. Briefly she thought of Dahiya, commanding her men across the sands of Africa, and felt another stab of something like envy. It would be so much simpler, she thought, if she could ride as Dahiya did, answering to no man.

Then she felt the thrill of Theo's presence at her side and thought that this, too, was something. More than something. It was everything she had fought for, everything she had lived for, since the day he sailed away from Spania.

She rode through the day intensely aware of Theo's proximity, laughing and listening as she came to learn something of the man he had been, of the men amongst whom he rode. She felt his eyes upon her when he thought she was not looking and treasured every one of his quiet questions. That night, when they halted in a small town along the road, she knew they had chosen it because of the tavern there in which she could find a proper bedchamber. She was grateful for the consideration, but she knew the men, had she not been in their midst, would just as easily have camped on the roadside. She wanted to say she would be just as happy to do so, but she felt still a strange awkwardness between her and Theo, so instead she took the chamber and lay awake throughout the night, Jadis heavy and alert at her feet, staring at the wooden beams and longing for the high, stark clarity of the mountains.

* * *

THE FOLLOWING two days followed a similar pattern. She and Theo spoke little, not least because finding privacy amongst men who were long accustomed to riding at each other's side was not easy. It was only on the third day that Lælia insisted they ride past the small town they reached in the mid-afternoon.

"It is the last tavern before Corduba," said one of the handful of Illiberis men who rode with them.

"And there are still good riding hours left in the day." Lælia urged her horse forward. "We will make camp at night-fall. It will leave fewer miles to ride in the morning." Her new companions raised their eyebrows, but the Illiberis men knew their mistress too well to argue, and so on they rode.

They made camp amongst an old Roman ruin set back from the road, high on a hillside with a good view of any who might approach. They had come across more than one band of limping, defeated soldiers returning from the battles to the north. Such meetings had brought little in the way of encouraging news. There was always the chance that opportunists might ride the roads also, especially those who hoped to find women alone in the smallholdings they passed. A guard was set up as soon as they unsaddled the horses.

Lælia had felt a strange tension build during the day. Tomorrow they would be in Corduba, and whatever measure of privacy she and Theo had would be gone. Her aunt Riccilo would want answers to questions Lælia herself had not yet broached, nor Theo hinted at. She knew, as night fell and the men cooked over a low fire, that she needed to discover at least some truths before she faced her aunt's scrutiny.

She caught Theo's eye across the makeshift circle of saddles and baggage and tilted her head toward the darkness beyond. She saw him murmur something to Silas, whose dark eyes moved to her and back to Theo. The big man nodded and leaned in, distracting the other men so they did not notice Theo's departure nor hers as she slipped into the night. Jadis moved through the darkness at her side, silent and watchful.

Lælia walked a distance from camp and leaned against a chestnut tree, watching the hobbled horses as they grazed. The man guarding them was a low shadow at a distance opposite, out of earshot.

Lælia felt rather than heard Theo's approach. She took a deep breath and turned to face him.

"Your cat." Theo tilted his head toward Jadis, a half smile on his face, though his eyes were wary. "She does not yet trust me." As if in answer, Jadis gave a low growl and slunk around Theo's legs, eyeing him with gleaming topaz eyes.

"I rescued her as a kitten. She has never shared me with another and is wary of strangers."

"Is that what I am to you, Lælia?" Bending down, Theo met Jadis's eyes. The cat came to complete stillness, long tail straight out behind her, every sense alert. "A stranger?" He reached out with one hand, and Jadis edged her face forward, sniffing at the proffered hand warily. "I understand it," Theo said tersely, still looking at the cat. "But I wish it were not so." Jadis took a tentative step forward. She touched her nose delicately to Theo's hand, then stepped back. She glanced once at Lælia, who nodded, then she streaked off into the darkness. "Still undecided, I suspect," said Theo dryly, standing up. But despite his levity, the eyes he turned to Lælia were shadowed and cautious.

"I told you in the stables that we fought for you," she said without preamble. "The foals, and I."

Theo nodded, his eyes barely visible in the gloom.

"It was not only the foals who sensed you." Lælia fought to keep her voice steady. There was no time for fear. They did not have time.

They never had.

"I dreamed of you, too," she said. "I saw you. Even when others believed you dead, I knew you were not. In my dreams I knew your pain, and your struggles. I may not have been at your side during the times you drew steel, but I lay with you in the nights when you wondered if you would ever come home. And I promised myself that when you did, I would not hold you to anything." She could not see his face clearly, but Theo stirred slightly at her last words, clearly uncomfortable. "Let me finish." Reaching inside her tunic, she pulled out the amulets she had worn for so long – the entwined serpents carved from horse bone that formed the Illiberis symbol, the original coin of Geila he had gifted her, and the other coin, his own, that Theo had sent back as proof that he lived, before he sailed from African shores. "You promised to return, Theo, and you kept your promise. But I hold you to nothing more than that." Lælia stepped forward slightly, trying to discern his expression. "In those dreams," she said quietly, "I saw her, Theo. The woman you knew. The one you took. She stood between you and me, like a guard." Theo stiffened, and she saw his hands clench into fists, but he didn't speak. "I do not mind that you took a woman." Lælia's voice was low, and fierce. "I am glad you found comfort in that place. But I won't compete with her." She withdrew the parchment she had brought with her from Illiberis. "This is the contract of our betrothal. It is yours, now." She held it out before her. "You agreed to marry me to protect Illiberis. I release you from that obligation. Illiberis is mine. My soul. My responsibility. But I will hold no other than myself hostage to it."

After bracing herself to speak, Lælia found the words

suddenly painful in her throat, and she was unable to form any more.

"Is that what you wish?" Theo's voice was low and rough. "To end our betrothal?" He took a hesitant step toward her and his eyes swam into focus from the gloom. They seemed to glitter in the dark, piercing her heart and the defences she had built around it. When she didn't answer, Theo reached beneath his leathers to a cord that had been hidden from sight. It was worn smooth, the old braid barely discernible, but Lælia remembered it instantly. She recalled the day they had woven it together from the foals' manes, the way Theo's hands had felt over her own, the sensation that they were weaving magic into being. On the end of the cord was the Illiberis amulet she had given him.

"I, too, dreamed of you." Theo's eyes didn't waver from hers. "You came to me everywhere. When I thought I could not live another day; amidst battle when I thought myself lost. I felt you inside me, so close it seemed I could touch you. At times I thought I would go mad with dreaming of you." He gritted his jaw so the vicious scars gleamed in the moonlight. "I did take a woman. There is nothing I can say of it, other than that she has no place in my heart. To my shame, I don't know that she ever did."

Lælia's pulse slowed and then thudded in a jagged beat. She waited.

"When I left here I was a son of Aurariola, heir to an honourable name. I am returned the son of a traitor who may yet face the rope. If you wish to end our betrothal, I shall respect your decision." He touched the contract lightly, his fingers stroking it like the most precious ornament in a fine villa. "But I do not wish to end it, Lælia. I wish to marry you as soon as we find a priest to say the words. I want you by my side and in my bed, every day until my days are ended. I want never to be apart from you. Not for another day, nor another night." When she did not speak, he stepped still closer. His hand closed over hers on the contract. "You speak to me of obligation, as if I see marriage to you as a burden. Is that how you feel, Lælia?" He swallowed, and when he spoke again his voice was low and pained. "Do you no longer wish this marriage?"

Less than an arm span lay between them. It seemed to Lælia no less than the river Bætis, a gulf that, once crossed, could never be returned from. A gulf made seemingly unnavigable by the murky questions that lay between them. But Lælia had been stranded too long alone to think of hesitating. Whatever dangers lay in those depths were nothing, she thought, to the desperate loneliness of being without Theo at her side.

She stepped forward, and into the gulf.

"I wish it," she whispered. "I have wished for nothing else from the day you sailed. I will be your wife, Theo. Now, and every day from now."

Then his hands were in her hair and his mouth was on hers, and there was nothing gentle about it. His body told her what no words could, and she answered him, her hands gripping the scarred face fiercely, the years of pain and doubt and isolation flowing between them like the river itself.

The night slipped away. The reality of his hard, leather-clad body was nothing like the boy who had once kissed her in the stables. That had been dizzying, intoxicating as wine and bittersweet raw with leaving. This was deeper, darker, and so consuming that it was only when Theo pulled away, breathing heavily, his eyes glittering with a hard light, that she realised she was pressed against the rough bark of a chestnut, her tunic half off her shoulder.

"Tomorrow," Theo said hoarsely, "as soon as we reach Corduba, we will find a priest. Do you hear me, Lælia? The moment we arrive."

"I don't care about a priest." Lælia pushed off the tree and swayed toward him. "What do priests know of this?"

Theo inhaled sharply. "I will not dishonour you in the eyes of any man. We will have the words said, and men to witness, that none may accuse us of breaking any law." He touched her face, his hand rough with a warrior's callouses, leaving a trail of heat on her skin. "We did not come so far to let priests and their laws gainsay our marriage." He half smiled in the moonlight. "I told you once, long ago, that if I started with you, I would not stop. Do you remember?"

"I remember everything." Her words were hot and fierce in her throat.

Theo nodded. "I, too." His thumb stroked the tension in her jaw. "And it is truer now than it ever was then, Lælia. Xristus, but I want you." His voice had roughened, deepened, and this time when she swayed toward him he caught her, groaning as his mouth took hers again.

When he finally stepped away from her, Lælia could barely stand.

"Tomorrow," Theo rasped, his steps unsteady as a newborn colt as he backed away from her. "Tomorrow, Lælia. And by God, I will kill any man who gets between us."

7

THEO
MARCH, AD 693

Corduba, Spania
Cordoba, Spain

Theo rode into Corduba the following morning with his body aflame and only one thing on his mind. "Find a priest," he growled to one of the Illiberis men as they crossed the long Roman bridge. "Bid them come to Theodofred's villa. Immediately." The man nodded and turned away, barely able to hide his grin.

Leofric rolled his eyes. "You have less sense than horsefly. Have I teach you nothing of women?"

"You have no lessons to give that any man of sense would wish to hear, *wenkai*." Silas rode up on Theo's other side. "Do you have stones for eyes, Slav? The only wonder is that it has taken so long." He cast slow eyes at Theo. "Any fool could see she would have married you amidst battle and covered with blood, had you been smart enough to ask her."

Theo bore their joking with good humour. It hid his own misgivings. He could barely look at Lælia, riding tall before him, Yosef at her side. The memory of her mouth under his own was a sweet torture that had kept him awake throughout the night, unbearably aware of her breathing barely ten paces from where he slept. And yet, despite the savagery of his longing for her, his absolute certainty that he could no more walk away from her than he could take his own life, Theo was rent in two by guilt.

His eyes rested on Yosef. He wanted to speak to him and yet he knew that the desire to do so was no more than a man seeking absolution from his priest, absolution it was neither Yosef's job nor obligation to give. There was no God in heaven that could ever forgive Theo for the deception he was about to practise. Marrying Lælia was the most selfish, dishonourable action Theo had ever taken, and he despised himself for it, even as he knew he was utterly powerless to walk away.

I must tell her. His teeth clenched, grinding hard enough to cause pain, which he welcomed. *I will not marry her with this lie between us.* He was already spurring Titus forward when Silas caught the horse's reins. "For a man trusted by Apsimar himself for his strategic intelligence, you can be a fool, *wenkai.*"

Theo glanced to his other side, but Leofric had fallen back to talk with one of the men. "It is not like you to counsel against honesty," he said quietly, glancing at Silas then looking away. He could not bear the understanding in the steady dark eyes.

"And I do not do so now. It is the timing of this truth, rather than the truth itself, that I would question." Silas tilted his head in Yosef's direction. "And if I know your Jew at all, he, too, advises you to wait." When Theo did not answer, Silas made a gruff sound. "The Jew gives good counsel," he said slowly. "If he knows this thing and does not stand between you and your bride, just as I know this thing and do not stand in your path, why do you think to know better?"

Theo's mouth hardened. "Was it not you who once told me that a man such as Oppa does not change his nature? He will use that parchment, Silas. And Lælia will never forgive me when she discovers it."

"Your bride has many hard lessons ahead, *wenkai*. This is but one of them." When Theo looked at him in surprise, Silas was not smiling. "The Lady of Illiberis is a woman of worth, a woman of bravery. But she wins one victory, using an army that is not hers, against a small force, where she has the advantage of land and defence, and believes herself now a warrior. Whereas you and I, *wenkai*?" Silas lifted a shoulder. "We have fought a hundred battles and more, and we know that such a victory is no more than the first rung of a ladder she has neither the forces nor the coin to climb. You know this, or you would be in Illiberis still, preparing men to fight for it."

"You do not understand what Illiberis means to her." Theo swallowed and looked out over the still, brown river. "I fear," he said, more to himself, "that even I had forgotten that."

Silas snorted. "Do I not, *wenkai*?" When Theo turned back to him, Silas's face was uncharacteristically grim. "Do you think I came to the fleet from the air, that a stray wind blew me from my homeland and into the emperor's service?" Taken aback, Theo stared at him. In fact, he had never given great thought to Silas's origins, other than to know that he was African. "The home I had is long gone." Silas held his eyes. "All I knew from that time are dead. I will perhaps never see the home of my childhood again, and if I did, perhaps I would not so much as know it, for I know now that a home is only such when it is filled with those we love. If the whispers along the road are true, soon enough both you and your bride will be standing before a council with this king you hate. When you do, that parchment Oppa holds may well be the only thing standing between the two of you and death." His eyes darkened. "I like the subterfuge no more than you, *wenkai*. But after seeing you wait so long to find her again, I like even less the idea of you losing her once more. And lose her you will, if she knows you have already used her homeland to trade with the same man she recently risked everything to defeat. The loss of those she loved is too raw, her victory too recent. She will likely turn and ride back to her lands, choose a fight over diplomacy. And then, *wenkai*, it can only end in blood."

"It is wrong to lie to her." Theo's voice rasped in his throat as he said the same words he had to Yosef. "You know it is wrong, Silas."

"Yes." Silas nodded slowly. "It is wrong. It may also be the only way to keep her alive." He took his hand from Theo's horse and turned his eyes back to the road. "I do not like it any more than do you, *wenkai*. And your Jew; for all his love of subterfuge, I think he does not like this lie, either. But I think that he, like I, prefers the lie than to see you both torn apart by Oppa's games; or, worse, to watch Lælia waste her courage and strength upon wielding steel in a war she cannot hope to win." He hardened his mouth. "The time will come for confessions, *wenkai*. But today is not that day."

As Leofric rode close, Silas raised his voice to a more jocular tone. "Today," he said, "you stand before a priest and take the girl whose name you have whispered in your sleep every night since I pulled you from the water." The large hand clapped Theo's shoulder hard enough to almost knock him from his horse, and he nudged Leofric with the other. "At least then we might all get some sleep, no?" Laughing in a deep, rich rumble, he spurred his horse ahead to Lælia's side, taking Leofric riding with him and leaving Theo to ride into Corduba alone.

* * *

THEO HAD MET Riccilo only once before, many years ago, and briefly. But even he could tell the strain of war had taken its toll. Though still tall and proud, her elegant features uncannily like Lælia's own, there were lines at the edges of her mouth and on her forehead, and silver streaks marred hair that had once been raven black. She greeted them perfunctorily, with little regard for either Theo's long absence or his and Lælia's recent bereavements. Theo, who was long accustomed to the aftermath of war, was neither offended nor shocked by her brevity. It was, in some ways, a relief to simply discuss what lay before them all. Or it would have been, had Riccilo not rounded on Lælia the moment they were alone.

"The messenger you sent told me there was a battle. Against Oppa himself, no less."

"We did not know to whom the army belonged when we mounted a defence." By the stubborn tightening of Lælia's expression and the mutinous set to her mouth, Theo guessed this was not the first time the two women had been at cross purposes. "We defended Illiberis from an attacking force. Any man would have done the same."

"Men are fools with more steel than brains, and you, Lælia, were raised to have more sense." Riccilo shook her head in frustration. "Theodofred is even now captive in Egica's dungeon for doing no more than looking the other way when his men rode with Paulus. What do you think Egica will do to you, if he discovers that you not only raised arms against his own son but, if your messenger is to be believed, used foreign mercenaries to defeat him?"

Put like that, Theo thought, Lælia's position was shown in stark relief.

"I do not think Oppa will allow his father to hear so much as a whisper of his defeat at Illiberis." Lælia's face had settled into a cold, blank mask. "His men, too, are paid mercenaries, loyal only to him – now that Giscila is dead."

Riccilo blanched visibly at the name. Lælia nodded grimly. "It was Giscila who led the army against Illiberis. And it was in taking his life that Acantha lost her own."

For a moment, Theo thought he detected a softening in the older woman's face, but a moment later the hard, brittle expression was back. "Revenge." Riccilo almost spat the word. "For this Acantha lost her life and endangered yours? Revenge is for children." She shook her head angrily. "All she has done is give Egica yet another reason to kill you, should he hear of it."

"I could have killed Egica's son." Lælia's voice was hard. "I had him, Riccilo. I could have held Oppa hostage, and the Crown to ransom. Do not think I did not consider it." Lælia's voice was hard. Theo hid his surprise. They had not spoken of this, apart from in those early moments following Oppa's flight, and he had wondered more than once what she had thought at the time. "But I did neither of those things. None can say that I waged war upon the Crown. I defended Illiberis with every means at my disposal, until I knew it was the king's son who rode against us, and then I let him go. A hundred men can testify to that. Egica will likely condemn me as a traitor either way, even if, as I suspect, he never learns the truth of what happened at Illiberis." She shrugged with an insouciance Theo suspected she did not truly feel. "There is no escape from that, Riccilo. At least I know that I did what was needed to defend our land. I would do it again." Her brows drew down. "I *will* do it again."

"Do it again?" Riccilo stared at her. "Have you lost every wit God gave you, child? The rebellion is over. Your grandfather lost and paid for that fool Sunifred's arrogance with his life, as did too many good men. Egica has my son. He has Theo's sister. And he holds all our futures in his hands, to do with what he will. Even if he learned it was his son who launched the attack, it would not matter, not now that he is victorious. You are right about one thing: he will name you traitor either way. Illiberis is lost, Lælia —"

"Illiberis will never be lost! Not to me!" Lælia's fists clenched at her sides, her topaz eyes flashing.

"Illiberis is lost," Riccilo repeated more loudly, as if her niece had not spoken, "and you will be fortunate if your life, too, is not forfeit, for I would not be at all surprised if Egica ordered his tame bishops to sanction the murder of women as well as men." She was quivering with rage and fear as she finished speaking, and Theo, long familiar with such shock, said gently to Lælia, "The servants told me the bathhouse fires are lit. Perhaps you might enjoy some time there, whilst I speak with your aunt?"

She opened her mouth and for a moment he thought she would refuse, but then she closed it abruptly, turned on her heel, and stalked away, not bidding her aunt goodbye.

"Well, at least she listens to you." Riccilo sank into a chair, her face flushed. "It is thanks to God, and Paulus's foresight, that the two of you are wed. That may be the only thing that saves her."

"I may yet be condemned alongside her," Theo said quietly. "It is possible that Aurariola will be taken."

"Possible!" Riccilo snorted. "It will be a miracle if it is not."

Theo thought of the parchment Oppa held, the deal they had once made. Would Oppa hold to it, even after what had taken place in Illiberis? Might he yet save Aurariola? *He may hold to it. And he may not.* Either way, Theo's stomach churned at the knowledge that it would be Oppa who held his fate in his hands. *I should have killed him,* he thought viciously, as he had a hundred times since he had watched Oppa ride from Illiberis. But if he had, they would even now be riding to their deaths, with nothing to save them. It might well have been that he and Lælia had both drawn the same conclusion, though for different reasons: Oppa alive was the best chance they had. The thought made him sick.

He forced himself to refocus. "I should tell you," he said to Riccilo, "that Lælia and I are not yet wed. I have sent for a priest."

"Not yet wed?" The colour drained from Riccilo's face. "Why, in the name of all the gods? Do you not know that Oppa himself is rumoured to be nearby?"

Anger twisted Theo's gut. "The bastard would do well to keep his distance from me," he said grimly. "And as I said, I have sent for a priest." He stood up, suddenly unable to remain still. "I am covered in dirt from the road. You will excuse me, Lady Riccilo." He strode from the room without waiting for a reply, Riccilo's sharp eyes boring into his back as he went.

"We are still waiting for the priest," said one of the Illiberis men hastily, seeing the dark expression on Theo's face as he came toward the stables.

"Then I shall find one myself." Aware that his tone was unnecessarily curt, Theo tried to soften it as he said, "Tell Silas and Leofric I've gone to the Basilica of Saint Vincent in search of one." He carried on before the man could reply, welcoming the chance to walk somewhere, anywhere, rather than sit contemplating the darkness of his future.

Theo had known he was returning to chaos, and possible death as a traitor. Oppa had said as much back in Sebastopolis, and though he knew not to trust a word the man said, that much Theo had not doubted. Oppa was too schooled in gathering information, and clever in his use of it, to lie about such a thing. Still, Theo had hoped. Hoped his father might somehow have been saved. That his brother might somehow have survived. That his sister might, by some miracle, have escaped Egica's clutches.

But if he was honest, Theo thought, striding grimly through the bustling streets that ran alongside the great basilica, ignoring the curious glances at his ravaged face with practised detachment, there had been one thing, or person, that had overridden every other doubt or concern. Theo had returned to Spania because he wanted Lælia more than he valued his own life. Because the mere thought of Oppa taking his place beside her, in life and in bed, sickened him to the point of madness.

What point, though, had there been in his grim determination to survive the hell he had lived through and return to Lælia, if the only future they faced lay at the end of a rope, a spectacle for the scum of Toletum to titter over as they drank their wine? Theo hit a stone wall in passing, hard enough to draw blood from his knuckles. Was he to marry Lælia, only to lose her, and his own life, in less than two turns of the moon? He stopped mid-stride, staring down the road but seeing instead the options that lay before him. *Should we run?* The thought had been there, Theo knew, since the moment he landed at Ilyan's court to the news that Sunifred's rebellion had failed. It had lurked in his mind through the long night he had sat beside his brother's broken body, and it whispered in his ear as he rode the misty way from Illiberis to Corduba. It had sat on the edge of his tongue when he spoke to Lælia, like a treacherous shadow he couldn't quite bring himself to name.

Somehow even the thought left a sour taste of cowardice and dishonour in his mouth. He felt his ancestors, the great general, Geila, and his own granduncle, King Suintila, after whom his father had been named, shrink in shame that any of their noble blood would flee the nation they had given their lives to build. Spania was Theo's home. Sooner rather than later, he knew, its very existence would be threatened by the might of the Arab army he had spent the past five years fighting. And where would he, Theo, be, when they came for his homeland? An exile, despised and hated by his own countrymen, unable to stand at their side?

No. He could not be that man. And after hearing her speak to Riccilo, he doubted Lælia would ever flee, either. *Even if you wanted to run, you know you don't have the strength to run away from her.* The thought twisted uncomfortably within. He shouldn't be surprised; her loyalty to Illiberis, after all, was the very reason she had agreed to marry him in the first place. No matter what else she might be prepared to lose, she would fight for that. To the death, if need be. How could he ever have doubted that? And why, he wondered, must coming home be so cursedly hard?

He kicked a stone, sending it flying down the road.

"Homecoming not quite what you'd expected?"

The cold, silky voice sent a shudder of revulsion through Theo's body. "I thought I'd made it clear in Illiberis, Oppa

Egicason," Theo said, without turning around. "You are not welcome near me, or any I call mine."

"From what I hear, you have been remarkably slow to make the Lady of Illiberis yours, given how hard you fought to return to her." Since Oppa's words mirrored Theo's own thoughts almost exactly, he found himself with clenched fists and gritted teeth, struggling not to draw a sword. He fought to get his emotions under control, but something of what he felt must have shown in his face, for when he turned, it was to find Oppa smiling coldly, a gleam of triumph in the flat obsidian eyes.

"You did not truly think your little bride's victory at Illiberis would be the end of matters between us, Aurariola, did you? Ah." Oppa cast his eyes skyward, as if struck by an idea. "Am I still to call you by that name, Theudemir? Will my father, do you think, call you by that name?"

"What is it you want?" Theo hissed. "Say it and be gone."

"You know what I want." Oppa stepped forward, his voice hard, all trace of levity gone. "You know the parchment I hold. It has your signature upon it. My offer stands. I will speak for you to my father. You will marry your whore and take your father's lands. Keep your title at court. None save I knows you were present at Illiberis, nor exactly what took place there. Should the conflict be spoken of, it will be said that the attack was led by my exiled uncle, whom all know to be a madman. The defenders were sent by the witch Al Kahinat, who all know buys horseflesh from Illiberis, and who had no love for my uncle. She saw a chance to dispose of him and sent her mercenaries to take advantage of Spania's chaos." He shrugged dismissively. "But really, there is no need for any of this to come to my father's ears. I can see that it does not – or that what whispers might reach him are easily explained away."

Theo stared at him through narrowed eyes. "Do not pretend that you tell such lies to serve my interests. I cannot imagine you wish your father to know that even with an entire army at your back, you could not take Illiberis from an inexperienced girl."

Oppa's eyes flashed with bitter fury, and Theo felt a savage stab of satisfaction that disappeared just as quickly a moment later, when, his brief display reined tightly back under control, Oppa said softly, "Careful, now, Theudemir. You and I both know that I hold the only sure way out of this, for you and Lælia."

"Why would you help us now?" Theo flung the words at him, sickened at the sound of Lælia's name on Oppa's lips. "Aurariola and Illiberis are both forfeit to the Crown for their part in the rebellion. You have no need to make deals. They are the Crown's by default, just as our lives are in your father's hands." The words tasted like dirt on his tongue, but such was his mood, Theo took a twisted pleasure in the pain of saying them. "You have Lælia and me at your mercy. What else could you possibly want?"

Oppa did not react to his hostility but went on in a matter-of-fact tone. "I told you once before that Spania will not always be under my father's rule." Theo knew too well the shadows that lived behind the man's eyes, the thin smile, to doubt there were games here of Oppa's device that he did not yet know. "When we face the threat you and I both know is coming," Oppa went on, "I intend to be in a position to fight it. Having you settled in Aurariola on the eastern coast is to my advantage." He smiled coldly. "Particularly when I know you are there by my favour."

"Fight it, you say." Theo repeated the words flatly. "The last time we encountered Arabs, Oppa, I do not recall you fighting them. Has something changed, since Sebastopolis?"

Oppa's smile was like oil on water, slick and transient. "Ah, but Sebastopolis was always going to be lost. And there, my family did not sit on the throne."

Theo stared at him in disgust. "Perhaps it might not have been lost, had you not actively worked to make it so."

"Perhaps." Oppa shrugged and smiled again. "And

perhaps you might take Sebastopolis as a lesson in what happens to those who work against me, instead of with me."

"Even if you manage to conceal the truth," Theo said amidst a rising tide of self-disgust that he was even having this conversation, "why would you think your father will grant you leave to take that as your own?"

"Because after the war he has just fought, my father has more need of coin than he does a troublesome southern province too far to ride in any comfort – yet another reason he is unlikely to listen to whispers about battles fought there. Particularly battles that may involve my long-exiled uncle." Oppa smiled grimly. "My father does not need ancient scandals tainting his fresh victory. In addition, I, you understand, have coin enough to buy his crown for myself – and a great liking for the privacy Illiberis affords."

"If you have coin enough to usurp him," said Theo, curious despite himself, "why don't you? Why plead for crumbs from a table you might instead eat from at your pleasure?"

"Ah." Oppa's mouth curled in a smile that didn't reach his eyes. "But now you ask questions beyond the rank of a common soldier, Theo, when your job is to take orders rather than question the strategy."

"And what is that strategy, exactly, Oppa?" Theo's voice was flat and hard.

Oppa's mouth curled. "Nothing so terrible. Only your help, Theo, to best prepare Spania for the threats that lie ahead."

"And again I wonder, what is it that you know, exactly, of these threats?" Theo's eyes narrowed. "Who is it?" he asked abruptly. "Your ally, in the Arab forces?" It was something that had bothered Theo ever since they sailed from Sebastopolis. Something even Yosef, for all his obscure connections, seemed not to know.

"Ah. Now why on earth would I tell you that?" Oppa was enjoying this, Theo knew, and it sickened him. "I think,"

Oppa went on, "that instead, we should speak of how to ensure that you keep Aurariola – and your head."

Oddly, it was not rage Theo felt, facing his old enemy in a crowded Corduba street. There had been too many taunts, over the years, for him not to see what lay behind them. Dangerous Oppa undoubtedly was. Vile, certainly. But he was also the boy Theo had once chased off with an arrow, and a man who had only recently left the battlefield of Illiberis after suffering a round humiliation at the hands of an inexperienced female commander. Theo might have hated Oppa Egicason with the force of a thousand men, but he knew him, too.

"It's a strange thing about soldiers," he said evenly. "They have an annoying habit of not only enduring long wars, but of winning them too, eventually. However long it takes." Holding Oppa's eyes long enough to see the sly smile disappear, Theo turned, ready to walk away.

"I have your sister, Egilona."

Oppa's voice stopped him.

"I have Rekiberga, too. Though she, I don't think I can save. My father has quite the creative taste for vengeance, you understand. I may be able to stop him from killing her, but beyond that…" He let his words trail off. Theo turned slowly back around, but he didn't speak. "And do not think I don't know your Jew rides with you." Something truly ugly crossed Oppa's eyes, and Theo almost took a step back, despite himself. "What do you think my father would do if he knew there was a treasonous snake travelling in your company, Aurariola, one who is in league with the bothersome Jewish dissidents who even now murmur of forcing my father's hands? How long would you remain out of a dungeon if he thought you part of their plot? But the Jew, too, I will let go unmolested, so long as he turns now and runs for Septem. I will find time for that Jew, one day," said Oppa softly, his voice almost a hiss. "He almost killed me, in Sebastopolis. Such things are not to be forgotten. It is not over between him and me. But not yet. Not yet." He stared at Theo. "Your uncle's fleet lies in the river at Hispalis." His voice lost its sibilant anger, becoming brisk and efficient, the sudden change of tone and topic taking Theo by surprise. "That fleet could be yours. You could take up the role you always meant to have – that of commander of Spania's fleet, an honoured and respected military leader, as your father was and his before him." Despite the slightly mocking tone, his eyes were steady on Theo's. "You can even pacify your bride with the lie that one day she might have Illiberis back, that this trade is no more than a temporary thing." He smiled coldly. "I will not betray your lie, Theudemir. You may tell her whatever you choose. None will know the truth but you, and I."

Goaded beyond restraint, Theo stepped forward, his hand on his sword hilt. He wanted to reach inside the black eyes and pull out every piece of the darkness that lived there. "What is the end you seek, Oppa?" he hissed.

Oppa smiled coldly. "Think on what I offer, Aurariola. You are yet to reach Toletum. You can arrive there the son of a traitor, condemned to death or disgrace; or an honourable man of Spania, who returned to his king in good faith, as ally – yes, even as friend – to the king's own son. All I wish, for the moment at least, is that our old arrangement stands. We tell the story Spania will understand: we fought together abroad, we return with our enmities laid to rest. We do not mention what occurred at Illiberis so recently, nor at sea, nor back on a distant battlefield in Sebastopolis." He met Theo's eyes. "Your future is in your own hands, Theo. Think carefully what you do with it."

"How do you imagine I would ever trust you to keep your word?" Theo's hand was still on his sword. "You lie with every breath you take. How do I know you will not expose that parchment to the entire court? It is the easiest way for you to achieve your ends. Your father would laud you for it. None would blame you. And I could not deny it. In one stroke you would achieve all you have ever wanted."

Oppa's smile did not waver. "I could have done that the moment I landed in Spania. But you and I both know the only real power in that parchment lies in the fact that you signed it without Lælia's consent or knowledge. It has value only so long as it is a secret you wish kept, Theo, and no further. I could wield it against you at court, but it does not of itself grant me Illiberis. Only an act of public concession will achieve that, followed by the signing of a formal contract, between you, Lælia, and I, handing over sole control of the latifundium to me." Oppa held up a hand, smiling silkily. "I do not expect this immediately, you understand. Such a demand might well shake the delicate balance you and I have reached. Your bride will need time to adjust to her new reality." His smile faded as quickly as it had come. "So long as you remember that I could have shown Lælia the parchment back in Illiberis. We both know that if I had, you and I would be having a very different conversation now. But I didn't." Turning, he began to walk away. "Think about that," he called over his shoulder to Theo. "I could have seen your destruction before you so much as drew a breath of Spanish air. Ask yourself why, if I meant to betray you, I did not do it then. Ask — and then make the right choice, Theudemir of Aurariola. Whilst you still have the liberty to do so."

* * *

Theo returned to the villa by a rear entrance. He needed to speak to Yosef, and he didn't want to chance an encounter with any other until he had.

The road ahead seemed darker than any other he had faced. On one side, exile. On the other, lies. In between those was Lælia. *It has value only so long as it is a secret you wish kept, Theo, and no further.* After Oppa's words, Theo knew, more than he had ever known anything, that the only right course was to tell her. But he knew, too, that doing so would mean the end of all they had.

74

When he had signed that parchment, back in the turgid morass that had been Sebastopolis, he had been able to convince himself that perhaps Lælia might understand his reasons. So many years into a foreign war, Spania had ceased, in his mind, to be divided into this latifundium or that; he had almost stopped thinking of Aurariola or Illiberis. To Theo, battle weary and focused on the Arab threat that had been his life for so long, home had become a distant concept, one that was a neat bundle of two things: Lælia and Spania. The two things had seemed intertwined: Lælia's life, and the future of his homeland as a whole. The truth was that Theo had, if not forgotten Lælia's bond to Illiberis, at the very least, underestimated the depth and power of it.

His return had brought the reality home to him with stark clarity, and with it, the terrible gravity of his betrayal. He had signed away Lælia's birthright, her heritage.

Her soul.

If he told her, there would be no marriage. There would be nothing of the future he had dreamed of. And Lælia herself — what would she do? Theo paused in the breezeway, thinking of the fury and scorn on her face as she confronted Riccilo. *Silas was right. She will run back to Illiberis, and then she will fight.* He knew it with a hard, horrible certainty. *And if she fights, she will die.*

He made a hard noise of frustration. It was not for him to decide what Lælia would or would not do. He had only one choice within his power: to tell her the truth, or to marry her on a lie. After that, he could only accept what she chose.

The thought sent a dark, terrible fear through him, worse than any battle eve he had faced.

A door opened to his right, and suddenly all thought fled Theo's head.

It was Lælia, come up the stairs from the bathhouse at the rear of the house. As the door opened, Theo was assailed with the steamy scent of her bathing — rose and almond, mingled with a hint of sharp, fresh citrus that brought so many memories back it made his senses reel. *It comes from her hair,* Theo thought in a wild snatch of recall, staring at the long damp tangle that fell down her back, stark black against the white linen. He remembered that scent. It had clung to his senses through his darkest nights, the promise of sunlit fields and home. She stepped hesitantly into the breezeway, her eyes on his, the curves of her body shaping the thin robe. Theo found he could barely breathe.

Lælia's hand touched his face, the smooth runnels of scar beneath his eyes, her thumb tracing them. "What troubles you?" She stepped closer, the warm heat of her body scented and intoxicating, and Theo was lost.

His arm went around her waist, pulling the slender warmth of her against him, whilst with the other he wrenched open the door behind her and pulled them both into the dark, scented intimacy of the stairwell. Candles burned in sconces on the wall, casting a flickering light in which nothing was clear. Her arms snaked around his neck and he took her mouth with the hunger and desperation of a man who knew well it might be the last time he ever touched her. The stone wall behind her was warm from the fires below and he held her against it, dipping into her mouth over and over, his hands travelling down her body to lift her against the stone. Her legs came around him and he groaned against her mouth as he moved into their cradle. She twined around him in lithe, scented warmth, her hands on his face and in his hair, pulling him fiercely to her, every muscle in her body drawing him closer.

The skin of her shoulder was velvet smooth, her neck rich with rose and almond beneath his lips, and she made a small noise that he thought, through the heady haze of her nearness, he could not bear to never hear again. The thought made him savage. His body was hard and fired, and he had no thought of pause.

The sound of footsteps flung him away from her as a long

shadow approached the bottom of the stairs. "Go," Theo said hoarsely, horrified at what he had almost done. "Go, Lælia."

Her eyes were dark and heavy lidded with desire, the hard buds of her breasts pushing through the thin robe, her skin flushed where his mouth had touched it. "Promise," she said roughly, her eyes searching his face, and the word broke him, because Theo knew she saw the darkness within and had invoked the one word that bound them more than any marriage contract ever had. His hand came up over his heart as if willed by itself, the old gesture they had once exchanged in a stable lit much as this stairwell.

"Promise," he murmured, and the word tore him in two even as it sealed them both into one, forever.

Lælia held his eyes for a long moment. Then, as the servant appeared at the bottom of the stairs, she opened the door and was gone.

8

YOSEF

MARCH, AD 693

Corduba, Spania
Cordoba, Spain

Yosef heard impatient footsteps pounding the stone and was facing the door when Theo thrust it open, then closed it with enough force to shake dust motes into the air.

"This is a conversation I do not wish overheard." Theo strode to the window and stared grimly in either direction before pulling the shutters closed, leaving the room dimly lit by the oil lamps on the wall and a lone candle on the small table. He turned to face him. "I spoke with Oppa." He said the words in a flat, expressionless tone, but Yosef, seeing the fiercely clenched jaw and the green fire in his friend's eyes, thought he had never seen Theo so close to the edge.

He poured wine and wordlessly handed Theo a full cup, which was tossed off with little more than a glance. Yosef refilled it and waited.

"He knows you are here." Theo met Yosef's eyes. When Yosef didn't speak, he went on. "His offer still stands: he takes

Illiberis; I keep Aurariola." He paused, holding Yosef's eyes. "And you will be permitted to leave Spania. Unharmed."

"My wellbeing is not your concern," began Yosef immediately.

"He knows about the Jewish plans to rise against the Crown, Yosef." Theo cut him off. "And, even more dangerously – he hates you. He hates you even more, I think, than he does me. The encounter between you back in Sebastopolis got to him. You humiliated him, made him feel powerless. I know Oppa. He cannot let such things go, even when he wants to. Which means he has games planned for you still." His words were dull and hard. "If we hesitate now, Oppa will see you dead before you ever see Sarah again, Yosef. There are two reasons he has not yet done so: because he does not yet know the truth of your journey – and because he uses you as a pawn to gain what he wants from me."

Yosef felt the colour drain from his face. Part of him had known the rebellion was a fool's game, one that had no hope for success. But to hear aloud that Oppa already knew of it enraged Yosef in a way he himself hadn't anticipated.

Theo, seeing his face, nodded grimly. "He means to kill you. But before he does, he will discover what you went east to learn, and torture you until you tell him the whole." One of Theo's hands touched his face in reminiscence. "And if you think these scars tell the full story of Oppa's penchant for torture, believe me when I say he has only learned more sophisticated methods in the years since he practised upon me. We have come too far, Yosef, and both endured too much, to see all we have worked for lost under Oppa's whip. You cannot fall into his hands."

Theo spun away. Three short paces took him across the room. He turned and stalked back, his chest rising and falling in hard, uneven breaths. "I can't do it, Yosef." Theo's voice cracked on his friend's name. "I can't marry her upon a lie. Not after all this time. And after seeing her in Illiberis…" His voice broke. "I had forgotten, Yosef," he whispered hoarsely.

"I had forgotten how close tied she is to that land. What I did…" He broke off, shaking his head in self-recrimination. "It was unforgiveable." This time, when Theo met his eyes, Yosef saw the red-rimmed exhaustion in them, the toll that the lie had already taken. Theo, Yosef realised, had not slept an easy night since the day they had ridden into Illiberis and seen Lælia staring Oppa down.

"We could kill him." Yosef said it flatly, and Theo did not blanch.

"Do you imagine I haven't thought of that?" Theo shook his head again, wearily. "He holds too much in his hands, Yosef. I have not existed alongside the man for the past years without knowing something of the manner in which he operates. If Oppa should die here, we would be arrested before we returned to the villa, hung as traitors before dawn. Oppa does not leave such things to chance. If we killed him, it would be exile – and even then, I could not guarantee our safety. All we have fought for would be lost. Your journey would have been for nothing. All of it… all those years. Wasted." His voice broke with frustration and he gripped the back of the *lecta*, staring grimly at the wall.

Yosef clenched his fists. "Then we will tell her. Some of it, at least."

Theo's eyes narrowed, but he didn't speak.

"We don't have a choice." Yosef spoke slowly, the words helping him form his own thoughts. "You do not have the character to maintain a lie, and Lælia is too observant to be long fooled. Better that we address this now, take control of it." He turned away from Theo and walked slowly to the closed shutters, his mind separating the issues with the diplomatic dexterity years of travel had taught him. Not for the first time, Yosef observed the ability in himself with a certain amount of distaste. In counterpoint to Theo's white-faced strain, his own diplomacy seemed dishonourable, contemptible even.

Yosef pushed aside his qualms and thought rapidly.

He had to be in Septem when Athanais arrived from Constantinople, which she would do as soon as the weather turned warm. He had entrusted her with the silkworms he had carried from Serica, and he was the only one amongst them who understood the process of their cultivation. If they were lost, all he had risked would be for nothing. He could not take that chance.

The Jewish rebellion was another problem he did not wish to be long away from. He knew well the foolhardiness of men emboldened by a small victory. Even now, the Jews of Garnata began to believe themselves capable of actually waging a war, at least for long enough to fight for changes to the laws governing them. Yosef knew their hopes were ambitious at best, foolhardy at worst, and he could not bear to see them sacrifice themselves against Oppa's brute steel. But Lælia, he knew, would never accept the loss of Illiberis. *Unless,* he thought, *she believes it a temporary measure — one that would save lives.* Yosef turned back to Theo.

"The only thing Lælia cares about more than Illiberis itself is the people for whom she feels responsible. Particularly those who are vulnerable: the Jews of Garnata; the tribes of the mountains who guard the Illiberis horses. We will tell her that Oppa's deal is a short-term solution, the only way to protect them until we can regroup and take back Illiberis. We tell her that I will return to Septem, to better organise the rebellion there, and to gain Ilyan's help in gathering a stronger force with which to return."

"She will never forgive me for signing Illiberis over to Oppa without her consent." Theo shook his head. "Never."

Yosef took a deep breath. "Then we don't tell her."

Theo's head snapped up.

"We don't mention anything of the parchment you signed in Sebastopolis. We don't tell her the whole." Theo's face darkened, and Yosef felt his own words corrode something inside him.

"We will say that we are only pretending to relinquish

Illiberis to Oppa and have no intention of allowing him to take it permanently. We tell her that the reason Oppa is prepared to make a deal, rather than condemn you both as traitors, is, firstly, because he is afraid of what you might say of his role in the attack on the fleet, and secondly because he does not dare openly admit to his father that he attacked Illiberis and lost." He forced himself to look steadily at Theo with his next words. "We tell Lælia that I return to Septem only to gather a greater force upon which to build a rebellion."

Theo visibly blanched. "This is not one lie we tell now, but two," he said roughly. "First we tell her nothing of the parchment, and then we say that we intend, eventually, to regain Illiberis."

Yosef saw his own self-disgust mirrored in his friend's eyes. "Perhaps it may prove true," he said quietly. "Neither you nor I know what the future holds."

Theo made a harsh sound. "It is no more than a fairy tale, Yosef. You know that as well as I. The moment this deal is done, Illiberis is gone."

"Perhaps." Only his long years of diplomacy helped Yosef maintain an even tone. "But what we do both know, without doubt, is that Illiberis cannot be held now. And if Lælia tries to hold it, she will die, Theo."

"It is not my right to make that decision for her." Theo's voice cracked. His body had hunched in on itself as Yosef spoke, as if every word were a stone weighing his heart down.

"Is it not?" When Theo glanced up, startled, Yosef forced down his own qualms and met his eyes steadily. "Do you think she would not make the same decision for you, if it meant saving your life?"

Theo searched his face, frowning. "Why are you so sure this is the right thing, Yosef? It is not like you to encourage a lie. Yet both you and Silas counsel this." He shook his head. "I do not like it."

The room blurred before Yosef's eyes. For a moment he

was back in Paulus's study, sitting beside Lælia as her grandfather spoke of Illiberis: *Your family settled this valley, Yosef, just as Lælia's settled in Illiberis. Together, we will preserve both.*

Lælia's eyes glittering topaz as her hands moved, in the gestures that were once her words: *If anyone wishes to take them from us, they must first pass the tribes – and me...*

The memory was so clear it was as if he could see the patrician's hawkish, stern features, his own father's quiet pride. But most of all, he saw Lælia as she had been then, wild and fierce, utterly linked to the earth from which she sometimes seemed, to Yosef, to have sprung.

"Illiberis is not just land to Lælia," he said slowly, still staring into the distance. "You and I, Theo – we have lived a long time outside of Spania. And I am not certain either of us ever felt defined by the soil of our birth. We understand land as do most men, as an asset." He pulled his eyes back to Theo. "But I rode for a long time with Dahiya. Land, to her, was not an asset. Altava, the kingdom for which she fights, is her soul. It is who she is and what she lives for. Without Altava, there would be no Dahiya; and without her, I believe the dream of Altava would die." He paused. "I think it is the same for Lælia and Illiberis. That land is her mother, and her child, but never has it been simply an asset. And if she believes, even for a moment, that you traded it as one, I think it would break something inside her that cannot be repaired." He held Theo's eyes. "I am afraid if that break happens now, Theo, that she will burn Illiberis, and herself, to the ground.

"But Lælia is no fool. She knows as well as any of us the capricious nature of kings, and of war. She already knows she faces charges of treason, and I believe she will accept conceding Illiberis as a temporary measure. Particularly if it means saving your life." When Theo made a furious noise, Yosef held up a hand. "Wait. I am not suggesting she does this for you, but if Illiberis is her soul, Theo, you are her heart. I would not see both broken." Theo looked up sharply at that, his eyes narrowing, and Yosef knew his words had found their mark. "And they would be, Theo, if she ever learns that parchment was signed back in Sebastopolis. Nobody needs to know you agreed to this, and that Oppa holds your agreement in writing."

"Oppa will know." Theo's voice was hard. "That parchment is a weapon he will wield without mercy, Yosef. I know him. He will hold it, taunt me with it, and in the end, destroy both Lælia and me with it."

"You can't know that. You know as well as I how fates change." Yosef gripped his arm. "All I know is that if you admit this to her now, Theo, you will never even have a chance at that life. It will be gone, forever; and worse, Lælia will be broken. She will ride from here, head for the home that she loves, and if she does, it is as likely as not that she will die as a traitor. I don't think I can live with that. Can you, Theo?"

Yosef and Theo stared at one another, the words hanging in the dim air between them.

"I can't do this." Theo's voice was a hoarse whisper. "It is a lie, Yosef."

"A lie that will save her life – and the lives of countless others." Yosef's mouth twisted. "Do not think I like it any more than you, Theo. For I do not." For once, Yosef did not try to mask his inner turmoil but let it show on his face, in the eyes that Theo held. "I act as much from my own interests as do you, in this. And I despise myself equally. But you and I both know what is truly at stake. Lælia is my oldest friend. I honour her as my sister. I know her bond with Illiberis and I honour that, also, for I have lived alongside it all my life. But I have also walked to the furthest edges of our known world, as have you. I know that when the Arabs come, such pagan bonds will matter not at all – even less, perhaps, than they do beneath the Christians. If there is no united front to protect Spania from invasion, Illiberis will cease to matter, as will Garnata. I cannot put aside that knowledge any more than you can, Theo." He paused. "Even if I believe that Spania may well be better served by Arab masters than it is by Christian ones." His mouth twisted at Theo's visible surprise. "Do not forget," he said softly, "the laws your people continue to pass against my own. There is good reason the Jews of Garnata plot rebellion, Theo. And when the day comes that Spania is threatened, do not expect them to fight at your side. The Gothic kings have given us little reason to love them."

A knock at the door saved them from what Yosef suspected might, in another time, have been a hard argument. "The priest has come," came the muffled voice of a messenger. "The Lady Riccilo says the *œca* will be ready in one hour."

Theo wrenched the door open and issued a stern, one-word command: "Wait." He shut the door and strode restlessly to the window. "There is another solution," he said roughly. He braced himself, one hand either side of the window, and his head slowly bowed, until he was staring at the floor, his powerful shoulders tensed as if for war. "If I do not marry her – if I break the betrothal – that parchment has no power."

The words hung in the air between them, suspended as if time itself had stopped. In their weight, Yosef saw and felt all that had come before this moment: the years of separation and longing; the torture and terror of slavery; the blood and steel of war; the hard, horrible fear that Theo would never return, or that if he did, it would be to find Lælia dead, or taken.

"No," Yosef said.

Theo did not look at him. "It is the honourable thing to do, Yosef."

"It would also destroy you both." Theo turned slowly around, his eyes searching Yosef's face. "If you leave her now," Yosef said, "she will never forgive you. Even if you tell her the reason why; perhaps especially then. She has lived all these years waiting for your return." He shook his head. "You have lived enough of your lives apart, Theo. Now it is time to face your future together, whatever that might bring."

"Whatever that might bring," Theo echoed hollowly. He

shook his head. "I wonder if any good can come of something that is born of lies." But Yosef knew he spoke to himself, and when he straightened, his face was already closing over. "I must talk to Lælia before we are wed."

Yosef nodded. "Together, Theo. We will tell her together." He waited a moment. "It will be better coming from us both," he said, and he could hear the pain in his own voice.

Theo's mouth hardened. "Of all the roads I have taken," he said bleakly, "never have I chosen one more against my own conscience − nor loathed myself so much for the taking of it." Shaking his head, he opened the door to face the messenger. "Tell the Lady of Illiberis that her betrothed would speak with her before the ceremony," he said brusquely. The man, seeing the expression on Theo's face, swallowed any objections and went silently to do his bidding. "Come," said Theo grimly. "Let us have this over with."

* * *

"And Oppa agreed to this?" Lælia's eyes gleamed with a hard, golden light. Jadis, at her feet, growled softly.

Lælia was wrapped in a cloak that covered her gown, with a hood over her hair, and Yosef suspected she did not want Theo to see her before they stood before the priest. Her modesty was a reminder of the girl he knew lived within her, who still believed in Theo, in love, in the bond between them, and his heart ached for the betrayal they were enacting upon that innocence.

"He sought you out here, in Corduba," Lælia went on, "only to ask you not to betray his actions to his father?"

"Not only that." Yosef did not dare look at Theo as Lælia's eyes swivelled to him. "Oppa does not wish to admit a defeat, it is true, nor be openly exposed as the architect of the attack on the fleet. But it is more than that. Oppa is ambitious. He wants a stake in Spania's future. Egica already has a legitimate son. He has no need for an ambitious bastard with

86

resources to rival his own. Should Egica suspect Oppa's true power, the size of the force he landed and with which he attacked Illiberis, he may well decide to dispose of him. If Oppa is to remain his father's confidant, he must prove his allegiance, and his worth, to the Crown."

"So Oppa will speak for us both at Toletum," Lælia said slowly, looking between them, "in exchange for my saying that I willingly surrendered Illiberis to him, and you saying nothing of his part in the attack on the fleet?" Yosef nodded grimly, aware of Theo doing the same, but neither of them spoke. "You like this no more than I," Lælia said. It wasn't a question.

Yosef, waiting for Theo to speak, realised his friend couldn't bring himself to answer her. "It sickens both of us." He did not have to feign the harsh disgust in his voice. "But it may also be the only way both we, and the people of Illiberis, survive this, Lælia."

Lælia frowned. One hand went down to Jadis's head. The lynx sat silently, staring up at her mistress with golden, speculative eyes. Expecting fury, Yosef was taken aback when Lælia looked back at them and said thoughtfully, "I think you might be right."

Theo's head snapped up. "You do?"

Lælia's mouth curled slightly at the incredulous note in his voice. "I am not a child, Theo. I know there will be retribution for our fathers' role in the rebellion. And I know, too, that we do not yet have the forces to defy Egica. My grandfather knew it, as did your father. It is the reason they waited so long to join the rebellion. I will not repeat their mistakes, and I will not see those I am sworn to protect die for nothing." She looked at Yosef. "But you believe the Jewish forces in Septem might soon gain Ilyan's support." Yosef was grateful that she phrased it as a statement to which he needed only to nod agreement. He did not trust himself to speak. "And the deal is only words, something to appease the court, and Egica. Illiberis was not defeated and occupied as Sunifred's lands were. To take it formally will require time. Official agreements, a public concession. Without those, he will have little chance of securing the co-operation of the neighbouring nobility, and he will need that for Illiberis to mean anything. Without them, he can't access ports, nor trade with any ease. To the northern court my victory may never be known, but all the south knows Oppa was defeated at Illiberis. War may have cowed the southern lords. It hasn't erased their memories, however, especially of their sons lost at sea by his hand. They will not easily, if ever, accept Oppa as a neighbour. They certainly will not do so without a formal concession, written evidence of his claim." She was staring at the wall thoughtfully, speaking her thoughts aloud rather than to them, to Yosef's sickened relief. Lælia's easy acceptance of their story, her absolute trust in their word, hurt more than any knife cut could have. He did not dare look at Theo. He could not begin to imagine how the other man felt.

"I will send word to Zdan asking him to remain a time longer, whilst we wait to see if Ilyan plans to help us now, or later." Lælia's mouth tightened, and she looked up at Yosef. "You must tell Ilyan he cannot wait long. Oppa will not long be content with a deal in name only. The time will come, soon enough, when he takes over Illiberis, and every day he is there will make him more determined to formalise his arrangements. The southern lords will only hold out for so long; Illiberis is too valuable for them to ignore forever, both for defence and for trade. We have some time," she went on, her brow furrowed in concentration, "for they will not easily betray my family, but if they come to terms with Oppa as lord of Illiberis, it will be that much harder to win them back." She glanced at Theo, waiting, it seemed, for a sign, anything that might indicate his agreement with her thinking; Theo, however, remained stolidly silent, his expression carefully schooled into neutrality. It was, Yosef thought, a step too far for Theo to actually encourage her in his deception, and when he didn't speak, Lælia went on.

"Zdan and his men have already done more than I asked of them. They are not safe there, and it is unfair of me to ask them to tarry. I will not needlessly endanger them, Yosef. A few weeks, no more. You will return to Septem and then send word, yes?"

"Of course." Yosef was ashamed of how easily the lie slid from his lips.

"And you." Lælia turned to Theo. "Are you sure you can stomach Oppa lying about what he did to you? Stand in court and let him claim you as an ally, rather than taking responsibility for his crimes against you – for this?" She touched the scars on Theo's face, her own twisting with sympathy when Theo jerked away as if he had been burned. Yosef winced, feeling Theo's shame and self-disgust as if it were his own. To have Lælia believe them was bad enough. That she should feel sympathy for Theo whilst he betrayed her was a step further, and Yosef, seeing the agony Theo could not hide, felt sick.

"We will all do what we must." Theo's voice was hard as shattered glass, his movements mechanical. "We have no choice if we wish to survive."

Lælia nodded, her face grave. "At least we do it together," she said, and her sad smile broke Yosef's heart.

Theo nodded, but he did not speak.

They left Lælia standing in the room, her face soft with love and trust.

* * *

THEY WERE some way down the corridor when Theo finally spoke. "I will send Silas and Leofric to Aurariola the moment this day is done. Ensure that, at least, is safe. You will return to Septem and discover if there is any merit to this rebellion. If there is a way to make our words to Lælia less than a lie, we must find it."

Yosef nodded, though he knew the answer already. He

knew that Theo, too, knew, but that he had to at least ask, for his own heart's sake.

Outside the door to his chambers, Theo paused and turned to Yosef. "This filth remains between you and me," he said roughly. "Not because I will not own it. But because I will not have her shamed any more than we have already." He put his hands on his hips and looked away. "Lælia is not an innocent to be protected. She is intelligent, and brave. Honourable." His eyes turned back to Yosef. "I could have told her the whole."

"No," said Yosef quietly. "You could not, Theo, and you know it. Nothing you could say will ever make Lælia understand how, or why, you signed that contract without her agreement. It will break her heart and destroy the only thing that she will have to sustain her in the years to come: her love for you. All of this works only if Lælia believes in her heart that she is doing the right thing for Illiberis." He glanced around to make certain they were not overheard, but the long corridor was deserted. When Theo turned back to him, Yosef saw the resignation in his friend's eyes, and the beginning of the implacable mask starting to fall over it. Theo, he knew, was a soldier. He would find a way to mask his pain – even if it almost killed him to do it. "You have taken the only course open to you," Yosef said quietly. "Do not doubt it, Theo."

"I do not doubt it." The mask had fallen, and Theo's eyes were arctic chips of ice in his face. "But I will never forgive myself for it."

He opened the door and stepped inside. "Now leave me," he said, his back to Yosef. "And let me bathe before my wedding."

9

LÆLIA
MARCH, AD 693

Corduba, Spania
Cordoba, Spain

Lælia knew Theo was in the bathhouse. She had heard the servants talking amongst themselves as they carried linens down the stone stairs, their hushed whispers as they spoke of Theo's ravaged face. But it was not his face Lælia thought of when she imagined him in the bathhouse, which she could not seem to cease doing.

Riccilo's bathhouse, just as that in Illiberis, was a relic from an earlier, more lascivious time. It was a measure of the Duke of Corduba's influence that the priests had not yet closed the bathhouse, for they claimed bathing was an affectation of the wealthy, sinful against God. Lælia suspected it was Riccilo, who had been raised in the luxury of Illiberis, who had refused to allow them access. Certainly if they had seen it, those worthy men of God would have been horrified at the lewd scenes depicted in mosaic on the walls. It had been in Riccilo's bathhouse as a young girl that Lælia had first realised the nature of the images, the acts shown by them. In the years since she had looked askance at them, barely daring to examine the ways in which the naked figures were joined. Earlier, during her own bath, she had floated on her back in the dim light and allowed the water to hold her, shivering at the thought that in barely hours, she herself would be as those entwined bodies, lost in pleasures she had hitherto been able only to imagine.

Now Theo, too, was naked in that same water, looking upon the same scenes. Despite the savage pain she had once felt at the knowledge that he had lain with someone other than herself, Lælia found, as the moment of their wedding approached, that she was grateful that one of them, at least, had some experience of that which she had seen only in mosaic form.

It was easier to think of the wedding night ahead than the other matters they had just discussed. Even pretending to ally with Oppa sent dark fury racing through Lælia's veins. Then she would think of Theo, and what he had suffered at Oppa's hands, and chastise herself for her immaturity. If Theo could set aside his qualms after all he had endured, she thought, then surely she could do the same. And Illiberis, after all, was not gone forever. It was a ruse, nothing more, a necessary lie to save them both from execution. She shivered. That threat had not been spoken between her and Theo, nor by Yosef. But she had seen the shadow of it behind their eyes. Seen the fears they thought to shield her from. She was both touched by their regard for her, and mildly impatient that they should think her unable to face such stark realities, especially after the battle she had just experienced.

She wished, too, that Theo might speak to her of how he thought they should proceed in saving Illiberis. But once again, she thrust the thought aside. It was not for Theo to make such decisions. She was grateful he trusted her to make them herself. Most men, she knew, would never allow such autonomy.

Pulling a brush through her hair, Lælia wished that she

might feel easier about their impending reckoning at the capital, more certain of how to manage their eventual return to Illiberis. She began to plan the routes they might take, where they might hide with the tribes in the mountains whilst they planned to retake her home. And she would be with Theo, after all.

The thought sent the same delicious thrill through her as it always did. The miracle of his return was too great for anything else to cast a shadow for long. His touch blazed through the darkness that had surrounded her all the long years of his absence, his mouth on hers driving thought of any other concern, even Illiberis, to the far reaches of her mind. They had not yet so much as shared a bed and still Lælia thought she understood how nations had been won and lost for love. Her desire for Theo's presence seemed to occlude all other priorities, deem everything else irrelevant.

Riccilo's knock on the door made her jump. Lælia realised she had been sitting for some time with the brush in midair, her mind already lost in thoughts of the night to come.

"Lælia." Riccilo entered the room without pausing for permission, closing it firmly after her then crossing the room and closing the shutters, too, against any unwanted ears. "There is none left but me to counsel you." She drew up a stool next to Lælia and, taking the brush from her niece's hand, began pulling it through the long black curls with swift, efficient strokes, her face in the reflection of the polished bronze mirror wavy and indistinct. "There are things you must be made aware of before you bind yourself to Theo. For believe me – once you are wed, your fortunes are tied. No matter what those fortunes may be." Her mouth tightened and the brush tore through Lælia's hair with a force that made her wince.

"I thought you wanted me to marry Theo?" Lælia met her aunt's eyes in the mirror.

"I had thought you already wed. But if you are not, we have time still to consider your options." Ignoring the darkening expression growing on her niece's face, Riccilo went on: "You need protection. Nobody knows what will happen at Egica's council. Theo may be condemned as a traitor alongside his family, even if he was not directly involved in the rebellion. He could be dispossessed, even executed. Have you thought of that?"

"If he is dispossessed, we still have Illiberis. Or we will, soon enough."

Riccilo's hand stilled. "Illiberis?" Her eyes in the mirror narrowed. "Lælia – I told you on arrival: Illiberis is lost. You will never return there, or at least, not during Egica's reign. Certainly he will not allow the son and daughter of traitors to rule there together. Illiberis is a lost dream, Lælia. The sooner you recognise that, the easier your life will be."

Lælia fought the familiar tide of resentment and hostility she felt whenever Riccilo spoke of her future. "I will marry Theo, and we will make our decisions together."

"There is another way."

Lælia frowned. "Another way to do what?"

"Illiberis is a rich prize. There are other men at court who would pay dearly for access to it. Men who fought at Egica's side, and who have his favour."

Lælia turned on her stool and stared directly at Riccilo. "After all this time," she said flatly, "after all we have gone through – you would dare suggest such a thing?"

Riccilo pinched her lips. "Less than a year ago, I was married to the Duke of Corduba, the second most powerful man in Spania beside the king himself. A man descended from the most venerated of Spania's royal families, one who held a position all thought unassailable. Now my husband is in a dungeon, my son is held hostage, and I will enter Toletum under palace guard to watch a trial with no more idea than a common servant what the outcome will be. I dare suggest such a thing, Lælia, because I know how easy it is to lose everything." Jadis uncurled herself from the hearth where she lay and stalked slowly to Lælia's side, butting her hand with her large head. Lælia's hand rested on it, feeling the cat's taut power as if it were her own.

"And if there is a lesson to be had in what you say, is it not that marriage to a powerful man is no protection against fate – or Egica?" Lælia threw the words back at Riccilo. "I will marry Theo in less than an hour, Aunt. And we will face whatever comes together. Whether that is exile, war, service to a king we both despise – or, yes, even execution. Do you think I am blind to such possibilities, Riccilo? After all I have seen?" She shook her head impatiently. After so long making her own decisions, it was a difficult adjustment to be cast once more in the position of a child in need of advice. "I will say this, so you might know it: I did not face down the Toletum court, nor fight an army at Illiberis, merely to marry a man in order that he might protect me. I am marrying Theo because I love him. Because he is my choice. And because I trust him, no matter what we might face once we leave here." Jadis, curling about her legs, growled softly in agreement.

Riccilo took in the twin pairs of topaz eyes staring at her, and eventually her own face fell into resigned lines. She raised the brush and gave Lælia a half smile in the bronze. "Well," she said wryly, "it seems he can swing a sword well, at least. You may be grateful of that, in the end." Reaching into the bodice of her gown, she pulled out a small bag.

"Your grandfather sent me these, long ago, for safekeeping." She upended the bag onto the table, and two gold rings fell out, dull with age. "They are the rings that were exchanged at your betrothal. After Oppa tried to nullify it, the rings were kept with a copy of the contract, in the event you may again need evidence."

Lælia stared at the solid gold circles. They were nothing like the gaudy rings the Goths favoured, with rich stones and carvings at the centre. These were of the old Roman design, fede rings: plain bands, with two hands clasped at the centre.

She ran her thumb over the ridges of the design and shivered.

* * *

THE ŒCA WAS SPARSELY DECORATED, with none of the rich furnishings that would have accompanied such an occasion in another time. Lælia didn't care.

She wore a gown of crimson wool. Her hair was unbound, falling to her waist in smooth waves of midnight black, brushed to a sheen by Riccilo and threaded with night jasmine. Acantha's ruby, a long-ago gift to her grandmother from Dahiya, hung from a webbed chain in the centre of her forehead, gleaming like blood in the candlelight. Lælia paused at the door. She had insisted on entering alone, declining both Riccilo's and Yosef's offers to walk with her. Taking a deep breath, she entered.

Theo was standing below the dais, facing the door. His eyes met hers as she stepped through the entrance. They glittered arctic green, hard and rich at once, roaming slowly over her from head to foot. When they returned to her face there was a depth in them that made her breath catch.

Lælia walked toward him across the marble tiles, barely aware of Silas and Leofric off to one side, Yosef's watchful dark eyes, Riccilo's worried ones. She stood in front of Theo and drank him in. He wore his military tunic, a brilliant crimson that matched her own, the bronze plate on his forearms polished until it shone, his white hair gleaming in the candlelight.

Lælia barely heard the priest's words. Her eyes were held by Theo's, the Latin washing over her inconsequential. It was not here that they were married, not truly. It was long ago in a stable when the foals were born. When Theo had kissed her goodbye. A day earlier, when he had kissed her against a chestnut tree, with the scent of the woods all around them. Long before that, when, as little more than an infant himself,

96

he had ensured she drank enough to stay alive until they were found in the caves.

The priest's words were no more than a surface gloss upon a bond far older and deeper than words could describe. And yet, they mattered; as Lælia gave her oath and held her hand out for the rings that had long ago been exchanged by their parents, she felt a sense of completion. The ring felt warm and familiar on her hand, as if it belonged there, the clasped hands at the centre seeming to embody the promise that had bound them for so long. When the priest finished his words, Lælia's hand rose of its own accord, and Theo's gesture matched her own, covering his heart.

Promise.

His lips lingered on hers, just long enough to make the priest clear his throat, and then the ceremony was done.

Lælia would never recollect their wedding meal with any clarity. She was too aware of Theo beside her, the hard length of his thigh burning through her dress, the touch of his fingers on her mouth as he fed her the first mouthful, as was tradition. She heard the good-natured banter of Leofric and Silas, saw Yosef's quiet, warm smile. She was mesmerised by Theo's long fingers on the knife next to her, the way the light gleamed on the twisted folds of his scars. She ached to touch him, was impatient for the meal to be done, and when he looked at her his own eyes darkened with a desire that matched her own.

Finally the interminable evening was done, and raucous shouts followed Lælia's exit, in Riccilo's company, to the bedchamber that had been prepared for them. Riccilo opened the door, but when she would have come inside, Lælia halted. "You may leave me here."

"You will need to be undressed." Riccilo frowned. "Prepared for what is to come —"

"Theo will do it." Lælia flushed but stood her ground. Somehow, she wanted this for herself, the privacy of their own chamber, a place nobody but they inhabited. "Leave me here." Riccilo shook her head but, after another look at

Lælia's set face and glittering eyes, did not argue but simply walked away without comment.

A moment later, Lælia heard footsteps enter and the door close quietly behind her. She did not turn around.

She felt him as Theo approached. The heat of his body seemed to reach out, enveloping her before she felt the first touch of his hand on her waist. She looked down and saw the fede band on his hand, the clasped hands gleaming in the low light. Her own came up beside it and she looked down at his long, lean, burnished hand, hard with swordplay, beside her own, lithe and calloused from the bow.

"Fighter's hands," he murmured, his lips so close to her neck she shivered. She felt him smile against her skin. His fingers twined through her own. Her head tilted to the side as his mouth trailed along it, his other hand roaming down, across her hip to her thigh and back in a maddeningly slow path. "I remember the first day I saw you." His thumb grazed the curve of her breast and Lælia gasped. "I thought you were too tall, too slender, for one of the tribes." His hand traced the long curve of her waist. "You seemed to flow like water when you moved." His mouth was on the soft place beneath her jaw, and Lælia could think of nothing but the touch of his lips, the low, husky sound of his voice. "I wanted to catch you, hold you forever. Even before I knew who you were, you fascinated me. These hands." His fingers, twined in hers, brought their joined hands up her torso until they lay over her thudding heart. "The way they moved when you talked with them." He splayed their hands wide over her heart. "Promise," he murmured against her throat. "You don't know how that word has haunted me."

In a swift movement Lælia spun in his arms, her own twining about his neck as she faced him. "Do I not?" she said fiercely. "Do you think it has not haunted my every moment since you sailed?"

He pulled her against the hard bulk of him, his eyes heavy lidded and dark as he looked down at her, one of his hands delving into the mass of black hair as he held her head, drinking her in; then he was kissing her.

It was long, and sweet, and ached with the years that had held them apart. Raw edges became deep and heated, a liquid fire that consumed her, racing through her veins until she was molten and aching, clinging to him. With a rough noise Theo lifted her against him, her dress hitched up and her legs around his hips, carrying her to the wide bed covered in furs. Lowering her to it, he stood between her legs and pulled his tunic over his head, the scarred expanse of his chest, hardened with muscle and war, glowing like burnished copper in the candlelight. Her hands rose to the neck of her gown and he stopped them, pulling them apart and holding them above her head with one hand. The other hand came to the woven cord of her bodice and, with sure, steady movements, unlaced it and pulled it through one eyelet after another, his eyes never leaving hers.

Finally the dress lay open, the linen chemise beneath transparent and open wide enough to expose her. Lælia felt the air on her skin like a shock. When Theo's thumb moved slowly over the mound of her breast, his eyes burning into her own, she moaned aloud, her hands closing around his forearms as she pulled him toward her.

Instead he slipped his thumbs beneath the woollen dress and hooked it down, throwing it in the direction of his discarded tunic, stripping the bronze cuffs from his arms and the last of his clothes so that he stood before her naked and hard, and when Lælia reached for him he lay beside her and teased her flesh with lips and tongue until her chemise had joined the rest of their clothes and she felt the decadent stroke of the skins beneath her, and his hands upon her until she was writhing and calling his name.

"I want you," he said hoarsely, his eyes glittering hard green as he looked down at her, his hand relentless between her legs, her breasts sweet and aching from his mouth. "I want you more than I've ever wanted anything in my life, Lælia."

"Then take me," she said fiercely, staring up at him without fear or hesitation. "I've dreamed of it, Theo. I've dreamed of this. Of you." And this time when she surged up toward him, he met her. He held her as if he might hurt her, holding himself slightly aloof as if to gentle her, but Lælia had waited too long and wanted him too badly to hold back. She rose toward him and drew him into her, aching for this, for the joining that had haunted her nights and left her tangled and heated in imagining. Theo surged into her with a fullness that took her breath away and made him give a hard, hoarse cry. The moment of pain was sharp and oddly satisfying, and then he was deep inside her, holding her from beneath as he took her in long, hard strokes that seemed to radiate through every pore of her body, his mouth on hers and his body amongst hers as her legs twined about him.

Heat surged between them and he drove harder as she rose against him, pulling him into her further and deeper until sensation ripped through her and she cried out, clinging savagely to him; he held himself hard inside her, gripping her against him, and she felt the fierce pulse of him within her.

"I love you," he murmured against her face, still moving slowly inside her, and she twined herself closer to him. "Xristus, Lælia, I have loved you every day since I met you."

"And I you."

He rolled onto his back, pulling her with him, and she came atop him, her mouth still hungry on his. "I knew it would be like this," she whispered against him. "I knew how it would feel with you. I dreamed it... sometimes, alone, I touched myself and imagined it as you."

Theo groaned, taking her mouth harder, holding her against him and moving beneath her, still hard. "Tell me," he said roughly. "Tell me what you would do."

And as the candles guttered in the corner and the night birds called beyond the window, Lælia murmured in his ear, telling him of the visions she had seen on the long-ago night when Acantha had taken her to the caves, of the bull they had hunted in her dreams, and the way he had taken her. Dream or not, she told Theo, in the nights following her vision, the remembrance of how he had felt, surging inside her, had driven her near insane, and her hands to learn her own body until this night could come and make it reality.

"It was on that moon that we fought at Barca." Theo held her close and told her of the ferocity of that, his first battle, and of the savage bolt of lust he had felt in the aftermath. "You were there with me." His lips moved restlessly on her skin as she arched toward him. "I felt you beside me as I fought, and I wanted you so badly in that moment I was mad with it."

They did not sleep until the grey light of dawn crept through the window, and when they did, it was with joined hands, twin rings side by side on the pillow, black head next to white, bound forever.

10

———

LETTER FROM SAFIA TO COUNT ILYAN

MARCH, AD 693

Toletum, Spania, to Septem, Mauretania
Toledo, Spain, to Ceuta, Morocco

My honoured father,

We arrived in Toletum not a quarter turn of the moon ago, but I have so much to relate I fear there may be neither parchment nor ink enough for the telling.

We are in the palace, waiting, as all Toletum does, for the Sixteenth Council and Egica's reckoning. None know who will survive his revenge. Theodofred, Duke of Corduba, languishes in the dungeons, his fate uncertain. His son Roderic seems oddly oblivious to the danger his father is in. Never have I met someone so certain of his place in the world as Roderic. He laughs with Wittiza as if they were the equals they always have been, secure in his belief that his position is somehow unassailable.

There has been no word from Egilona's mother. It is said that both her father and her brother Alaric died in the rebellion. She does not, however, cry for any of them. If Roderic is oblivious to the danger he is in, Egilona is not only fully cognisant, but uncannily composed. She does not speak of her family and devotes her energies to keeping the attentions of her three young suitors fully engaged. She seems to have charmed even

102

the king himself, who bestows upon her that rarest of gifts — the occasional dark smile of genuine amusement. Egica, I suspect, sees in Egilona that which he most admires in others: ambition and intelligence.

She will need both. Her allies are few, her enemies many. Laurentius Severianus sought her out in the days following our arrival. Despite his best efforts, the strain upon him was easily discernible to one such as I, who have been taught by my mother and you to see what men wish to hide. His friend, Shukra, the Persian who has done much business with Septem in the past, has been imprisoned in the same dungeon as Theodofred. Shukra's crimes are rumoured to play a central role in the debates at the upcoming council. It seems that the former archbishop, Sisebut, was discovered by the new archbishop, Felix, as a corrupter of young men — and that Shukra is guilty of the same Christian sin, of lying with men. Do not forget that I was raised in the women's quarters of your palace, amongst concubines, a great many of whom have enjoyed the pleasure of Shukra's company during his visits. I never knew him to take a man, even when it was offered, or as part of a debauch. Nor can I envisage him deliberately corrupting an innocent. He lives by the code of Zoroaster, holds himself to it, I believe, as stringently as any man does to his god. It would contradict all I know of him to believe him capable of seducing and manipulating against another's will.

Nonetheless, he stands accused of not only doing exactly that, but of fomenting insurrection and nurturing foreign alliances. Given Sisebut's own plots, the crime of homosexuality now seems equated with treachery also. It is rumoured that the bishops will debate the merits of excommunicating those found to be guilty of homosexuality — and that both Shukra and Sisebut face almost certain execution.

Laurentius Severianus said little of the situation during his visit, which he made to lend Roderic and Egilona comfort, though he could offer little reassurance. At least Egilona's brother, the priest Athanagild, is here in Toletum. He, too, seems deeply concerned for Shukra's fate. Neither he nor Laurentius said much of it other than that they believe Shukra to be innocent of the charges against him. I write all this not to apprise you of meaningless gossip, Father, but because I know you have entrusted Shukra with a great deal of information in the past and considered him a valuable ally and resource. I believe his fate to be almost certainly death. If *you wish me to take any action on his behalf in this matter, you must send word immediately.*

Of equal, if not greater concern, is the arrival at court of Oppa, the king's bastard son. He, I believe, is more dangerous than any other of the king's retinue – more dangerous even than the king himself.

Oppa does not often appear in public. He is not given to ostentation, preferring the anonymity of shadows and secrets. He has been in Toletum barely longer than we, but I have already discovered he has every servant in our small company in his direct employ. It is said he owns every tavern and whorekeeper in Toletum, as well as opening several new places stocked with exotic attractions that cater to the darkest and most perverse whims men (and women) can envisage. Wittiza, who has ever had a taste for the lascivious and sensual, is quite in thrall to his sophisticated older half-brother. Oppa has gifted him with every manner of luxury designed to delight a young man – a warhorse marked with the emperor's own brand; a curved scimitar with a jewelled handle rumoured to have been taken from the dead hand of an Arabic general on the battlefield; armour made to order by artisans in Constantinople, with Wittiza's own name writ upon it. Even Roderic's and Pelayo's eyes gleam at Oppa's stories, despite the rumours all have heard of his dark proclivities. If anything, such rumours add to his standing in their eyes. He has yet to introduce them to the pleasures of the flesh, though he has already installed in Wittiza's household a servant girl perfectly designed to titillate and enthral him. The princeling, of course, is too young to understand he is being primed for slaughter. The girl is bait. When Wittiza reaches for it, Oppa will reel him in to one of the many houses he owns and see to it that Wittiza is seduced, pampered, and thoroughly made Oppa's own creature.

Egilona wisely makes herself scarce when Oppa visits. She has an instinct for self-preservation. Oppa is not an enemy she wishes to make, so she makes herself invisible when he comes, and murmurs only admiration from beneath demurely downcast lashes when Wittiza speaks of him.

She uses the time when Wittiza is occupied to write to the old queen, Liuvgoto, who remains with her daughter Cixilo sequestered in the monastery outside Toletum. I have been careful, since arriving in Egilona's employ, to maintain the pretence of deep piety, attending church daily. It aids in the sending of these letters, but now I see it serving a different purpose: that of gaining access to the old queens. I made it a practice to visit every monastery upon the road here, to pray and give alms. Egilona began to join me. Our piety drew the benevolence of the priests, and universal praise, for these Spaniards prize prayer almost as much as coin. We have maintained our practice here in Toletum. It is helped by the fact that Egilona's brother, Athanagild, is a respected priest with, it is said, the ear of the archbishop himself, while Laurentius Severianus is a relative of the famed Isidore of Hispalis. Egilona's piety is accepted and encouraged as natural and right from one of such illustrious religious credentials, and her recent passion for languages is considered in the same light. I, however, knowing Egilona as I do, suspect her newfound passion for God is much more to do with her desire to seek advice from the old queen Liuvgoto than from any true revelation, and her sudden interest in learning Arabic a result of her listening more closely to Oppa's stories than she might admit. (In this, of course, I am able to be of benefit, something that serves to draw us even closer.) Egilona craves power. Liuvgoto understands it. Both have the same goal, I believe — to see Wittiza safely crowned, and controlled by their guidance in his every decision. Liuvgoto sees in Egilona an opportunity to extend her control to the next generation. Egilona sees in Liuvgoto the mentor she needs. The rest of the world seems to have forgotten about Liuvgoto. A dangerous mistake, I believe. I will soon visit the monastery, and Egilona, I expect, will join me.

Meanwhile, we await the judgement of the council, along with the rest of the capital. Only then will we learn what Egilona's fate will be — and Roderic's.

As I wrote earlier, Shukra's fate would seem grave indeed. I do not know how I might help him, but I am yours to command in this matter, as I am in all things.

Ever your servant,
Your daughter

11

LAURENTIUS

MARCH, AD 693

Toletum, Spania
Toledo, Spain

Laurentius gripped the wrought-iron lattice at his library window and stared unseeing into the hard March sunlight. The sky was a pale wash of blue, high and light, and the air had yet to lose winter's chill. Beyond the walls of the villa, Laurentius knew the city bustled, but inside was an oasis of calm that had nothing to do with the turmoil in his own heart.

"You have been visiting him. Why will you not let me do the same?" Laurentius did not turn at the sound of Athanagild's quiet voice at the door, though the even timbre sent a shiver down his spine that had nothing to do with the words themselves. He felt rather than heard Athanagild step inside the library and close the door. "I cannot bear to think of Shukra in that cell, awaiting punishment for crimes that are mine, not his, without so much as a word from me."

"It is too dangerous." Laurentius's words came out more snarl than answer.

"But not for you?"

"I am not implicated in this." He turned to face Athanagild with his fists bunched at his sides. "Felix believes that Sisebut and Shukra were fighting a perverted battle for your affections when he came upon them in that bathhouse. He believes you the unwilling victim of their sexual depravities. Why would a victim visit his torturer?" He saw Athanagild's face, already pale, go ashen, the wide hazel eyes gleam with a hurt that flooded him with guilt. None of this was Athanagild's fault. It was his actions that had led to this. He who had been unable to control his own damned lust…

Laurentius spun back toward the window, breathing hard. "You cannot visit Shukra." He stared bleakly at a pomegranate tree that had one last red fruit clinging stubbornly to the branch. After a long pause, Athanagild spoke again, his voice calm and quiet.

"You will raise suspicions of your own if you remain in Toletum much longer, Laurentius. The fleet is rotting in the river at Hispalis without crew to man it or you to command it. You left neither orders nor men to protect what you have created. The fleet was the pretence upon which you returned to Spania. If you ignore it, people will begin to talk —"

"Let them." Laurentius's voice was flat and hard. Who else, he thought dully, should bear the whispers and accusation, if not he? When Shukra was rotting in a dungeon, accused of sins he himself was guilty of? "There is no point to the damned fleet. Not anymore." Taking the floor in hard strides, he reached the wine jug, poured himself a cup, and tossed it off in one long swallow, pouring himself another immediately. Athanagild's eyes on his back scorched in silent accusation, making him feel even worse. "Don't look at me like that," he muttered, staring at the wall.

"Like what?" Athanagild's voice was quiet and pained. "You never meet my eyes to see what is in them." When Laurentius didn't answer, he went on: "Do you think I do not understand your anger, Laurentius? I cost Shukra his freedom, and probably his life. I know you cannot forgive me. God knows, I cannot forgive myself. Tell me what you would have me do, and I will do it. Give myself up, tell Felix the truth, that Shukra was my confidant, nothing more —"

"He would never believe you." Laurentius forced himself to turn and meet Athanagild's eyes. "Such a confession would achieve nothing but make Felix lose respect for you and think you in thrall to Shukra's seductions." He spat the last words with all the self-contempt that had kept him awake and half-drunk every night since Shukra's arrest. "Not to mention the fact that Shukra would kill me himself for allowing you to do such a thing."

"We cannot leave him there." Athanagild's mouth was a tight, hard line, his eyes blazing in the way that fired Laurentius's blood regardless of his guilt and anger, his self-loathing. "I will not let him die to protect me, us. We have to think of something, Laurentius."

"Do you think I don't know that?" Laurentius was across the room in three strides, his every muscle taut with rage and frustration as he held himself barely inches from the lean figure who stared back at him without flinching. "That I don't spend every waking minute trying to think of a solution?"

"Then speak to me!" Athanagild's customary composure fell away, his voice raw with hurt and anger. "Make me part of your plans, instead of your enemy. You've barely spoken so much as a dozen words to me since the night he was taken. I know nothing of what you think, of how you feel. I can do nothing to help —"

"If I wanted your help, Athanagild, I would have asked before now." Seeing hurt and rejection flare in the rich hazel eyes, Laurentius tasted the pain he had caused as if it were his own and felt both sick and savagely satisfied. He nodded tersely as Athanagild stepped back. "Do not come here again," he said coldly as he walked to the door, reaching for his cloak. "You can't help, Athanagild, and your presence is more pain than joy."

He stalked from the room without looking back, savouring every stab of agony his words caused. Laurentius knew he did not deserve the happiness he felt in Athanagild's presence, could take no solace in the lean arms and blazing heat between them. His oldest friend was paying with his life for his, Laurentius's, inability to control his heart or his nature, and Laurentius would never again allow himself to indulge either.

* * *

THE GUARD at the entrance to the dungeons smiled knowingly as Laurentius came toward him. He had grown accustomed to the coin Laurentius paid to access the darkness below. But the smile today verged on insinuation, and Laurentius, with the unerring instinct that had guided him through wars and diplomacy men such as this could never understand, looked at him with hard disdain. "I am here to see the Duke of Corduba. Show me to him."

"The duke?" The man lifted his eyebrows. "Not the little Persian, today?"

"The Persian is of no more use to me. He has given all the information we might expect. Until I verify it, he can rot, until such time as my king sees fit to kill him, as all men of God have a right to expect." He spoke carelessly, looking down the stairs as if already focused on the next target, and had the satisfaction of seeing the man's insinuation give way to slightly fearful respect. "Why am I still waiting?" Laurentius shifted his eyes back to the man. "Do you grow greedy for coin, man? I assure you, it is an easy enough matter to arrange your replacement." He saw the man's eyes stray to the purse at his waist and glared at him. "You have taken enough of both my time and money. Let me pass, before I report your insubordination."

The man stepped aside with alacrity, his face now pale and afraid. "Do your job well," murmured Laurentius as he passed, "and I will ensure you see solidi rather than tremisses on my next visit." The guard flushed with pleasure and Laurentius continued down into the stinking dungeons, content that he had reset the balance of power between them. It was a dangerous game he played. One in which he could not afford even the slightest hint of suspicion, even from a palace guard. And especially not since that whoreson Oppa had returned, and with him a web of spies to rival even Shukra's.

He turned right at the bottom of the stairs, not game to so much as glance in the direction of Shukra's cell lest the guard was watching. He drew a deep breath, forcing himself to inhale the foul odours despite his distaste, and made his way through the dank stone to the cell at the far end.

"Theodofred," he said quietly. "How are you?"

The mound slumped against the far wall did not move, nor respond. Theodofred's once proud mane of golden hair lay in lank tangles about his bearded, gaunt face, his eyes dark sockets in his skull. The bowl of brown sludge that served as his rations sat untouched where the guard had placed it. Laurentius knew for a fact that every bowl met the same fate. Theodofred had not eaten since his capture. He opened his cracked lips now to ask the only question he had since the day he was thrown in here: "Riccilo? Roderic?"

"Safe, still. Roderic is at court now with Wittiza. Riccilo will ride to Toletum for the council."

It was always the same. The two names, said as a question, then nothing. Today, though, Theodofred frowned and opened his mouth again. "Riccilo should not come."

"And you know nothing will stop her." Encouraged by even the slightest animation of the listless figure, Laurentius went on: "She sent word that she will come to see you as soon as she reaches the capital —"

"No." Theodofred's answer was so swift and hard it cut Laurentius off. "On your life, Severianus, swear she will not see me here, like this. I do not care what you do to prevent her.

Neither she nor Roderic is to enter this place. Swear it." For a moment his eyes flashed arctic blue, and he was once again the son of Chindasuinth Rex, a warrior who had led men beneath the Chrismon and peacock onto a hundred battlefields.

"You have my word," said Laurentius quietly. Theodofred regarded him with the same hard scrutiny for a long moment then, seeming to see what he needed, slumped back and faced the wall, his momentary fire gone. Laurentius knew he would not speak again. Nonetheless, he remained by the cell for almost a full turn of the hourglass, talking of inconsequential matters, telling Theodofred of Roderic's prowess with horse and sword, of the petty happenings at court. He did not expect a response, nor did he get one.

A stir at the top of the stairs paused his monologue and he heard the change of guard, the man he had recently reprimanded giving his replacement stern orders to treat Laurentius with respect and ask no awkward questions. He smiled tightly and waited to hear the man's retreating footsteps. Then, bidding Theodofred a farewell that went, as he expected, unanswered, he made his way silently through the stone to the other end and the cell in which Shukra was kept.

In stark contrast to the desolate duke, Laurentius found Shukra stripped to the waist, somehow almost impeccably clean, and engaged in imaginary swordplay that involved a series of remarkably athletic movements for someone who was existing on the meagre scraps of a prison diet. The floor of his cell was neatly swept. When Laurentius had once asked how Shukra achieved this, he had shrugged and pointed to the tall boots that he kept neatly turned upside down by the wall. Shukra had an innate ability to make his prison cell seem as orderly as a palace state room, and his presence in it as if he were the master of his own home.

"*Aziz-am!*" he said now, smiling in welcome for all the world as if they were two equals meeting in a tavern. "How does this day find you?"

"How do you think it finds me?" Laurentius stared at his old friend, unable to maintain his customary pretence of going along with Shukra's charade. "The day of the council comes ever closer. Egica means to execute you, Shukra." He knew it was brutal. But for weeks since Shukra's capture, Laurentius had pretended to himself that there was a way out of this. It was only now, as the day of reckoning approached, that he had to admit there was no such way. It was time Shukra knew that. "Did you hear me?" he demanded when Shukra did not react.

"I am thinking the entire dungeon heard you, *aziz-am*." Shukra's voice was light and playful, his face as unconcerned as ever. "The years are granting you lines on the face but yet no subtlety."

"Do not joke, Shukra. Not about this." Laurentius grasped the metal bars. "You have to tell them the truth, Shukra. That you were there to kill Sisebut, and not to fight over Athanagild."

"You are already knowing how stupid this is." Shukra's tone was gently chiding. "I am a foreigner and condemned already for being such. I could shout my innocence from the highest tower. It would not change Egica's mind and would serve only to endanger – others." It was not necessary for him to stipulate who those others were. Laurentius gripped the bars harder.

"I do not believe those *others* require your protection," he muttered fiercely.

"Do they not?" Shukra raised his eyebrows. "Because it is seeming to me, *aziz-am*, that those others are being as stupid as ever they were."

"Stop this," Laurentius began.

"No, *aziz-am*." This time there was a note of authority in Shukra's voice that made Laurentius pause. "It is you who must *stop this*, as you say. Stop with these visits. With the drinking so much I can smell it upon your breath as if you were a common soldier." Shukra's eyes flashed with distaste.

"With not sleeping at the nights, and do not tell me you sleep, for I know that face you have and it is not one of a man who is sleeping, *aziz-am*." He leaned forward and lowered his voice so only Laurentius could hear it. "I did not find my way to this cell because I am innocent. For months I knew what that damned priest was doing to that boy and did nothing. For that alone I deserve to sit here – and take whatever punishment finds me. And know this." He held Laurentius's eyes, his own for once free of dancing humour. "I would do it again, *aziz-am*, and a hundred times again, if I knew it would keep you safe. So you will be doing nothing to jeopardise this that I have done, nor to ruin it. I have made my peace with Ahura Mazda, the one who sees all. This is my right path. I have chosen it, and walk it I will. But I no longer wish you to walk it with me." He held up a hand as Laurentius began to speak. "No, *aziz-am*. It is enough now. Do you think I do not know that the guards begin to whisper, to say that for a man who claims to be a patriot, you visit a condemned traitor too often? That I don't know you well enough to know that you push away all who would give you comfort in this time, and think only of how to free me?" When Laurentius could not find his voice to answer, Shukra's face softened into a compassion that broke Laurentius's heart more than any hard words ever could. "Do not act in a way that will make my choice mean nothing, *aziz-am*. Walk out of here today and do not return. Let us say our farewells as men, and be done. If I know you come again, I will do as Theodofred does, and hold my silence."

He held Laurentius's eyes in the gloom, until he saw reluctant acceptance creep into them.

"Very well," said Shukra. "Now, then. Clasp my arm, brother, one last time, as the soldiers we have been together." His arm came through the bars and Laurentius gripped it, trying with every muscle to convey to the small Persian who was his oldest and dearest friend, his mentor and confidant, all he felt: the gratitude and the love, all that had been between them from the moment they first sat beside one another on the boards of a dromon, two scared boys far from their homes.

"It has been an honour." His voice was a husky rasp and Laurentius did not pretend to hide the tears in his eyes. "The honour of my life, Shukra."

"And of mine, *aziz-am*." Shukra smiled, gripping the arm with his lethal, wicked strength one last time, then stepped back. "Guard!" he called. Still holding Laurentius's eyes, he smiled sardonically. "This man tires me with his questions! Beat me, whip me, but I beg of you, man, remove this fool from my presence!"

At the clatter of footsteps on the stairs, Shukra retreated to the rear wall of his cell, his eyes flashing with mischief. "What is this, now?" the guard demanded, panting and red faced as he approached. "Is he bothering you? Shall I beat him?" he asked Laurentius, looking between them. Seeing Shukra wrap his hand surreptitiously in linen, Laurentius's mouth twitched, and he assumed a stern, disdainful expression as he turned to the guard. "Do your worst, man," he said, loudly enough that his words reverberated off the walls. "The man is a traitor and a fool. I am done here."

Behind the guard's back, he nodded once at Shukra, whose mouth curled slightly in appreciation. This one thing, Laurentius thought, he could give to the man who had given everything, including his own life, to Laurentius: one last chance to be the soldier he was.

He walked away up the stairs, smiling to himself as he heard the guard's first yelp of pain. "Now, *aziz-am*," he heard Shukra say in a conversational tone, "I am not certain who is training you to be fighting, but they are clearly not skilled in their duty, are they, if I might do this?" Another sound of pain was accompanied by the clatter of multiple guards on the stairs responding to their companion's calls for help. Laurentius, casting a practised eye over their portly figures, guessed it would take double their number to finally wrestle Shukra into obedience.

* * *

He returned to the villa with his heart oddly full, to find that, to his surprise, Athanagild was still there.

"Athanagild," he said hesitantly, trying to find words to repair the damage of earlier; but when the tall figure turned toward him, his words were halted by the blazing triumph in the young man's face.

"Lælia," breathed Athanagild, waving a parchment, his eyes glittering fiercely. "She lives. This came by messenger from Corduba this morning, carried by one of the Illiberis men. Lælia is safe, Laurentius − and she is riding now with Riccilo, for Toletum. And, Laurentius." He stepped forward, and Laurentius realised the glittering in his eyes was not just excitement, but unshed tears, held back by the last of Athanagild's restraint. "Theudemir is with her," he said in a low, hard voice. "My brother has come home."

12

OPPA

APRIL, AD 693

Toletum, Spania
Toledo, Spain

"Brother!" Wittiza was plump for his age, and Oppa, who loathed indiscipline in all matters, had to quell his distaste as he embraced the adolescent's soft figure. Wittiza's eyes lit on the gleaming helmet in his hands. "Is that for me?" It was studded with rubies and far too gaudy for Oppa's taste, but he had learned that his half-brother's tastes ran to the Gothic penchant for glittering ostentation, and so gold and jewels it was.

Oppa bowed his head in feigned homage as he held out the offering. "It is indeed, *princeps*. It was won on the battlefield at Sebastopolis, taken from the head of an Arab who thought to defy your Spanish thiufa." In fact, it had been made to Oppa's specifications by a workman in Cartago Nova, but the man had been paid well for his silence, and no-one at court would know the difference.

"If all the emperor's men had been Spaniards that day, Sebastopolis would never have fallen," said Wittiza, with all the pompous authority of a thirteen-year-old boy who had been cosseted since birth and never so much as smelled a battlefield, even from a distance. "Your people would follow you into the fiercest battle." Oppa bowed his head once more.

He raised his eyes to find both Pelayo and Roderic staring at him, their eyes gleaming with the eagerness that only talk of battles could rouse in boys on the verge of adolescence.

"You were really there," breathed eleven-year-old Roderic.

"You fought the Arabs," said Pelayo at the same time.

Oppa inclined his head gravely, as if the two children in front of him were honoured lords of the court instead of the disgraced sons of traitors who would soon find themselves friendless and disinherited. Observation of Wittiza's small court had taught Oppa that the three boys were close as brothers and fiercely loyal to one another. Regardless of how soon their status might change, Oppa was too astute to dismiss them yet. Gaining Wittiza's trust meant charming his friends also – and it was not a difficulty. The boys had been so long isolated that they were starved of outside company, and when that company brought gifts of fine horses, gleaming swords, and stories of distant battles, any hesitation they may have harboured about Wittiza's somewhat elusive half-brother was dispelled. The only member of the close circle Oppa had not yet found opportunity to beguile was the daughter of Aurari-ola. Nine-year-old Egilona seemed even more elusive than Oppa himself, somehow always otherwise occupied on the days he chose to visit. Oppa would have thought nothing of it, had it not been for the frequency with which her name was mentioned by all three boys. Any girl who held such a familiar role in the future king's household was a threat to Oppa's own control. Not to mention her relationship to Aurariola, and to Theo.

"Is the lady Egilona here today?" he asked in an offhand manner, proffering a box of candied fruit which the boys fell upon eagerly. "I brought sweets for her, also."

"Egilona never eats sweets," said Wittiza around a bulging

mouthful. Oppa felt a twinge of unease. For some reason, the knowledge that Egilona practised abstinence, as he did, was unsettling. It implied a tidy, disciplined mind. Oppa tucked the knowledge away for future reference. "That is a pity," he said lightly. "I seem always to miss the opportunity to make her acquaintance."

"Egilona likes going to church." Roderic shrugged, as if such a desire was entirely foreign to him. "She goes to visit all the monasteries hereabouts. It's boring."

All the monasteries? Oppa's previous feeling of unease increased. He made a mental note to put more eyes on Egilona. An abstemious girl, a reputed beauty, and the sister of his sworn enemy, who had begun visiting monasteries nearby – when Liuvgoto herself was inside the walls of one? That was a danger too far.

"Ah, well," he said lightly. "Next time, perhaps. Ataulfo," he said, turning to his old childhood companion who had reassumed his old place at Oppa's side since his return, "take Pelayo and Roderic to see the horses I brought my father as a gift from Africa." Thus ensuring the boys would remain occupied for some time, Oppa drew Wittiza slightly away from the others. "I know you, too, have a love for horses," he said quietly, "but you are no longer the boy your friends are. I thought that today, we might explore some other delights." He paused at the door, looking carefully up and down the corridor, as if he were about to embark upon a forbidden mission. Wittiza instinctively drew close to him and lowered his voice as he said, "Where are we going, brother?"

"Not far, today." Oppa put a faint emphasis on the last word. "But if you like what I show you, the next time, perhaps we will venture further." Having thoroughly captured the young prince's attention, he led Wittiza out of the royal chambers, opening a door hidden behind a tapestry in an alcove, which led to a room at the bottom of a set of winding stone stairs.

"I did not know this was here," panted Wittiza behind

him, and again Oppa felt a twinge of disgust. The boy was so fat he could not take stairs without catching his breath. And yet soon he would sit beneath the votive crown, as king of all Spania. Oppa restrained himself from shaking his head.

"The room is a secret known to few." Oppa paused outside the wooden door. "Do you remember the Frankish servant I sent you – Clotilde?"

Wittiza's pale-blue eyes widened. His tongue came out and wet his lips, and a faint sheen of sweat glistened beneath the fringe of brown hair cut straight across his forehead. "She is very beautiful," he said, his voice slightly wheezy. "But I do not see her often. She serves Egilona for the most part."

Oppa's lips tightened in annoyance. Egilona again. The girl definitely needed watching. "Today," he said, careful to show no hint of his thoughts, "she is here to serve you." He pushed open the door and had the satisfaction of hearing Wittiza suck in his breath behind him.

Clotilde was wearing no more than a thin, almost transparent chemise. Her blonde hair tumbled over one bare shoulder in a gleaming waterfall of curls, and her blue eyes peeped up at them through long, dark lashes. She reclined on a lecta, one leg demurely forward, but not far enough to conceal the faint shadow of the triangle at the apex of her thighs. She looked the very picture of innocence. None would suspect she was in fact a highly practised whore, whom Oppa had trained from childhood. "*Princeps*," she said now, popping a grape between plump, red lips, "it has been too long since I have been permitted to serve you."

Wittiza could do nothing but stare at her, his lips slightly parted, the bulge at the front of his robes evidence of his appreciation for the form before him. "I did not send Clotilde here to wait upon Egilona," murmured Oppa over Wittiza's shoulder. "She was sent as a gift for you. And not only to be your servant."

Clotilde patted the lecta. "Come, *princeps*," she said huskily, her lips parting in a seductive smile. "Sit beside me a time."

Her eyes travelled suggestively down Wittiza's body, coming to rest upon the bulge in his robes. Wittiza shifted awkwardly, colouring. "You seem uncomfortable, my lord," Clotilde said, raising her eyebrows. "Let me help ease you." Wittiza shot Oppa an awkward glance, clearly unsure what he should do.

"She is yours." Oppa smiled darkly at his half-brother. "As everything in this city – this country – is yours. Today is the day you begin to enjoy what belongs to you, brother." He put his mouth closer to Wittiza's ear. "And the next time," he murmured, "I will take you to a place where there are a dozen Clotildes. All waiting to serve only you, *princeps*." When Wittiza's eyes widened even further, Oppa laughed softly. "As a king, there are the duties you have to your people – and then there are the rewards you deserve for fulfilling those duties. I returned so that I might help you with both. For what else are older brothers for, if not to show their younger the pleasures their parents might disdain?"

Wittiza was already moving toward the inviting figure on the lecta. "You are good to me, brother," he said breathlessly.

Oppa waited until the plump figure was ensconced on the lecta, his attention entirely absorbed by Clotilde's clever hands, before turning for the door. "I am good indeed," he murmured, closing it behind him with a hard, dark smile.

* * *

With Wittiza occupied, Oppa made his way to his father's chambers, knocking on the door and waiting for the low command: "Enter."

Egica was seated at the table for his midday meal, and he waved Oppa carelessly into the chair opposite. Oppa sat, accepting a small plate of meat, then waited until his father dismissed the servants. "Well?" Egica demanded, staring at his son through dark, implacable eyes. The recent war had aged his father, Oppa thought. The eyes might still hold the flat darkness they always had, but the jowls were slightly fuller than they once had been, the tall figure a little stooped. There was grey at his father's temples and deep lines in his face, and when he raised his wine glass, his hand trembled ever so slightly.

All this Oppa noticed, for he had long learned to notice all there was to see in men – even his own father.

Particularly his own father.

"Illiberis." He said only that one word and had the satisfaction of seeing his father's knife pause halfway to his mouth, and Egica's eyes narrow.

"Go on."

"As we speak, I have a force riding south. By the time your council convenes, my men will have total control of Illiberis. None will threaten our hold. I have made a deal to take it."

"Made a deal with whom? Paulus's hellcat? She is beholden to the Crown as the daughter of a traitor. We do not trade with traitors."

"Not with her. With her husband."

Egica paled with anger.

"Theudemir of Aurariola has returned. He and the Illiberis girl are married. I have promised him Aurariola, in exchange for Illiberis. The girl, however, does not know of our arrangement."

"You promised the son of a traitor that he could keep his family lands?" Egica glared at his son. "That was a promise you had no authority to make."

"Theudemir of Aurariola is a dangerous enemy." Oppa's face was flat and hard. "He knows a great many of our secrets. Perhaps enough to see rebellion rise again, if not here, then on foreign soil."

"Then why does he live?" Egica slammed a hand down on the table, but Oppa did not jump. "I thought you assured me he would die long before returning here?"

"He is more valuable to us alive. And now you have him as an ally."

"Explain," said Egica coldly, "how the son of a traitor could ever be an ally."

"Theudemir has spent the past five years reaching the highest ranks in the emperor's fleet. He has trained under the best warriors in Christendom, has contacts at the highest levels in Constantinople, and led an entire squadron of the Karabisianoi. Now he has returned – and he is beholden to me for his life." Oppa held his father's eyes. "In Hispalis lies an entire fleet of dromons with no men to man it. And as we speak, forces gather against us in Septem. Sooner than you might think, we will need to guard our southern border. What better man to do that than one who has trained with the emperor's own – and who owes us a favour?" *And what better way for me to ensure our military forces are under my control, rather than yours?*

Oppa paused, waiting for Egica to absorb his words. He was careful always to use "we", rather than "I", to leave his father with the illusion of control. Egica had not yet realised that the power in his rule was subtly shifting to favour his bastard son, and Oppa intended it to remain that way. His plans relied upon Egica believing in his own absolute authority.

"Forces gather in Septem, you say?"

Oppa nodded, smiling to himself at how easy it was to have his father take the bait. "Your spies have uncovered a Jewish conspiracy there against your rule. They work with the Jews in Garnata, and others, plotting another uprising." It did not matter that the Jewish rebellion was no more than the pathetic dream of a few weak men. Whatever Ilyan and Yosef ben Arun were hiding was unlikely to be either pathetic or a dream. Perhaps they were connected to the whispers of rebellion, and perhaps not. Either way, he needed Theudemir of Aurariola's focus safely elsewhere, and the ability to take sudden action if necessary. Better that he lay the groundwork for that with his father now, in a way Egica would understand.

"I will crush them." Egica's face was hard and uncompromising. "I will kill every one of them." A brief flash of real fury flared in his eyes. "Too many in the south managed to sidestep the recent rebellion. Waited to see who would triumph. They are as ungovernable as they ever were, and they deserve to die…"

Oppa kept his contempt well hidden as Egica expounded on the deceit and treachery of the southern lords. He found it pitiable that his father could be so disturbed by the recalcitrance of a few petty nobles from mountainous backwaters. After all Oppa had faced, such men were no more than the most minor pieces on a board, easily interchangeable, certainly expendable. It was another reminder of his father's fallibility.

"Better, perhaps," he interjected smoothly as Egica drew breath, "that we expose them, just as you so wisely did your enemies during the recent rebellion." Flattery, as ever, worked upon Egica. It was a fine balance – his father, Oppa knew, was too intelligent for sycophancy. But subtle flattery, carefully wrought and sparingly administered, worked to keep Egica docile. "In your dungeons you have, at the moment, a certain Persian spy."

Egica nodded sharply. "He is accused of sodomy, as well as spying. He will be condemned to death."

"Might I suggest you make an example of him – then let him go?"

"What has this to do with a Jewish uprising in Septem?"

"It is the Jews of Septem with whom the Persian is allied." This was not strictly true; it was Yosef ben Arun with whom Oppa knew Shukra to be allied, but that part of his plan his father did not need to know. Oppa had chased the Jew and his secrets for too long. He meant to solve the puzzle, once and for all, and take whatever treasure it was the Jew and Aurariola had so carefully guarded all this time. "If you release the Persian," he went on, "he will run straight back to Septem, and to the rebellion against you. Then we need only watch, and wait, whilst here at home we deploy Theudemir of Aurariola to work with his uncle Laurentius to build up the fleet to a force no army of Jews can hope to attack." Oppa knew the likelihood of the Jews of Septem launching a fleet was next to laughable, but his father, he was well aware, would easily believe in such a threat. In reality, Oppa would have Theo on a tight rein, the fleet he managed a force Oppa himself could deploy as he saw fit, against or for whatever enemy he desired. Theo would be a weapon to which only he, Oppa, held the key. The thought was intoxicating on every level.

"When they come," he went on, forcing himself to focus on his father, "we will be ready for them. You will expose Ilyan as your enemy, the Jews as enemies of Spania, and take whatever wealth they have as your own. There will be no more opposition from the provinces to your wishes to bring heavier penalties against the Jews of Spain. All their trade will be yours, their resources forfeit to the Crown."

Oppa forced himself to stop, aware that he was perilously close to dictating a course of action his father should take, something it was never wise to do with Egica.

His father steepled his fingers and frowned. Oppa had to hide a contemptuous curl of his mouth. He knew that gesture. Egica already knew he was going to agree to his son's plan. He simply wanted to make certain Oppa knew it was his authority that commanded it.

"And you are certain that Aurariola will do your bidding?" Egica's eyes narrowed as he asked the question.

Oppa felt the visceral surge of excitement, almost bordering on arousal, that he felt every time he remembered his encounter with Theo in the street in Corduba. He had already forgotten his moment of humiliation in Illiberis. What did a moment in the dirt matter, when soon he would have Theo in his power, utterly dependent on his goodwill? For a moment he had a childlike desire to confide his triumph to his father, to seek approval for the masterstrokes he had wielded to get to this place. He suppressed the urge before it had fully taken hold. Such confessions were beneath him – and would serve only to weaken a position of strength he was building carefully, step by step, conversation by conversation.

"Aurariola will do exactly as I ask," said Oppa quietly. "I told you — I saved his life. He never would have escaped Sebastopolis had I not aided him in doing so. He owes me his life, and you his allegiance. You hold in your power the ability to give him back his family lands and allow him to keep his name. Believe me when I say both of those things mean more to him than any old grudge he may bear me." He met his father's eyes and forced sincerity into his own. "Theudemir and I fought together," he lied. "We have learned to live with our past."

Egica looked at his son for a long time, then he tilted his head and twisted his mouth. "You are much changed, my son."

"War changes men, as well you know, Father."

It was generous flattery, given Egica's lack of military experience, but his father accepted it as his due. Egica inclined his head loftily but did not answer.

"It also teaches us about the fragility of rule, how easily it may be shaken." This, Oppa knew, was dangerous ground — but this seed was one he had to plant, and the earlier, the better.

Egica raised a disdainful brow. "You cannot inherit my crown. You know this."

"Of course." Oppa dipped his head, concealing his irritation with long practice. "It is not for myself I speak, but for your son, Wittiza." He turned the wine cup on the table thoughtfully. "He will be fourteen soon. Age enough, your council would agree, to be associated with your rule, Father."

"Associated with my rule?" Egica stared at him. "You know the council's will as well as I. Our kings are elected. They do not inherit."

"They do if the council belongs to you." Oppa met his father's gaze squarely. "Any on the council who might have opposed you are already dead, or awaiting death, for their part in the rebellion. Any others who dare question the decision can be bought with coin, or secrets, both of which I can aid you with, should you need it. The Church has been cowed for its part in the rebellion, and even the south, now, will lie subdued under your command. I say make Wittiza co-ruler at your side, and let it be widely proclaimed. Cement our family's legacy, Father, as your grandfather Tulga intended it to be, and allow me to help you."

"And what is it that you want, in exchange for this help you offer?" Egica's eyes were calculating.

Oppa smirked, turning the wine cup again. "For now," he said, "I believe Illiberis needs a bishop."

"A bishop?" Egica's eyebrows shot up. "You would wish to take up the robes of a priest once more?"

Oppa shrugged. "I have become accustomed to the wearing of them. And, in time, I might aim higher than Illiberis. Hispalis, perhaps."

Egica was looking at him as if he was trying to make him out. "You have coin, men, and lands. What do you want in a backwater like Illiberis, wearing the robes of a priest?"

"Illiberis is close to Septem. And in Septem, rebellion brews." Oppa met his father's eyes with every pretence of transparency. Egica did not need to know of the trade links Oppa had established, nor of his son's desire to have an open route to the sea, should it be needed. Illiberis was far enough from Toletum to conceal Oppa's endeavours, close enough to Africa to ensure a free flow of information, and the best-guarded base in all of Spania's south. It was the perfect place to take his brother, to seduce Wittiza with all the debauchery a young man might desire.

And, perhaps above all, it had the added advantage of fulfilling a desire for revenge that Oppa had harboured since the first day he had faced Theudemir of Aurariola and the silent heiress of Illiberis across a wooded glade, a humiliation he had never forgotten. So long as he controlled Illiberis, he controlled both Theo and Lælia. That outcome was one no money could ever buy.

"I believe Illiberis is where I might best serve you, Father," he said dutifully. "Give it into my care, and I will uncover this rebellion – and safeguard your southern borders."

Egica hesitated, but this time, it was only for effect. "Very well, my son," he said, raising his wine cup to Oppa. "Illiberis you shall have."

* * *

The hour was late when Oppa finally returned to the house he maintained, beyond the palace walls, by the river. It amused him to take quarters amidst the squalor in which he had been raised, barely a stone's throw from the brothel in which he had been born. Oppa's years abroad had taught him the value of existing on the fringes, that power was rarely decided within palaces, but more often than not in the places where men drank and whored. It was there they exposed their weaknesses and boasted of what they knew. Oppa might wear the robes of a priest, but he had an ear in every bed in Toletum. Between the two, he already wielded more power than Wittiza ever would.

A light burned still in his chambers. When he pushed open the door he found a slender blonde girl stretched across his bed, eyeing him seductively beneath long lashes, looking so similar to the girl who had welcomed Wittiza earlier that Oppa's mouth curled in distaste. "You shouldn't have waited up."

"But I tire of waiting indoors for news." The girl pouted. She spoke in Greek, and her robes were both too rich and far too immodest to have been cut by any Gothic seamstress. "You promised you would take me to court."

"And I will." Oppa forced himself to smile and sat beside her on the bed, tracing the fullness of her lower lip as he cast

127

an assessing eye over her figure. "But not yet, *dulcissima*. It is not time yet."

"When will it be time?" There was a petulant note to her voice.

"I am waiting for a very special visitor to arrive in Toletum."

"Do you wish me to seduce him?"

"Oh, it's too late for that, *dulcissima*." Oppa stroked her cheek, feeling power surge through him. "You have already seduced him. Many times over, in fact."

The girl's eyes widened. "Theo? He is coming here?"

"He is indeed." Oppa's eyes darkened. "And when he does, I promise you this: you will be dressed in the finest of gowns and paraded before the entirety of the Toletum nobility – Elpis."

And the girl who had once seduced Theudemir of Aurariola, on far distant shores in a time he surely thought would be forgotten by all, looked at Oppa with eyes that were suddenly hard as a winter sky, her previously soft lips tight and vengeful.

"And I, my lord, shall look forward to it."

13

ATHANAGILD

25 APRIL, AD 693

Sixteenth Council of Toledo

"**A**re you certain I cannot attend?" Theo was leaning up against the wrought-iron window in Laurentius's library, his arms folded, frowning thoughtfully. Athanagild's eyes ran over his brother's face, as they had done every day since Theo's return. He had tried not to stare at the fierce scars that ravaged the once almost perfect features, but they were difficult to ignore. Somehow, though, Athanagild thought they suited Theo in a way perfection never had. Nobody, looking at Theo now, could doubt what he was – a warrior, a survivor, and a man who had known pain.

His eyes lingered on his brother's tall form as he said, "I am certain, Theo. The council will be opened to the nobility on the day sentence is passed, but not whilst the bishops debate the matters Egica brings before them. He wishes their decisions to be confidential until he stands in judgement over those who defied him, when he will wield his revenge with their full authority." He met Theo's eyes. "And he will have their authority," he said quietly. "Egica has left nothing to chance. He knows the outcomes he needs, and he has stacked his church with those who will deliver them. Sisebut's scheming disgraced the clergy. They are Egica's slaves now, humbled and prepared to do whatever he bids."

Theo pushed his long form away from the wall and strode to the wine jug, pouring himself a cup. "Perhaps it is fortunate, then, that neither Alaric nor Father survived to see judgement at his hands."

"Perhaps." Athanagild felt the sharp pang of loss and took a deep breath to steady himself. "But I do wish they had both lived to see your return. Especially Alaric. He never stopped fighting for you, Theo. Never. He went to war because of what Oppa did to you —"

He broke off abruptly and swung away, not wishing Theo to see the crippling grief he felt every time he faced the reality that Alaric would never again stride into the room, his eyes flashing, throwing a careless arm about Athanagild's shoulders. Even his joy at Theo's return could not eclipse the shadow of his elder brother's passing, especially since he had learned that Rekiberga had not only been captured, but was even now held captive in the palace, a piece, no doubt, Egica would take pleasure in playing before the entire court.

"I am sorry."

At Theo's quiet words, Athanagild turned back to him, frowning at the expression on his brother's face. "I did not mean to imply that Alaric's death was your fault." He spoke clearly, looking directly at Theo. "Do not mistake my meaning and do not, Theo, make Alaric's death your burden. Our brother knew always why he raised his sword, and against whom. Your suffering was but one more weight on a scale already heavily stacked in his heart against Oppa, Egica, and the Spania that killed all our mothers."

He felt another stab of pain, swift and furious, at the thought of his own mother, Elsuith. Her heavily pregnant body had been found dead on the ground, throat cut, and stabbed through the belly to ensure neither she nor her child could live. None knew who had committed the crime, or rather, none would speak of it. Athanagild, however, knew that Oppa had landed his dromons along the coast near Aurariola.

And Athanagild knew Oppa.

His mouth tightened. "Alaric's death lies on only one set of shoulders," he said grimly. "And if it takes until I am grey, I will find a way to avenge it. Oppa will pay for what he did. To you, to Alaric – to Lælia."

Theo stirred uneasily by the table. "I have spent much of these past years living at close quarters to Oppa." There was a dull shadow over the eyes that met Athanagild's, a darkness he could not quite read. "He is a dangerous enemy, Athanagild. Be cautious how you attempt to play him." Theo's mouth twisted bitterly as he tossed off the cup in a swift movement. "He does not follow any path honourable men might recognise." At Athanagild's harsh cough of laughter, Theo frowned and put down his cup.

"If you think me an honourable man, Theo, you have been away from Spania for too long." Reaching for the rich outer robe that denoted his recent rise in status, Athanagild pulled it over his head and faced his brother with hard eyes. "I have seen corruption beyond anything a man such as you might imagine. I have lived a lie and appeased men I despise to gain intelligence. I have traded with evil and betrayed every oath I have ever taken. Do not think me unequal to a man such as Oppa, Theo. You may have spent these past years waging war with steel and fire, but I have spent them in the same shadows Oppa thinks he owns. Whatever games he plays, I will discover them, Theo – and I will see them, and him, undone."

"Athanagild." Despite the many hours they had spent talking since Theo's return, Athanagild thought that he had not before seen the expression that twisted his brother's features now. He frowned, waiting for Theo to continue, but as Jadis's appearance at the door announced Lælia's entrance, Theo's voice was abruptly cut off, his ravaged face suddenly the bland, implacable mask Athanagild recalled well from their childhood days.

"Lælia." The shadows wrought by Oppa's name were banished as swiftly as they had come. As Lælia's tall, slender figure entered the library, Theo's eyes were once again the deep, rich green of summer pasture, the scars on his face seeming to fall into softer lines as he strode forward, his hands outstretched. Athanagild, seeing the soft glow of love turn Lælia's eyes to burnished bronze, slipped from the room unnoticed, leaving them to the comfort of each other, Oppa's name scattered to dust beneath their visible joy.

* * *

ATHANAGILD, head whirling, strode downhill along the busy, winding road that led under a horseshoe arch and out of the city walls to the Basilica of Peter and Paul, which lay beside the old Roman circus. He felt terribly unprepared for the ordeal ahead. Theo's arrival had been overwhelming, in more ways than one.

First there had been the long hours of talking, the effort of trying to pack years of deep change into a handful of late-night conversations. Lælia had already told Theo much of the political machinations of the past years, but there was much she herself did not know and, Athanagild suspected, much she had not relayed. She and Theo were so visibly, almost blindingly, in love with one another that Athanagild doubted either of them had much mind for the events during the years they had been separated. Even the knowledge of Paulus's death, and the recent tragedy of Acantha's, had been ameliorated for Lælia by the long-awaited miracle of Theo's return. Though she had listened quietly as Athanagild spoke of Shukra's captivity, Egilona and Roderic being held hostage, and the long litany of deaths on the Toletum battlefield, he had the sense that Lælia was insulated from all by the gleaming mantle of love she and Theo shared. She showed none of her customary savagery, the sharp precision normally present in her questions, seeming uncharacteristically content to allow Theo and him to talk uninterrupted, and often without being present. Athanagild, accustomed to Lælia taking a decisive role in any matter even loosely pertaining to her own future, had been somewhat surprised at her silence. Part of him wondered if Theo truly knew all she had done in the years he had been away.

He felt, too, the familiar shadow of his own lies. After greeting Theo and Lælia warmly, learning news of the fleet, and joining them at meat, Laurentius had barely been seen in the villa. When he did appear, he and Athanagild moved about one another with the wary caution they had long mastered, careful always to maintain cordiality without any trace of the familiarity they shared. The effort of maintaining the façade had never felt more trying than in Theo's sharp-eyed presence. In the face of Theo and Lælia's blatant joy in one another, never had Athanagild wished more to speak of his own feelings, and never had he felt so heavily the burden of silence. He could not tell the truth of Shukra's capture, nor of the reasons for Laurentius's often grim silence. Athanagild, in recent days, had, quite unusually, found an unlikely solace in the monastery's solitude.

Amidst the emotional tumult, he had had little time to think upon what the council would hold, and he entered the basilica feeling uncharacteristically unprepared. As was customary, the king was to open the council with a speech that would set the tone for the deliberations.

"There are likely to be few surprises," murmured one of his colleagues, a priest from Tarraconensis, as the bishops filed in to take their places beneath the rich votive crowns dripping a dazzling array of jewels from the ceiling. They stood behind their chairs, leaving only the central chair of the archbishop empty, its former occupant being now on trial for treason. "Egica will demand the power to condemn the traitors, confiscate their property, and excommunicate all those involved in the rebellion. His speech is likely to be swift enough."

Remembering, too late, that Athanagild himself was the son of one of those about to be condemned for treachery, he coloured. "Nobody knows how he will deal with the offspring of the accused," he added uncomfortably.

"If past examples serve," said Athanagild composedly, "we will be condemned alongside our fathers."

The priest looked at him askance. "Are you not afraid of what that will mean, for you?"

Athanagild shrugged. "My fate is in God's hands – and the king rules with God's blessing. Whatever he decrees will be right."

The man crossed himself, unable to argue with such immutable logic, but the eyes he turned from Athanagild's were sceptical. His were not the only eyes to look Athanagild over curiously. Athanagild did not much care. Felix, he knew, would soon be archbishop. And Felix believed Athanagild an innocent victim of Sisebut's sodomy, and thus of the Church's disgrace. Athanagild's eyes rested on the bishops Idalio, Maximo, and Mumulo, all equally pale as they met his eyes. Men whom Athanagild had once seen plot Egica's downfall in a midnight chapel with Sisebut. He held their lives in his hands – and he had made certain, since Sisebut's capture and imprisonment, that they all knew it. Athanagild was not concerned about his own fate. If his long years as Sisebut's plaything had taught him anything, it was how to play the game of power in Toletum.

No, Athanagild was not worried about his own future.

But he was afraid of what Theo's, and Lælia's, would hold.

As Egica entered the chamber and prostrated himself on the floor before the assembled bishops, as was custom, Athanagild found himself paying less attention to the king's speech and thinking instead on his brother's somewhat conspicuous silence regarding his and Lælia's future. All Theo had said, when Athanagild pushed him, was that he had reason to believe he would not be held to account for their family's treason.

"You should not have come," had been Athanagild's first words after his initial, passionate relief at seeing both Theo and Lælia alive. "Alaric rode south to take you to Septem, Lælia, and you should have gone. Toletum is not safe, for either of you." Laurentius, on seeing them both, had made a similar remark, taking Theo aside. "It is a miracle you are not imprisoned already," Athanagild had heard him say grimly. "The only solution now is for you to flee before the king sends guards for you both. There are whispers that Illiberis not only fought in the battle for Toletum but mounted a full-scale defence against the king's own forces."

Theo and Lælia had said little to those accusations, and even less of their own plans. "You yourself have not fled," Theo had said, turning uncomfortably piercing eyes to Athanagild. "Clearly you have found a way around the punishment that is coming. I believe I, too, have done so."

"But not one you might share with me?"

"Do you wish to share your own methods with me, Athanagild?" In the long silence that had followed this exchange, Athanagild had the bittersweet realisation that regardless of their mutual joy at being reunited at last, the gulf that lay between him and Theo now was one far wider than that created by years and foreign lands. They were no longer held by the unspoken bond of familial trust. The loss of it hurt him more than he could have imagined, even as he knew that he was as guilty of creating the breach as Theo. They both, Athanagild suspected, harboured secrets that condemned and saved them in equal measure.

He wished it were different. But such wishes were, Athanagild thought bitterly, the stuff of childhood fantasy. Reality was darker and more complex, and every man must find a way to navigate it according to his own conscience.

As if to punctuate his thoughts, Athanagild was suddenly aware of Oppa, standing slightly off to the side of the council, mouth curled in slight amusement as he watched the proceedings. He did not sit amongst the senior bishops but his robes, Athanagild noted, showed his status as their equal. He had heard that Oppa was to take up a bishopric. He wondered that even the most corrupt amongst his brethren could stomach such blatant hypocrisy. Seeing the heavy-lidded eyes watch the king with barely disguised contempt, a sharp, burning hatred twisted Athanagild's chest so he found it difficult to breathe. As if drawn by his rage, Oppa's dark eyes fell upon him and Athanagild felt the shock of his attention like cold steel in his flesh. For a moment the two men stared at one another. Then Oppa's eyes, having given nothing away, moved on, leaving Athanagild wondering if the man had even recognised him at all.

Unsettled, he dragged himself back to the present and tried to make sense of the king's overly florid statements.

"I think," said Egica sharply, pinning the assembled bishops with a gimlet eye, "your paternities are unaware of how many evils strike the earth every day because of divine indignation, and how many stripes and crimes of the infidels destroy it." Having thus set the tone, he embarked upon a searing catalogue of the Church's failings. "We have come to know," he said, raising a portentous finger, "that in many basilicas of God, sacrifices are not offered to the Lord; the structures remain abandoned and without a roof, and collapse."

Egica droned on, setting out clear directives that bishops must follow in the upkeep of their churches, all underpinned by dire warnings of Jews mocking their Christian counterparts for the disrepair of their places of worship. Athanagild wondered why, given the gravity of matters before the council, Egica would spend so much time concerned with the manner in which bishops maintained their churches. A moment later, however, it became clear.

"You must try chiefly that wherever you find idolatry or diabolical superstition, or are made aware of them, you hasten to uproot such a crime, as true worshipers of Christ." The bishops from Gallæceia all moved uneasily at this, and a low murmuring broke out around the basilica. Athanagild suppressed a knowing grin. All present were aware that the lords of Gallæceia paid only the loosest lip service to the Christian faith. One could walk barely a mile along a road in that wild country without falling over a stone cairn or pagan statue; even the priests themselves were often more aligned to local pagan worship than to the scriptures they preached. But now, after Gallæceia had risen so spectacularly against Egica during the rebellion, the king clearly intended to use those transgressions to impose his own will on the Church in that area. Athanagild would place all the coin he had that Egica had already sent men of his own north to take the place of the rebellious clergy there, and to remind the northern lords of their allegiance to the Crown. "All that you will find to have been offered to these idols," Egica went on sternly, "you will deliver entirely to the churches closest to the place."

Athanagild fought to keep the cynicism he felt from his face. He could only begin to imagine what Egica's priests might deem to be pagan offerings. The people of Gallæceia would soon, he thought, discover that any coin they might have could be deemed pagan offerings – and confiscated in God's name.

As Egica carried on, Athanagild's eyes roamed to Oppa, resplendent in his white robes edged with subtle gold thread, and stopped abruptly at the smug expression on the pointed face. *This is Oppa's plan,* he realised with a cold shock. *It isn't only the north that is known for pagan offerings.* Athanagild recalled the abbey high in the mountains above Illiberis; the dilapidated state of the church in the township, compared to the Jewish temple at Garnata. *He will take control of the church at Illiberis, be the Church's control on pagan influences and lax clergy. Doing so will ingratiate him with the highest levels of the Church, for nobody wishes to deal with the pagan south. He will appear not only dutiful, but pious, and all the while, he will be seeking ways to manipulate the southern lords and consolidate his power.* Oppa was using the Church as his avenue to control not just Illiberis, but the entirety of the south, though at the thought of those fierce lords behind their impenetrable mountain passes, Athanagild could not help but wonder how successful even Oppa would be in bringing them to heel.

He was still contemplating this when Egica's sonorous tones delivered the next blow: "But there is still something more important than the above: to uproot, with the zeal of God, the infidelity worthy of extirpation of the Jews of both sexes."

Not the admonition, or the conversion, of the Jews, Athanagild thought. *The complete excision.* Egica was putting the Jews of Spania on notice that they must convert, flee, or die. Leaving no room for doubt, Egica went on to explain that any Jew who remained unconverted and who dared trade would not only incur taxes, but that those taxes would have to be paid by his converted brethren.

Again, Athanagild saw behind the curtain of the pompous decree. Any converted Jew could expect, at any moment, to be taxed into poverty, for the crimes, real or imagined, of those amongst his people who had not converted. Egica meant to place a burden of tax so heavily upon the Jewish community that their continued existence was impossible. Glancing at Oppa once more, he saw the slight curl to the man's thin lips. Unseen by any, Athanagild clenched his fists beneath his robes. None of this was Egica. This council was being run by Oppa, and Oppa's ambitions. If he had suspected before that the balance of power was subtly shifting in Toletum, today was all the proof he needed. It was Oppa who now held the reins of power, wielding them with a lethal dexterity even his own father could not combat.

Egica's next words dragged Athanagild from his specula-tions with the savagery of a body blow. "Likewise," said Egica silkily, his eyes flat and black as they regarded the assembled men of God, "amongst other crimes, you ought to order the extermination of that obscene crime of homosexuality." The bishops stirred uneasily. Athanagild, willing his expression to remain neutral, his face not to flush, could not look at Felix and barely dared breathe. "The horrendous practice," Egica went on, "that taints the grace of an honest life and provokes the wrath of the Supreme Avenger, who is in heaven."

And where, thought Athanagild savagely, *was that Supreme Avenger when Sisebut would force me to his bed? It was not God who avenged me, but Shukra; and he rots in a cell because of his actions.* Athanagild shivered. He was a man of God, first and foremost, and he was aware that his thoughts were perhaps the closest he had ever come to outright heresy. He knew Egica's words would see Sisebut dead when the bishops were finished with their deliberations. But his dark satisfaction at that prospect was destroyed by the knowledge that Shukra, who was innocent of any such crime, would meet the same fate – whilst he, Athanagild, the very reason for this decree in the first place, and even more guilty, perhaps, than Sisebut himself, would walk free, at continuing liberty to indulge his sins with the man he loved. At the thought of Laurentius's stern, strained face, every muscle in Athanagild's body tensed. He was responsible for Laurentius's pain. For Shukra's imprisonment. And he would walk from this room with no man suspecting him of anything other than piety and patriotism.

The hypocrisy curdled in his gut.

"From now on," Egica was saying, as Athanagild forced himself to focus, "any nobleman who tries to engineer the death of the king, or the loss of the nation or the homeland of the Goths, or to excite any disturbance within the borders of Spain – both he and all his descendants will be excluded from holding any office. They must serve the treasury in perpetuity, also losing all their own property, which the king's clemency will freely attribute to whomever he wishes."

It was not unexpected. No traitor could hope to retain his lands or title. But still, hearing it said so bluntly amongst stone and frankincense, echoing across the assembled heads, Athanagild felt a dull sense of finality.

Aurariola was gone, as was Illiberis.

Whatever they faced now, they would do so as supplicants to the Crown – and at Oppa's mercy.

14

THEO

MAY, AD 693

Toletum, Spania
Toledo, Spain

Theo woke from dreaming of Lælia with the familiar, bittersweet clench in his heart. Then he became aware of the long limbs entwined with his own, the faint citrus scent of her hair, and felt a wave of relief and joy sweep through him just as he did the sudden, fierce arousal of his own body.

"*Liefs*," he murmured against her neck. She stirred within his embrace. He moved against her, that slight movement all it took to light the savage flame of desire that seemed always just beneath the surface, flaring into a raging blaze that never ceased to take his breath away and swallow him in sweet heat. In the pale light of dawn, he looked up at the long, supple lines of her body atop his own, her head thrown back and hair rippling about her. "You're so beautiful," he said wonderingly, his hands holding her as she rode them both higher, into a place beyond any he had ever, in his wildest fantasies, envisaged; then, as she began to buck and shudder, flipping her

141

over, he drove deep inside. Her eyes were heavy lidded and glowing topaz as he surged to the hilt until he lost himself in her body and soul, going to the place where only they two existed, and then fell to sleep once more, their limbs twined so closely they were one.

The shadows of dawn had fled when she turned to him and said, "It is today that we will know our fate."

"*Ja.*" Theo lay with an arm under his head, staring unseeing at the beams above them. Normally he would play the coming day in his mind, searching for strategy, envisaging how he might manage it. Instead he turned his head on the pillow and, reaching out, drew one finger along the slow curve of Lælia's waist. "I do not want to bring it forward by speaking of it," he said roughly. "Soon enough it will be all we talk of."

"We have not spoken of how we will manage this." Theo forced himself to hold her searching gaze, but he felt himself retract, the hated mask of his lies falling over his eyes to hide the truth from her. Lælia's eyes narrowed. "I know we agreed to deal with Oppa. But we have not spoken about how it is to be done, nor what will follow. I know you want to protect me." Her hands were under her cheek, her face barely inches from his own. "But I do not need you to do that, Theo. I need you to trust me. We should speak of how we will face this, what we will say."

"What is there to say? The deal with Oppa has been done." Turning abruptly away from her, Theo swung his legs over the side of the bed and strode, naked, to the jug and basin on the side table. Washing without looking at her, he eventually turned back to find her propped up on one elbow in bed, watching him with disquieting scrutiny.

"You have spoken with him already?"

"I have." Theo tried and failed to keep the tension from his voice.

"And you didn't tell me?" Her eyebrows drew together, a dangerous light gathering in her eyes.

"We agreed on the course. I confirmed it with Oppa. That is all." Seeing her face darken, Theo sat back down on the bed, forcing himself to meet her eyes. "I can't bear to so much as think of that bastard in the same room as you." *That much, at least, is the truth.* "I was not trying to shield you from the truth. But I am not certain I could have said what had to be said if he was staring at you during the conversation." It had been hard enough, even brief as their meeting had been. No more than the time it had taken for him to curtly agree to the terms Oppa had outlined in Corduba. They had not shaken hands, nor talked on it further, but even that much had been enough to send Theo to a riverside tavern, where he had proceeded to drink enough that he had wound up spending the night on Athanagild's couch. "I should have told you." He stared at the floor.

Her face softened, her arms snaking about his waist as she pressed her lips to his bare skin, sending a shiver through him. "Yes, Theo. You should have. But I understand why you didn't."

Her understanding only made his deception worse. Theo went on before she could notice his discomfort.

"Athanagild has already told us what Egica directed his bishops to find. The Church is cowed, Lælia. They will do his bidding. We will be dispossessed, either completely or partially, as traitors, or as the descendants of traitors. Shukra will be sentenced to death." Frowning, he wrapped linen about his waist and stood, bare chested, with hands on hips, staring at the floor. "I don't understand why Shukra won't fight for his innocence," he said. It was the one thing amongst all he had learned that Theo didn't understand. Shukra − accused of homosexuality? It made no sense, and it made even less that both Laurentius and Athanagild seemed so resigned to Shukra's fate. Theo looked up to find Lælia still watching him, though now with a strange, secret smile curving her lips.

"Do you not?" she said. Swinging her own legs out of bed, she moved across the room, deliberately brushing his body with her own as she passed him. All thoughts of Shukra or anything else fled Theo's mind. He reached for her and she danced out of his reach, laughing softly. "Go. I have to make myself presentable for our king."

Despite her light-hearted tone, even an indirect mention of Egica was enough to turn Theo's stomach. He dressed in a grim silence, stealing the occasional glimpse at Lælia as she washed, wishing only that he could draw her back to bed and lose himself in her body and ignore every cursed moment of what was to come, for them both. Taking a last look, he smiled when she waved him away. Closing the door behind him, he moved into the silent corridor and toward the sounds of the villa stirring, bracing himself for the ordeal to come.

* * *

THERE WAS nothing like the scent of blood to draw a crowd.

The streets leading to the palace were teeming with merchants selling everything from water to religious relics purported to protect a man from God's vengeance. Bunches of rosemary to ward off evil; frankincense to protect against the devil's judgement. By the time Theo reached the palace he was heartily sickened by the carnival of spectators, all of whom recognised him by the savage markings on his face and murmured to their friends as he and Lælia passed. They entered the reception chamber and crossed themselves with holy water, leaving Theo's sword by the door; then they came into the main hall.

Riccilo stood with Roderic at her side, stiff backed and tall, close to the dais. The other nobles maintained a wary distance, unwilling to stand too close to one so surely condemned for treachery. All knew Theodofred languished in the dungeons below. Theo and Lælia drew close and Riccilo's eyes flickered to the side. Despite her position, Theo could not help but admire Riccilo's pride. She wore a crimson wool gown that plunged at the neckline, and around her throat was the serpent torc of Illiberis, ruby eyes gleaming at the centre. Her hair was dressed high on her head. When Lælia came to stand beside her aunt, heads turned, for she, too, wore the serpent of Illiberis at her neck, the sapphires complementing her indigo wool gown. The two women stared directly ahead, chins uptilted, meeting the disapproving eyes of the bishops on the dais with unapologetic defiance, as if to directly countermand the king's own speech at the opening of the council, when he had railed against pagan practices. Glancing sideways at the twin figures, Theo could not help but suppress a smile. If Egica had thought to humiliate the south, he had reckoned without the women of Illiberis.

Then he caught sight of Oppa, lurking to one side of the dais, and his own smile faded. He had not allowed himself to dwell upon what today might bring, but he should have foreseen that Oppa would seek to twist the knife. Green eyes met black. Oppa raised his eyebrows once; Theo gave a reluctant, almost imperceptible nod. The answering flash of triumph in Oppa's eyes made him long for Silas and Leofric at his side, and a sharpened sword. But Silas and Leofric were gone to Aurariola, and Theo had left his sword at the door.

The bishop Felix, recently and in unprecedented fashion declared archbishop of Toletum and thus of all Spania, entered the chamber, Egica following behind. Beside him walked a shorter, slightly plump adolescent, self-conscious in his stiff, formal robes. His face was round and soft, his eyes watery blue, and though he wore the ostentatious eagle symbol that proclaimed him Egica's son, by comparison to Oppa's dark eyes and angular features, Theo thought Wittiza bore little resemblance to the king. The boy's eyes flickered to the side of the dais as if searching for something. Theo followed his gaze and frowned when he saw Oppa nod reassuringly, and the way Wittiza, in turn, seemed to relax, taking strength from his half-brother's presence.

That, Theo thought, *is a dangerous alliance indeed.*

The king and his son prostrated themselves as Felix

intoned a prayer that God's will might be done in the chamber; then both sat, Egica in the great carved chair beneath the jewelled votive crown, his son in a smaller chair to his right side. The assembled nobles, silent, watched them expectantly.

"The council of our blessed fathers," said Egica, gazing coldly around the chamber, "has made wise and just decisions. The judgements we carry out today are not mine but belong to God, and to our mighty fathers of blessed memory, Chindasuinth and Wamba, who made the laws upon which we now act."

We, Theo thought, noting the way Egica included his son in his rulings. *He is setting the stage to name his son as co-ruler, then.*

From the corner of his eye, Theo saw Riccilo tense at the invocation of her husband's father's name. Chindasuinth had chosen her as wife for his son. The old king had made of Riccilo something of a favourite, admiring her spirit, and laughing off her pagan beliefs with the careless disdain he had ever shown the Church. Chindasuinth may have loved the law, but he had little time for the Church fathers who promulgated it. To hear his name said aloud now, alongside that of Wamba – the same king, it was rumoured, that Egica himself had conspired to poison – was nothing short of a deliberate provocation. By the muttered asides in the chamber, everyone there knew it.

A dark light gleamed in Egica's eyes. "Bring forth Rekiberga, daughter of Sunifred."

Beside him, Lælia sucked in her breath as Rekiberga was pulled unceremoniously onto the dais and pushed roughly before the king. Rekiberga did not fall to the floor in supplication but remained standing, staring defiantly at Egica. She was dirty and dishevelled, her gown torn and bloodstained, and had clearly been held in grim circumstances. Theo, glancing at where Athanagild stood amongst his peers, saw his brother's face set in hard lines, his eyes glittering as he took in the pitiful sight before him. Theo had never met Rekiberga, but he knew his brother Alaric had loved her fiercely, and that Athanagild considered her a sister. To see any noblewoman so degraded was disturbing, a stark reminder of how ruthless a king's justice could be. Theo, seeing the satisfied gleam in Egica's eye, knew that was precisely what this ugly piece of theatre served to demonstrate.

"Rekiberga, daughter of the traitor, Sunifred." Egica addressed her without any of the titles to which she was born. "Your father plotted to murder his king. He led a rebellion against the man chosen by a council of his peers and anointed by God, and thought to place himself above all other men of the Gothic nation. As his last living relative, you are disinherited of all property and title. You have no place at court, and no dowry." Rekiberga stood quietly as he spoke. She did not flinch, and although Theo could not see her face, there was a certain defiant set to her shoulders that did not speak of submission. Egica's face darkened. "You should be on your knees before me," he spat, leaning forward.

Rekiberga went obediently to her knees, but still she did not speak, and though her head was bowed, her gown torn and dirty, her quiet figure radiated a certain dignity.

Egica stared at her then finally sat back, looking at her through narrowed eyes, stroking the short beard on his chin. "Gisclamundo," he said eventually, beckoning the man forward. "You have a son, do you not?"

"Ataulfo." The nobleman nodded.

"Ataulfo. Of course." Egica looked meditatively at Rekiberga. "I think Ataulfo would do well with such a bride, do you not agree?"

"Indeed," said Gisclamundo, almost stammering in his excitement to get the word out.

"It would be easier, after all, for the new duke to take the reins of his new lands with the daughter of the former duke at his side. For continuity, you understand."

"Of course, *reiks*. I thank you —"

But Egica was already waving him away, the moment having achieved the public humiliation he sought. Rekiberga stood to leave. As she approached the side door, Egica said sharply, "No! You will leave through the front doors, that all may look upon the face of treachery."

Slowly Rekiberga turned. Pulling the tattered remains of her gown across her chest, she began walking down the aisle made by the crowd parting for her, watched in silence as she went. Her face was pale as milk, her eyes stark as an icy sea. She moved slowly through the crowd with her head high and her jaw set hard. Only as she reached Lælia did her mask falter for a moment, pain and shock appearing like a sudden cloud.

"Courage," Lælia breathed. The word was barely audible, but whatever Rekiberga saw in Lælia's eyes must have given her strength, for when she turned back she was upright and tall once again, her face a hard shield against a world that was, Theo knew, about to become uglier than any she could previously have imagined.

As the door closed behind her, Theo released a breath he had barely been aware he was holding, only to suck it in again when Egica's man announced, "Theodofred, Duke of Corduba."

The man who stumbled into the council chamber between two of the king's *gardingi* bore no resemblance to the tall, proud warrior Theo recalled from the days before he had left Spania. This man was thin and stooped, face drawn with weariness and defeat, his once impressive frame so diminished Theo would not have recognised him had it not been for the brilliant blue eyes staring out at the crowd, searching, Theo realised when they paused on Riccilo, for his wife and son. Riccilo trembled slightly but she did not falter as she held her husband's eyes, though two hectic spots of colour flamed in her cheeks and her lips were a bloodless, tight line. Theodofred's eyes dropped to his son and a spasm of pain crossed his face. Roderic, Theo thought, watching the boy from the corner of his eye, looked at Theodofred as if his father were a stranger.

"Theodofred sunau Chindasuinth." On Egica's lips the name was almost a slur. It was Chindasuinth, after all, Theodofred's father, who had once dethroned Egica's grandfather, King Tulga, in a humiliating public spectacle of tonsuring, banishing the fallen nobleman to ignominious retirement in a monastery. Theo could only imagine how long Egica had nursed his revenge. Now he had killed one of Chindasuinth's sons, Favila, in open rebellion, and had the last living son on his knees before him.

Revenge, indeed.

Egica did not attempt to hide his triumph as he stared down at the humbled figure, his black eyes gleaming. "You held one of the most prestigious titles in all Spania, are descended from the most distinguished of lines."

Held, Theo thought. *He means to kill him, then.*

"And yet you sent men to fight against the very king you are sworn to defend. Do you deny that men from your own thiufas fought alongside Sunifred's rebel army?"

"*Ne.*" Theodofred's voice was rusty with disuse. "I do not deny it."

"Your own father murdered over two hundred nobles whom he deemed traitors, after he took the crown." Egica's voice was harsh, the gleam in his eyes savage now. "If it was Chindasuinth who sat on this throne today, do you think he would show you mercy?"

"My father showed no mercy to those he considered enemies."

"No." Egica's eyes glittered. "He did not." He paused for effect. "Spania has only one punishment for traitors, Theodofred sunau Chindasuinth," Egica said slowly, "and that is the one your father carried out with such ruthless efficiency."

Riccilo gave an involuntary gasp, reaching instinctively to draw Roderic close. Wittiza, Theo noticed, flinched when he saw this, biting his lip worriedly. The assembled nobles muttered uneasily amongst themselves. The law for treachery might indeed be clear, but Theodofred was not just any nobleman. He was duke of the most powerful province in Spania, the last living son of a legend. Execution might well be in accordance with the law, and it was certainly the method Chindasuinth had employed to keep the unruly nobles in order; but those had been savage, blood-soaked days, and despite the recent rebellion, Theodofred had long been a voice of reason and moderation in council. Theo noticed Laurentius, grim faced and silent, standing with arms folded by a pillar, staring at the dais with burning eyes. None could speak in Theodofred's defence. The punishment of traitors was the king's decision alone.

Then Oppa stepped forward. "*Reiks*." All eyes swivelled to the white-robed figure who stood before Egica, his head bowed respectfully. "*Princeps*," Oppa formally addressed Wittiza, who smiled uncertainly at his half-brother.

"Oppa." Egica's eyes narrowed. "Do you wish to speak?"

Theo folded his arms and regarded the dais speculatively. He knew enough of Oppa to know there was nothing spontaneous about this interruption. *Oppa has a plan for Theodofred.*

"Theodofred's son, Roderic, is your own son's closest companion." Seeing the smile of relief on Wittiza's face, Theo's mouth twisted scornfully. Oppa was ingratiating himself with the son. Allying himself with the next king. "As I rode north to your capital, *reiks*, I met many of those men from the south who had fled the battlefield after your glorious victory." Oppa's tone was respectful as he addressed his father, with exactly the right mixture of deference and authority. "All said they had fought with Sunifred of their own volition, not under Theodofred's own banner. And Wittiza himself told me the Corduba thiufa fought alongside your own forces – even against Theodofred's own brother, Favila, in putting down the northern rebellion."

The nobles stirred, muttering amongst themselves, and Wittiza's eyes widened eagerly, moving between Oppa, on the dais, and Roderic, who stood stiff and red faced at his mother's side. Theodofred remained kneeling on the dais, seeming almost indifferent to his fate.

"*Reiks.*" Oppa's head was still bowed but slightly raised to meet his father's eyes, and by the look on Egica's face, it was clear his bastard son had his full attention. "Your son will one day, with the blessing of God and of the Gothic nation, lead us at your side. When he does, he will need strong allies – and I believe he and Roderic sunau Theodofred to be bound as tightly as any brothers might be. Is it not true, Wittiza?"

Theodofred's head snapped up at the mention of his son, and for the first time since he had entered the hall, his face showed some remnant of the fierce man he had once been.

Wittiza nodded eagerly. "Roderic is loyal to me," he said, his voice tight with excitement and high pitched, his face flushed. "He would never betray us."

Egica's eyes moved between his sons, then to Theodofred. They narrowed thoughtfully. "Roderic," he said, raising a hand. "Come forward." Roderic glanced uncertainly at his mother. Riccilo, white faced, gave the slightest of nods. Theo guessed she did not trust herself to speak. Roderic moved jerkily forward, stumbling slightly on the stones as he went, coming to stand beside his father's kneeling figure. It was telling, Theo thought, that Roderic did not so much as think of going to his knees before his childhood playmate – and that Egica did not ask it of him.

"You have long been companion to my son Wittiza, have you not, Roderic sunau Theodofred?"

Roderic nodded, glancing at Wittiza, then at Oppa, both of whom nodded encouragingly. *Roderic knows Oppa,* Theo realised suddenly. *Sees him as a friend.* He felt an altogether too familiar feeling of creeping unease as he looked at the tableau on the dais. Theo had watched Oppa play these games before, knew what the bastard planned almost as well as Oppa himself. He saw the power base Oppa was building, the web of allegiances he was weaving under his father's very nose, in the guise of helping Egica consolidate his son's position.

"Roderic." Emboldened by Oppa's proximity and the presence of his childhood companion, Wittiza spoke with more confidence. "Will you swear your allegiance here, now, to my father, and to me?"

Roderic neither hesitated nor so much as glanced at his father as he said, in a clear voice that carried around the hall, "With my life, *princeps*, now and always, I pledge to you and your father, my king, my allegiance, and that of my family, and of the lands we govern with your blessing." The answer came so readily, with such fluency, that Theo suspected it had been rehearsed. Seeing Oppa's head turned slightly toward Roderic, the satisfied curl to his mouth, Theo thought he knew precisely who had coached the boy.

Egica's black eyes roamed the room, noting, Theo thought, the approval and eagerness on the assembled faces, and seeing, undoubtedly, the moment in which he could cement his son's presence at his side. "Wittiza," he said, turning speculative eyes to his son, "if you would accept Roderic as your ally, what sentence would you impose upon the father, who betrayed your crown?"

Wittiza, flushed with importance and the gravity of the moment, stroked his hairless chin in imitation of his father, but it was to Oppa his eyes slid. It was such a subtle glance it was barely perceptible, but Theo, who had, over the years, developed an unerring awareness of Oppa's presence, knew exactly to whom the glance had been directed and saw the faint inclination of Oppa's head. *This, too, they have discussed,* he thought, with the same dull sense of inevitability.

"Theodofred saw the treachery of his men and did not seek to turn them away from their path." Wittiza's voice was still high but stronger now, as if he knew himself to be on more certain ground. "He saw the treachery of his friends, men who should have been loyal to you, *reiks*, and he did nothing to stop them. He saw much that no man should ever see – and so his punishment should be that his ability to see be taken from him."

"No!" Riccilo cried out before she could stop herself, then she clapped her own hands over her mouth, her eyes wide with horror. Theodofred was looking at his son, his face agonised, but Roderic did not meet his eyes, standing stiffly and staring directly ahead, at Wittiza. Egica took in Riccilo's stricken face, Theodofred's pained one, Roderic's wooden, set features, the shocked, and equally avid, expressions of the assembled nobles, and Theo saw the dark eyes gleam with satisfaction.

"*Gut*," said Egica. "You are merciful, my son, and also wise." The compliment was meant for the benefit of the assembly, not Wittiza, but the plump prince still flushed with pleasure. It was to Oppa, though, Theo thought darkly as men brought forth a brazier of hot coals, that the credit was due. He was both the inspiration for, and architect of, this particular horror.

"Roderic." Egica smiled coldly at the boy before him. Though tall for his age, Roderic, Theo knew, could be no older than eleven. "Your father has been pronounced a traitor. You say you are our loyal ally, sworn to obey the Crown in all things, with your life if necessary. Is that true?"

Roderic nodded. "*Ja, reiks.* I am sworn."

"Then you will prove your allegiance by carrying out the sentence your prince has decreed your father suffer." There was a collective gasp. Wittiza visibly blanched, his eyes flying to his father in confusion and then, when Egica did not return his glance, pleadingly to Oppa. Oppa, however, remained stolidly silent. Oppa, Theo thought, knew better than Wittiza just how far Egica could be pushed. From the corner of his eye, Theo saw Lælia put her arm around Riccilo; it seemed to an observer a gesture of comfort, but Theo, seeing the corded muscle in Lælia's shoulder, knew it was one of restraint.

Egica nodded at the poker gleaming red in the coals. "You will take the poker, Roderic sunau Theodofred, and put out your father's eyes, that he may look upon neither his king nor those who would betray me, ever again."

Roderic turned uncertainly toward his mother. He was a handsome boy, with his mother's angular, even features, and he looked now at Riccilo as if seeking her approval. Riccilo, white faced, nodded at him, and Roderic, pale and set, turned to his father.

"Do as your king commands." Theodofred spoke for the first time since he had admitted his guilt to Egica. His voice rasped in his throat, but his eyes blazed vivid blue, as if in defiance of their imminent death. "Do not hesitate, Roderic."

"You will not speak." Egica's voice was sharp as a whiplash. "And you, boy, will do as your prince and king command." He leaned forward in his chair, watching Roderic with an anticipation that Theo found sickening.

Roderic glanced once at Wittiza, who was pale faced and sickly looking, then around the room, as if searching for something. Following his gaze, Theo came to two small figures, both standing with guards on either side, by a far wall. One was a dark-haired boy with an intelligent face and resigned, cautious eyes. The other was a stunningly beautiful girl with startling blue eyes, hair so white it gleamed in the marble hall, and a face so achingly familiar it froze Theo to the spot.

Egilona.

Roderic stared at the pair across the hall as if they were his anchor, and the two returned his gaze as if they willed their own strength into his veins. Roderic's chest rose in a deep breath, almost as if he inhaled their strength, and when he reached for the poker, his hand was steady. He stared directly into his father's eyes and said, in a clear voice easily heard throughout the hall, "Theodofred sunau Chindasuinth, Duke of Corduba, you are accused of betraying your king and the nation of the Goths. For these crimes you are sentenced to the loss of your eyes, that you may never again in this life look upon the king you betrayed." Pulling the poker from the coals, Roderic plunged it deep into his father's right eye.

Theodofred's scream was raw as the stench of burned flesh, and just as sickening. Riccilo cried out and would have fallen to the floor had Lælia not held her upright. Roderic, his face grim with shock, held the poker deep, until the eye was a blackened, revolting socket; then he returned the poker to the coals like a sleepwalker, no longer, Theo knew, seeing what was before him. The silence whilst he held the poker back in the heat was thick with tension and horror, Theodofred rocking back and forward on his knees, his one lone eye fixed on his son as he bit his mouth to stop crying out. When Roderic turned back with the poker in his hand he paused, staring at the agonised remaining eye, and for a terrible moment it seemed he might falter. Then, as if gathering what last remaining strength he had, he drove the poker down into his father's face and held it there as Theodofred, writhing beneath the burning iron, screamed again, an inhuman noise that sent ice through Theo's veins. When Roderic withdrew the iron, the great frame slumped forward, finally and mercifully unconscious.

Riccilo, in Lælia's arms, sobbed helplessly, all trace of her former dignity gone amidst the horror of her husband's punishment. Roderic stared at her, his face stricken with guilt, and when Egica finally dismissed him, he returned not to her side but to stand between the two figures by the wall, watching silently as his father's inert figure was dragged ignominiously from the dais.

"So." Egica's eyes ran over the shocked faces below, seeming not at all perturbed by what had just transpired. "The Duke of Corduba will be returned to his home to live out his days, and his son will assume his title and lands, to rule over both under the guidance of my own counsellors until he is of an age to serve my son as he is sworn. And now we will consider the other traitors who stand in this room."

Theo's heart quickened and he tasted salt in his mouth as he did before every battle. But the king's dark eyes moved over him and Lælia, lingering only a fraction – just enough, Theo thought bitterly, to garner just such a reaction – before moving to the figures standing either side of Roderic by the wall.

"Pelayo sunau Favila."

The dark-haired boy at Roderic's right side moved toward the dais and knelt before it, head lowered respectfully. *"Reiks."* His voice was low, clear, and studiedly neutral.

"You, also, are the son of a traitor, another disgraced descendant of Chindasuinth himself. Your father rode into pitched battle against me, led the might of his forces against his own king. Such actions cannot stand unanswered."

"My father died for his treachery." Pelayo spoke without inflection, and although he could not see his face, Theo suspected his expression was bland as his tone. "His body was dragged behind your horses from Gallæcia to Vallisoletum, that all might witness his defeat. His lands were taken, are ruled now by lords loyal to you – *reiks*." There was nothing in either tone or posture that indicated anything other than respect. Perhaps because of that, Pelayo's calm statement of fact fell into the room with devastating simplicity. One son of Chindasuinth's had just had his eyes taken from him; now another's tattered remains seemed to lie on the flagstone floor before the assembled nobles, as present as if Favila had lived to face his own punishment. And there was something in the way Pelayo said "reiks", almost as an afterthought, that seemed to strip the title of all meaning.

Egica's eyes narrowed thoughtfully. "I believe there is only you and a sister left of your father's children?"

Pelayo nodded.

"And your sister remains in the north?"

"Under care of your men, *reiks*." Still there was nothing but calm respect, but this time Theo saw the boy's shoulders, already wide for one so young, stiffen, and Egica, too, must have seen, for he sat back in his carved chair and stroked his beard with the attitude of a man satisfied with his own thoughts.

"My son tells me you are loyal to him."

At this, Pelayo's head came up proudly and turned to meet Wittiza's eyes. "I am, *reiks*. I am sworn to your son, now and forever." There was no mistaking the sincerity in his tone, nor the readiness and pride with which Pelayo spoke his allegiance. Wittiza smiled and nodded at his friend.

"Well, then." Egica nodded. "It is well that my son should inspire such loyalty." Theo inwardly rolled his eyes. Egica, it seemed, would waste no opportunity to showcase his plump son's apparent fitness to rule to the assembled nobility. This, perhaps, was the most tediously predictable part of the proceedings. "Your sister," Egica went on, his dark eyes gleaming unpleasantly, "will remain in the north under the supervision of my own men and, in time, will be married as I or my son see fit. And you, Pelayo sunau Favila, will remain at my son's side, sworn to protect him, though holding none of your father's titles nor any honour other than that my son, in time, may choose to bestow upon you."

It was no more or less than anyone had expected, Pelayo least of all, Theo thought as the boy bowed his head, murmured his thanks, and moved back to stand against the wall beside Roderic, his features as carefully composed as before Egica had started speaking. Pelayo, Theo thought, watching the cautious, impassive face, was one to be watched. Such composure was a rarity in one so young.

"Egilona dauhter Suinthila."

Theo stiffened. He felt Lælia's fingertips touch his own, but he would not give Egica the satisfaction of seeing him take her hand. Theo's eyes flickered to Athanagild, standing amongst the bishops. His brother's face was as bland a mask as Pelayo's had been. He did not react when he met Theo's eyes. Egilona moved away from the wall and through the crowd with a composed elegance that, like Pelayo, seemed far beyond her years. Despite her youth, her gown was made of quite the richest cloth Theo thought he had seen since arriving in Spania, an ice-blue brocade threaded with rich gold and silver embroidery. A jewelled chain was threaded through her hair, which, though worn loose as befitted a girl of her age, was artfully designed in a series of white-gold curls that frothed down her back. She walked through the crowd like a princess rather than a prisoner, and Wittiza, Theo noticed, watched her with such glowing eyes and colour in his cheeks that it would be easy to think she came before him as a bride rather than for judgement.

Egilona swept down before the king in such an elegant prostration that the women in the chamber sighed in admiration, and the men looked at her indulgently. There was something unbearably touching about her quiet dignity, as if Egilona seemed to contain in her exquisite features and perfect decorum the very essence of the Gothic ideal.

"You have been companion to my son since infancy, have you not, child?"

Egilona nodded but did not speak, keeping her eyes respectfully downcast.

"When did you last see your home, in Aurariola? You may answer."

"I do not recall, *reiks*." Her voice was just the right mixture of sweetness and hesitancy to make the assembly smile in sympathy.

"Two of your brothers are present amongst us today. Can you point them out to us?"

"No, *reiks*." This time there was a slight catch in her voice.

"And why is that?"

"I do not know them, *reiks*." Her voice was just timid enough to garner the sympathy of the hardest heart in the room before she went on quietly, "My brother Theudemir left Spania when I was very young. Athanagild has been in a monastery since that time. I had one other brother, but he betrayed his king and country and died a traitor."

"As did your father."

"*Ja, reiks*."

"Your mother?"

"I do not know my mother's fate." There was the catch again, almost, but not quite a sob, enough to make the assembly move restlessly, shaking their heads and clicking their tongues that such beauty and innocence should suffer so. Wittiza was sitting forward in his chair, his face twisted in sympathy, clearly longing to reach out a hand to Egilona. Theo fought an urge to stride forward, take his sister, and walk from the chamber, striking down any who might cross his path. He steadied himself by imagining Silas's voice in his mind: *"Such a man does nothing without thinking, wenkai. Your sister is not the object. All this man does, he does to provoke you. Do not be his plaything."*

Theo breathed deeply and slowly, forcing himself to focus, to withdraw his eyes from the small figure at the dais and instead see the larger game play out.

Oppa was watching him. He could feel the man's eyes the same way one magnet sensed another. Egilona was a prelude to him and Lælia. Oppa would not allow Egica to harm her; his need for control over all aspects of Theo's life was too great to allow such a valuable piece to be pawned as Rekiberga had been.

"Perhaps," said Egica silkily, "we might decide your brother's fate before we do yours, child."

Now it comes. Theo was almost relieved. The entire cursed day had been leading to this moment. Now that it was here, Theo found himself facing it with the same icy composure he had a thousand battles.

"Theudemir sunau Suinthila."

Theo strode forward without hesitation, cutting through the swathe of curious eyes with not so much as a side glance, still wearing the crimson tunic of the Karabisianoi with his rank at his shoulders. He knelt with military precision. *"Reiks,"* he said respectfully, rising again without waiting for permission and facing Egica directly.

Egica regarded him blandly, his dark eyes giving nothing away. The king let the silence stretch out uncomfortably. Theo was aware of Egilona's small figure beside him. He wanted to smile at her, to offer some kind of comfort, but instinct told him to show nothing under Egica's scrutiny. Instead he stood in the attentive but neutral stance of a soldier, wide legged, hands clasped, eyes forward but without direct focus.

"Your father betrayed his country."

Theo said nothing.

"Your brother was a general in the rebel Sunifred's army. One of his greatest leaders, it is said. He was part of the rebellion from the beginning."

Still Theo did not speak.

"The men from Augusta Emerita joined the rebellion at your brother's command. The entirety of the military headquarters, riding against their sworn king, beneath your father's banner." For the first time there was a hint of real anger in Egica's voice, a dark fury that was horribly reminiscent of Oppa's own. "Do you deny it?" Egica demanded.

"Of these events I know nothing." Theo did not look at Egica as he spoke. He answered the question with the same neutral tone he would have reported to his superior in the Karabisianoi. "I did not land on Spania's shores until long after the events of which you speak. I had neither knowledge of them nor any part in them. By the time of my return both my father and brother were dead, and the rebellion ended."

"And you think to use this as your defence?" Egica leaned forward in his chair, studying Theo's face closely. "You think you should escape your family's guilt merely because you did not wield steel at their side? Speak!" he commanded when it seemed Theo would not answer.

"I am a soldier, *reiks*." Theo spoke evenly. "For many years now I have served in the imperial fleet with but one goal: to return to Spania and help create a fleet of our own, to defend Spania's shores. Of her internal affairs in the years I was absent, I know nothing. You are my king, and my commander. I am returned now to your service and will do as you command, and take what punishment you decree on behalf of my family, if that is your will."

There was a silence during which, despite the knowledge of the deal he had made with Oppa, Theo felt his future teeter before him. He had neither steel at his belt nor ally in the room, but still, he thought, he could possibly fight his way from it should he have to. He could feel Lælia like a tidal force behind him. He knew she had a concealed knife, just as he did; he had never seen her face a day without it. They would leave carnage in their wake but it could, if it must, be done. Theo became aware that some part of him had faced today knowing it might come to this, that the only possibility might be to fight his way from this hall and the darkness that ruled it. He realised that he had, unconsciously, noted the position of every one of the king's *gardingi* in the hall, and he found himself making cold calculations as to how swiftly he would need to move to dispatch enough to clear his path to the door. His muscles tensed reflexively. He had, he thought coldly, only seconds to act if the king ordered him taken.

There was a movement from the shadow at the edge of the dais. Egica's eyes flickered sideways to Oppa's dark face, then back to Theo. "My son," Egica said smoothly, "reminded me recently that you fought beside him for some years, on foreign shores."

In an instant Theo was back in the ruins high on the hill above Sebastopolis, facing Oppa's dark eyes, hearing his cold voice saying, *I have decided it will serve me infinitely better if you reconsider your position and return as my ally.* His face tingled where Oppa's whip had once cut it, the smooth runnels of flesh seeming alert to their creator's presence. Oppa was in his flesh, in his soul, and for the first time in many years Theo felt the sickening connection between them, the complex ties that bound them. *Fought beside,* he thought bitterly, was a strange way to characterise what Oppa had done to him.

But his face showed none of his thoughts as he nodded courteously in response to Egica's words. "Yes, *reiks*," he said respectfully. "That is true."

"Oppa tells me," Egica went on, "that you both served the emperor in his wars abroad, predominantly against the forces of the Arabic caliph." He cast his eyes around the hall as he spoke, well aware of the awe in which the imperial forces were even now regarded amongst the nobility. Theo's eyes cut to Oppa, who stood to the side, his head modestly bowed, to all intents and purposes humble as his father extolled his talents.

Theo had to swallow hard on his contempt and keep his own eyes carefully averted. He was grateful so many of his father's old allies from the south had found reason to avoid being present here today. At least they would not see his hypocrisy, this fake alliance with the man who had seen their sons go to a watery grave.

"Oppa informs me that news from Spania came infrequently," Egica said for the benefit of the watching nobility, "often greatly delayed due to the dangers posed to seagoing vessels. Such trials make unlikely allies of men when they are far from home; my son and Theudemir, it seems, put aside their differences, as men in war together do." There was a murmur of respectful agreement to this. *As if any of the men in this room understand war,* Theo thought scornfully. *I would bet all of them watch battle waged from the safety of a nearby hilltop.*

Egica turned to where Oppa stood in the corner. "To your knowledge, Oppa, did the man before me now know of his family's treachery?"

Despite all that had passed between them, despite his knowledge of their agreement, still Theo found he was holding his breath as Oppa stepped forward. In an instant, the bastard could see him dead. It must, Theo thought, be a temptation, after all that had passed between them. He realised his fists were clenched. *God knows, in his shoes, I would not hesitate.*

"When word came that war had broken out," Oppa said respectfully, "both Theudemir and I made haste to return to Spania. There were rumours Spania herself was threatened, by foreign forces."

There was a murmur at this. Egica's face darkened. "I assure you," he barked, "there is no such threat."

Oppa inclined his head. "Of course, *reiks,*" he said blandly, but Theo, seeing the nobles stir uneasily and the dark gleam of satisfaction in Oppa's eyes, knew the bastard had achieved his objective of sowing seeds of doubt in the minds of the assembly. To Theo's annoyance, he found himself temporarily sharing Oppa's satisfaction at seeing the king's smug certainty slightly shaken.

"To your knowledge," said Egica, clearly intent upon regaining the ascendancy, "did Theudemir sail with the intention of joining the rebellion?"

"We sailed at the same time from Anatolia." Oppa was once more the dutiful son. "I can attest to the fact that Theudemir played no part in the recent rebellion. He was highly regarded in his role in the Karabisianoi, rising to the rank of *komes* and winning many accolades in battle. To my knowledge he returned only to serve his country by playing a role in Spania's defence."

There were more mutterings, this time of admiration. Though it had been a generation since the last of the imperial forces had been expelled from Spania, still there was, amongst the aristocracy, a type of reverence for imperial approbation. Theo's accolades, his position in the emperor's own forces, loaned him a level of prestige bordering on the magical. Oppa's words raised the essence of patriotism in the heart of every Spaniard present, who looked at the men before them and saw heroes of Spania, who had represented their country bravely abroad, amongst the almost mystical ranks of the emperor. Theo, who had watched men bleed in mud far from their homes, fighting wars they did not understand nor care about, knew the farce for what it was. But to these Goths, so far removed from the colossal business of imperial wars, it was a world that seemed full of romance – and in this, Theo thought cynically, lay Oppa's manipulation.

"Whatever role Theudemir of Aurariola might have played on foreign shores," said Egica thoughtfully, stroking his chin as if in serious consideration, "his family were traitors on their own. Should their lands and title then be passed on to this man, whose loyalty we cannot guarantee, a stranger to Spania, after so long?" It was a rhetorical question, but one carefully designed to make the nobility believe the king was actually treating the matter with respect. Theo could almost admire the farce.

There was another murmur, this time of interest and agreement. Oppa remained diplomatically silent. Egica tilted his head in every imitation of deep thought. "You spoke of rumours of foreign enemies, my son," he said gravely. "What form did these rumours take?"

Theo stifled a grim smile. This was Egica taking back the power he had lost in Oppa's earlier comments, framing it for his own outcomes.

Oppa clearly understood what was expected, for he answered obediently: "It was said there is a Jewish conspiracy." At this the murmurs swelled to open chatter, above which Oppa said clearly, "In Septem, *reiks*, where many of your enemies have fled during the rebellion."

"A Jewish conspiracy!" Egica's brow darkened, and he allowed his voice to deepen with anger. "It is not the first time I have heard of such a thing." His eyes shifted over the assembly. "Lælia *faldenreis* Paulus, of Illiberis. Stand before your king." Every muscle in Theo's body tensed. He did not dare look at Oppa. This was it; the moment they had planned, and suddenly Theo knew, with a deep, horrible certainty, that Oppa had crafted every moment of the upcoming scene with the masterstrokes of manipulation he had long mastered. Egica and Wittiza, Theo and Lælia, they were all puppets on Oppa's string, dancing in the roles he had cast them. He felt impotent and furious and yet – and this sickened Theo profoundly – relieved. Egica was no match for his son, not anymore. They would walk from this hall today, after all.

Though what they would be after they did, Theo did not dare think.

"Illiberis deployed every resource against us in the recent rebellion." Egica glared at Lælia. "It is said your grandfather

tolerated Jewish trade in Garnata and even that he profited
from it. That he made foreign alliances, traded with Jews in
Septem."

"I know nothing of such alliances." Lælia's voice was cold
and flat.

"But of your grandfather's treason, surely you do know.
Did he not leave you to hold Illiberis yourself, in the event that
war moved south?"

"He left me to defend Illiberis against foreign invaders."
From the corner of his eye, Theo saw Lælia glance at Oppa,
but she said nothing more.

"To defend Illiberis *against* such invaders – or to ally with
them?" Egica's question was rhetorical, and he addressed the
crowd, now, rather than the woman in front of him. "Our
council of blessed fathers," said Egica, "amongst other
matters, decreed that we must show greater discipline in our
churches, and against the Jewish enemy in our midst. To this
end any Jew who does not convert, and who is discovered to
be trading in defiance of our Church, will incur taxes that will
be paid by his converted brethren. No Jew will escape the
tribute they owe to God and the true faith. To this end, I will
place bishops of faith and discipline in the wildest and most
unbowed of my provinces – the pagan nest that is Gallæcia –
and in Illiberis itself, a land all know is plagued by *baguadae*
and savage tribesmen who practice dark magic. Fráuja Oppa
is both a man of the Church, and one that knows war."

Lælia stiffened beside him, and Theo could not look at her.
He knew what was coming and equally that there was no way
to stop it, nor to lessen the pain it would cause. He could only
watch, now, as Oppa's drama unfolded.

Egica leaned forward. "I am informed that you,
Theudemir, are now wed to Lælia of Illiberis. Is this true?"

Theo nodded. "It is."

"Under Gothic law you are entitled to one-third of your
wife's property. This, I will take to be held as forfeit for your
family's part in the recent rebellion, until such time as I see fit.

I do so on the condition that you take up the role for which you are certainly qualified, at your uncle's side with the fleet in Hispalis, training men to fight as you have learned. If you agree to both these conditions, I will allow you to take your father's title and your family's lands in Aurariola, and thus your place at court, as one of my *seniores*." He did not wait for Theo's assent but shifted his eyes to Lælia. "For your family's treachery, you will forfeit the remaining part of the Illiberis latifundium to Fráuja Oppa's care," he said coldly. "Your life is spared only by virtue of your marriage to this man, Theudemir of Aurariola, and his word that he will take responsibility for you. You will not return to Illiberis. You will claim no goods from your home, nor any of the horseflesh for which your family is known. You are stripped of all titles and honour associated with the province of Illiberis, and the right to take income from it. Until further notice, the custodianship of Illiberis will fall to Fráuja Oppa, who will assume management of it in the name of the Church. I shall leave it to him to make the arrangements to settle the estate in his own name." Once again, Egica did not wait for Lælia's assent, but he moved his eyes instead to Egilona. "Your sister," he said to Theo, "will remain at my court, as companion to my son. Let her presence in my household serve as a reminder to you of where your allegiance is best placed – and what is at stake should you forget to whom you owe it."

He said more, but Theo could no longer hear him. He was aware only of Lælia at his side, silent and still, as all she loved in the world was stripped from her and given to the one man to whom she had sworn never to bow.

Count Theudemir of Aurariola took his place in King Egica's court upon the shoulders of his wife's dispossession, and as he signed his name to the cursed edicts of the Sixteenth Council of Toletum, in the recesses of his soul, he knew he had committed a sin that no confession could ever extirpate.

15

LÆLIA
MAY, AD 693

Toletum, Spania
Toledo, Spain

The dream came in the small hours.

Lælia was in her grandmother's caves beneath the abbey in the Illiberis mountains. The underground stream and pool of water she remembered had grown, become a vast, still indigo sea, fed by an unknown source. The cave walls were there but invisible, existing somewhere beyond sight in her dreamscape. Lælia sat on the flat rock she recalled from childhood, and from a fissure in the rock above, a single moonbeam shone down onto the water's surface.

As she watched, the moonbeam seemed to grow, to cast a wider gleam across the blackness. The water began to stir. At first it was no more than a ripple on the surface. Then, as if an unseen force stirred from beneath, it became more turbulent. The water churned and surged, and from above the light grew to an almost blinding brilliance, turning the sea to a wild, roiling torrent that reached for the rock where Lælia sat.

Suddenly she was no longer on the flat stone but far out to

sea, drenched at the very centre of the moonbeam. The light was exhilarating and invigorating, seeming to permeate every inch of her body and soul, entering her and filling her with an almost unbearable sensation that made her want to cry and scream at once, so overwhelming she was lost in it. For the longest moment she was caught in the maelstrom, so she did not know where she was nor what happened. Then it was gone, the light and the turbulence, and Lælia was back on the flat rock, the cave walls visible once again, the black pool of water still and silent before her.

She opened her eyes.

The night was still, the bedchamber silent. Theo's long limbs sprawled beside her, his head turned slightly away, his hand barely inches from hers on the linen. He breathed evenly and deeply, the scarred, twisted flesh on his back rising and falling steadily. Feeling suddenly bereft without him, Lælia curled into his side. He stirred, murmuring her name, and gathered her fiercely to him in his sleep, his legs twining with hers, his mouth finding her own before he was fully awake. Her body still restless, Lælia lost herself in his hands and mouth, in the miracle of his presence, before they both returned to a dark, silent sleep in which her earlier dream was forgotten.

* * *

It was morning, after they had breakfasted, and Theo was pulling on his cloak by the door. "I don't like leaving you here alone, like this."

Lælia had fallen ill the day after appearing before Egica. A week later, and despite the unrelenting desire for Theo that haunted her nights, she was still listless. It was a dragging, lingering exhaustion that seemed to dull her senses during the day, leaving her uncharacteristically weak. Her mind felt slow and clouded, her ability to think clearly oddly muted. Jadis lay at her feet in Riccilo's Toletum townhouse, growling softly

168

when any but Tosius approached. Even Theo was not exempt from the cat's hostility. Jadis's growls may have been less audible, but the eyes that followed him gleamed warily, the long tail moving slowly behind her. Theo adjusted a pillow behind Lælia on the lecta and said tentatively, "Riccilo left the names of ladies who can come to sit with you —"

"I don't want them." Hearing the hard note in her voice, Lælia forced herself to smile. "I don't need people," she said, striving for a more even tone. "I need to leave here, Theo. I hate this city. Egica has had his day of triumph. There is nothing holding us here." Despite her efforts, Lælia heard the bitterness in her voice. Theo's face set into bland lines, as it inevitably did at any mention of Egica's ruling. She reached for his hand and met his eyes. "Do not think I blame you," she said quietly. "I do not, Theo. It was my decision to feign surrender. One I would make again." But she did not have the energy to comfort him, to reassure Theo they had done the right thing. The truth was she felt numb and dispirited in the wake of the council, dispossessed in more than just name. She felt adrift, her only anchor Theo himself. Having so long had the charge of Illiberis as her guide, she was not sure, now, how she was supposed to progress. Her mind constantly worried at it. Nor did Theo seem inclined to discuss it with her, changing the subject whenever Illiberis was raised, an evasion she found increasingly painful. The weight of her responsibility felt heavy and lonely, but then, she imagined, Theo must feel the same about Aurariola.

Now, as her mind drifted again, her eyes slid away from his. "The sooner we leave here, the sooner we can ride south," she said, her voice growing stronger as she saw in her mind the crystalline light and high, clear air of the mountains. "From there we can begin to make plans." Her hand clenched involuntarily around his. "There is nothing for us here. We should ride whilst we can — whilst Oppa remains here with his father. We can make plans from Aurariola."

Theo's fingers tightened briefly around her own before he

withdrew his hand and stepped back, turning away as he did. "I have been asked to remain until Egica has apprised me of his expectations for the fleet and finalised the tribute Aurariola must pay to compensate for my family's rebellion." He paused. "And I am still waiting for permission to meet with Egilona."

Lælia didn't answer. She felt suddenly sick, as she seemed to daily since she had stood before Egica at court. Sometimes she wondered if the loss of Illiberis had somehow made her ill. She knew it was fanciful, but then, she had lived many things others would deem magic. Was it so foolish to think her own body was tied to the earth that had been part of her family from time immemorial?

But she said nothing of this to Theo. It was he who had to face Oppa daily across the palace floor. She still did not know how Theo contrived to maintain civility with the man who had wrought such destruction on his face and body, who had done so much to destroy him. And she knew the thought of his sister being held in the palace, under Oppa's control, turned his stomach. She forced herself to smile as she said, "We will speak when you return, then. I hope it is today you are granted permission to speak with Egilona."

He nodded briefly from the door, but his smile was strained, his stride jerky as he left the room. Toletum, Lælia knew, was no easier for Theo than for her. It was not fair of her to ask of him what he could not give. For now, they were all Egica's puppets.

The sickness surged again and she ran for the basin, moaning as her stomach lost the thin gruel she'd tried to swallow to appease Theo. She slumped against the wall, her woollen gown feeling uncomfortably tight and restrictive. She longed with a sudden, hard desire for the wild spaces of Illiberis, or even the vast expanse of Dahiya's desert. Anything but this cloistered stone and the stench of humanity.

The logical part of her mind knew that the temporary surrender of Illiberis was the only realistic path they could have taken if they hoped to walk from that palace chamber alive and unharmed. If she needed any confirmation they had done the right thing, the unwelcome memory of Theodofred's smoking flesh and Riccilo's devastation was vivid enough. Her aunt and uncle had left for Corduba the day following Egica's brutal punishment, a moaning Theodofred, barely conscious, transported by wagon. There was no guarantee he would survive the journey. Lælia knew Riccilo did not care, wanted only to be far from the stench of raw flesh and Egica's contempt. Roderic had remained at court. He had not come to bid his mother goodbye, and Riccilo was not permitted access to the palace to see him.

But the loss of Riccilo's regal demeanour, the pride that at times had bordered on arrogance, had not affected Lælia nearly so much as watching Rekiberga stumble from the palace chamber, the stricken look in Alaric's bride's eyes when they had met Lælia's in that hall. The memory made the sickness surge again and Lælia retched helplessly over the basin, her stomach bringing nothing forth. She had not once recalled Rekiberga's pale, desperate face without illness from the moment she had left the palace. In reality, Rekiberga's humiliation in court had been only the beginning of a day of horror.

First, they had been forced to line the streets and watch as Sisebut, the archbishop who had schemed with Sunifred to bring down Egica's reign, had been dragged through the Toletum streets behind Egica's own horse. It was a punishment normally reserved for rebel lords or soldiers, and in times past, to punish a man of God in such a way would have been unimaginable. But these were different times. Sisebut had thought to place himself amongst temporal affairs, had allowed ambition to supersede God. He had shamed the Church and in doing so empowered the Crown. Dragging him to his death along the Toletum road, whilst watched by the sixty bishops who had assembled for the council, had been Egica's brutal reminder of the consequences should ever the clergy think to place themselves above his rule again. The

Church in Spania had, for a time at least, been brought under harsh control – and Felix, who had, in an unprecedented move by the council, been unanimously appointed the new archbishop, seemed more than willing to bow to his king.

The savagery of the spectacle had driven the city into a frenzy. All of Toletum had drunk the city dry that night, a wild bacchanal worthy of the old gods of war, high on the tension of the day. Lælia had sat behind the walled garden of Theodofred's domus and listened to the raucous cries from the road beyond. It was only the following day she and Theo had learned from Athanagild that Rekiberga had been forcefully taken from her bed, carried through the streets like the prize of war she was, and a priest summoned to marry her then and there to Ataulfo, accompanied only by the drunken, triumphant shouts of his men.

Athanagild's white-faced fury and Theo's silent, set face had been nothing to the gut-wrenching revulsion Lælia had experienced. *That could have been me*, she thought, over and over, each time the mantra making her stomach rebel, and she did not know if the violent sickness she felt was because the thought frightened her – or because a part of her, strangely, wished it *had* been her.

At least Rekiberga fought, Lælia thought savagely, as she had many times since learning of the girl's fate. *She stood before Egica without shame or apology. She never surrendered. She rode for Alaric, would have left everything behind without a thought.* Despite the horror of what Rekiberga must now endure there seemed, to Lælia, a strange honour in what the girl had done, by comparison with her own choices. No matter what logic Lælia knew lay behind their strategy at court, still she could not escape a corrosive feeling that she had betrayed all to which she owed loyalty, a sense that whatever came after this could never replace what had been lost the day she rode north from Illiberis.

Possibly hardest of all, she was unsure that, even if she were free to do so, she could find a way to hold Illiberis. Was this, she wondered, why she could not find the strength to insist that they return? Worse, was her inability to formulate a strategy the reason that Theo avoided the topic? He was a soldier, after all. Perhaps he saw her indecision, her lack of experience, and read it as a lack of commitment to her home. Lælia retched again. She could see no way to hold Illiberis, and that failing made her deeply ashamed.

Her inner turmoil had made her uncharacteristically withdrawn in Athanagild's presence. There was something in the way he looked at her when the rest of the room talked, or touched her hand as he passed her a wine cup, that threatened to undo her completely. Athanagild and Alaric had been her companions in the long years without Theo. They had known her better than any other. She feared that if she let Athanagild see even the slightest crack in the careful façade she maintained, the entire lie would crumble. Because no matter how she understood the logic that had led to them conceding Illiberis, the truth, Lælia knew, was that every day she did nothing to fight for its return she felt both bitterness and shame rise closer to the surface, and she could not bear the thought of having that darkness erupt and destroy the happiness she and Theo had waited so long to find.

"Lady." The servant who put a tentative head around the door was from Corduba and had known Lælia since childhood. She was the daughter of Riccilo's own maid and had stayed in Toletum after the rest of the household had ridden south with Theodofred's broken body. "I have brought a drink that will soothe your belly. It is made from a rare root, hard to find, but I sought it in the market this morning." She held out a bowl of boiling water with thin slices of a pale, slightly yellow root floating on top. Lælia took a tentative sip. It had a pleasant taste, slightly spicy, and fresh, as if it enlivened her insides.

"Thank you." She smiled wanly at the maid and drank a little more. "It seems to help, a little. What is it called?"

"The merchant said it comes from the Arab countries. He

calls it *zanjibayl*." She smiled as Lælia sipped it. "My mother used to buy it for Lady Riccilo when she was with child. She said it was the only thing that would soothe her morning sickness. Perhaps it is the same for you."

Lælia halted with the bowl halfway to her mouth. "Morning sickness," she repeated blankly.

"Yes." The maid was bent over the bed and didn't see Lælia's stricken face. "Though your aunt was ill for only the first few months. I believe all was well for her after that, and God willing, it will be thus for you, also." She chattered on cheerfully as she changed the bed linens, oblivious to the stunned silence behind her, pausing only to take the bowl from Lælia's unheeding hands and promising to return shortly with a refill.

Lælia heard her footsteps retreat down the stairs through a fog. At her feet, Jadis sat up with her ears pricked, staring intently at her mistress, her tail very still. Lælia met the cat's eyes. She put a hand over her belly as if it were a foreign land. The cat's gaze followed her gesture. Jadis made a low sound, like a moan. Rising from the floor, she rubbed her head against Lælia's legs then twined herself between them and dropped to the floor again.

I am with child.

A sudden recollection of last night's dream came to her. Her grandmother's cave. The vivid light that had seemed to drench every inch of her body, inside and out. *Yes,* she thought, with dawning certainty. *That is what the dream signified. The soul of my child, come to the cave of my body.*

Lælia wanted Illiberis with a sudden, hard longing, a visceral pull as savage as her desire for Theo had ever been, the same surge she had once felt deep in the desert when she had thrust her hands into the earth and felt Illiberis pull her home. She was carrying a child of Illiberis within her. She could not grow it here, in the cold stone of a hostile city, where the scent of the earth was drowned in man's waste and the sky was grey with cooking fires. *That is why I am sick,* she thought, still holding her belly. It was not just the morning illness of pregnancy. She knew it wasn't. It was because her body needed the solace of Illiberis, of mountain air and clear river water. And because of the shame she felt every time she accepted the loss of her home.

Lælia rose with more energy than she had felt in days and strode to the polished bronze mirror. Glittering eyes stared back at her, face both pale and flushed with hectic colour. Her gown, she noticed clinically, was not just tight in sensation and imagination. Already her body had swollen, thickened with the life inside it.

I cannot stay here. She knew it with absolute certainty. *I cannot bear this child here.* Calling for the servant, she began to fold her belongings, feeling excitement and trepidation in equal measure.

A child. Her and Theo's child.

The day grew, and Lælia made her plans to leave.

* * *

THEO DIDN'T RETURN until late afternoon, by which time Lælia had packed the entire villa and was almost out of her skin with restless excitement.

"What is happening?" Theo looked around at the piles of belongings with a bemused smile. "I left you barely conscious on a lecta, Lælia." Jadis growled, a low, warning snarl. Theo ignored it.

"I had the servants pack my things."

His eyes narrowed but he didn't answer, and Lælia hurried on, her carefully thought-out words lost in the emotion driving them. "I had a dream last night. I didn't understand it, not then. But this morning, after I was sick, the maid said something, and suddenly I understood. I dreamed of Illiberis, Theo." She met Theo's eyes and laughed shakily. "I am saying this poorly, making little sense, I think." She drew a deep breath and tried to steady herself. Theo watched her but

175

didn't speak. She couldn't read the expression in his eyes; Theo, she had learned, had a disquieting ability to shield his thoughts from even her. "I am with child." Seeing wonder dawn on Theo's face, she raced ahead before he could respond. "I know you said we have to be here in Toletum. But I know what my dream meant, Theo. I can't grow this child here. I have to go back to Illiberis. This child is of my blood. It needs my earth to grow. That is why I have been so sick." She spoke feverishly, trying to get the words out, aware of the slight frown on Theo's face, the fact that the flare of wonder in his eyes had faded, replaced by a wary caution. If she could just explain what she meant, make him see as she did.

"The maid thought I had morning sickness. But I know it isn't the child that is making me ill. It is the fact that I am with child *here*, Theo, away from the place it belongs. It is longing for home just as I am. That is why I have packed my things. I understand that you may have to remain, to pacify Egica. I don't wish to endanger you, after all you have endured, nor burden you with my problems." He blanched, and she felt a stab of guilt, that she should add Illiberis to the list of things he must consider. "But I can't stay here. I must go, Theo. Oppa is still in Toletum. Tosius tells me he has not yet even sent his men to Illiberis. I have friends in the south; there are lords who escaped Egica's wrath but remain faithful to our cause. Zdan is still there. Once back in Illiberis, I can contact Yosef, and those in Garnata who are part of the rebellion. I will go to Septem if I must. I must start to make plans now, before Oppa arrives to take control. None need know that I have not gone to Aurariola. It is so far east they are unlikely to send scouts —"

"Lælia, wait." Theo's voice was neither gentle, nor with the edge of humour it usually carried. His eyes were piercing, hard green, his face uncharacteristically grim. "You cannot go to Illiberis. You could not have done it before, but certainly, you cannot do it whilst you are with child. Surely you must see that it is impossible."

Taken aback, Lælia stared at him. "I did not think to ask your permission," she said slowly. Jadis, growling softly, began pacing by her feet, twining between her legs. "And nor do I ask anything of you. I had thought we were in agreement on this – we would bow to Oppa at court but make our plans all the same. I do not ask you to leave Toletum, nor renege on your agreement with Egica. I am practised in moving with stealth, Theo. Tosius knows every tribal path through the mountains. None can track us once we are in them, nor know of our presence in Illiberis unless we wish it to be known. I can be in Illiberis before Oppa is even aware I have left the capital, and I can live in the mountains for as long as necessary without detection. He need never know I did not ride to Aurariola." She searched his face, frowning at the remote, hard expression on it. "You do not think I can do it," she said flatly, feeling her face colour.

"I did not say that." The scars on Theo's face had never seemed deeper, his expression more forbidding. "But even if you make it to Illiberis, Lælia, what then? You live in a hut amongst the tribesmen, whilst I pretend you are with me in Aurariola? How long do you think such a pretence could be maintained? Whatever Egica's paranoia and the whispers from Septem, there is not yet a Jewish army landing on Spanish shores. Eventually you would have to sail for Ilyan's court, running the risk of attack at sea, and go into the very exile we have just risked everything to avoid. How could you think that is something I would ever agree to?"

"*Agree to?*" Resentment churned inside her, made worse by her suspicion that he simply didn't have faith in her strategic ability. Jadis growled again.

"Tyr!" Theo swore in exasperation. "Might we at least speak of this without your cat growling at me?" When Lælia stared at him in silence, Theo made a visible effort to get himself under control, forcing a smile that, despite his best attempts, did not approach his eyes. "Lælia." He grasped her arms. Jadis's growl grew more dangerous, and Lælia had to fight not to recoil from a touch that, to her shock, felt suddenly like a trap binding her, rather than a gesture of affection. "You are with child. It – this is a dream, Lælia." Now the smile truly did reach his eyes, the hard green softening, deepening. "A miracle, even," he said quietly. "Something that even in my wildest dreams, I barely dared imagine."

His grip loosened, his thumbs stroking her upper arms, and Lælia felt the familiar warmth of his presence steal through her, calming her and firing her blood at the same time. "A child," he said again, wonderingly now, his eyes searching her face. "Is it a boy, Lælia, do you think? Or a girl?"

Lælia felt a reluctant smile spread over her face. "I do not know," she said softly. "I had not thought of it. But, Theo –"

"No." Theo began to laugh. "You thought only of packing your possessions and riding more than two hundred miles through war-torn country." Shaking his head, he drew her close, kissing her temple, laughter still rumbling in his chest. "You are the fiercest, wildest creature I have ever known," he said, holding her against him, his hands feeling the curves of her new form with both wonder and hunger. "Yes, and that damned cat of yours too, even if it hates me." He put a hand out to Jadis, who reluctantly sniffed it, gave him what could only be construed as a disdainful look, then slunk sullenly from the room. He turned back to her. "You are braver than any man I have fought beside – and even more reckless." Drawing back, he swept a long curl of her hair from her face, cradling it between his hands. "I know you miss your home," he said quietly. "I wish, more than anything, that I could take you back there now, Lælia. But regardless of my loathing of Oppa, he is not a man to cross. At present, all whispers of the battle at Illiberis have been silenced, any murmurings that you might be guilty of treason quelled. But do not think we are not watched, more closely, perhaps, than ever before. If either of us leaves here with any hint of intention to return to Illiberis, or to reassemble the forces that opposed him and his father, Oppa will destroy us both – and more than just us, Lælia." Holding her face, Theo shook his head, dark shadows moving behind the sea green, echoes of a past Lælia had not shared with him and could not see. "I know Oppa."

"And you think I do not?" Lælia frowned, searching his face, not understanding what she saw there. Despite her softening at his touch and words, shame and anger burned at the pit of her stomach. After all she had done to hold it, still he called her reckless, thought her as impulsive as a child. Did Theo even believe her capable of talking rationally of her home, of formulating logical plans? "I fought Oppa too, Theo. Perhaps I did not endure what you did at his hands. But I fought him, and I outwitted him. I can do it again."

"I do not doubt it." Theo stroked the tension in her jaw. "But not like this, Lælia. Not whilst you carry our child, and whilst our every move is watched. Not whilst –" His voice, suddenly rough, cut off, and he looked away. Frowning, Lælia watched him, then, replaying the scenes at court, slow realisation dawned.

"Not whilst Egica has your sister." Lælia remembered Egilona's beautiful young face and then thought again of Rekiberga's pale face, her torn gown, and blanched. "He would use her," she said, feeling revulsion steal through her as she realised the truth of her words. "Oppa. He would use Egilona without hesitation."

"That is not the reason I don't want you to go," Theo began, frowning.

"But it is one of the reasons." For a moment Lælia saw the woods in Illiberis long ago, felt the insidious stroke of Oppa's whip on her face, and she shuddered. Suddenly she understood at least some of the shadows behind Theo's careful composure. The by now familiar shame rose in her, that she should think only of Illiberis, whilst Theo must every moment consider the futures of so many. "And you are right to think of Egilona," she said quietly, feeling the stone walls crowd in upon her again. "We both know enough of Oppa to know of what he is capable."

"Do not think I ask this of you for my sister." Theo's face was strained and hard, his eyes clouded with those old shadows again. "I would not have you blame any but me for this —"

"I do not blame you." Lælia shook her head, moving back into the circle of his arms. "I could never blame you. This is Oppa's evil. I may hate everything about the thought of him on my land, but making this agreement was my choice, for which I will always remain grateful to you. I will stand by it. If you, who have endured so much at his hands, might swallow your pride, then I, too, must."

The darkness in his face didn't lift at her words, seemed instead to deepen, become more pained, and though he did not pull away, Lælia thought he wanted to, and it hurt her. Did he think less of her, she wondered, for so easily relinquishing that which she swore she loved?

I must think more of his concerns, she thought, *than my own.* She thought of Riccilo's long-ago warnings that marriage was a battleground; she did not wish hers to be such. It was selfish to ask more of this impossible situation than could easily be given. Her home would wait. It must. For Theo's sake. For the sake of their unborn child.

"Theo." She touched his face, feeling him tremble slightly, almost as if he wanted to pull away. "We will do what we must. And one day, I will find a way to regain Illiberis, I promise. One that does not endanger you, nor those we love." She held his eyes. "You said the Arabs are a formidable force," she said tentatively. "Laurentius said the same thing, and Dahiya, also. She believed that the day is fast approaching when they may even fight their way to Spania's shores. Do you believe that, too, Theo?"

He tilted his chin, his eyes staring somewhere over her head, to wars she could not see. "Yes," he said finally. "I do."

"Then one way or another," Lælia said, "Spania will need

a strong south. And there is no greater stronghold than Illiberis. One way or another, Theo, Illiberis will be ours again." She did not know what she expected him to say, only that she needed something, in this moment, to reassure her that all she had been born to was not gone forever.

There was a long pause. Beyond the lattice over the window, the cries of city sellers bounced from stone, and the scent of wine and waste rose from the sewers. A baby cried somewhere, the sound like a door clanging shut on the life Lælia had led.

"I think," said Theo slowly, "that with time, anything is possible, Lælia. I think we have to believe that." He met her eyes, but no matter how Lælia searched his, she could not see in them the reassurance she longed for. "And until then," he said, a warmer note entering his voice, "we have Aurariola, to which we will soon return. It is not Illiberis, that is true. But it is far from this cursed city. And it has a beauty and freedom of its own to offer you – and our child." He covered her belly with his hand, and Lælia felt it, the visceral connection between Theo, her, and the new life within. But although she wanted to lose herself in it, to fall into the comfort of that small circle, she felt pulled, dragged from it by a power just as strong. She knew the comfort as a lie that would hold her and trap her, promise her joy but not fulfil that part of her soul that forever roamed the high places with the herds in Illiberis. Despising herself for her weakness, she nonetheless felt a sudden, desperate need for Theo to know her true heart.

"I promise you," she said fiercely, twining her arms around Theo's neck and staring into his eyes, "that no matter what the future brings, I will find a way for this child to know Illiberis. No matter what I might have given to Oppa for now, I will never betray Illiberis in my heart. Never. One day, our child will know my home as I do, Theo. No matter how long it takes."

Theo held her close about the waist, his eyes guarded and

solemn on hers. "I know," he said roughly, "that Illiberis will never be forgotten, Lælia."

And then he kissed her, his words lost in the sweet rush of mingled joy and wonder they shared, and Lælia gave no thought to the qualified nature of the promise he had given.

* * *

LATER THAT EVENING, though, when Theo had gone to speak with Laurentius and Athanagild, she found Tosius in the stables. The little man's face was drawn and pale. Tosius did not like the city, nor the people found there, any more than did Lælia herself. "How fast can you ride to Illiberis?" Lælia asked.

Tosius's eyes gleamed. "This I can do in four days." Jadis rubbed her body against the tribesman, nudging him and purring, and he leaned down to stroke her head absent-mindedly.

"Four?" Lælia frowned. "So quickly?"

Tosius shrugged. "If I have the good horses, yes."

"You will take the best from here, and money to buy more on the way."

"What message do I bring, *dauhter*?"

Lælia leaned on the haunches of the bay gelding he had been grooming. The horse grunted softly and she smiled, stroking it. "Tell the tribes they are not forgotten," she said slowly. "I will return. Not yet, for it is not safe. But as soon as I can."

"And what of the son of a king who plans to ride there and take it?"

Lælia's face hardened. "He may take the fields and crops about Illiberis, Tosius, for there is nothing I might do about that. But the horses" – her eyes gleamed fiercely in the low light – "they are of the tribes, Tosius. Of Illiberis. Oppa will not have them." Jadis's purring grew louder.

Tosius's face stretched in a sly smile. "This is easy," he

said, dipping his head once. "Horses, they are hard to discover in the mountains. And there has been a war." He shrugged. "Much has been lost that cannot be easily found."

"Take my greatest gratitude to the Riders of the desert. Their obligation to me is finished, and they must return to their *adwaar*, with honour and my thanks." She swallowed hard, feeling something break inside her as she said the words.

Tosius nodded gravely. "It is right that they return to their lands."

"Yosef will be preparing the Jews of Garnata for rebellion. Tell him I will come as soon as I may."

Tosius ducked his head, still smiling. "This the tribes will be pleased to know, *dauhter*. Garnata, also. I am proud to take this message."

"And tell them this, Tosius." Lælia's hands stole to her belly, and she smiled grimly. "Tell them I carry the next generation of Illiberis women inside me. And Illiberis women will never surrender their earth. I must soon go to Aurariola. There I will wait, Tosius, yes. But I will return. You tell them that."

Tosius's eyes gleamed, and he bowed his head respectfully.

"I will tell them, *dauhter*, and the tribes will dance for you, and for your young. We will wait for you – and we will guard what is yours. I will ride to Aurariola after I have given your message."

Lælia watched him ride from the stables as the sun fell. "Soon," she whispered, frowning as the small figure disappeared in the city crowds. "Not yet, Tosius, but soon."

16

YOSEF

MAY, AD 693

Garnata, Illiberis, Spania
Granada, Spain

Yosef stood in the cave above Garnata, allowing his eyes to adjust to the gloom.

The last time he had stood here was the night he had fled Oppa's men. The night his parents had been taken and then murdered, and when he had been made exile.

The cave smelled dull and old, undisturbed. The layer of dust on the wooden chests was thick, and the boulder Yosef had placed at the entrance had been there so long grass had grown about it. None had entered this place since he had left. Yosef wondered what would have happened if he had never come back. Perhaps these chests would have lain here for centuries, their contents of old trade agreements and scholarly writing forgotten, lost to the world of men. Would it have mattered, he wondered, if they were?

He pushed the thought impatiently from his mind. The time for such musings was long gone. Yosef had chosen his course the day he killed the man who raped Sarah, and again when he had fled Spania with the stench of his father's burning flesh in his nose. He had chosen it with every footstep he had taken on foreign shores, and the day he had helped Theo escape the Arab army. It was too late now to wonder at the rightness of his actions. They were taken, and he must find a way to walk the path they had laid for him.

He touched the wooden chests, wondering what he should take. Much of it was now outdated, superseded by the agreements he had himself made on his journey, which were held now either at the Illiberis latifundium or in Septem, with Jewish merchants. These treasures were largely his family's heritage, records and writings that dated back to Roman times.

In the end, Yosef took only a few personal mementos, things that reminded him of his father and mother, or that he thought might serve some use. The rest he sealed inside the chests. When he left the cave, he did so mindful that none watched, rolling the rock carefully back into place. Perhaps, one day, he, or his descendants, might return to Spania and claim the contents. If not, this cave would remain, a reminder that Jews had once called this place home.

He entered Garnata at night, much in the same manner as he had once left it. He travelled the quiet streets to Hasdai's door and paused outside. For a moment he truly considered simply leaving, walking away, and leaving the Garnata Jews to what pointless schemes they might wish. But then he saw Sarah's face in his mind, her feverish excitement at the prospect of fighting back against the forces that had so torn their world apart, and chastised himself for his lack of commitment to a cause that he should, by birth and upbringing, be sworn to aid.

He pushed open the door.

Hasdai, Haym, and several of the Garnata Jews were crowded around the kitchen table. By their red-stained lips, the half-full jug of wine on the table was not their first, and by the glittering eyes and high colour in their faces, the conversation had been heated for some time.

"Is it true, then?" Hasdai demanded almost before he had closed the door. "Is that murdering bastard to take control of Illiberis, barely weeks after we fought him to humiliation?"

How quickly they claim the Illiberis victory for their own, Yosef thought, *when it was the hardened men of the desert, and those of the tribes, who won it for them.* Hasdai and the others, as he recalled, had done little other than shake their crude weapons from the walls of the old fortress and watch as other men did the fighting. But he said none of this.

"Yes." He nodded his head. "Lælia was forced to concede Illiberis to Oppa, in court, at least." He spread his hands out, palms up. "If she had not, we would even now be facing the wrath of Egica's forces."

"And would that have been such a bad thing?" Hasdai's face shone with righteous anger. "Perhaps such an attack would force Ilyan's hand." When Yosef didn't speak, Hasdai appealed to the others at the table. "Must we wait upon the Lady of Illiberis to make our decisions for us, like children? Perhaps it is time we simply acted ourselves."

"With what?" It was the old man who spoke, the one Yosef recalled from last time they met – Moshe, he thought the man's name was. "You are too young to recall what war truly looks like. I recall it well. And I will say this: a dozen men unskilled in combat, armed with pitchforks, are a laughable excuse for an army. We are not equipped nor prepared to defend Garnata – and we cannot so much as consider it without the support of Illiberis."

"Then what do you propose?" Hasdai glared around the room.

"If I might make a suggestion?" All eyes turned to Yosef. "Perhaps you might leave Garnata," he said. "For now, at least. Come with me, back to Septem. There are many more there who share our convictions. There we can trade and make a life as well as a plan. In Septem we might live as men

– until, of course, we return to take back our home." Mentally he apologised to the God of his heart for the subterfuge. The reality was that Yosef doubted the Jews of Septem would see their cause through. In truth, once men found a good income, and the means to create more, in his experience the desire for bloodshed rapidly waned.

And in his inner soul, Yosef knew no good could come of this uprising. Not unless it was part of a far greater effort. The Church in Spania was all powerful, and though the laws might be made by the king, their power was given by the Church. The chances of seeing those laws overturned, under the present regime at least, were not good, not unless they were backed with all the coin and swords in Ilyan's arsenal, and somehow, Yosef could not imagine that wily politician risking so much for such an uncertain outcome.

What Yosef did know was that he would rather have those discussions take place in Septem, where at least they were all safe, than worry about what might occur in Garnata in his absence.

"Leave," said Hasdai, staring at him blankly. "Leave our homes? Our businesses?"

"What little business is left to us." It was a woman who spoke, a plain-faced, middle-aged woman Yosef vaguely recalled as married to a baker. "With every new law that is passed, our trade is further restricted. Where are the southern lords now, who have profited from us for so long? I do not see them coming to our aid. We cannot gather at temple. And now, with that evil monster coming to take Illiberis, we are likely to be dipped in oil for the mere suspicion of practising our faith." All eyes flickered to Yosef, his father's ghost hanging like a grim spectre in the room amongst them. For a moment Yosef was back there, a boy lying on a rooftop, watching as his father was burned. His mouth tightened, and he met their eyes.

"Do not think," he said grimly, "that I do not understand your rage. I do. Better, perhaps, than any in this room. Did I not lose both of my parents to Oppa's savagery?" *And my wife something even greater.* The words ran through his mind with the blood-red rage he always felt but would never verbalise, not again, not ever. The memory of Sarah's ravaged body was one he had learned to discipline, but it was harder, here, amongst the streets where such horrors had begun. "I understand, well enough," he said again, and now every eye watched him. "But I have travelled far since those days. I have seen much, both of war, and of men. I say this: that we do as our people have always done. We go where it is safe. We band together. We build our resources – and we wait for the right time."

The eyes gathered about the table looked at him, and then at one another. The woman who spoke earlier shook her head slightly. "I cannot go," she said bitterly. "My husband is ill, and my parents aged. But if I could, I would not hesitate."

Hasdai covered her hand briefly with his own. "Then it will be our duty to prosper that we may return. For you, and for all the others forced to pretend to a faith not our own." He looked up, his face tired. "Very well, Yosef ben Arun. We will go to Septem – and there, we will await your orders."

* * *

It was late when Yosef left. He stood across the street from his family home, hidden in the shadows. A light burned in the window, and the sound of voices came from the rear garden. It was occupied now by a family of converted Jews, given to them with Yosef's blessing. They would welcome him, he knew, if he asked to enter, but his presence would make them uneasy. In such times all had eyes upon them and were wary. Some might support the ideas of the rebellion, but most, he knew, simply feared for their lives and pretended to conversion to save themselves.

And what, Yosef thought, did he want inside his family home, anyway? What purpose would it serve, to stand inside the rooms of his childhood, his father's study? Arun's astrolabe; his great codex of the *Lex Visigothorum*; the works of Isidore of Hispalis – all had long been in the villa at Illiberis, and they seemed far less important to him than they once had. Yosef smiled now to think he had once been in awe of such tools and texts, thinking them the height of sophistication. In the years since, however, he had seen the great libraries in the caliph's palace, learned medicine from physicians in Persia, seen scrolls in Serica far older than anything the Goths possessed. He had learned that the Spania of the Goths was a poor remnant of richer cultures, a world where learning had become the sole preserve of priests, and thus was made and recorded by men of God rather than those of knowledge. Even saying such a thing would be enough to have him executed. Not just in Spania, but anywhere in Christendom. For Yosef, however, the Circle of Lands, and Christendom itself, was no longer his world, if, as a Jew, it had ever been. And now he could no longer be awestruck by anything in it – only despairing and strangely lonely.

He had come home, it was true. To the immeasurable gift of Sarah, Arun, and his unborn child. But the fact was, Yosef was as homeless as ever he had been whilst on the road. And a part of him, hidden deep from sight, was afraid he might never truly come home again.

He took a last look at the home of his childhood, mounted his horse, and rode toward Illiberis.

* * *

THE FOLLOWING day Yosef stood in Paulus's study in Illiberis, staring blankly through the wrought-iron lattice to the blazing spring day beyond. The air smelled of fresh grass and turned earth, and the familiar sounds of the daily routine at the villa floated through the window as they ever had. If he closed his eyes, Yosef could envisage his own father sitting here, bent over the large leather codex with the accounts, and Paulus striding down the corridor bellowing orders at the servants.

Nostalgia, it seemed, was even more potent here than in his own home. If he turned his head, Yosef could see Lælia as the child she had once been, yellow-eyed and silent, gesturing wordlessly for Yosef to slip from the room and join her, roaming the high places when they should be learning.

Tyr! The Gothic curse was not his god nor his language, but in this room, in this villa, it was the one he thought of. Yosef turned to look at the heavy leather volumes on the stands by the wall, and the chests on the ground before him. He had no time to waste. Oppa's men were not far behind him on the road according to the scouts he had sent to keep guard, and he must remove what he could before they arrived. The less Oppa knew about the workings of the latifundium, the better. Yosef had entrusted the servants with most of it, but this, the study, was his responsibility.

"I had the servants pack what they thought Lælia would want, to be sent to Aurariola." Yosef turned to find Gratimo in the doorway, his craggy face grim and shadowed.

"Who will you send with them?"

"I will ride to Aurariola with them myself, as soon as I have met with Oppa's men." Gratimo grimaced on the last words as he stepped into the room. "There are several of us from the Illiberis thiufa who will take them."

"But then you will return here, to your lands, your families?"

"*Ne.*" Gratimo shook his head. "Most of us are old men, with children who might work our lands. We were sworn to the Count of Illiberis. Now we are sworn to his daughter. If she returns, we will also. If not…" He shrugged. "Aurariola is as good a place to die as Illiberis."

Yosef swallowed hard, his throat full of an emotion he could not express. Bending to the chests, he wrapped the rolls of vellum in leather and packed them carefully amongst wood shavings. "As soon as these are done you must send men to carry them to Sexi," he said. "We can't risk Oppa finding them."

Gratimo nodded. "Consider it done." He paused, and Yosef looked up at him.

"What is it?"

"Zdan." Gratimo held his eyes. "The Riders from Africa. Perhaps they could take the chests with them."

"When they ride from here, you mean." Yosef straightened up and met Gratimo's gaze. "I know they can't stay," Yosef said quietly. "Lælia knows it, too."

"They would, I think, if you asked." Gratimo shook his head. "But it is not fair to ask it."

"We do not run from battle."

Both men swung around at the sound of Zdan's deep voice. The warrior entered the room, his lean height a quiet, but nonetheless impressive, presence. "If there is more fighting to be done, we will stay."

"There is not." Yosef met Zdan's eyes. "It is done, for now, at least."

Zdan frowned. "Then the rumours are true? You are to give this land to the same army we defeated?"

Gratimo and Yosef exchanged a glance, and it was Gratimo who answered. "It is given that other land may be held."

"And this is customary, in your wars?" Zdan's tone made it clear what he thought of such custom.

"It is what must be done," said Gratimo woodenly.

"And Lælia of Illiberis, she agrees to this?" Zdan's eyes narrowed as he regarded the two men. "Dahiya will ask, you understand. She sent us to hold Illiberis, under Lælia's command. I do not wish to return to her with the news that we surrendered it."

"Lælia herself gave the order," said Yosef. "In this, I speak for her."

Zdan looked unconvinced. Yosef was wondering how to

proceed when a small shadow slipped in through the door. "Tosius," he exclaimed in surprise. "When did you come?"

"In the night." Tosius waved a hand, dismissing Yosef's question. "Men are coming," he said, in the short manner of the tribes. He turned to Zdan. "The Lady of Illiberis says go." He put his hand over his heart and inclined his head. "She sends this, her respect, and gratitude."

Zdan nodded slowly, covering his own heart with his hand. "It was nothing," he said gravely.

Yosef, looking between them, shook his head, smiling. "You have known me for years," he said, addressing Zdan, "yet you do not listen to this from me, but from Tosius?"

"You have many allies, many masters to serve." Zdan nodded at Tosius. "He has only one: Illiberis, and the lady who belongs to it. He has the same heart as we," he said simply.

His words stung, and Yosef turned away, busying himself with the chests. He had thought, when he left Illiberis long ago, that the fortunes of Garnata, his own journey, and Illiberis would be forever entwined, one and the same. Yet with every day that passed, he felt those paths splintering off toward different futures, whilst all he could do was look on helplessly, knowing he did not have enough feet to walk each and must eventually choose.

Tosius turned gleaming brown eyes to Yosef. "Your people here in Garnata, and in Septem. They prepare to fight?"

"Eventually." Yosef maintained an even expression with the practice of many years. "For now, they will come with me to Septem. We must be careful."

"The Lady says she will return as soon as she may." Tosius's eyes were uncomfortably sharp. "To fight for what is hers. She will be waiting to hear news from Septem. She hopes you will be ready."

"Of course." Never had Yosef liked the double speak of diplomacy less. He had heard enough of the talk from the Septem Jews to suspect that even if they did fight, it would be to win Illiberis for themselves, not to hand it back to Lælia. After all that had been done to them, the exiled Jews of Spania were unlikely, in Yosef's opinion, to go to war merely to swap one overlord for another, no matter how old their alliance. The men who had once worked together, men such as Paulus and Arun, were gone, and those who had taken their places did not share the same unquestioning allegiance. It was a disquieting truth that Yosef had yet to process, let alone share with Theo or Lælia. It was yet another layer of complexity in a situation already labyrinthine with conflicting ambitions.

Wary of Tosius's sharp-eyed scrutiny, Yosef did not look up as Zdan said, "You wish us to take some of these chests to Ilyan?"

"Yes." Yosef carried on packing. "And you must leave today, I think, so make ready."

Zdan and the Riders left before sunset, the scrolls and codices of Illiberis packed on their horses. Yosef, watching the silent band wend away from the villa, led by a man from the tribes, wondered if any of the chests would ever see Spanish soil again. *If they do,* he thought, *still it will never be the same. I wonder if Lælia knows that?*

The long years away had taught Yosef something of return: that one never truly did. The place one left was never found as it was, as it had been. Time and place belonged together. The same place years later was a different one, because the time was not the same. It was a curious conundrum, one Yosef sometimes thought men such as Tosius and Zdan understood better than did his own people, or the Goths. Men of the earth seemed to understand that time was all there was, every moment its own place, and that one moment could not be held beyond when it was lived. Such thinking was, in the modern world in which they all lived, both blessing, Yosef thought, and curse.

* * *

THE SMART THING, Yosef knew, would have been to have left before the arrival of Oppa's men the following day, at noon. Perhaps, he thought, as he eyed the newcomers from beneath the ragged hood of a torn old cloak, a part of him missed being an anonymous stranger in a crowd. There was no doubt he felt a certain familiar thrill in disappearing into the shadows at the rear of the Illiberis square, to all intents and purposes a bent, wizened peasant come to hear from the new priest of the future that awaited the people of Illiberis.

The priest's name was Ulric. He was a stolid, stern-faced man, to whom the soldiers all deferred. Ulric wasted no time in gathering the tenants of Illiberis, the townsfolk, and even the lowliest of peasants, into the church behind the town walls. He said a long, arduous prayer, then rose and looked about at the crumbling stone with distaste.

"Much will change in this place," he said. He launched into a long discourse on the rulings of the Sixteenth Council in Toletum. Yosef, standing in the shadows at the rear, listened with barely disguised amusement as Ulric informed his congregation that pagan offerings would no longer be tolerated, tithes to the church would be enforced to make repairs upon it, and the church in Garnata would be restored entirely as a Christian edifice, with all traces of Judaism eradicated. The sermon was in fact little more than a recital of the decrees from the council and was received with dull indifference by a citizenry who knew already that their lives were to change irrevocably. There were none in Illiberis alive who knew any life but the one they had lived under Paulus and Acantha. They knew only that now they were to obey a lord from Toletum, of whom they knew little other than that they had recently fought to defeat that same man. What manner of lord he would be, they would not know until the seasons had turned, and in the meantime, if a priest told them to mend the roof, they would mend the roof.

When the interminable lecture was done, they went into the sunlight and on their way, subdued and with little to say.

Yosef joined the rear guard of Ulric's retinue as they rode back toward the villa. He slipped into the group with the stealth born of long practice, walking alongside the horse of a junior cleric who took his new posting with a conscientious piety that Yosef, despite the danger of his current position – or perhaps, he could privately admit, because of it – found amusing.

Some distance on they came to the pathway that led uphill, to the abbey where Acantha had once dwelled. As they passed, the cleric stared uphill in fascination. "Is it true," he said to Yosef in a hushed whisper, "that a group of heretics live up there, under the guise of being women of Christ? I heard they are witches who lay pagan offerings beneath trees and perform spells at water pools."

Yosef thought of Acantha's tall, proud figure, riding down from the mountain heights, her face fierce and bronze and proud, and felt his heart twist with longing for a time that would never return. "The heretic woman who led that community," he said quietly, "gave her life fighting for it. For this land that she called home."

The cleric crossed himself. "Then she died as all like her will die," he said, looking around fearfully. "Defeated by God's forces and the might of the Cross."

Soon after, Yosef slipped away from the road and into the fields. He came close once again when the procession reached the field beyond the stables, where Gratimo met them, with Tosius and a small delegation of the tribes. Ulric stared at them disdainfully. From the cover of a nearby clump of trees, Yosef watched the exchange, his heart twisting at the sight of Tosius's staunch, defiant little figure facing down the flock of dark-robed priests.

"The tribesmen are the guardians of the Illiberis horse-flesh," Gratimo said hastily as Ulric approached, clearly concerned by the uncompromising glare in the other's eyes at the sight of Tosius and the other tribesmen.

Ulric made a disparaging noise. "Tell them I want the herds brought down to the villa without delay."

Tosius stepped forward before Gratimo could speak. Smiling as if he were delighted to meet Ulric, he chattered away brightly in the language of the tribes, making no effort to use either Latin or Gothic, both of which, Yosef knew, he was perfectly able to speak.

"He says," Gratimo translated, "that the herds were taken by the barbarian army that attacked Illiberis. Even the tribe's own horses, he says, were taken. What you find here in the stables is all that is left."

Storm clouds gathered on Ulric's face. "The Illiberis herd is much of its wealth. I do not believe it simply gone."

Though Gratimo's face remained set in a soldier's stolid indifference, his mouth twitched slightly as he conveyed this to Tosius, and even from a distance, Yosef detected a glimmer of amusement in the dour lines as Gratimo translated the tribesman's reply: "He says that your men are welcome to join them in searching the mountains, but he fears you will find nothing. He says many horses were taken south by the barbarians, and that men from his tribe saw them loaded aboard dromons bound for Africa."

Ulric glared at Tosius. "You will instruct this man that I will soon be visiting his people. Unlike my predecessors, I do not tolerate pagan superstition – and I will show little mercy to those who practise it."

Gratimo turned to Tosius and made a pretence of translation.

The little tribesman's face maintained its merry, slightly unfocused expression, but when he spoke, Yosef saw the deadly gleam in Tosius's eyes. "You may tell this imbecile," said Tosius in the light, chirruping, sing-song cadence of the tribes, "that he may search until his feet are raw. He will never find the horses of Illiberis, and he will never see my people in his stone castle. You can tell him that our people wait for the Lady of Illiberis. That no matter who sleeps under this roof, this land belongs to us, and to those of our blood, who know its songs and its magic. You tell him he may speak words to whatever god he chooses. The spirits who live in trees and water do not care to whom he sings. They were here before he came and will endure long after he is gone."

He finished speaking and, turning to his companions, gave a short command. A moment later they were gone, melted into the gloaming.

"Well?" Ulric demanded. "What did he say?"

Yosef looked after the shadows disappearing into the mountain folds, his heart twisting with longing and sadness as he heard Gratimo speak.

"He said to tell you," Gratimo said softly, "that he understood."

17

THEO

MAY, AD 693,

Toletum, Spania
Toledo, Spain

"I don't understand why Shukra doesn't simply proclaim his innocence of these charges." Theo strode across the mosaic-tiled floor of the œca in Laurentius's Toletum domus and poured himself a cup of wine from the stand in the corner. "Why would he sacrifice himself needlessly for a crime any fool can see he is not guilty of? Surely there are whores enough in Toletum who will attest to the fact that his tastes run to women, and not men?" Frowning, he turned to look first at Laurentius, then at Athanagild, who stood quietly on the other side of the room. "Wasn't Sisebut discovered in a bathhouse behind a brothel? That in itself should surely be enough to make it clear Shukra is no sodomite."

"Felix has already testified against him," said Laurentius quietly. "And Felix is now archbishop. Shukra was condemned not only for the crime of − sodomy, but also for spying." His face twisted slightly on the word "sodomy". Theo entirely understood his distaste. He had not fought amongst men for so many years without being aware of the manner in which some chose their pleasure, but familiarity had not lessened the disgust he felt for the act itself. To be condemned of such a crime seemed to Theo to be the greatest disgrace he could imagine, a crime against God as well as man. It galled him that Laurentius and Athanagild seemed so passive.

"And yet," he mused aloud, "despite having been condemned of these crimes, Shukra was not amongst those sentenced to death. Why has he been spared?"

"Shukra will never be released." Laurentius's voice was unexpectedly harsh. "He has resigned himself to his fate, Theo. I suggest you show him the courtesy of respecting his choice."

His uncle, Theo thought, not for the first time, was changed by his time in Spania, and by the loss of his oldest friend. He had grown more stern, with less of the light touch of humour that had once existed beneath the surface. There seemed also between him and Athanagild a grim understanding that was both bond and division. At times Theo saw them exchange glances filled with the same unspoken understanding he had shared with Silas and Leofric, the bond of men who had seen war together, though he suspected the two did not always enjoy the same oneness of mind he shared with his men. He supposed that made sense, when one was a soldier, the other a man of God. But for the life of him, Theo could not understand why neither his brother nor his uncle would fight for the little Persian who had so tirelessly shown them all such loyalty. He himself would never abandon Silas or Leofric to such a fate. He did not know what to make of the fact that Laurentius seemed so ready to do so.

"What is it that concerns you, Theo?" Athanagild moved away from the wall and toward his brother, effectively blocking Laurentius's face from Theo's view. Theo pushed his concerns about Shukra to the back of his mind with the efficiency he had learned during years of combat, focusing instead on the shadow that was never far from his conscious thoughts: Oppa.

"Oppa does not leave anything to chance." He folded his arms, frowning at Athanagild. "If Shukra hasn't been executed, then Oppa has a plan for him. We need to discover what that plan is."

"Oppa?" Athanagild was looking at Theo curiously. "Why are you so certain he is behind this, Theo? Could it not be Egica, or the Church, who is deciding Shukra's future?"

"No." Theo heard the flat certainty in his own voice, saw Athanagild's rather startled expression, and, not wishing either of his relatives to suspect why he was so familiar with Oppa's motivations, forced his tone to soften as he went on. "Egica has no reason to pardon a traitor, and in the wake of the council, the Church has been merciless in punishing those amongst its ranks it suspects of sodomy. There is no reason to spare Shukra unless he might serve some purpose. I suspect that Oppa has such a purpose in mind."

"And do you have a notion what that purpose might be?" Athanagild was looking at him with the same disquieting scrutiny Theo recalled from their childhood. He turned away, unwilling to let his brother see too much.

"Oppa's purposes are inevitably dark," he said curtly. "Whatever his reasons for sparing Shukra, rest assured they are not benevolent." He was silent for a moment. "I suspect," he said slowly, "that Oppa sees in Shukra another link to Septem, and to Yosef's mission to the east. He is determined, I think, to uncover the source of the sudden surge in Jewish confidence, the reason they might believe themselves able to fund a rebellion. Oppa knows Shukra is linked to Ilyan, and to Septem. He hopes to use those ties, I believe."

"I can see Apsimar's influence upon your thinking." Theo swung around to find Laurentius regarding him with a twisted smiled reminiscent of his old, dry humour. "You have acquired his habit of looking for what is hidden."

"I have you to thank for his favour, I believe." Theo's own

mouth curled reluctantly. "A mixed blessing, as I suspect you know."

Laurentius gave a brief cough of laughter. "My influence would not have been enough to win Apsimar's trust. You must have proven yourself, in more ways than one, for him to take you into his confidence." His eyes ran over Theo and for a moment, Theo remembered the boy he had been, riding at Shukra's side toward Illiberis, listening wide eyed to stories of Laurentius and Shukra on foreign shores, unable to imagine himself living half of what they had together. Yet in the years since, he had been slave, soldier, spy, and sailor – and now, he was something he suspected neither Laurentius nor Shukra would ever recognise. His face tightened, the familiar mask falling over his eyes, sheltering his heart from Laurentius and his brother. As it did, he saw a similar veil fall over the eyes of the other men. *We are all changed,* he thought wearily. *And not, perhaps, for the better.*

"I had news of Apsimar," he said, more from a desire to change the nature of their conversation than any other reason. "Yesterday." He did not mention that the messenger had come from Septem and also borne news of Zdan and Yosef's safe return.

"What news?" Laurentius's face lit up with interest.

"It seems that Leontios, the *strategos* who lost the battle at Sebastopolis, has incurred the emperor's wrath. Apsimar sends word that Justinian II has imprisoned Leontios as punishment."

"Imprisoned!" Laurentius shook his head. "It is unwise to imprison a man for losing a battle. Such decisions will not sit well with the Karabisianoi."

"Certainly not with Apsimar." Theo grinned. "Apsimar has no love for Leontios, it is true – I heard him more than once refer to the man as a fool – but he has even less, if possible, for Justinian II. Not least because it seems that after their success in Anatolia, the Arabs are launching another expedition to Africa. The longer Justinian delays his response, the harder it will be to dislodge an Arabic army. Apsimar is impatient to sail, I take it."

"All this, your messenger relayed?" Laurentius was looking at him with the same curiosity Athanagild had a moment ago. "Then Apsimar does, indeed, trust you a great deal."

"Sebastopolis was a sordid mess." Theo's face tightened as he recalled the tension and layers of conspiracy that had characterised his years in the Anatolian port. "Apsimar needed eyes in every alley. And he alone amongst the emperor's commanders puts the Karabisianoi first, the lives of his men ahead of imperial ambition. Such a man is easy to give allegiance to."

"Yes," said Laurentius thoughtfully. "Apsimar was always able to inspire such loyalty." His eyes travelled over Theo, lingering a moment on the deep, twisted scars on the younger man's face. "And he has an unerring instinct for men who will lead well. Clearly he sees in you such a man, even if you are no longer under his direct command."

Theo pretended not to notice the subtle question, and he avoided further interrogation on the exact nature of his relationship with Apsimar by turning to an easier discussion of the state of imperial conflict, and speculation over what the emperor and caliph might do next. Such topics were both easy and interesting, and Theo found himself impressed again with Athanagild's grasp of international politics, something even more exceptional given his brother's position inside the suffocating environment of the clergy.

He could, he knew, have told Laurentius more of his communications with Apsimar. There was no great secret to it; Theo had left the service of the emperor to return to his homeland, as Laurentius once had. If he had left amidst a war, still none blamed him, Apsimar least of all. Sebastopolis had been a rout. The fact he had survived at all was a testament to his skill. But in the time since he had returned, Apsimar's messages had found Theo with increasing regularity. Messages that, he sensed, might once have found their way to

Laurentius, now came to him, often aided by Ilyan's hands. And every message suggested the same thing: the Arabs were coming. Not yet, perhaps, but they would come. And when they did, Theo knew Apsimar expected Spania to be ready.

Expected Theo to be ready.

The worst of it was, deep within, Theo knew he craved war the same way some men did drink. He had not, perhaps, known it before he left Sebastopolis, for he had for so long been fixed upon his goal of returning to Lælia that he had given little thought to what he might do once he achieved it. Now that he was home, however, he was coming to the realisation, albeit reluctantly, that part of him was still fighting the war he had left behind. He found himself thinking of strategy, considering what the Arabs might do, where they might, even now, be stationed. He felt starved of information, wanting to know the particulars that might one day mean survival or defeat: the number of dromons the Karabisianoi now manned; where they were stationed; the fighting readiness of the men. He wanted to stand in a room with men such as Apsimar and markers on a table, analysing and planning.

He wanted to be leaping from the prow of a dromon onto a stony shore, knowing he had done all he could to prepare himself and his men for victory. Theo missed war in a way that made him feel almost ashamed, and to consider the decisions he had made in a different light. He had been forced to realise that the man he had become was not the one his father had raised, nor even one his uncle and brother might respect.

Apsimar, Theo knew, would see nothing wrong in the deal he had made with Oppa. Would see it, in fact, as a wise play in the imperial game of whispers and subterfuge.

Laurentius, however, would not.

And so Theo talked genially with his uncle and brother, aware that both watched him, in their quiet moments, with disquieting scrutiny.

After they had enjoyed a good meal and the late afternoon turned to evening, he and Athanagild bid their host goodnight and walked together through the city streets. The brothers made an odd pair, drawing more than one set of curious eyes: Theo, with his fierce scars and still wearing the crimson military tunic of the Karabisianoi; Athanagild, red headed and in priestly robes. Theo strode through the street looking neither right nor left. He had long ceased to allow curious eyes to concern him.

"You are well informed, brother." He smiled at Athanagild as they walked, ignoring the whispers and wide eyes of two small boys nearby. "It is unusual to find men of the clergy so well versed in military affairs."

"Abroad, perhaps." Athanagild did not return his smile. "In Spania, war does not discriminate between laity and clergy." Theo nodded, unsure what to say to that. Many times since his return he had been made aware that his brother had endured a war of his own, one he shared no more than Theo did the stories of his scars. In some matters, they were brothers as they had ever been. In others, a gulf lay between them that Theo sometimes feared could never again be spanned – one of secrets and lies. With uncanny prescience, Athanagild said, "Lælia, too, has fought a war of her own. And not just the battle at Illiberis."

"I know that." Theo knew he sounded curt. "I wish I could have been here," he said, trying to soften his tone.

"But you weren't." Athanagild's tone wasn't accusing. It was calm and matter of fact, as Theo's own might have been in the same circumstances, but no less devastating for being so. "And whilst none blame you for that, Theo, do not think she is any less scarred by the years of your absence than you are yourself. Lælia has won the right to decide her own future, and to fight for what she believes in."

Theo, taken by surprise, looked sideways at his brother. "What makes you think I doubt that?"

"I think that for a long time now, you have had to make difficult decisions with none other to consult than your own conscience." Athanagild's hazel eyes met his own, their sharp perception jolting Theo more than he cared to admit. "I know something of that," Athanagild said quietly. "I, too, have been forced to make decisions alone. It is hard, in such circumstances, to believe any other worthy of trust."

"What is it you are trying to say, Athanagild?"

Athanagild halted some distance from the entrance to Theodofred's domus, where Theo and Lælia were still staying. "I am saying that lying to Lælia is unwise. You were not here to see how she fought, for you, and for Illiberis. Whatever your plans, she deserves to be included in them. And her own ideas to be heard." Theo frowned but did not answer. Athanagild stepped closer to him, his eyes still on Theo's. "Lælia has endured much," he said quietly. "She has always found a way to triumph, even when the odds seemed hopeless and all doors were closed to her. She is relentless in her pursuit of truth and ruthless with those who lie to her. She is both one of the most loyal people I have ever known, and one of the least forgiving. She demands honour of herself, and thus has no understanding of dishonour in others, no tolerance for it." He paused, giving his next words careful emphasis. "If she discovers you are lying to her, Theo, she will never forgive you."

Theo's heartbeat was painful in his chest. It took every ounce of his self-control to maintain an even expression. "What makes you think I am lying to her?"

"Initially, it was because the deal you made with Oppa was too easily done to be an accident." Athanagild's eyes were no longer calm but shards of hard gold that Theo found difficult to meet. "But after listening to you and Laurentius speak tonight, I would imagine that there is little you would not do to save Spania from facing the Arab army you have fought for so long. To be in a position to do that, a man needs powerful allies – and the commander of a fleet requires a coastal port." His pause was unbearably long. "Aurariola has one," he said softly, "whilst Illiberis does not."

Theo stared at his brother, for once bereft of words.

"Lælia has been lied to many times already," Athanagild continued without waiting for a response. "You are the person she trusts above all others." Theo felt every word like a dagger in his heart, striving with all his years of military discipline not to let Athanagild see how much they hurt. "In the years you were away," Athanagild went on quietly, "Lælia was as my sister. She still is. Even more so, perhaps, than my own sister, whom I barely know. I have seen Lælia stand in court before the nobility and triumph over them, win the admiration of Archbishop Julian himself. I've seen her take body blows that would have felled many a man, and rise, determined to overcome. And through it all, her faith in you, her loyalty to you, has remained unwavering. I would not wish, Theo, to see such trust betrayed."

Utterly unnerved by his brother's prescience, when he finally did speak, Theo's response took even him by surprise.

"When I was abroad," he said, "I fought for a time alongside Dahiya — a woman the Arabs call Al Kahinat."

Athanagild's eyes narrowed. "Lælia told me of her time with her in the desert."

Theo nodded. "Did she tell you that it is Apsimar who is said to be father to Dahiya's children?"

"I had heard that, yes."

"Dahiya fought for her lands whilst she carried both children, barely pausing to give birth. Those boys, by all accounts, were raised in baskets at the side of a camel. They carried a sword before they walked."

He looked up to find Athanagild watching him closely.

"Lælia is with child." The words sprang from Theo almost unbidden, rough on the evening air. Athanagild stared at him, his own eyes widening. "She is carrying my child, Athanagild."

"I am happy for you," Athanagild said slowly. "Truly, brother, I am."

Theo made an impatient noise. His hands gripped the stone wall at the entrance to the domus hard enough to turn the knuckles white. "I know you have all endured much," he said harshly. "But I have seen war in a way that even you have not, Athanagild. I have lived it day and night from the moment I left these shores. And I would not have our children raised amidst that chaos. Not if there is any other way." His jaw clenched hard. "It may yet be avoided, but I cannot focus on securing Spania if I am also destabilising it from within. I cannot see how we might regain Illiberis. Not without losing all else, our lives included."

"Then tell her that." Athanagild's answer was swift and direct. "I doubt Lælia is blind to the issues you face." When Theo did not respond, his brother's expression became thoughtful. "Ah. But that alone is not the lie between you, is it, Theo?"

Theo's face hardened, but he could not bring himself to tell his brother of the parchment. It was enough, already, that Yosef should know it, and Silas. They at least were part of that far-away world in which such a vile deed had been done. But Athanagild was part of Lælia's world. To tell him the truth when Lælia herself did not know it seemed, to Theo, an even greater betrayal, one he could not bring himself to make.

"Perhaps you think my dissimulation about Illiberis a lie, and mayhap you are right, brother," he said, sidestepping his brother's accusation with a politician's dexterity. "But it is a lie I will tell a thousand times and more if it will keep Lælia, and our child, safe." Part of him expected Athanagild to press for answers, so when his brother's response came, it was so unexpected as to disarm him.

"I would not see her heart broken, Theo." Athanagild touched his arm gently. Theo shuddered, almost flinching from the kindness. "To do so would break my own."

"And you think I wish that?" Theo's voice rose despite himself. He stepped away, stiffening his resolve. "Do not concern yourself with my marriage, brother. Perhaps your concern is better off focused on the man who is at this moment imprisoned beneath the palace for a crime he did not commit – a man to whom we both owe everything, and yet whom you and Laurentius seem perfectly content to see rot in a dungeon! Do not speak to me of honour and loyalty whilst Shukra dies a slow death."

He had the dubious satisfaction of seeing Athanagild's face pale, two hectic spots of colour finally penetrating his brother's unsettling composure.

"You know nothing of Shukra's sacrifice." Athanagild's voice shook slightly.

"You're right." Theo nodded, aware that he was taking a measure of revenge for the blows Athanagild's own insight had recently inflicted. "I know nothing of the secrets you and Laurentius clearly share, just as you know nothing of mine. This is our life now, Athanagild – secrets we none of us might share, no matter the ties of blood and loyalty that might hold us. What is it that your scriptures say – *judge not, lest ye be judged?* You know nothing of what I have had to do, and even less of how much I love my wife, and my unborn child." Athanagild's face was no longer simply pale but entirely bloodless, the mention of secrets somehow seeming to suck all expression from his eyes, leaving them blank, empty voids of a pain Theo neither recognised nor understood. But his own guilt manifested in an anger so fierce he gave no thought to what might cause such pain, instead seeking only to wound as he himself was pained by his brother's uncomfortable perception and unerring accusation. "I will do what I must to protect Lælia," he said grimly. "And you, brother, will say nothing that may endanger her – for if you do, mark me, my answer will be ruthless indeed."

Anger and guilt twisting inside him, Theo swung on his heel and stalked down the road, his brother's eyes seeming to burn accusing holes in his back as he went.

18

———

LÆLIA

JUNE, AD 693

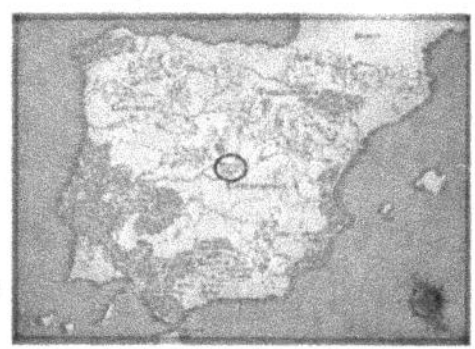

Toletum, Spania
Toledo, Spain

The nights had grown cool, and clouds covered the half moon. Lælia fingered the moss-green wool of her gown with distaste. It was not a colour that flattered her and was hardly what she would have chosen for a feast in the king's hall. Unfortunately, it was the only gown in Riccilo's wardrobe that still fit her swelling waist.

"You are beautiful." Smiling, Theo moved to slip his arms around her from behind.

"I am heavy as a carthorse."

"You are barely three months with child. It will be a wonder if any even notice."

Lælia gave a hollow laugh. "The women at court notice everything."

"Rekiberga will be there. Egilona, too. You will not be alone."

"Poor Rekiberga." Lælia shook her head, her gown forgotten. "It is cruel that Ataulfo should parade her at court so soon

209

after her public humiliation. Every time I see her I think of Alaric —" She broke off, turning to Theo worriedly. "I am sorry. I forget, sometimes, that he was your brother."

"Do not be sorry." Theo drew her close. "He was your brother, too." A smile twisted the scars. "Sometimes it seems both of my brothers became more yours than mine, in the time I was away."

"They always believed you would return, as I did." Her arms twined about his neck. "Even when all others told us to forget you, still we believed."

"Well, tonight will give the doubters ample chance to look upon the face they all thought lost." His mouth tightened briefly, and Lælia touched the smooth folds of scarred skin with one hand.

"It is one night," she said, unsure if the words were for herself or Theo. "One feast, and then we might leave this cursed city."

"*Ja.*" Theo kissed her, and they stood like that, for a long time, until night fell and it was time to leave.

* * *

THE PALACE WAS TEEMING with people. Every nobleman had brought members of his thiufa to Toletum, and soldiers lounged in every alcove of the palace reception hall and corridors. Lælia nodded to those she knew, doing her best to recall their names. Some returned her greetings, but most coloured and turned away. None knew how to address the daughter of a traitor, or the niece of the recently humbled Duke of Corduba. Theo strode through their midst looking neither right nor left. Men did not colour when they looked at him, Lælia noticed. They watched him with mingled admiration and curiosity. Even if he was Suinthila's son, somehow Theo had escaped the stain of treachery. Perhaps it was the crimson tunic of the Karabisianoi, the unconscious air of command he seemed to carry, or maybe it was simply the grim scars that spoke of suffering and survival. Whatever the reason, Theudemir of Aurariola, Lælia thought, strode through the palace of Toletum with all the authority of the highest noblemen in Spania, and not the slightest hint of apology.

The feast was laid out not in the airy palace council chamber, but in the square hall that had been built during Wamba's reign. It boasted a barrel-vaulted, coffered ceiling that curved above a series of sturdy pillars, and a horseshoe arch at the entrance. The floor was dark stone rather than the delicate mosaics of the old Roman houses, and the only decorations in the blunt stonework were simple geometric patterns or friezes depicting religious scenes. Despite the flowers and branches hung for the celebrations, Lælia thought the hall resembled a church rather than a place of festivities. She shivered as they entered.

The nobility were seated at long tables set in a square formation around a centre table upon which lay a lavish display of fruit and flowers, lit from above by an iron circular candelabra. Together with the braziers on the surrounding pillars, the hall was lit well enough to clearly show the curious faces turned to the door as Theo was announced.

Not I, Lælia noted as a member of Egica's *gardingi* said her husband's name. *I am merely his wife. No longer the Lady of Illiberis, nor even Lælia of Illiberis. I am a wife, now, and known only by my husband's name.* It was a hollow feeling, disquieting, and Lælia was relieved when they moved out of Egica's direct gaze and to their seats which, she noticed, were uncomfortably close to the king's own. It seemed odd to her that they were seated in a position of such honour. She guessed Egica wished to show off his power and benevolence by condescending to Theo. Lælia saw Rekiberga sitting across the table that she was shown to, but her smile of relief disappeared when she recognised two of the other women, one seated beside Rekiberga, the other on the bench next to Lælia's own place.

"Lælia of Illiberis." Amalfrida's pale-blue eyes were as hard and cold as Lælia recalled from the last time they met.

"Oh – but do forgive me; of course, you are no longer known by that name." Pausing long enough to ensure her barb had found its mark, her mouth twisted nastily. It was a reminder to Lælia of the days before she had discovered her voice, when she had thought Theo lost to her forever, been alone and friendless at court.

But those days were long behind her, and Lælia was no longer the girl she had once been.

"Amalfrida." Lælia inclined her head coolly, remembering that long-ago day when Jadis had knocked Amalfrida to the ground amidst a royal festival, and Lælia herself had taken a horse and thundered from the old Toletum circus, drawing arrows from the king's own guard as she went.

There was nothing in the memory in which to rejoice, and she put it from her mind.

"Gisa," she added, nodding with slightly more warmth to the girl next to her on the bench. Gisa's heart-shaped face had filled out somewhat since they last met, as had her waistline, but a little plumpness suited her. She and Amalfrida both wore their hair covered beneath coif and veil, the richness of the material proclaiming their status at court. Lælia met Rekiberga's eyes across the table. "Rekiberga." She smiled warmly for the first time since taking her seat. "I am so very pleased to see you."

"And I you." Though Rekiberga returned her smile, her once sapphire eyes were dull and listless, her face colourless against the veil that hid her auburn hair. Her body seemed thin beneath the voluminous robes that were nothing like the brilliant jewel colours Lælia recalled her wearing, but by the way her hand rested on her belly, Lælia guessed she, too, was with child. Her heart twisted in sympathy. How must it be, married to Ataulfo, a man Rekiberga could not possibly love, carrying his child, when only months before she had been riding to Alaric, prepared to ride into exile if it meant being by his side? Briefly Lælia saw again the moment Alaric had fallen, the arrow appearing through his body as he raced behind Rekiberga to the gates that would have meant safety. Rekiberga, still holding her eyes, flinched slightly, as if the same memory passed her own mind.

"Rekiberga." Theo, having already greeted the others close by, smiled across the table. "I am so pleased to see you."

"Theudemir." Rekiberga's voice trembled slightly. "It is… a miracle." She tried to smile, but the expression was wooden, her lips stiff. "Truly a miracle," she whispered.

"A miracle indeed!" Amalfrida reached across her husband, a portly man with a thick black beard that was lavishly woven with jewels, popped an olive into her mouth and stared at Theo. "You were thought dead," she said, in a tone that suggested she took Theo's return as a personal affront. Ignoring Lælia entirely, she went on, "And yet here you are. And permitted to inherit, I understand." This was said disdainfully, in a manner that made it clear Amalfrida thought little of the king's benevolence. "My father died at Toletum," she said, loudly enough to be heard by several people nearby.

"Mine, also," said Theo quietly. "Alongside my wife's last remaining relation, and Rekiberga's own father."

"Traitors, all," hissed Amalfrida, her eyes glinting with spite. In the uncomfortable silence that followed, Amalfrida's husband, a count from Tarraconensis whose name Lælia vaguely recalled being Wimar, coughed uncomfortably. Just as it seemed the scene might take an ugly turn, a high, silvery voice interrupted them.

"Amalfrida. What a lovely dress! I believe I saw Queen Liuvgoto wearing a similar material on my recent visit – but no. Now that I think of it, she was using it as a runner on her table… but fine, indeed. From Frankia, if memory serves? Yes, I thought so." Egilona's small figure was inside the square made by the tables, behind Amalfrida, and the mere fact that she was on her feet whilst the assembly were seated was evidence enough of her standing at court. If any doubt remained, she smiled now at Theo, the perfect pink bow of her mouth curving sweetly, and said, "Brother. My lord Wittiza has requested the honour of meeting you. Will you and your lady wife" – she smiled prettily at Lælia – "join us at our table? We have much to speak of now that you are returned."

Amalfrida, her face flushed with fury, seemed about to respond when Egilona turned to Gisa. "Your father's gift to my lord Wittiza was received with great joy," she said, nodding her head gravely at where Count Vitulo smiled indulgently at her from his place close to the king, raising his cup in admiring acknowledgement of her words. "It is a fine horse indeed. We hope you might join us, during the coming days, when we ride out to hunt?" Whatever biting retort Amalfrida might have wished to deliver was superseded by Gisa's stuttering, blushing acceptance of Egilona's invitation, as if the diminutive figure before her were queen, rather than the ten-year-old daughter of a dead traitor, and king's hostage at court.

"My dear sister." Theo rose, extending a hand to Lælia, his mouth twitching at the corners. "You are extraordinary, indeed."

Egilona's eyes, as clear and piercing as Theo's own, looked directly at him. "Am I not?" she said archly. And though her words received an indulgent ripple of laughter from those close by, who clearly dismissed them as the precocious whim of a child, Lælia, observing the high, arched brows over sloping blue eyes, and blonde ringlets dressed in a remarkably sophisticated style for one so young, thought there was nothing even remotely childish about Egilona.

"Sister." Egilona extended a hand of her own to Lælia, guiding her through the gap in the long tables and speaking high enough to be easily heard. "I was thrilled to learn I shall soon be an aunt, as will be all in Aurariola when they hear your news. When do you return to our family lands?" Chattering merrily for all the world as if they were two long-lost acquaintances on a summer's walk rather than watched by the eyes of every member of Spania's haughty nobility, Egilona led Lælia directly across the stone floor to the head table, where four spaces remained empty. One of them was between Egilona and Roderic, who sat next to Pelayo, who was in turn beside Wittiza. The other vacant seats were on Wittiza's other side, between him and the king. "Come, sit with me so we might become acquainted," said Egilona, drawing Lælia down beside her. "I know Roderic, too, is eager to speak with you after so long." Grimacing at Lælia behind his sister's back, but nonetheless still grinning, Theo obediently took the seat between Wittiza and the king, where he was reluctantly persuaded to relay to the *princeps* detailed descriptions of his overseas battles. Roderic and Pelayo both craned their heads to try to listen in.

Deeply uncomfortable to be both separated from Theo and so blatantly the centre of attention, Lælia made polite responses to Egilona's questions, impressed despite her discomfort at the girl's self-possession. "I heard you mention you have visited Queen Liuvgoto," she said quietly when the attention of the table was focused on a particularly daring tale of Theo's. "How is she? I heard of her sufferings during the time Toletum was under siege."

"She is quite recovered, God be praised, despite the traitor Sunifred's attempt to poison her." Egilona shook her head. *For all,* Lælia thought, *as if her own father had nothing to do with Sunifred's rebellion.* Lælia wondered if Egilona was aware that it had been her own brother, Athanagild, who had carried the poison to Liuvgoto's chambers. Poison that would have been successful, had it not been for Shukra's expertise with herbs to ameliorate it. Then she found herself almost choking on her soup as the sloping blue eyes flicked her way and one long-fringed eyelid winked slyly. "You should join us on our next visit to the monastery, sister," Egilona said innocently, for the listening ears. "It is a fine place for prayer."

She is a witch, thought Lælia, her initial wariness giving way to outright admiration. *One who has already learned to weave her spells.* Her eyes flickered over Egilona's head to where the slight, nondescript figure of Egilona's maidservant hovered in the shadows. Not by the slightest mannerism did Safia betray any recognition of Lælia. Her eyes remained demurely on the floor, her presence all but invisible. *And you,* Lælia thought, *see everything, and understand even more. What a pair the two of you make!* Instinctively she reached down to stroke Jadis's head and remembered, too late, that her cat was at that very moment prowling Riccilo's domus, undoubtedly terrorising the servants.

"What is it?" Egilona asked, and Lælia was again reminded that nothing escaped the wide blue eyes.

"I was thinking of my cat, whom I could not bring tonight," she said ruefully. "Jadis. She's a mountain lynx and doesn't enjoy being confined in the city."

"Is that the same animal that once pinned Amalfrida to the ground?"

Lælia grimaced. "It is a memory I would prefer to forget, but yes, that was Jadis."

Egilona sat back, her eyes gleaming. "I wish I had seen that."

"It was, by all accounts, quite the sight."

Lælia stiffened, the skin on the back of her neck crawling at the flat, silky tone. *I will not give him the satisfaction of turning,* she thought, bracing herself for Oppa's greeting. But to her surprise, the king's bastard did not pause at her chair and force her to greet him, as she had expected. Instead he continued past her, to the vacant seats between Theo and the king. "*dulcissima,*" he murmured, drawing forward a slender, very pretty girl with white-blonde hair and pale-blue eyes, and gesturing to the place beside Theo. "Please – sit."

As the girl took her seat, she turned to Theo, giving Lælia a clear view of her face. Seeing the hard, almost vicious triumph flash in the girl's eyes, Lælia frowned. Her own gaze slid to Theo, whose body had gone rigid with tension. The colour drained from his face as he stared at the blonde girl, and his eyes grew darker, until they glowed with a feral fury Lælia could not recall seeing in them before. Then he glanced back at her, and if Lælia had been left in any doubt as to whether he knew the girl, the hurried way Theo's eyes slid away from Lælia's own told their own story. He turned his head quickly aside, but not before Lælia had clearly seen the extent of his shock.

He knows her. Lælia's eyes shifted between the blonde girl and Theo, her mind moving rapidly. *And whatever lies between them, it isn't a small thing.* Then she glanced at Oppa, only to find him watching the girl and Theo with a half smile of such obvious delight that it turned her stomach. *Whatever their secret, Oppa knows it, and he has brought her here purposely to discomfort him.*

She felt Oppa's dark eyes watching her, waiting, and Lælia knew he had planned this, was waiting for her reaction.

I will not give him that satisfaction.

Sitting tall in her seat, schooling her face into the impassive mask she had mastered during her long years of silence, Lælia met Oppa's gleaming black glance with flat disdain. Holding it long enough for him to note her lack of emotion, she turned her attention deliberately back to Egilona, though keeping half an eye on the figures down the table. Theo, having regained his composure quickly enough that Lælia doubted any but Oppa and the girl had noted it, had managed to greet both politely and turn his attention back to Wittiza.

Unfortunately, his captive audience had been lost the moment that the girl sat down. Wittiza was no longer listening to Theo's stories. "Brother," Wittiza addressed Oppa, "won't you introduce your companion to us?"

Oppa inclined his head with every pretence of deference. "You do us both honour, *princeps*. This is the lady Elpis, whom I rescued from the smouldering ashes of Sebastopolis after the Arabic army's victory over the emperor's forces."

Sebastopolis. Lælia felt a faint ripple of shock. *Then he knew her over there, during his years at war.* She felt an uncharacteristic stab of something almost like jealousy, the gulf of those years she could never be a part of separating her from the others at the table. She may have been Theo's wife, the mother of his child, but when it came to the years he had been abroad, she felt as a stranger. "Like so many of us that day," Oppa continued, "Elpis was sorely wounded. I could not leave someone so delicate to the ravages of the Arab barbarians."

"You did an admirable thing, brother." Wittiza's expression of glowing admiration was mirrored in the faces of the watching nobility, some of whom even applauded at this speech. Lælia, however, was oblivious to all else but Theo. Accustomed to him being always composed, no matter the provocation, she was startled to see the savage fury growing on his face as Oppa spoke. She was about to intervene when she felt the slight pressure of Egilona's hand at her side.

"Careful." Although Egilona's eyes were downcast and her lips barely moved, Lælia heard her clearly when she went on, "Oppa brought that whore here to goad you both. Do not allow him to succeed."

It was not the crudity of Egilona's language that shocked Lælia, but rather what it signified. Her eyes slid between Theo's face, hard and furious, and Elpis's, glittering and oddly triumphant, and a sickening suspicion began to grow. As if drawn by her words, Elpis's eyes slid to Lælia and lingered there for a brief moment, spite gleaming in their depths.

I know your husband, the eyes said.

Lælia held them. *You know nothing,* she returned silently, forcing herself to maintain the impassive smile of diplomacy.

Any doubt she might have had about what the nature of Theo and Elpis's relationship might once have been was dispelled by the sight of Theo, on her peripheral vision, almost quivering with tension. Elpis's eyes held Lælia's just long enough to make her point, then they moved on. They reached Egilona and paused. Something flared in the pale blue, a kind of despairing pain so at odds with the spite of a moment earlier that Lælia almost found herself feeling empathy for her.

Almost.

"My lady," said Egilona courteously, when the eyes lingered long enough to be remarkable.

"I did not mean to stare." Collecting herself, Elpis smiled prettily. "You just – reminded me of someone." Seeing Oppa's eyes narrow, the curl of his mouth, Lælia felt a prickling of danger. *He is setting a trap*, she thought, trying to catch Theo's eye; but he was turned away from her, the rigid set of his shoulders the only indication of his fury.

"Egilona is Theo's sister," Oppa said, smiling down the table at Elpis, for all the world as if he were making polite conversation.

"Your sister!" Shock and something else passed Elpis's face as she turned to Theo. "The one you told us about, the day we met –" She stopped abruptly as she realised what she had just said, her eyes flying to Oppa, then to the assembly, to see who had heard. Most, however, were engaged in their own conversations and paid no mind to what was taking place on their table. Wittiza, fortunately, had been briefly distracted by Pelayo, and seeing Pelayo's eyes flicker to Egilona, Lælia thought she knew who had given him his cue. Glancing at Theo's stiff back, she guessed, by the hard gleam in Oppa's eyes, that her husband's legendary composure was, for once, completely lost. When he spoke a moment later, she knew it was so.

"Yes, Lady Elpis." Theo's voice was low and lethal, his emphasis on the word "lady" just enough to convey his contempt. "Egilona is my sister. Does she remind you, perhaps, of someone you once knew?"

Lælia kept her expression blank with no small effort, straining to hear their low-voiced exchange, her heart thudding with tension, aware of Oppa's eyes noting her every move.

"Someone you knew?" Wittiza, hearing the end of their

conversation, turned back to Elpis eagerly. "Who does Egilona remind you of? She must be a beauty, *ne*?" He smiled indulgently at Egilona.

"Oh, she was." Oppa's voice was lazy, almost lascivious, and Lælia, at a sudden recollection of his hands on her skin many years ago, the insidious caress of his whip handle across her body, shuddered involuntarily. Oppa's eyes flickered to her and flared once more. "Unfortunately," he went on in the same low, suggestive tone, "Elpis's sister died in the same battle from which Elpis and I – and Theudemir of Aurariola, of course – escaped." Oppa nodded at Theo, for all appearances, Lælia thought, as if they had fought the same battle, side by side. The thought curdled amongst her fury like sour milk, her hands clenched so tightly beneath the table that her nails cut the skin.

"What a day it must have been, to see the Arab army so close!" Wittiza's eyes were shining as he looked between the two men, seemingly oblivious to the cold gleam of satisfaction in his brother's eyes, or of Theo's tightly held fury.

"It was, indeed, a terrible day. One of savagery – and betrayal." At the cold hostility in Theo's tone, Lælia wondered that Wittiza and the rest of the assembly remained oblivious to the drama unfolding between the three figures. "However, I believe I may have some news that will bring you joy, Lady Elpis." There was nothing in the steel precision of his tone that spoke of tenderness, however, and Lælia, seeing the way Elpis shrank from him, began to feel truly concerned. If this was the woman he had told her of, the one he had lain with during those years, there was more to the dynamic than he had owned. She heard his words again, as he had spoken them on the hillside outside Corduba: *I did take a woman. There is nothing I can say of it, other than that she has no place in my heart. To my shame, I don't know that she ever did...*

The echo was replaced by his actual voice, here and now, cold and hard, saying: "There was another rescue that day. A young girl, who does, indeed, look remarkably like my sister. Is it possible that the child Pelagia is the sister you believed lost to you, Lady Elpis?"

Had Lælia not been watching Oppa closely, she might not have seen the momentary betrayal of shock in his expression, mingled with something else. *Is it fear?* she wondered. The game, it seemed, was no longer Oppa's alone. Whatever the emotion behind Oppa's reaction, however, it paled in comparison to Elpis's.

"Pelagia?" The colour drained from Elpis's face. "Oh, Theo! You mean she is alive?" Her manner of address was unmistakably intimate, and when involuntarily she grasped Theo's forearm, it was with such familiarity it sickened Lælia to the core. Even if she collected herself as quickly as she had lost herself, and although Pelayo rapidly distracted Wittiza again, Elpis's slip had not gone unnoticed. Wittiza's eyes were not the only ones moving between Theo and Elpis with narrow speculation, and when inevitably they turned to Lælia, gauging her reaction to what was clearly a lover's touch on her husband's arm, it took all the willpower she had to remain blank faced and courteous.

This was Oppa's trap. He intended for Elpis to unmask herself, to reveal her and Theo's intimacy.

Lælia was damned if she would show the tumult within, even if she could feel Amalfrida's gleeful eyes like brands on her skin. She did not dare look at Theo. That, she knew, would betray her, more than any other thing. Beneath the table Egilona's hand, cool and strong, covered her own, both settling and restraining.

It was Egilona, in the end, who brought the interminable agony to a blessed close.

"Brother," she said, smiling gaily down the table to where Theo sat woodenly beside Elpis, who was equally pale faced and silent. "Your wife knows much of war horses, I believe. Would you and Lælia like to see the one recently gifted to Wittiza?" Fluttering her eyelashes at Egica, she said breathlessly, "We can leave, can we not, dear *reiks*? You have no need for children at your table, do you?"

Lælia was already gathering herself to rise when Egica, who had imbibed a great deal of wine, uncharacteristically smiled at Egilona and said in an almost avuncular tone, "In a moment, yes, child, you may. But before you go, I have an announcement to make."

Inwardly cursing, Lælia forced herself to sit back in her seat as the eyes of the assembled nobles turned expectantly toward the royal table.

"As many of you acknowledged with your recent generous gifts, our son, Wittiza, recently celebrated his fourteenth birthday." Egica bowed his head briefly at the ripple of applause. "In accordance with the laws of our revered forefathers, Wittiza is now of age to sit beneath the votive crown and lead the proud nation of Spania."

There was a muted murmur at this, though not nearly, Lælia thought sourly, the outcry there would have been prior to the rebellion. Every nobleman present knew that kings were elected by council and clergy. Inheritance was not the Gothic way, and Wittiza had no more right to sit on his father's throne than any other amongst those gathered.

"Of course, should the situation arise when a king is needed, such matters are for the council of seniores and our esteemed clergy to decide," Egica went on, appeasing the murmurers somewhat. "In the intervening time, however, I wish to take this opportunity to announce that in months to come, I will ask Archbishop Felix to formalise my son's role by appointing him co-ruler at my side, for so long as I might humbly serve our great nation."

Co-ruler. Across the tables Lælia unconsciously sought Athanagild's eyes. Her brother-in-law was seated at the far end of the hall. He was not looking at her, Lælia saw, but at Laurentius, his face grim. His expression was mirrored in others around the hall. Co-rulership was not unheard of; it had, in fact, been used by Chindasuinth with his own eldest son, Reccesuinth, who had then been elected unopposed at his father's death. But Reccesuinth was a grown man, a proven warrior already approaching senior years when his father made him co-ruler. Wittiza was a spoiled child who had never seen anything more challenging than a practice ring. Appointing him co-ruler was a blatant bid for succession by lineage, and an open provocation to the established order.

But after the recent spate of brutal punishments and executions, there was not a man present in the room who dared challenge the king, and so they lifted their cups and toasted their *reiks* and *princeps*, and though it tasted like sawdust in her mouth, Lælia said the words with them and even pretended to drink, for she could feel Oppa's eyes upon her still and would not show him her inner turmoil – not if it made her sick to do so.

Then she followed Egilona from the hall, walking behind the rigid, tense shoulders of her husband.

Following him.

For all the world, she thought bitterly, *like any other obedient wife.*

* * *

Lælia waited until the door had closed on their bedchamber before she allowed her mask to finally slip. Untying the cords that bound her cloak, she noticed with a certain detached pride that her fingers were completely steady. She and Theo had walked from the palace in silence, inches of space between them, and now he stood at a distance from her, across the room, by the door. He had not removed his own cloak, nor bent to untie the lacings on his boots. Lælia had left Jadis outside the bedchamber. She did not trust either her own emotions, or Jadis's reaction to them.

"That was the girl you lay with, in our time apart." Lælia turned to face him. His earlier fury had receded, the scarred face grim and closed in a way she had not ever imagined seeing when he looked at her. "Do you deny it?"

"No." The word was hard and final. At least, Lælia thought, he did not insult her by lying.

"You said she had no place in your heart. That she never did." Carefully she untied her cloak and laid it over the end of the bed. "It did not seem, tonight, that your heart was untouched, Theo. It seemed to me – and to the rest of the court – that at one time, at least, that girl occupied a very large place in your heart. A place that still bears scars from her actions. Or did I misunderstand the moment when you accused her of betrayal? Or, perhaps, the one where you saved her sister?" She looked around the room as if searching for something. "Where is the sister, now that we speak of it? Pelagia, I believe you called her. Is she also here, in Toletum, hidden away, another piece to be sprung upon me before the ladies of the Toletum court, when I least expect it?"

She had planned to keep her voice emotionless, but by the time she had finished Lælia's hands were clenched as tightly as they had been in court, heat burned her cheeks, and though her voice did not shake, it had sped up, her articulation low, hard, and unmistakably furious.

"I did not know Elpis was here. I would never have seen you subjected to such humiliation –"

"Humiliation?" Lælia took a step toward him, fury rippling through her body like fire. "You think me small enough to be humiliated by a creature such as *Lady Elpis*?" She felt a stab of savage satisfaction at Theo's frown of confusion as he watched her. "I do not care that you take a hundred whores, Theo. I care even less for what the fools at court think of me, or of you, for that matter. I am not one of those fine court ladies, Theo. I do not require your lies, nor your protection. But I do require honesty. So I will ask you, now, for the truth. Why does Oppa have Elpis? Did you save her sister, and if so, why? Where is she? What games do you and Oppa play that you have not told me of?"

Theo drew a sharp breath, but his eyes were opaque, something inside him hidden from her, and Lælia again felt the crumbling within, the erosion of a part of her she had hitherto thought indestructible.

"Elpis was Oppa's creature." His voice was flat and expressionless, his eyes giving nothing away. "Not at the beginning, perhaps, but when I ended our… arrangement, and for a time before that, I believe, she took his coin, though I did not know it. On the final night in Sebastopolis, Oppa took Elpis's sister, Pelagia. A child who did, indeed, remind me of my own sister. A child I cared about as one would a sister. I knew what Oppa was…" His voice broke off and for a moment the iron composure slipped, his head dropping and shaking. "I knew what Oppa was capable of," he muttered. "I remembered that day in the woods, with you…"

"I know what you remembered. I may not bear his scars, but I know the feel of his whip on my skin." Lælia heard the snarl in her voice, was powerless to soften it. "Go on."

"But you do not know." There was an edge to Theo's voice, a darkness, that momentarily halted her. "Oppa's depravity has grown, Lælia. Become the lure by which he draws other men to him. In Sebastopolis he kept entire stables of children such as Pelagia, to serve those who desired such things. Pelagia only narrowly escaped being one of them. The unfortunate result of that was Oppa recognising her value as a piece in his game."

Lælia did not answer, but she tensed at the picture his words painted.

Theo went on: "Elpis made certain I came for them, but she did so at Oppa's bidding. We walked into an ambush. Elpis wanted to see me punished for slighting her and, I believe, thought Oppa would spare both her and her sister. Of course, Oppa cares nothing for anyone who cannot serve him. He ordered Elpis to leave, and then he told me that Pelagia reminded him of you, of that day in the woods. That he intended to – enjoy Pelagia – all the way back to Spania.

He said it with a whip in his hand and Pelagia bound to a chair. He wanted me to watch." His mouth twisted in distaste.

Despite her anger, Lælia found herself caught in the scene, her eyes on his face as he continued.

"Yosef and the rest of my men arrived at that point. In the fight that followed, Oppa fled, taking Elpis with him, and my men and I were imprisoned by Arab soldiers. I thought Oppa had taken Pelagia also. It was only when we sailed from Sebastopolis, and our captors were revealed as Dahiya's sons, Yosef's friends, that I discovered Pelagia had been smuggled aboard the dromon and sailed with us. When we reached Septem, I left her in the care of Ilyan's palace women." This time his twisted smile contained a certain wry humour. "Courtesans are something Pelagia understands well. The women's quarters in Ilyan's palace are her natural home." He met Lælia's eyes and the smile faded. "Neither Pelagia nor I thought Elpis still alive. Oppa is not known for his mercy. I had thought Elpis either long dead, or abandoned in a distant port when Oppa tired of her."

Lælia frowned at him. "And it did not bother you, that this woman, with whom you had lain, the sister of a child you obviously care about, was lost, or abandoned?"

"Elpis betrayed us, Lælia." Theo's voice was quiet. "Not just me, but her own sister, also. Good men died for her that day. Honourable men, who stayed to rescue Elpis and her sister, because they knew Oppa for what he is and did not wish to see any woman or child suffer at his hands. Elpis knew the manner of men who fought with me. She knew they would not stand aside whilst her sister – a favourite of the soldiers who live to see a child's smile, something that might remind them of the children they have left behind – was held by a man they universally despised. Elpis knew all that – and still she did not care. She led us into an ambush knowing we would die, and many did. She traded her own sister for Oppa's word that Pelagia would be safe. And even after he broke it, still she sits beside him, his creature." His face twisted in disgust.

"So when you ask me if I cared that she was lost, or perhaps dead, my honest answer is no, Lælia. I did not care if Elpis was dead. And if I gave it any thought at all, I hoped she was dead, simply because I would not wish Oppa's depravity upon any human, and particularly upon any woman. But had I known, for a single moment, that Oppa would bring her here, to Spania…" His voice roughened and though he did not look away, colour flooded his face, and his eyes on Lælia's own were dark with shame. "I would have done anything to spare you what occurred tonight," he said simply. "I do not expect your forgiveness. I certainly do not deserve it. But I would have you know that I was, at least, honest in what I said to you that night. Elpis has no place in my heart. She never did. That is the very reason she hates me so much, the reason she wished for revenge."

"Elpis does not hate you, Theo." Lælia felt suddenly flattened with exhaustion, barely able to stand. "She loves you. I expect that is why she remains with Oppa: because she hoped it would bring her back to your side. She loves you still, and that makes her very dangerous."

She saw his eyes narrow, and she held up her hand when he would have spoken. "Is that all, Theo?"

Theo frowned. "What do you mean?"

Lælia gestured impatiently. "Is that the only story between the three of you?"

Something passed over Theo's face, a shadow, there and gone, but enough. Lælia stepped closer. "Did something else happen between the three of you, over there? Are there other secrets that I might one day be forced to face?" She watched him carefully, her eyes searching the dark shadows behind his eyes, wondering, for the first time, if they held more than just hard memories of a difficult past. "Why does Oppa still seek to goad you?" she asked softly. "Why, if you have acquiesced to all his demands, kept his secrets from the court, never denounced him for attacking the fleet, or Illiberis – after all that, Theo, why does Oppa bring your whore to court and seek to humiliate us both?"

"You know the games he plays." Theo's rejoinder was harsh and fast, but he turned away as he spoke, and Lælia felt a twinge of unease.

"Yes, I know the games he plays. I, too, have been forced to play them with him, more than once. But do you know what I have learned from those games, Theo?" She waited until he was looking at her again before she continued. "I learned that Oppa never plays a game unless there is something he wishes to win. So my question is: what was the purpose of his game tonight? What does Oppa still want from us?"

Theo met her eyes, but his own were a hard, implacable green, utterly unreadable, and Lælia, staring at the bland mask, thought she had never expected to find herself on the other side of it. Involuntarily her hand went up to his cheek, touching it fleetingly. "Let me in, Theo," she whispered, searching his face. "Whatever it is Oppa wants from you, tell me, and we will fight it together. Even if that means running." This time when she reached for his face she held it between her hands, forcing him to look at her, and for a moment she thought she saw something behind the glacial mask in his eyes begin to soften. "I will run with you, Theo, if it comes to that, and never once look back. All that matters to me – all that has ever mattered to me – is Illiberis, and you. The rest is nothing but smoke. If we must raise this child in a foreign court, swap horses for camels, and give our allegiance to Ilyan until we can raise an army of our own, then that is what we will do. But we have come too far, endured too much, to let Oppa's games rule our lives for a moment more."

Too late, she felt the rigidity of his jaw under her hands, saw the softness flee his eyes, and the mask come down once more. "What?" she whispered, her hands falling away. "What did I say?"

Then Theo's arms were around her, his large hands gentling her, soothing, stroking her hair, and he was murmuring words of comfort against her ear that felt like stones on her heart. "You said nothing wrong," he murmured. "And I wish the answer to your question were simple, Lælia, but it isn't. Oppa and I have been playing at this game for years now, across seas and battles I can't begin to explain. He played Elpis tonight for the same reason he holds Egilona, or plays my benefactor at court: to ensure I know it is he who holds the power now. No more, no less." It was his turn to take her face in his own hands. "Oppa needs me for his own stature at court, Lælia. He wants me doing his bidding, and for other men to know I do as he wills. And frustrating as it might be, if it means you stay alive, and our child is born safe" – he covered her belly with a warm, reassuring hand – "then it is a small price. And I would never ask you to flee, Lælia, nor take you from your home and go into a foreign land, heavy with child. No man of honour would ever willingly do such a thing."

For a moment Lælia wanted to argue, to tell him that she would run a thousand times, even from Illiberis, if she must, and happily, if it meant she never had to sit across a table from Oppa Egicason again. But then she thought of all Theo had suffered to come back to her, the fact that he was unexpectedly now heir to Aurariola only because his brother had been killed trying to save Illiberis, and she chastised herself for so lightly dismissing his sacrifice. She had a sudden recollection of Elpis's spiteful, hard face, and the emotions she felt hardened into a savage wave of fury toward the girl who had dared to betray Theo. Pulling back, she looked up into Theo's face.

"Do you know where Oppa keeps his whores?"

Theo frowned. "Why would you ask such a thing?"

"Because," she said, her voice fierce, "I want you to go there. Tonight. I want you to face Elpis. Face them both."

"You can't mean that." Theo shook his head, searching

her eyes. "What if someone saw me? After tonight, the entire court will already be talking –"

"I *want* them to see you. And let them talk." Lælia felt anger rise in her with savage satisfaction. "Do you think I care what they say? I want you to storm into whatever damnable hole Oppa hides his dirty secrets in and make a scene that will be whispered in every alley corner and courtly salon come tomorrow. I want every nobleman in Toletum to know that we aren't afraid of Oppa, or of any whore he brings to court." She stared at him, letting him see her anger, and her pride. "If we were not married," she said fiercely, "and if I did not carry your child, I would walk in there myself, and to hell with the Toletum court. I would face that fool of a girl down and make her regret every moment she dared touch you, only to betray you. I do not hate her for lying with you," she said, taking Theo's face between her hands again. "Once, I was even grateful to her, for ensuring you were not lonely. But lying *to* you? Betraying you?" Righteous anger flooded her heart. "That, I will never forgive. And nor should you, Theo." Stepping back, she smiled at him. "So go. Face down Oppa, and make sure he knows that if he should ever dare humiliate either of us like that again, he will die – and his whore with him."

19

OPPA

JUNE, AD 693

Toletum, Spania
Toledo, Spain

Oppa's brothel was set along the river, at something of a distance from any other establishment. It had large gardens bound by thick stone walls, and the domus itself offered no windows through which men might accidentally gain a glimpse of what lay beyond. Oppa had learned much from his years abroad. The Toletum establishment was the pinnacle of those experiences, a place offering both the greatest luxury and the most exotic wares of any in Toletum. Girls arrived weekly from distant ports, where they had been recruited with whispers of coin greater than any they might earn servicing sailors on a dock. In a land that had long been closed to foreigners, Oppa's brothel offered men a glimpse of the world beyond Spania – and delights of the flesh that, if known, would chill the marrow of the priests who held Spania so tightly in their conservative grasp.

"I have never come this way before." Wittiza looked

around the darkened streets a little nervously. "I wish you had allowed Roderic and Pelayo to accompany us."

Oppa hid his contempt behind a bland smile. "In time, you will bring your companions here and bestow upon them favours that will bind them even closer to your side. But first, you must become master of the darkness yourself, at home amongst men and scenes other men shy from. Like this, you can own those you wish to keep by your side, anticipating their needs before they themselves know them. In this way you will bind them with their own secrets, keeping them loyal to you above all others. Such is the way power works, brother. And tonight is your first lesson."

They had arrived at a wooden door in the wall that marked the entrance. Oppa handed their horses to his man and ushered Wittiza into the darkened gardens, where the soft sounds of girlish laughter were muffled by thick foliage and the men who held them close. Wittiza stumbled along in Oppa's wake, staring about him with wide eyes, trying to make out the shapes in the darkness. "Is Clotilde here?" he asked, and ahead of him, Oppa smiled into the darkness.

"I have a treat for you tonight that will make Clotilde no more than a distant memory, brother." Leading Wittiza around to a rear entrance, he turned to the boy. "When you visit this place – and you may, Wittiza, any time you choose – always you will enter by this door. Like this, men will know you were here, but they will never be certain when you come, nor how you arrive. A prince should never be predictable, nor common. This door is yours only and will always be manned by loyal men who are discreet."

Men loyal to me. Oppa smiled to himself. Pushing open the door, he nodded at the man there, then led his brother down a stone passageway that led to a wide room with a generous balcony beneath which the River Tagus moved on its slow path. Oil lamps flickered in filigree sconces on the stone wall. The centrepiece of the room was a tremendous bed Oppa had commissioned from Toletum's finest carpenter. It was wide enough to comfortably accommodate half a dozen bodies with room to spare. The posts at each corner were carved with carnal scenes that would do a Roman bathhouse proud, the two mattresses were stuffed with Oppa's own blend of down and feathers, and the entirety was covered with sheets of fine linen.

Wittiza looked around the room, his face visibly falling when he saw it was empty.

"Before I introduce you to tonight's delights of the flesh," Oppa murmured, moving to a marble side table, "I have brought you another treat – one I came across in Anatolia, carried by merchants from the distant east, and almost impossible to acquire here. I brought this back especially for you to try, my brother, and have a limited supply I am happy to share with you, should you take a liking to it." Watched by Wittiza's curious eyes, Oppa opened a small pouch and poured some seeds into a bowl. "They come from a poppy grown in lands to the east," he said as he ground them up. "Smoking the powder will enhance your pleasure." Packing the brown substance into a pipe, he lit it and passed it to his brother.

Wittiza inhaled the smoke then coughed violently. Oppa smiled. "All do that, on the first inhalation. Try again."

Wittiza did, holding the smoke in his lungs this time, as Oppa instructed. Oppa repacked the pipe and the boy inhaled again. "That is enough," Oppa said, taking the pipe away. "Too much, and your pleasure will be lost in dreams."

"I feel nothing," Wittiza said, frowning.

Oppa handed him a cup of wine. "You will."

Not half the cup was gone before Wittiza's eyes became distant, his face slack. Oppa, seeing the smoke dream begin to take, murmured an order to the serving girl and quietly withdrew into the shadows. Moments later, the door opened, and two veiled women entered, their bodies swathed in layers of flimsy cloth that did little to cover the ripe curves beneath. Slowly they began to move in a seductive dance, their hands roaming intimately over each other.

The shadows had grown long indeed, and the room heady with smoke, when the veil of one of the women dropped, to reveal Elpis's face. By that time, Wittiza was naked and plump on the bed, so astonished at his fortune and lost in his smoke dream that he did not notice when Oppa slipped silently from the room.

It had been altogether a remarkably successful evening, Oppa reflected as he made his way back to the main room of his brothel, an airy expanse with a dozen small alcoves in which men lounged, women draped over them. Pouring himself a cup of wine, he cast a practised eye over the various clients, making mental notes of which man liked what, who drank more, who was free with his coin, as at the same time he replayed the scenes from earlier that night, when Theo had first seen Elpis's face.

At the recollection of the stark shock in the other man's eyes, Oppa felt a surge of visceral excitement that no touch from a woman could ever rouse in him. No matter how Lælia had tried to hide it, he had seen in her face, too, the recognition of what Elpis had once meant to her husband. Oppa sipped his wine slowly, savouring the taste as he did the memory of Theo and Lælia's mutual hurt and fury. It had been impressive, he could admit, the way in which they had both, in their separate ways, managed the situation. But he would dearly have loved to have been lurking in the shadows of their bedchamber, he thought, when they had closed the door behind them. Oppa thought he would have given half the coin in his very full coffers to have heard that particular exchange.

So lost was he in imagining what might have passed between Theudemir of Aurariola and his wife that Oppa did not notice the front door opening until a low, furious voice addressed his back: "Oppa Egicason."

Smiling to himself, Oppa tossed off the wine, composed his features into polite disinterest, and turned around. "Why, Theudemir of Aurariola," he said, loudly enough to be heard by several of the clients present. "I did wonder when you would come in search of your old friend. Although, it pains me to tell you, she is at present servicing my younger brother, Wittiza. Elpis's tastes, it seems, have grown rather more expensive since you tumbled her in a Sebastopolis whorehouse." His words drew a murmur of laughter from the surrounding alcoves. Oppa stepped forward, smiling. "I take it your wife no longer wishes to enjoy your presence in her bed." He clicked his tongue remonstratively. "It is never wise, my old friend, to mix one's wife and one's whores. A lesson learned by all noblemen, in time. Take tonight as your first instruction."

Theo's face was still as carved marble. Only his eyes stirred, glittering a hard, brilliant green that sent a thrill of answering savagery through Oppa. When Theo spoke, there was no mistaking the lethal menace in his low tone that nonetheless carried clearly to every ear in the salon. "My wife," he said, placing a faint emphasis on the word, "is not so feeble as to find your whores offensive, Oppa Egicason. Though she did comment that it seems a shame that with all your coin, you cannot yet afford to buy one untouched by other men." There was a low ripple of uncomfortable laughter as men stared eagerly between them, waiting for the next insult. Oppa felt a familiar, corrosive anger curdling within but was also so taken aback by Theo's mode of attack that he found himself oddly frozen.

"My wife did speak of coming to see you herself," Theo said, again loudly enough to be clearly heard. "And we both know she is more than capable of getting past your guards, Oppa. Even of putting a knife through your throat, should she choose." The murmur of conversation had stopped entirely, every eye in the room utterly fixated on the exchange. Theo lowered his voice to a lethal hiss. "We both know it would not be the first time she has bested you, Oppa Egicason. Would you like me to draw a picture for the men in this room of the last time she held a sword to your throat?" His eyebrows raised, and he looked around, holding one set of eyes after another. "He does not like to speak of such things, you see," he said, in a conversational tone. "No matter the fine words he uses at court, Oppa's only successful battles are waged in places like this" – he gestured at the ornate furnishings contemptuously – "and with whores as his weapons." He stepped closer to Oppa, lowering his voice. "If you thought the Lady of Illiberis would be humiliated by a fool such as Elpis, then you have learned nothing from your encounters with my wife."

For a moment the years slipped away, and Oppa faced Theo across the wooden board of a slaver's dromon, the tails of his whip slick with Theo's blood. *Even now, you dare taunt me… even as I hold the thin rope of your life in my hands…*

Theo, staring at him with that same glittering, strange smile he did now: *You can take my life… It matters not at all. Lælia will never have you. She is mine. She will always be mine…*

And then, barely fourmonths ago, when he had found himself lying in the dirt, Lælia's sword at his neck, her voice contemptuous: *Let him go. He's not worth it…*

"That's right," hissed Theo, his face so close Oppa could see the shards of ice in his eyes. "Do you remember how it felt, that day, Oppa? Do you think any petty display at court can ever remove the taste of my wife's steel from your mouth?"

Oppa stared at him, not trusting himself to speak, but not backing down, either. He was given a brief reprieve by a high, thin voice, saying tremulously from the doorway, "Theo? They said you were here – that you came for me…"

Theo did not move, his eyes not wavering from Oppa's face as he said, in a sardonic voice that carried clearly across the room, "I came to give you news of your sister, Lady Elpis." He put just enough emphasis on the title to bring colour to her face, and a ripple of nervous laughter spread through the salon. "She is in Septem, where she is being raised by the concubines of Ilyan's court."

"Concubines?" Elpis's voice wavered.

"You have no need to fear." Theo's smile was hard and unpleasant. "Unlike your current benefactor, Ilyan does not deal in children. Pelagia is safe." He turned his head, staring at Elpis with eyes as hard as flint. "I shall ensure she knows you live – though I doubt, after your betrayal nearly cost her life, that she will much care."

Elpis gave a low cry, but she had already been forgotten by the two men, though the exchange had given Oppa time to collect himself. He had moved away from Theo, and when he spoke now, he was pleased to hear his voice did not shake.

"This is the problem with soldiers," he said mildly, smiling easily around the room. "They lack humour. They are so *honourable*, are they not?" The watchers laughed obediently, but Oppa, who knew better than most the mood of a room, knew it was too late to mend the damage done. "Perhaps, Theudemir," he said, inclining his head for all the world as if he had invited the man into his home, "now that we have dispensed with the business of whores and wives, you might join me for a glass of good wine, so we can discuss matters of state in private?"

Theo's lips curled. Oppa thought he might stalk from the room, and for a brief moment he found himself wondering what would happen between them, then; but Theo, clearly weighing the room and knowing he had won at least a temporary victory, nodded curtly. Before he left the room, however, he turned back to Elpis. "You will never address my wife again," he said coldly. "Should you go near her, I will kill you myself – for her honour, and for that of the good men who died that night to save you."

Had Oppa any capacity for pity, he might have felt it at the sight of Elpis's pale, shattered eyes as they watched Theo walk from the room.

* * *

Oppa led them down a passageway, opening a heavy door and ushering Theo inside with exaggerated courtesy. The room was his own, an oasis of leather and stone quite distinct from the overly sensual silks of the outer chamber. "Wine?" He reached for the jug on the sideboard and poured himself a rather large cup, proud that his hand didn't shake. "No? It is very good, I assure you." He tossed it off in one swallow, welcoming its heat with uncharacteristic relief. Oppa walked across to the fireplace. Leaning on the mantle, he stared into the flames.

"Have you forgotten the parchment I hold?"

When Theo didn't answer, Oppa pushed a log with his foot, leaving it in the fire long enough to feel the sting of the flames through the leather. "You should think carefully about publicly insulting the man who holds proof of your deceit."

"You have Illiberis now."

Oppa felt an odd thrill at Theo's flat tone.

"We both know I cannot undo what is done. But it is me you control with that parchment, Oppa. Not Lælia." Oppa heard the shift in the air as Theo took a step toward him, and he had to exert every ounce of self-control not to flinch. "If you ever dare humiliate my wife again as you did tonight," said Theo, his voice shaking with fury, "I will kill you, Oppa, and take what comes next."

"Such loyalty." Oppa took a leisurely sip of wine, trying to ignore the sudden rush of adrenaline through his veins. "Such theatrics. And yet you are right in one thing: your wife is far more difficult to control than you, Theo."

Turning to face Theo's rigid figure, Oppa tapped one finger against his wine cup thoughtfully. "I realised something at court tonight, Theo. In some ways, I know your wife better even than you." Seeing Theo go rigid with fury, Oppa laughed softly. "You were right when you said she had bested me before. And not just the day of your return, Theo. You forget that in the years you were away, your wife and I fought our own battles, back here in Spania.

"She slipped into my room as I slept, once. To steal back the contract of betrothal between you and her. Can you believe that?" He shook his head, ostensibly lost in his thoughts, though in reality his every nerve was attuned to Theo's proximity. "She could have killed me, that night. I think on it, sometimes. Did she pause for long, at my bedside? Did she look down on my sleeping figure and consider driving it through?" He turned and met Theo's eyes, and despite the other's composure, he saw the turbulence in the green depths. "You didn't know that," he said slowly. "Did you, Theo? She never told you about that night. I do not wonder at it; I am unsure that she ever disclosed to anyone that it was she, herself, who retrieved the contract. She is not one to boast of her triumphs, after all. It is one of the qualities I have learned to admire in her. No deed matters to her." He paused, allowing a small smile to play upon his mouth as he held Theo's eyes. "Not," he said softly, "if that deed is done in the service of Illiberis." He sipped his wine deliberately, allowing his words to sink in. "That is why she agreed to marry you in the beginning, is it not? It is the same reason, I think, that she did not kill me that night – nor, though God alone knows she wanted to, the day she had me at sword point at Illiberis. Because this is what I know of your wife, Theudemir. With every breath she takes, Lælia has only one purpose: to serve Illiberis. She is bound to it, body and soul. Perhaps, though I daresay it is hard for you to hear, more even than she is bound to you." He did not move toward Theo; he did not need to. Every fibre of the man's being was focused on him, Theo's burning eyes searing straight into Oppa's own. "I think," said Oppa softly, "that you forgot the depth of that bond. I think the years away lessened your memory of Lælia's loyalty to her home.

"But whilst you were away, I was here, watching. I saw your wife's loyalty to her home. I lived it, Theo. I suffered for it." He smiled grimly. "And then" – he raised his wine cup – "I used it, Theo."

Theo's fists clenched hard enough to turn the knuckles white, but still he did not speak.

"The truth is," Oppa said, and now all trace of softness had gone from his tone, "you are just now beginning to understand the enormity of the betrayal your signature on that parchment represents. You are reminded every time you look at your wife that you signed away the one thing for which she has, over and again, risked her own life. No, Theo, I might not control Lælia, you are right. But you have done the one thing she never would: given me control over the two things she loves the most. And that, my old friend, is close enough."

Theo's face was stark white, his body taut as a drawn bow. Oppa saw the long-ago boy Theo had once been, staring him down despite the whip Oppa held. Saw him saying, *Lælia is mine.*

But now, Oppa thought with savage satisfaction, *you have, in your own way, given her to me – and you know it. Every time you lie with her, I will lie in the bed between you. And that is a far greater victory than any I might once have desired.*

He tossed off the wine cup in a single swallow, his eyes never leaving Theo's. "My priests in Illiberis tell me," he said lightly, "that the women of Illiberis have long adhered to a pagan tradition, of taking their newborn infants to caves for some arcane ritual. How will your wife feel, Theo, now that she is to bear a child of her own, knowing that you have deprived her of the chance to perform a ritual her family has kept alive for centuries?"

Oppa had known it was a step too far; perhaps part of him had simply wanted to know just how far Theo could be pushed.

Mention of his unborn child, Oppa realised as Theo lunged, was the tipping point.

But he had expected it, and Theo's steel fell on empty air as the door flew open and two burly guards crashed through. Oppa held up a hand, halting their raised sword arms.

"A misunderstanding," he said smoothly, smiling at Theo's

heaving chest and glittering eyes, "nothing more." He waited until Theo lowered his sword, however, before dismissing his guards with a curt gesture.

"They are both deaf," he said, shrugging. "I pierced their ears so that they watch but do not hear. It is safer."

"You are a monster." Theo's voice rasped like old metal.

"A crude term, but I will take it." Oppa's smile was gone as quickly as it had arrived. "But I am the monster that holds your future in my hands. I think we have finally established that."

Theo's eyes narrowed, but he did not answer.

"Of course I was aware of your wife's condition before it was made public tonight, Theudemir. Toletum belongs to me. I own the ears upon its streets, and more importantly, the whispers between its sheets. And what I hear from those whispers makes me quite certain that now is a good time for you to go to Hispalis and begin the work we agreed upon – that of restoring the fleet."

"Hispalis," Theo said flatly.

"Well, that is where the dromons lie, is it not?"

"Whilst Lælia goes to Aurariola."

"I have always thought your wife better suited to a rural environment than cities. Surely the coastal air is better for her condition than the foetid swamps of Hispalis?" Oppa's mouth curled. "That parchment is not the only piece I hold, Theudemir, as well you know. Your sister sleeps at this very moment under my father's roof."

Theo's fists curled again. "Egilona." The name fell into the room like a stone.

Oppa tilted his head in acknowledgement. "Do not mistake my father's indulgence for weakness. Your sister is held in his court as hostage. As such, she is a piece to be played at will, no matter how my brother might idolise her." He met Theo's furious eyes coldly. "Do not doubt my willingness to play that piece, Theo, nor my power to do so. Your sister's safety is entirely dependent on your actions." He paused for long enough to allow Theo to see the deadly intent behind his words. Then, with the unerring instincts that had led him to make a fortune from a bag of coin, friends in distant empires, and his father's court his own, Oppa played a hunch that until now had been no more than an itch at the back of his mind.

"Then," he said, watching Theo carefully, "there is the matter of your Persian friend. A friend, I might add, who lives still because I spoke for him. A courtesy I might withdraw at any moment." He had the satisfaction of seeing Theo's eyes narrow further. He paused, allowing a small smile to play over his lips. "Have you realised, yet, why it is that the Persian does not deny the charges against him, fight for his innocence? Who, I wonder, might be exposed if he did? Whose secrets might the Persian be prepared to die for?"

Seeing confusion shadow Theo's eyes, Oppa stepped back, satisfied with his handiwork. He was not yet entirely sure of his suspicions regarding the Persian, but so far, the whispers he had heard had been more than a little interesting. If he was correct, the Persian might prove to be his most valuable piece yet.

"Whatever game you play with Shukra," Theo said flatly, "I would advise you to play it with caution. You might be a monster, Oppa, but Shukra is a magician." He smiled coldly. "As for my sister, know this: should she ever come to harm at your hands, I will see you dead. Even if it means losing my own life."

"Such loyalty," Oppa repeated, smiling sardonically.

Theo's eyes flashed, but he did not rise to the bait, saying instead, "As for your desire to see me in Hispalis, I had planned to go there anyway, but only for so long as it takes me to rebuild the dromons and have them sailed around the coast to Cartago Nova, near Aurariola. The river at Hispalis is no place for dromons to rot, and no place from which to defend Spania's coastline."

Oppa shrugged. "An admirable plan. One of which I approve, Theudemir."

"Your approval," said Theo icily, "is the least of my concerns."

"It should be your greatest." Oppa eyed him, turning the cup in his hands. "The southern lords," said Oppa idly, "are less welcoming to their new neighbour than I might wish. I think you and I will both agree that I have been more than gracious in allowing you and your wife time to adjust to your new reality." Theo did not speak, just watched him, hostility coming from him in waves. "At some point in the coming months I will have the contract drawn up," said Oppa softly. "It will require both your names, as you well know, and the public concession these savages seem to require. There is no rush, of course. Such things take time. And I would not wish to cause you unnecessary domestic strain. Not when we have such – important – work to do together."

"Why?" This time when Theo looked at him, there was something different in his expression, a certain curiosity Oppa had not seen before. "Why are you so determined to establish a fleet in Spania – and to have me head it?" Theo asked bluntly. "All this – Illiberis, the parchment, your games at court – none of them are needed to make me head a fleet, Oppa. It is what I was trained to do. What I think is best for Spania. I would be doing it whether you blackmailed me or not. And as for the rest of it – your attack on the fleet, even your attack on Illiberis." His eyes on Oppa's were genuinely searching. "What do they matter now? The rebellion is over, and we both know it could not easily rise again. I can understand you wanting Illiberis, a base of your own. But you have it. Why wield the parchment over my head this way? Tell me what you want, Oppa, why you have this obsession with me, and with the fleet." He shook his head, staring at the wall beyond Oppa, over the mantlepiece. "If we agree on nothing else," he said quietly, "surely we can both at least acknowledge that the world we are facing will not be the same as the one in which we were children – or even, for that matter, the one we inhabit now. What is it that you think the future holds, Oppa? And what part do you expect to play in it – or expect me to play, for that matter?"

Oppa did not answer immediately. He sipped his wine, turning back to the fire to conceal his face from Theo's. It wasn't that he hadn't given a great deal of thought to those exact questions. It was that this conversation, standing here in a grand room he himself owned, speaking of the future of Spania with Theudemir of Aurariola, was so close to the fantasy he had only recently abandoned as to be deeply disquieting to him. Oppa did not want to see Theudemir of Aurariola as an ally. He would never allow himself to feel again the dangerous intoxication of hope; those boyish dreams had died amidst the filth and corruption of Sebastopolis.

"Tell me something, Theo." He spoke without meeting the other's eyes. "Do you believe the Arabs will one day threaten our shores?"

"You know that I believe it is possible." The answer came fast, and hard.

"Of course you do. That is why you signed that parchment. Why even if she asked you outright, you would not fight at your wife's side for her lands. Because you believe, as I do, that soon enough, such things as titles will not matter."

"We have already had this conversation. More than once." Theo's tone had hardened. "Back in Sebastopolis. Again in Corduba."

"Perhaps." This time Oppa met his eyes steadily. "But perhaps it is time we had it again, Theudemir." He put the wine cup carefully down on the table. "I have not risen to where I am without learning how to know a man's worth. You are heir to Aurariola, which has one of the most strategic ports in all of Spania. Far enough north that no attack can easily surprise it; the perfect place to train and harbour a defensive fleet." He looked at Theo meditatively. "You are a soldier, Theo, to your core. And a soldier will always be preparing for war, searching for one, or fighting one. No; there is no point in denying it. Whatever your skill at politics, Theo, it is at the head of a fighting fleet that you belong, and whether I might like it or not, you, with your uncle's support, are by far the best man to lead Spania's. But now we come to the point." He held up a finger, his mouth curling slightly as he held Theo's eyes. "Once, long ago, Theo, we agreed to be allies. I think, for a moment in time, that I even believed it. But I learned a lesson then that I will never forget: no alliance is iron clad unless one controls it." He smiled mirthlessly. "You ask me what part I expect to play in Spania's future, and what part I expect you to play. My answer is this: I expect to *be* Spania's future, Theudemir. And to do that, I need you as an ally. One that I might count upon."

Theo stared at him. "And you think," he said slowly, "that after Sebastopolis, I could ever see you as ally again?"

"Ah." This time, Oppa's smile touched even the darkness of his eyes. He raised his cup to Theo. "But this is where our game lies, Theo. It no longer matters how you see me. All that matters is that I can count on you to do as I bid. You would say that alliances are a lofty thing, forged in blood and loyalty. I would argue I hold proof that they are not."

For a long moment, they stared at one another across the room. Oppa wondered if Theo felt it, the moment when Spania itself teetered in the balance, their mutual future hanging by the thinnest thread. They had been here before, long ago. Back when he had thought there was a chance he and Theo might fight for Spania as equals.

Hope.

It was, Oppa knew, the most dangerous fault line in a man's heart, and the most lethal weapon he could wield over another.

And Oppa had already learned his lessons about hope.

That was why this time, he had left nothing to chance. It was time to remind Theo of that.

"You could, of course, tell Lælia the truth." He raised the cup to his lips, and the moment was broken. "But I do not think you will. Her allegiance, as I think you know, is not so easily for sale."

Before Theo threw the door open and stormed from the building, Oppa had the satisfaction of seeing something he had never thought to see in Theudemir of Aurariola's eyes: shame.

20

LETTER FROM SAFIA TO COUNT ILYAN
JUNE, AD 693

Toletum, Spania, to Septem, Mauretania
Toledo, Spain, to Ceuta, Morocco

My honoured father,

By now, I believe you will have welcomed to your court those who have recently fled Illiberis. You are ever better informed than any other man, so I am certain the warning I am about to give is unnecessary, but I would be remiss if I did not relay it.

Oppa has left Toletum, riding for Illiberis. He has taken Wittiza with him, ostensibly to see the harvest and meet his southern lords, but in reality, I believe, to bind him more closely. Oppa has many plans, in all of which Wittiza plays a central part. Illiberis is where those plans begin.

Despite being fully cognisant of the burgeoning Jewish rebellion in Septem, Oppa allowed the Jewish merchant, Yosef, to leave Spania unharmed. We both know Oppa is not a merciful man. He made the deci-sion consciously. Before they rode south, I heard Oppa tell Wittiza that Illiberis was important because, and I quote: "the Jews there are the greatest threat your rule will face; and already, they gather force against you." It is a story he has impressed upon Egica also, that the Jews gather in Septem, allied with their brothers in Garnata. It is the reason he gives for taking control of Illiberis, but I suspect there is more to his tenure there than either personal vengeance or a desire for land.

Illiberis is the most powerful latifundium so close to the coast — and to you, Father. Oppa is no friend to you, nor to Septem. He craves power alone. I believe he intends still to uncover the reasons behind Yosef's journey, and to profit from it. He intends to take any Jewish trade or wealth as his own, build a stronghold in the south, and cauterise Jewish power in Spania. The rulings of the Sixteenth Council against Jews are fertile ground upon which Oppa can sow the seeds of division, suspicion, and, ultimately, complete annihilation. He allowed the Garnata Jews who fought alongside Illiberis to flee to Septem, with Yosef. This is my warning, Father: the Jewish rebellion is as doomed to failure as was Sunifred's. At court, it is spoken of with open contempt. Spania is pious, and there is little love for the Jews amongst the nobility. Any actual armed rebellion by a Jewish army will be abruptly, and savagely, put down. Oppa has done much to fan the flames of paranoia. It serves his own interests to have the nobility aroused in righteous anger at the thought of foreign invasion, whilst he quietly goes about consolidating his own power within Spania.

Lælia has left Toletum for Aurariola. She left in a blaze of scandal, which I relay here only to give you the backdrop to the current dynamic. Oppa thought to humiliate Lælia by flaunting an old concubine of Theo's at court. He might have succeeded, had Theo not turned the tables by going to Oppa's whorehouse that same night, with Lælia's open blessing, it seems, and by all accounts, humiliating not only Oppa himself, but the concubine in question. Toletum talked of nothing else for days, and though the event may not have made the ladies of the court like Lælia any more than they ever have, they certainly have now a healthy respect for her.

But I watched all parties closely in the days following, and I suspect something else took place that night, something even darker. I believe there is division between Theudemir and Lælia, perhaps fed by Oppa, though I do not know how. Whereas Theudemir seems to believe that Aurariola will be their home, Lælia seems driven still by the ambition to recover Illiberis. She said as much to Egilona, though unthinkingly, I believe. In their final visit, Egilona asked Lælia how she felt about making Aurariola her home, the land her child will inherit. Lælia answered thus: "All women of my line are daughters of Illiberis, no matter where they might be born." It was an odd answer, one Egilona noted, as did I. Egilona later remarked to me that she believes the loss of Illiberis weighs heavily upon Lælia. She said she did not believe a woman raised to war, as Lælia has been, would ever be content to be merely the Lady of Aurariola, her brother's wife, mother to his heir. I believe her to be right in this. If Lælia rides to Aurariola, she does so only as a temporary measure, a place from which she can, perhaps, ally with the Jewish rebellion to take back Illiberis. Should she do so, Father, it would certainly mean her death, something that clearly weighs upon Theo, for he never so much as speaks the word Illiberis in her presence. But after watching him with Oppa, I suspect the latter knows all of the above and uses the knowledge to make Theudemir dance to his bidding. There is something insidious in their relationship, a power dynamic that is more than simply old enmity. If Theudemir is a formidable soldier of war, Oppa is a puppet master almost to rival you, Father. I beg you not to underestimate him — and that you mind warily any communication between Lælia and the rebellion.

Egilona, Roderic, and Pelayo are all now pawns in Oppa's games. He excluded them from this journey south with Wittiza. Recently he has taken pains to gradually separate Wittiza from his childhood companions, seducing Wittiza with women and, I believe, other pleasures. Do you recall the house maintained by the Persian merchant, deep at the back of the market, in Septem, by the bath house? Recently I passed Wittiza in the corridor after he returned from a night with Oppa, and his clothes smelled exactly as did those who once frequented that house. Slightly sweet, smoky. You told me that the merchant sold a substance that gave the visitor a fever dream. By Wittiza's glazed expression, and that scent, I suspect Oppa has given him that same substance. It is yet another way to gain the boy's trust, and Wittiza is weak minded to begin with.

Egilona smiled sweetly when Wittiza bid her goodbye. One of Liuvgoto's greatest lessons has been to allow men their whores, their plea-sures. She has taught Egilona to value her own body and powers of seduc-tion as her greatest assets in the coming years. Of course, Egilona needed no such instruction. In Wittiza's absence she could have commanded the attention of any of the young men at court. Instead she has chastely with-drawn, spending most of her time at the monastery, and in Liuvgoto's company. Those at court nod approvingly at her devotion and chaste habits. Egilona, meanwhile, studies both languages and the strategies of power with as much diligence as her admirers believe she studies prayer. Egilona knows that if she is to survive Oppa's games and rival his place in Wittiza's heart, she must become as Liuvgoto once was — the silent force behind the Crown, the one person Wittiza trusts and admires. Oppa may have him now, but Egilona will win him back, I believe. She is the most determined person I know. She knows Oppa intends Wittiza to be king, and that Oppa gets what he wants.

She intends to be Wittiza's queen.

It is an ambitious plan, but one, I believe, in which she will succeed. Already in addition to her native tongue she is fluent in Greek, Latin, and Frankish — and, recently, thanks to my own tutelage, her Arabic, too, progresses. She has listened closely to the stories told by her brother and her uncle, and she begins to take an interest in the shape of the Arabic caliphate. I explained my knowledge of it by saying my mother was once a concubine to a powerful Arab. Truth, you always taught me, is the best basis for any lie.

I leave you with a reiteration of my early warning: the Jewish rebellion is doomed. Of course you will do as you see fit, but as your daughter, I can only plead that you do not ally yourself with something I know can end only in disaster. Not even if that request comes from Lælia of Illiberis herself — for she no longer holds that title and, I fear, may never do so again.

Your loving daughter,
Safia

21

LÆLIA
JULY–SEPTEMBER, AD 693

Aurariola, Spania
Orihuela, Spain

My esteemed friend, Ilyan, Count of Septem,

It has been many months since I have had news of you, or from my friend, Yosef, whom I know lives now under your protection.

Perhaps he has informed you of the surrender of Illiberis. I do not wish you to believe I willingly relinquished my home, especially after the aid so generously given to me by Dahiya and her Riders. As a master strategist, you will understand that —

LÆLIA'S HAND PAUSED, the quill dripping ink on the blotter beside her. What, exactly, was it that she expected Ilyan to understand? In his place, would she understand, or even care, about Illiberis's fate? What was his place, now? Was he thinking of Spania, or of the Arabic armies? Was Ilyan even to be trusted? Turning instinctively to ask Theo his advice, Lælia remembered first that Theo was not there and then, in a darker moment, that even if he was, she could not ask his opinion. Not on this. Never once had Theo asked about her plans to regain her home, or offered his advice. It was an acknowledgement, Lælia felt, of the esteem in which he held her, a respect for her as the Lady of Illiberis. Lælia could not bear for him to guess at how inadequate she felt to assuming that responsibility, nor how her terror grew, with every day that passed, that her right to so much as call herself by that title was no longer.

Theo was a warrior, a commander who was respected by his men without question. Aside from those early days, when he had asked how she wished to proceed before he dealt with Oppa on her behalf, he had never consulted her again. His decisions were made independently. He neither asked her opinion, nor laid his burdens at her door, though she knew he thought often of the Arabic war he had left behind. She suspected he worried that it would come to Spania's shores, and that he tried to plan what he might do if it did. In the face of such greater concerns, it felt petty to think of Illiberis. His autonomy made Lælia ashamed of her own indecision, of her desire for his counsel or advice. Dahiya, she was certain, had never relied upon Apsimar's opinion before deciding her course.

Thus it was that no matter how desperately she might have wished to, Lælia had never allowed herself to ask for his help, even though she felt a measure of frustration when she considered that Illiberis was, after all, one of the strongest holdings in the south. She needed to get it back, she knew. Not only because it was her home, and every day without it felt bereft and lonely, but because one day, Spania might well need her there as much as and more than it needed Theo's dromons.

She had to find a way.

Unwelcome as it was, Lælia forced herself to contemplate her position from Ilyan's perspective.

Sunifred's rebellion had failed. Illiberis was now, or soon

would be, under the control of the king's own bastard son, who had returned to Spania more powerful than ever. The Jewish merchant whose journey Ilyan had supported was now in Ilyan's court, meaning that whatever trade he had established could now flow through Ilyan's own coffers without the need of Garnata, or Illiberis.

But he will still need allies in Spania to make it lucrative. Jewish allies, or Christians willing to deal with the Septem Jews and provide cover for their trade. Unwillingly Oppa's face swam before her eyes. In a thought just as unwelcome as her doubts regarding Ilyan, Lælia grimly forced herself to confront the ugly truth: that Oppa would be more than willing to trade with the devil himself, if he thought it would bring him coin and power.

Ilyan hates Oppa, she thought, trying to counter her fears.

Then she thought of Ilyan's rapid shifts, his labyrinthine network of spies and coin.

Ilyan will deal with anyone he must.

Throwing the quill onto the blotter with a savagery that broke the point, she thrust back her chair, remembering, too late, the size of her girth as she rose, her belly bumping the desk.

The babe stirred, and Lælia put a hand over it. *Be still, daughter. I promise you I will find a way to regain what I traded for our freedom.* But the thought was dark, filled with the shadows of doubt and inadequacy she could share with no-one. Jadis, watching her mistress carefully from where she had been lying on the floor in the sun, rose and padded silently over to twine around Lælia's legs. She rarely left Lælia's side, now.

"Lady." Lælia turned to find Silas's dark bulk filling the doorway.

"Silas." She did not have to force her smile. Barely a month in Aurariola had given her intrinsic respect for Silas's calm, courteous manner that nonetheless, Lælia knew, concealed a ruthless killer beneath. She had known such men before; Zdan, for example. Silas's gentleness with her did nothing to make her doubt his efficacy in battle. It also reinforced her belief in his absolute loyalty to Theo. She had returned to Aurariola alone, bearing Silas and Leofric the message that her husband, the man she knew they considered their leader, had been commanded by the king himself to ride to Hispalis, and that he had bid them stay and guard Aurariola. They all knew that Theo's meaning was that his men should guard her. Whilst Lælia equally knew she needed no such chaperonage, she would not humiliate Theo by refusing it; and anyway, in truth, she was touched by his care. Having so long been reliant upon her own resources, she found a certain secret joy in the comforting mantle of Theo's protection – though simultaneously feeling guilt in her weakness for doing so, as well as for taking enjoyment, by proxy, in the esteem in which men regarded him. Her grandfather Paulus had shunned Toletum and had a reputation for hard, often unwelcome, counsel. Theo, on the other hand, was almost universally liked and respected. Whether she had wanted it or not, Lælia had benefited from his standing in Toletum society – particularly after word had spread of the manner in which Theo had taken Oppa down in his own whorehouse.

The memory of those whispers still had the ability to make Lælia smile.

She appreciated Silas's diplomacy in keeping his guardianship of her to an almost indiscernible presence, even though she knew well he had mounted patrols at every border of the lands, including extensive lookouts along the coast. It was no less than she herself would have done. Did it matter if it was Silas who gave the orders? She, after all, was free to focus on what she knew should be the only true priority: finding a way to win back Illiberis.

"A messenger has come from the mountains north of Aurariola, the furthest of your lands, my lady." Lælia noticed the careful use of her title, the way Silas referred to the lands as hers. They weren't. Aurariola was Theo's, would always be his. She was as much a stranger to the coastal cliffs and broad fields of barley as Theo had been to the wild peaks of Illiberis when first he came. But she appreciated Silas's courtesy and besides, he was right. She was Theo's wife. So long as he was absent, she ruled Aurariola in his stead. She would do her duty, no matter how much the doing of it felt hollow here, rather than upon her own lands.

"What news did he bring?"

Silas cleared his throat and gave her a half smile. "She, lady, not he."

"Ah." Lælia's interest piqued, she said, "Go on."

"There is a dispute, between the woman and a neighbour, regarding the division of labour for the upcoming harvest. Both families work the same lands. Both women lost their husbands during the recent rebellion. Now the women and children are left to bring in the harvest, but where one family has three grown sons, our petitioner has only one, a child no more than eight, and an infant daughter. She says the other family claims a greater part of the harvest due to the fact that they will do the bulk of the work. The woman argues that without her customary portion, she and her children will not be able to pay their share to the latifundium, nor eat this coming winter."

"Hmph." Leofric had appeared at Silas's side, his face, as ever, set in dour lines, his arms crossed across the bulk of his chest as if to defend himself against an imaginary foe. "Perhaps this woman needs to learn that her lords are not a charity, hm? She cannot bring the harvest, she cannot eat it." He shrugged at his own infallible wisdom. Silas rolled his eyes. Lælia bit back a smile.

"Where is she now?"

"Waiting outside, my lady."

"Bring her in." Stepping around the desk, Lælia smoothed her woollen gown, feeling a certain nostalgia, not for the first time, for her old garb of trousers and linen shirt. The dress felt confining and clumsy, especially given her burgeoning waistline. Silas and Leofric stepped aside, admitting a small woman with a slightly dark complexion, a babe in her arms. "Lady."

She nodded to Lælia with respect, but not obsequy. She spoke Latin rather than Gothic, and that with a faint accent. Lælia looked at her with some interest.

"Are you from the tribes?"

The woman's chin came up. "My husband was a Goth," she said, with quiet dignity.

"You mistake me." Lælia came forward. "I am from Illiberis, descended from the tribes in those mountains, and proud to be so. I do not think less of you."

The woman's face lifted, studying Lælia curiously as she took in the lean mountain cat silent and still at her side. "Then, yes," she said cautiously. "I am from the tribes. But that does not lessen my claim to the harvest," she added hurriedly, her face colouring.

"Of course not." Lælia glanced out of the open window. The afternoon sun gleamed across fields of barley, and a breeze that carried a faint hint of the sea drifted through the window. Theo's family villa was lavish, rich with Roman mosaics, as was Illiberis, but nonetheless she had felt trapped from the moment she entered it. She felt a sudden, visceral urge to escape, not only the walls of the villa, but the role that came with them. "I will ride north with you," she said abruptly. "I do not know my husband's lands, nor the fields over which this dispute has arisen. I would see them, and meet with your neighbour, in order to find a just resolution."

"I would be honoured, Lady," said the woman, looking both surprised and gratified.

Silas and Leofric exchanged a worried glance.

"I don't think –"

"You shouldn't be riding –"

Their predictable objections were quelled by a fierce look from Lælia. "I don't need you to think for me," she addressed Silas, "nor you," she turned to Leofric, "to tell me what I can or cannot do. We will leave in the morning. Please make the necessary arrangements. You may all go," she added, smiling at the woman to soften the command in her tone. Leofric's brows drew down heavily, and Silas clicked his tongue in clear disapproval, but neither lingered to argue, especially when Jadis growled at them. Jadis tolerated Silas, even going so far as condescending, on occasion, to rub herself against his leg. Leofric, however, she held in high contempt, a sentiment Leofric returned. Shooting the cat a resentful glance, Leofric closed the door behind them. Lælia stood rigidly before the desk until they had gone, then she closed the door and moved restlessly to the open window, staring down at the strange lands that spread all the way to the sea, which was a white shimmer on the distant horizon.

It was beautiful country, bountiful and peaceful. Lælia felt that in other circumstances, she might have enjoyed being here, riding it at Theo's side, as he pointed out his childhood haunts.

But Theo was not here.

He had offered to ride here with her, before leaving for Hispalis. "I do not like you riding there alone," he had said, several days after their encounter with Elpis at court and his ensuing confrontation with Oppa. "I would see you settled there, and comfortable, before leaving you alone."

"But you will still go to Hispalis."

"The king has ordered me to go, Lælia. I am hardly in a position to argue when the sole reason I have been spared is that I might best serve him by training and commanding the fleet. I will bring the dromons around to the port at Cartago Nova near Aurariola, as soon as they are repaired — and believe me when I say they will be repaired faster than any dromons in the history of the Karabisianoi, if I have to whip the workmen myself." Despite his attempt at humour, there had been a grim cast to Theo's face that had not escaped Lælia.

"Is it Egica who ordered you?" She watched him carefully as she asked the question. "Or Oppa?"

Theo's mouth had tightened. "Does it matter? It is the latter who pulls the strings of the former, as well you know."

"Was it because of what happened? When you went to see him? Because I meant what I said, Theo. I will not allow him to dictate our future. I would run −"

"To Septem, and your beloved camels, in an instant. Yes, I know." His smile had taken the sting out of his words, as had his large hand on hers. "You haven't suffered for my actions?" he'd asked, his smile fading. "Have the ladies of the court said something to upset you?"

"I told you." Lælia had waved him off impatiently. "I care about you, and Illiberis. The rest is…" She waved her hand in a spiral, and Theo grinned.

"Smoke," he supplied. "I recall."

"Exactly." Lælia had returned his smile. "But as for your encounter with Oppa − no, I have not suffered for that. If anything, quite the opposite. It is, I understand, quite unusual for a man of the nobility to prefer his wife's bed to that of a concubine." She had raised her eyebrows at him and had the gratification of seeing his eyes darken, his hand close on hers as he drew her close, his arms closing about her. "Especially when the wife in question is carrying his daughter."

"You seem very convinced our child is a girl."

"Of course it's a girl." She had smiled up at him, letting him see the wild places inside her, the part of her soul only he had ever laid claim to. "Why would I win back my home," she murmured, as she leaned forward to claim his mouth with her own, "only to give it to a man? Illiberis belongs to women − and so a daughter we will have."

Such small comments were her own way of raising the topic of her home. Always, when she did, she watched him from the corner of her eye. Waited, for something, anything, that would convey Theo's thoughts on the topic to her. But as ever, the mask concealing his thoughts had fallen, and he had simply pulled her against his chest with a faint smile. She had rested there, feeling the uneven tripping of her heart, hoping against hope he might ask what she intended, wondering if he, too, was considering what to say.

But when he had spoken again there was a catch in his voice, and as his lips moved against her hair, she realised his thoughts were fixed upon her, rather than Illiberis. "I can't bear to leave you." Despite her disappointment that yet again, the moment was gone, Lælia relished the rare moment of vulnerability, and she smiled against his chest before pulling back to look at him.

"But you are already thinking about your dromons, Theo. Don't lie," she said laughingly when he began to protest. "I can see it in your eyes. You can't wait to get your hands on those rotting timbers any more than I can to ride out of these cursed city streets."

"Lælia." His smile had faded. "About what happened – with Elpis, and Oppa –"

"No." Lælia had shaken her head, put a hand over his mouth when Theo would have gone on. "Elpis betrayed you, Theo. She lay with you, and then she betrayed you. I can forgive her lying with you. Betrayal, though – as I already told you, that, I do not forgive. Not from anyone. But particularly not from someone who loves you." Theo's face had whitened at that, and Lælia had felt a savage rush of fury toward the girl who had toyed with his honour in such a careless manner. The days after the feast at court had brought clarity to her thoughts, and understanding. Theo had not lied to her, had never lied to her. He had lain with a woman who had no honour, and what man, Lælia thought with an inward smile, could not be accused of the same crime? No; Theo was not to be held accountable for Elpis's lack of honour, nor made to pay for Oppa's manipulations. "If we allow Oppa to enter our marriage bed," she had murmured to Theo, "then he has won more than Illiberis. And I will not give him that, Theo. I will not give any piece of our life to him that he cannot physically take, no matter how many whores he parades at court. Oppa might pull many strings – but our hearts, those remain our own. And my heart," she had whispered fiercely as she drew

Theo toward the bed, "belongs to you, Theo. As it always has."

A soft gust of coastal breeze brought her back to the present, and Lælia turned away from the window, aware of the heat on her face and between her legs, the almost ever-present longing for Theo. Yes, she had told him to go to Hispalis. But that did not mean she liked it.

She did not like it. Not at all.

* * *

IT WAS DAWN the next morning, and the horses were almost packed to leave on Lælia's journey north, when Tosius arrived.

"You startled me!" Lælia swung around when he said her name. She was in her bedchamber, packing the last of her belongings into the roll she would tie to the packhorse. Tosius did not smile.

"You grow careless, *dauhter*, in a time when you should be vigilant."

"Why vigilant?" Lælia studied the ancient lines of his face. "What news do you bring, Tosius?"

"The herd is safe." Tosius moved into the room, glancing back to ensure the door behind him was fast closed. "But men came from the north. Illiberis is gone, *dauhter*. Gratimo rides even now with your belongings."

Even though she had known it was coming, even if she had tacitly given her agreement, still the words fell like stones upon Lælia's heart. She clutched the desk behind her, willing herself to remain upright. "Who?" she whispered, staring at Tosius. "Who came to take it? Was it Oppa?"

"*Ne*." Tosius did not flinch from her questions. "He sent a Gothic dog, Ulric. A tame priest." Tosius's expression was contemptuous. Father Iohannes, the previous priest, had been untamed enough to actually win the respect, if not the faith, of the tribes. He had ridden into their villages at Acantha's side and helped her in caring for their ill, turning a blind eye to the rock cairns by the river and the sound of drums beneath a full moon. Father Iohannes, Lælia had sometimes suspected, harboured a secret fascination for tribal lore. Certainly, he was wild enough to be considered by Tosius untamed, something the tribes would ever admire. Clearly this Ulric was the diametric opposite of Iohannes. Recalling the hard-faced priests who had accompanied Oppa upon his last foray south, Lælia's mouth tightened. Ulric's presence would not bode well, either for the tribes, or for the Jews in Garnata. Still, that did not explain the need for vigilance.

"What else did you see, Tosius?" she asked in the language of the tribes, watching the little man closely as she did.

Tosius clicked his tongue and looked away. Lælia waited. When he finally spoke, his eyes remained firmly fixed on the wall, and his voice was carefully neutral. "The Jews of Garnata have gone. Those who remain wear the cross now."

"The rebels who fought for us?" Tosius nodded briefly, as if even making the gesture hurt him. Lælia found herself reaching for the stable wall to steady herself, the ground beneath her seeming to sway. "Where did they go?"

"Septem." Tosius's response was swift.

"What news from there, from Yosef? Does the rebellion build?"

"No news, as yet. They are safe in Septem. That is all I know. Those who remain no longer speak of rebellion."

"I suppose it is too soon to expect much," she said, watching Tosius. She was unsure what she expected, but Tosius's stolid silence spoke louder than any words might have. "What other news?" she asked finally, when it was clear nothing more was forthcoming.

"The tribes send their message: they are yours, *dauhter*." This time Tosius's answer was swift, and he met her eyes, his wizened face grave. "They will keep your herd safe, and hidden. And when you are ready to fight for Illiberis again, they will be ready, *dauhter*. This, they tell you."

"And I am grateful." Lælia bowed her head in the traditional gesture of respect, and Tosius nodded.

She met his eyes again. "I am riding north today," she said. "To settle a dispute. Will you ride with me, or do you need to rest?"

Tosius, who had undoubtedly ridden night and day to reach Aurariola, made a contemptuous noise and rolled his eyes. Lælia stifled a smile. The mere suggestion that a tribesman might need rest was an insult not to be borne. Capable of extreme, and extended, laziness when the opportunity arose, Tosius was equally absolutely incapable of taking a rest when it was suggested to him.

An hour later, they were riding out of Aurariola, Silas and Leofric flanking her, Tosius a silent shadow at her side.

* * *

As she rode, Lælia thought of her last days in Toletum.

She had never before noticed the absence of friends in her life. In Illiberis, her life had been filled with too much to contemplate the need for friendship outside her own household. There had been first Yosef, and the tribes; then Paulus and Acantha. In the intervening times there had been Alaric, and Athanagild, and sometimes Laurentius or Shukra. Somehow, she had never felt alone.

But in Toletum, despite the bustle of the court, she had felt truly lonely for the first time.

Riccilo was lost to her. Theodofred's blinding had left Riccilo a crippled, grief-stricken shell of her former self. They had never really been confidantes anyway, but in the time following Theodofred's maiming, they had grown further distant. Rekiberga would have been Lælia's choice of companion, but Ataulfo guarded his wife jealously, especially against such a close associate from her previous life. Lælia had not been admitted to Ataulfo's domus when she called, even though she had it on advice from her servant that Rekiberga

262

was at home. Athanagild and Laurentius were so clearly strained and withdrawn that she had felt awkward approaching either of them. Egilona, oddly considering her age, would have been Lælia's next choice; but Egilona was almost as difficult to access as the king himself. She was considered a member of Wittiza's inner circle. As such, any request to visit with her passed through innumerable courtiers, even if the message came from her brother's wife. They had met only a few short times in the duration of Lælia's stay. She did not blame Egilona, for she understood the process, but the lack of companionship had been painful.

As a result, Lælia had ridden from Toletum feeling strangely isolated, an emotion that had yet to abate. Perhaps, she thought now, riding in the high morning sun, it was the pregnancy that made her so. If anyone, she longed most for Dahiya's company, which, she knew full well, was an oddity. Of all she knew, Dahiya was the least likely to indulge her sentimental feelings. And yet she craved the strong woman's curt presence like a person dying of thirst craved water. She craved it even more, perhaps, than she did Theo's return, though in a different way. Dahiya was the stick by which Lælia measured herself, and never more than now had she the desire for that measuring stick, for she no longer knew if she was rational or not.

She looked over at the woman who had ridden to Aurariola, and whose dispute they now rode to resolve. The woman's expression was still slightly stunned. Lælia knew her decision to ride north was both unnecessary and unexpected. The men of Aurariola who remained were all old, and infirm, but age had done nothing to soften their condescending smiles when Lælia had announced her intention to resolve the dispute herself. The reality was, Aurariola was perfectly capable of running itself without her, and Lælia knew it. The mundanities of organising the household were small matters that had, it was true, benefited from having a mistress, but a hired housekeeper could easily have done enough. As for the tenants themselves, most of the matters concerning them were small issues both Silas and Leofric were more than capable of settling in Theo's stead, with the advice of the aforementioned old men. No, Lælia's role at Aurariola was as superfluous as it was unsatisfying, and she knew full well that her decision to ride north had more to do with restlessness than any real desire to better understand her husband's lands. Lælia did not care for Aurariola any more than any other land upon which she had ridden throughout her life. It did not matter what attributes it possessed, nor that she was, in name at least, now its mistress. Aurariola was not Illiberis, and therein lay its fatal flaw, one no amount of time, Lælia knew, would ever serve to disguise. She had wondered, more than once, if that was how Theo felt about Illiberis. But Theo, she suspected, had been away so long that he no longer felt bonded to any soil in particular. Theo was allied to Spania, to the nation his ancestors had carved from a falling empire; he was welded to the sea, upon which he had lived so long; and he was bound to her, and to their child. But Aurariola, Lælia suspected, had, if anyone, belonged to Alaric, not Theo. She did not think Theo felt about land as she did. She was beginning to realise that few people did. The bond she had with Illiberis had nothing to do with politics or words on a page. It was a relationship of blood and soul that predated Spania itself – and even the empire that had existed before that. It was, she supposed when she could consider it rationally, unfair of her to expect Theo to understand how the loss of Illiberis truly felt in her heart, as if a part of herself were missing. Unfair, and, she feared, self-indulgent. Reluctant to place that burden on Theo, increasingly she had found it easier not to speak of Illiberis at all.

They arrived at the village late in the afternoon, and the dispute was resolved in the time it took to eat the humble meal, prepared, somewhat ironically, by the combined efforts of the two women involved. The woman with the sons who would do the labour was ordered by Lælia to take, and sell, a greater part of the harvest – as well as paying a greater tax –

but asked, also, to bear the responsibility of caring for the other woman as part of her own family until the woman's own children could carry their father's burden, at which time the arrangement would be revisited. The taxes payable by the original claimant would be reduced by Lælia to a negligible sum on the condition that she worked with the other family to ensure their labour was lessened. It was an easy arrangement, one that all parties received happily – and one Lælia could just as easily have decreed from the villa, as well she knew. But there was a freedom in sitting outside the small stone dwelling as the sky turned to rose, smelling the wild damp rise from the earth and hearing the lonely caw of a night hawk as dusk grew. Lælia thought she had been too long inside city walls, listening to the dry talk of men. It was a blessed relief to her, as night fell and her men made their way to other fires and the cups of liquor offered by the local men, to find herself seated amongst the women, many of whom bore the small stature and dark features of the tribes.

"Yes," she said, smiling as one of the women nodded at her belly and asked about her pregnancy. "When winter comes, all being well." As she had so many times, she began to think of how cold it would be when she carried the babe to the caves, as all women of Illiberis must; then she remembered, with the familiar stab of pain, that she could not.

"What troubles you?" The woman who had carried the claim to Aurariola asked the question under cover of the others' chatter.

"Nothing." Lælia forced a smile. "A small thing," she amended. "In Illiberis, where I am from, it is customary for us to take our children to the caves of their ancestors when they are newborn. That they might touch the paintings of our people, be known and protected by them as they grow."

"Ah." The woman nodded in understanding. "But you are far from these caves and cannot visit them." Without waiting for Lælia's answer, she turned to the other women and spoke in a quick, foreign dialect Lælia assumed belonged to the tribes there; it had a similar cadence to that used by Tosius. "We, too, have places such as this," the woman said, turning back to her. "Close to here we have caves of our own, places we, too, take our young and go to seek the wisdom of our ancestors. Whilst they are not your own, perhaps in that place you might still hear their voice, for in the afterlife all souls are one and no longer have the same divisions we do in life. I can take you there, if you wish."

Lælia glanced at Tosius, who was squatting at a respectful distance from the women but listening nonetheless. He met her eyes and nodded in tacit understanding, his face sober. Lælia turned back to the women. "Can we ride there tonight?" She nodded at where her men were gathered about a nearby fire. "I would rather not alarm my husband's men."

The woman smiled in understanding. "They will never know we are gone."

They left the increasingly raucous men as the moon rose, Tosius like a shadow at Lælia's side. They went on foot, climbing a narrow path that led upward from the barley fields into limestone cliffs carved in odd, twisted formations strange to Lælia. She found a curious, familiar peace in labouring up the steep track, focusing only on where to place her feet, her breathing, keeping pace with the women before and behind her. Despite the ground being profoundly different to that of Illiberis, still she could feel the ancient presence within it, sense her ancestors close by. When the woman ahead of her paused at a depression in the rock, Lælia already knew the sign of protection she would make and understood they had reached the entrance. She remembered Acantha making the same sign years ago, at the caves in the Valley of the Horse, and felt a savage pang of loss that she swallowed with difficulty. Lælia knew Acantha would approve of this visit. The thought made her strong, helped her breathe through the pain, say a silent prayer to her grandmother, lying at peace now in a cave of her own.

The pathway down into the caves travelled through

twisted limestone that gradually gave way to spears of rock hanging from the roof and growing up from the floor, the same curious, ancient formations of Lælia's own caves, the temperature stabilising to that of the earth, a warm, silent, timeless atmosphere that soothed her. Unlike her own caves, though, this pathway suddenly arrived on a ledge that over-looked a vast main chamber, with a wide, still pool of water at its centre. It was a dramatic space, so vast it was almost, Lælia thought, like being in the palace in Toletum. The woman ahead of her gestured to a narrow set of steps carved into the rock. She handed Lælia an oil lamp that lit the ancient forma-tions, finding strange, iridescent colours in their depths. "From here you go alone," the woman said. "We will await you outside the chamber."

Lælia nodded and stepped carefully down into the wide cavern. She glanced back once, but the ledge was empty, the women respecting her need for privacy.

Lælia settled herself on her cloak. The ground had the same curious life to it as that in her own caves, a faint warmth, as if it throbbed beneath her. She closed her eyes, allowing the deep peace of the place to steal into her body, the steady, time-less drip of water forming rock to become her lullaby. Time slipped away, and once again she was a girl in the caves at the Valley of the Horse, as Acantha played the bones and brought her visions forward. She could sense her grandmother's pres-ence as strongly as if the tall woman were playing them now, and the whisper of other voices, those whose hands had painted the shapes she had touched as an infant.

She cast her thoughts outward into their midst. *How am I to bear this child so far away from her own lands? How am I to raise a daughter of Illiberis when her first breath is of sea salt rather than moun-tain air, her first sunrise coastal haze rather than crystal brilliance? How can I raise her to be what she must when she will not touch the paintings of her ancestors? Should I be fighting, now, instead of waiting? What is it that I should be doing?*

All the pent-up frustration she had felt tumbled from her

mind into the dark stillness, like a purging of poison from her body. Releasing the thoughts was like lancing a wound, both painful and deeply relieving. Lælia tasted salt on her tongue, almost like blood, and gave up her dark questions to the wisdom of the eternal, opening her own mind to receive their answers, however they might come.

In her mind she saw a young child astride a horse, riding tall and straight, with the unmistakable grace and agility of Illiberis; but this child had not Lælia's dark, midnight hair, but a short cap of Theo's brilliant, gleaming white. The straight spine and determined shoulders did not belong to Lælia's daughter.

They belonged to Theo's son.

The boy in her vision rode beside his father along the coastal cliffs of Aurariola, nodding as the tall figure at his side pointed out over the sea below. Lælia's head turned as her son's did to look far below, where a thousand dromons were drawn up on the beachhead.

She rode onward, but the boy and his father drew away from her, until their tall figures were no more than pinpricks in a golden distance, as unreachable to her as a foreign land. The sea mist closed in around Lælia, filling her lungs so she could not breathe, choking her nose and clouding her eyes until she was lost in the dank, silent grey, shut off from all, spinning alone in the muffled nothingness.

All children are born as they are meant to be.

The whisper was inside her and around her, not Acantha's voice and yet redolent with her grandmother's presence, as it was rich with the presence of others, both familiar and strange. The words seemed to enter her as much as speak to her, becoming part of Lælia's being whilst also denying her true understanding of their meaning. Her eyes flew open to a dull, flickering light; the lamp had almost gone out.

With cold, shaking fingers, she tilted the lamp to draw the last of the oil. The lamp flared, casting shadows on the walls. Her heart beat unsteadily. One hand crept down to her belly, feeling the baby stir within. *My son,* she thought. *Theo's son.* She was not sad that it was not a daughter. Their son would be strong, she knew. A son to be proud of, a man in his father's image. She felt a surge of love and pride so visceral it almost hurt.

The words shifted inside her, and she tried to make sense of them. Did they mean that her son belonged not to Illiberis, but to Aurariola? To Theo, rather than her? Was Lælia herself now become no more than a vessel for her son's destiny, no longer required to fulfil her own? The thought was frighteningly disorienting, as if the entire perspective of her world had shifted. Accustomed always to thinking of what she must do to determine her own future, Lælia had the sudden sensation of her world tilting, so she must no longer determine and guide her future, but instead have it determined by following the destinies of others – Theo; her son. She felt a strange sense of being lost in their wake, becoming invisible in the grey, coastal mist, her voice silenced, her path no longer discernible. She took a deep, shuddering breath, impossibly relieved to feel the air slide unencumbered into her body.

She sat for a long time, but no further illumination came, and finally, as the lamp flickered weakly, she rose and climbed the limestone stairs to the surface, where Tosius and the women awaited her.

DAWN WAS TURNING the sky indigo and rose as the huts came back into sight. They were not silent and still as they should be in the pre-dawn, but rather a hive of activity, and Lælia felt the first stab of trepidation. Then she saw the large, sweating, dark bay horse, still panting from hard riding, and felt her insides twist with equal parts anticipation and dread. She knew who it was even before she heard his voice, calling orders in a hard, furious tone she had never thought to hear from him.

"I left her in your charge. She is with *child*, you damned fools, and you let her ride twenty miles through hard country – then lose her? Tyr!"

"*Wenkai*." Catching sight of Lælia behind Theo's stiff back, Silas's deep voice tried to stop him, but Theo was clearly beyond being reasoned with.

"Do not try to pacify me. One job, I left you. One. She is my *wife* –"

"*Schnecke*." Now it was Leofric's turn, his tone rough with amusement. Theo raised a fist, and Lælia, seeing he had reached the end of his restraint, said his name quietly: "Theo."

He stiffened, his fist still raised, then slowly turned. The man who faced her was not one she had yet known. This Theo, eyes glittering shards of sea ice, mouth a tight, furious line, every muscle taut and the twisted skin on his face gleaming savagely in the dawn light – this was the man who had led other men into war, the man she had heard whispered of, when others thought she did not hear. This man was the one who had been carved beneath Oppa's whip and in the depths of the ocean, through months of slavery and in countless battles. This Theo now strode toward her, his face twisted in fear and fury.

"What are you doing here?" He gripped her arms, not gently, oblivious as the others drifted diplomatically away, clearly sensing this was a scene that should be played out in private. "What were you thinking, to ride so far, with child? Why did you not deal with this in Aurariola – and why did you slip away in the middle of the night without so much as leaving word as to where you went?" There was not a hint of gentleness in his face as his brows drew further down. "Where *did* you go?" His eyes searched her face. "What was so secret that you did not so much as tell Silas or Leofric what you were doing?"

"To answer your first question," said Lælia, proud that her voice was steady, "I came because I was asked to settle a dispute in a part of your lands I had not seen, and I did not feel it fair to adjudicate without understanding the physical terrain involved." It was not strictly true, and Theo's dark expression did not alter. "As to your second – women from Illiberis have always ridden whilst with children. I was in no more danger on horseback than you are. I rode to Aurariola from Toletum without mishap – yes," she went on, before he could say anything, "I know you ordered me to ride in the litter, but I could no sooner bear the confines of that thing that I can the walls of the palace. I got rid of it as soon as we left the city walls." As his face began to take on a resigned cast, she continued: "I left last night to go to caves nearby that are sacred to the tribes here. It is customary, for the women of Illiberis, to take their children to certain caves, in the months after they are born. Since I have temporarily traded Illiberis for our freedom" – it was the most direct reference to the deal with Oppa she had ever made, and, seeing Theo blanch as she said it, she felt an unwelcome stab of satisfaction – "and cannot visit my own lands, it will not be possible for me to do this. The women here offered to take me to caves of their own. I did not tell your men because they are men, and Christians, and would not understand such things. They would have insisted on accompanying me, if they allowed me to leave at all, and such men are not permitted in places such as the one I visited."

"And what of me?" Theo's eyes narrowed, searching her face. "Is a man such as I permitted in these places, Lælia? Or must I forever remain a stranger to these secrets, one not permitted to so much as be informed of my wife's where-abouts – my child's?"

"You were not here." Lælia felt a surge of impatience, exacerbated by Theo's seeming refusal to so much as mention the name Illiberis, even after such a provocative comment. After so long being careful in her words so as to guard his feel-ings, a desire to assert her old independence rose to the surface, fed by the vision she had seen in the caves.

"You have not been here for many years, Theo. I have changed in that time, just as you have. I do not need to seek permission to go where I must, nor to consult what spirits I might regarding the future of our child. A child who will be born to your world, Theo, not mine. A son to ride at your side, learn your ways, not a daughter to inherit Illiberis." She did not hear the fierce pain in her voice until she saw it reflected in Theo's eyes, along with a dawning sense of wonder. "Yes," she said, her voice softening despite herself. "It is a son, Theo. Your son. And we are both to live at your side, on your lands. So, please, allow me these moments, in my caves, with those of my blood who would grant me their visions. For it is all I might have, for now at least, of the life I once lived. It is all I might carry, for now, of Illiberis." Stepping closer to him, she reached out and he caught her, holding her close enough that she could feel the frantic beat of his heart, the fear in his body. "Do not be afraid for me, Theo," she said quietly. "I will always come back to you, just as you came back to me." She covered his heart with her hand and looked up, seeing the dawn light shift in his eyes. "Promise," she whispered.

His hand covered her own, their matching fede rings gleaming dully, side by side. "A son." His voice was rough with exhaustion and emotion.

She nodded, her anger receding as fast as it had risen, taken away by the tide of love between them.

"Laurentius and I rode to Hispalis." He shook his head. "I could not stand it, Lælia. To be away from you again, after so long. Whatever Oppa's games, he can play them without me, for a time, at least. Laurentius and I agreed he would oversee the movement of dromons and men to Aurariola, and then I rode as fast as I could to here, to you. To arrive, and find you gone… then follow you, and find you gone again…" His voice broke off. "I was terrified, Lælia."

She cupped his face with her other hand, feeling in his skin the fear they had both lived with for too long, that the other might somehow be lost, that they might arrive too late.

"I understand," she whispered. "Next time, I will tell you, Theo. I swear it."

"Thank you." He covered her hand with his own, and they stood there, as the sun rose, their joined hands on Theo's heart and face, and Lælia felt as she held them that she saw their son's face and body shift beneath Theo's, the spirit of the boy's being already present in the Aurariola coastal morning, upon this land to which he would belong.

22

YOSEF

OCTOBER, AD 693

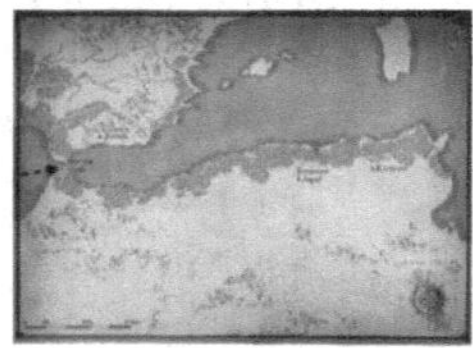

Septem, Mauretania
Ceuta, Morocco

"Yosef!" Sarah came clumsily to her feet, her eyes shining, as Yosef entered the low doorway of their Septem home.

"You should be resting." He drew Sarah close, closing his eyes and inhaling the hint of rose in her hair, savouring the feel of her rounded body against his own. It was a delight made all the sweeter for the years he had wandered alone, thinking her lost to him forever. He had married her the same day he and Theo had arrived in Septem after their voyage from Sebastopolis. Neither of them had wished to wait a day longer, and Yosef had been unsure what awaited him in Spania. He would not leave Sarah alone again, without so much as his name for protection – for what it was worth. It had been a prudent decision, given that he had returned from Spania to find her pregnant. In the time since, his sense of wonder had never faded, that this was his life now: a woman

274

he loved; a boy, Arun, whom he loved as fiercely as if the child were his own; and another baby on the way. If he had dared wonder what such a life might be like, the reality of Sarah had far exceeded his expectations. "Sometimes I think I could stand like this forever," he murmured against her hair, "just enjoying the reality of your presence."

"We could hardly launch a rebellion standing still." Her voice was rich with amusement, but when Yosef stiffened in her embrace, Sarah pulled back to look at him, her eyes narrowing. "Do not tell me you are doubting our plans, Yosef. Not again."

"Then I will not say it." He strove to keep his voice light, but Sarah was harder to fool than most. Yosef had discovered, since his return to Septem, that she was one of the very few who possessed the unerring ability to see beneath his carefully cultivated exterior.

"What has happened? You came back from Spania fired to galvanise our forces here. But then there has been delay after delay – and now you return from your visit with Ilyan looking as long faced as one of his horses. What did he say, Yosef?"

"Someone is arriving today. Someone Ilyan and I have both waited a long time to see." Releasing his wife, Yosef turned to the small window cut into the earthen wall. The shutters were open, only wrought iron covering the opening. He gripped the curlicued bars hard, almost relishing their unyielding pressure on his palms, staring unseeing at the narrow alley. An overladen donkey laboured past, staring mournfully at Yosef as it went. "We will join Ilyan for dinner tonight, and you will meet her yourself."

"Very well." It was one of the things he loved about his wife, her ability to be both measured and kind. Yosef had begun to realise, somewhat to his shame, that his travels had given him a certain mercurial veneer that kept his inner world hidden, and others at arm's length. Sarah seemed to have an ability to accept both his reticence and the secrecy that had become second nature to him, taking neither personally. Her gentle acceptance and the haven of her body were the places in which he found his only refuge, and that she allowed him that place was a gift that Yosef never, for a moment, took for granted. He kissed her now, putting into his caress all that he did not have the words to say, and Sarah, with her customary understanding, kissed him back, touched his face without comment, then said, slightly hesitantly: "Before we go to the palace, however, we have a meeting, Yosef. Hasdai and the others will be here any moment."

"Ah." Yosef nodded. "I had forgotten."

"I can tell them to come another day —"

"No." Yosef forced himself to smile. "They distrust me as it is." Drawing her toward him again, he kissed the top of her head to forestall the protest he sensed on her lips, and then he began to lay out cups and wine for their guests.

* * *

"IT HAS BEEN six months and more since the battle at Illiberis. Four months since we left our homes." Hasdai eyed Yosef across the kitchen table balefully, his arms folded. "Yet it is still you alone who meets with Ilyan on our behalf. And despite the amount of time you spend at the palace, it seems those meetings bring us no closer to a concrete plan."

"Ilyan has many visitors who are representatives for those with whom I have negotiated abroad. It is easier if I am there to meet them." Yosef maintained a courteous tone, though beneath the sleeves of his robe, his fists clenched. Ilyan, of late, had been even more irascible than normal, his mercurial diplomacy sorely tested. First by the influx of refugees and exiles from Spania following the recent rebellion; then pressure from Egica's diplomats to refuse the aforementioned sanctuary; and last but most certainly not least, a steady stream of worrying intelligence regarding the movements of the Arab forces to the east. To say that the concerns of the

Garnata Jews were low on his list of priorities was an understatement.

"You cannot be unhappy, here, Hasdai, surely?" Yosef turned quizzical eyes to the belligerent figure in his kitchen and then glanced around to include the others gathered there in his question. "You are free to trade once more. The agreements I negotiated during my journey are already bringing new goods to our warehouses, and there is no shortage of Gothic exiles happy to take our coin as intermediaries with Spania."

"We came here to prepare for war," said Hasdai bluntly. "Or at least to retake Garnata and force Egica to the table to hear our demands. I do not see those plans growing. No amount of coin changes the fact that Septem is not our home, Yosef."

The faces turned to him expectantly, Sarah's amongst them. It was her eyes, shining even now with love, that hurt the most. The fact that her own father had been forced to convert to Christianity, combined with the personal injuries she had suffered at the hands of so-called Christian men, had made Sarah one of the rebellion's most passionate advocates. He felt secretly ashamed that despite sharing her outrage, he could not, in all honesty, share her belief in the cause. He drew a deep breath. Whether he liked it or not, he would have to voice his doubts, sooner or later. He glanced again at the hostile faces in his kitchen.

Sooner, then.

"You are right," he said calmly, pouring the men cups of wine and waiting until Sarah had replenished the dishes of olives and nuts on the table. Diplomacy, he had long ago learned, was better served with full hands and bellies. Men were much less given to anger whilst being offered courteous hospitality. "Septem is not our home. But we are Jewish, and accustomed to making a life wherever the winds of fate blow us."

Haym, another of the Garnata Jews, frowned. "That

sounds a great deal as if you are giving up, Yosef." There was a general murmur of agreement. Yosef waited patiently until it had died down. It was time for some hard realities. He sighed inwardly. He had, he knew, been hoping to stave this off, for a few more days, at least.

"Before Ilyan launches forces upon Spanish shores," he said, "he needs us to bring him several guarantees. One." He gently tapped the table with his forefinger. "Pledges from the key lords on Spania's southern coast that they will join their thiufas to his cause, thus providing a geographical barrier that would seal the south against a northern army. This, despite our many overtures, those lords have not committed to do. Two." His middle finger went down. "Our guarantee that we have the coin to pay an entire army of mercenaries for as long as it takes to hold the south, consolidate our position there, and then repel what we might expect to be repeated advances from the north." He shook his head briefly. "No matter how well we thrive in Septem, we all know that even combined, we do not have anywhere near the resources required." Nobody contradicted this statement. "Three, and, possibly, most pertinent to our current position." He turned his palm upward, rubbing his thumb and forefinger together slowly. "A guarantee that the profits from Ilyan's prior investment in my journey east will benefit, and grow, as a result of supporting us. In short, that this war makes good business sense for Ilyan, and Septem." He stared slowly around the room, meeting each man's eye as he did. "This," he said quietly, "we cannot promise."

The men looked at him, then at each other. Sarah, heavily pregnant, folded her hands over her belly and regarded him thoughtfully.

"I thought," said Hasdai, glaring at Yosef, "that coin was the reason for your meetings with Ilyan. That he would support our cause and offer his own financial reserves to back our efforts, thus helping us create the channels to generate more wealth for us all."

"To launch a war," Yosef said, careful to keep his tone respectful and calm, "one needs to know exactly what one wishes to gain. Then, one must provide either the skills to fight it, or the coin to buy those skills. We are asking Ilyan to provide both, and to assume the entirety of the risk, all without a clear and achievable outcome. It is not a viable position. Not yet."

"Not yet?" Haym leaned forward. "I would say our objectives are clear as a knife edge, Yosef. We take the south, at the very least, the coast and mountains from Sexi to Garnata, west across to Malaka. We all know that once taken, these lands are not easily relinquished; had Sunifred based his rebellion there, as we had all hoped, we might hold the south still." It was a familiar refrain, one often voiced and debated, and none objected. "Once our position is secure, we force Egica to hear our demands. We negotiate different laws for the Jews, in the territory we hold at least, creating a trading base between Septem and Spania. We create a place where Jews are safe to worship and trade as they always did, far away from the primacy of the Christian church in Toletum."

Yosef listened carefully. When Haym finished, all eyes turned back to him. He nodded politely. "You are suggesting we create a Jewish nation within Spania. Redraw the boundaries of Old Bætica, the last-held imperial territory that was finally conquered two generations ago by the old king Suintila." There was a moment of silence as they all digested his words. "You would ask the current king," Yosef said quietly, "to dissolve the nation of Mater Spania, a feat that took the Goths three centuries to accomplish, and which remains still the idea for which all men in Spania are raised to die?" He looked around the room. "I am not saying this goal is not a worthy one. But I would be remiss if I said I thought it would, at this stage at least, be easily achieved."

"'At this stage'. 'Not yet'." Haym looked at him grimly. "You say these words as if a time is coming when you might think differently."

Yosef mentally winced at the dissimulation he was about to practise.

"Tonight, Sarah and I will go to the palace for dinner, and there we will meet an old friend of mine. Someone who holds the key to unlocking the profits from my mission east. If all has gone well, we may return with new hopes, and begin a new conversation."

"But you won't tell us more." Haym and Hasdai eyed him suspiciously, and the rest of the faces around the table scowled, though they didn't speak. It was always the Garnata Jews who ran these meetings; sometimes, Yosef wondered if the others came merely to drink his wine, and to be on the inside of what had become the inner circle of Jewish society in Septem.

"It is not wise to say more until I know of what I speak." Again, the silken words of diplomacy came almost too easily to his lips, and Yosef felt the familiar, jarring sense of his old and new worlds colliding. There were many times such as this, when he wondered who, exactly, he was now. Yosef the traveller, who had sat across tables from some of the wiliest and most dangerous men in the world and held his own; or Yosef the Jew from Garnata, upon whose shoulders the hope of an entire people rested.

Neither any longer felt entirely real. The only things that felt real were Sarah, Arun's smile, and the baby that even now stirred in her belly.

If Yosef had any real faith left, he thought, gripping his wife's hand beneath the table gratefully, it was to be found in those things.

* * *

"So this visitor we are to meet tonight. Why is she important?" Sarah was dressing her hair, and Yosef was lying on the mattress, watching her. Arun was with their neighbours for the evening.

"You are an incredible woman, *hachevi*, you know this?"

"Of course I know this." Her voice was rich with amusement once more.

"You do not ask what this woman is to me, only why she is important."

"I know you, Yosef ben Arun." Nothing more. No long explanations or modest blushes. Just that simple statement.

"That is true." Yosef smiled as she turned to him. "You do know me, Sarah, better than most. And the woman you will meet tonight – she, too, knows me. Not intimately," he said hastily, for much as his wife was incredible, some things, even he knew, were a little too much to ask tolerance of. "But Athanais knew me in the early days after I left Spania, when I was with Dahiya in the desert. We met again in Sebastopolis. It was she to whom I entrusted the eggs I had carried from Serica."

"The – worms?" Sarah could not disguise the curiosity in her voice. Yosef had tried to explain, to her and to Ilyan, the process by which silk was made; but even now, he knew, they doubted him. There were times when Yosef doubted himself. His time with Fei Hong in the mountains seemed like another world, an exotic dream that could not exist here, amidst the prosaic trappings of the life to which he had been born. Sometimes Yosef imagined himself explaining the making of tea, the exercises he had done every day, the way he and Fei Hong had fallen upon one another hungrily as the silkworms transformed through each of their stages. Such mysticism and sensuality, he felt, had no place here. When he had those thoughts, he wondered how the silkworms themselves might survive in such an environment. Which brought him back to Athanais's arrival.

"Yes." He nodded slowly. "I could not both return with Theo to Spania and save the silkworms. It was to Athanais that I entrusted them. I sent her to Constantinople with strict instructions, and to a Jewish cloth merchant there, a contact I had been given who once worked in the emperor's own

palace, where they also keep the secrets of silk. It was a difficult choice. Tonight we will discover if it was the right one –
or if we lost everything because I made it." Moving forward,
he took her hands. "No matter what news Athanais brings,"
he said softly, "I would make that same choice again, Sarah,
and again, if it brought me home to you."

She touched his face with her hand. "But you fear the
news she brings – that it might influence Ilyan, and our plans
to launch a force into Spania?"

Yosef nodded slowly. "Athanais will bring the first real news
we have had from Constantinople since we left. Apsimar sends
word to Theo, but the messages are sparse and relate strictly to
military matters. Athanais is different. She has made the gathering of intelligence an art form. She will bring a wealth of information, enough for Ilyan to make a clear decision about what is
the best course, for Septem – and for the Jewish rebellion."

Sarah stepped away from him, her eyes narrowing. "Your
words today did not leave our friends with much hope, Yosef.
And given what restrictive laws the Jews still in Spania labour
under, there are many here who think we have delayed too
long as it is. And what of Illiberis? Surely Lælia expects us to
help her win it back?"

"Yes." Yosef's tone was bleak. "I believe she does." He did
not flinch from Sarah's eyes. "But I have seen war, Sarah. The
Jews of Septem have not. Have no knowledge of what war
looks like. The Jews of Garnata fought one battle, did barely
more than hold a wall, and then ran into exile. Their prowess
has grown with every telling, but no amount of stories will
make warriors of them, Sarah. We talk of a *Jewish* rebellion;
but the reality, as I said today, is that any rebellion will be the
work of Ilyan's soldiers, not the Jews of Septem, or those of
Garnata. Ilyan will not commit that force without good cause.
And without it, Sarah, we have no rebellion."

Sarah's face had grown grave as he spoke. "I cannot help
but wonder," she said quietly, "why it is only today that you

openly voiced your reservations. After all these months of discussion." When he didn't speak, she went on, her voice rising slightly with hurt. "Were you ever truly committed to our cause, Yosef?"

Yosef took one hard step toward her then brought himself up short, his fists clenching in frustration. "Never doubt how much I want this, Sarah." His tone was low and fierce. "I despise everything about Egica, from his twisted bastard son to his rotten priests. To so much as think of Illiberis in Oppa's hands makes me sick to the stomach. But I have watched men die in battle, Sarah. Good men with as much cause as ours have, and a great deal more experience. I will not send such men to their death needlessly, even if they think me traitor for denying them their glorious end." He could not disguise the bitterness in his tone, and Sarah's face softened slightly as she heard it.

"And you think Ilyan will make his decision based on what this – Athanais – says?"

Yosef tilted his head, feeling a sudden wave of weariness wash over him. "I think he will listen to her, yes."

"But you believe our cause lost."

"Not lost, exactly." Yosef frowned. "I am just not certain that a war is the way for us to win back what we have lost, Sarah. I think we must try to plan for a different future."

"It is difficult," said Sarah, moving close and slipping her arms around his waist, drawing him toward her until the tension fell away from Yosef's body and he allowed himself the sweet respite of her embrace, "for me to imagine giving up the cause that has sustained me, and so many others, from the moment of our exile. And what of Lælia? What future does she face, without Illiberis?"

Yosef held her close but did not answer, losing himself, however temporarily, in the sanctuary of her body, allowing her questions to rest between them, unwilling, as he had been ever since his return to Septem, to break them both with a reality he understood – and which he feared both his wife and his oldest friend might never truly comprehend.

* * *

"Yosef." Athanais came toward him with her hands outstretched, her face lit with genuine warmth. Yosef felt something inside him shift. "Athanais," he murmured, his voice catching on the name. The Persian woman was as exquisitely beautiful as she had ever been, her woollen gown cut as daringly low as ever, her midnight hair unapologetically unbound, but it was not her beauty that Yosef saw. Athanais had known him when he was a boy, broken hearted and simply broken, about to set off through the sands. She had known him on the other side of that vast journey, was perhaps the only person, he felt, who truly understood the miles he had travelled, both within and without. It was an understanding too great to express and one he would never voice even if he could. "Athanais – this is my wife, Sarah."

Sarah came forward hesitantly, clearly intimidated by Athanais's exotic appearance, but she was met with an expression of such unmitigated affection that her polite smile relaxed almost immediately into one of genuine welcome. "Sarah," said Athanais, pressing her hands warmly. "The reason Yosef could not stay away a day longer – and a good reason, I am thinking, Yosef, no? Of course he is clearly unworthy of such a woman, but then, even the best of men are unworthy of their women, is it not true, *aziz-am*? But you must both sit with me and tell me of your life, for there is little more satisfying than to reach one's destination and find one's friends in a happy situation, is it not so, Yosef?" Chattering easily, she drew them both forward onto the dais, where Ilyan watched them, his eyes sparkling with amusement and interest.

"She is a witch, is she not," he murmured to Yosef in passing, shaking his head slowly in admiration.

"You have already spoken with her?" Yosef asked beneath the women's conversation. Ilyan nodded.

"The silkworms?"

"In this we are successful. The worms hatched, and bred. She brings both the mulberry trees and the worms themselves. We have the means to begin production, and a rich trade."

"But?" Yosef had not missed the conditional manner of Ilyan's response.

"But Athanais brings other news. And she met with Dahiya on the way here." His eyes when they met Yosef's were sombre. Aware the conversation between Sarah and Athanais had hit a natural pause, Yosef turned to them. "The silkworms are safe, then," he said, forcing himself to smile with an effort.

"Ah, your worms – truly, Yosef, I cursed you a thousand times for the care of these creatures!" Athanais cast her eyes to the ceiling in exaggerated theatre. "How such small things can cause so very much trouble, *aziz-am*. In Constantinople I must make an entire house, you understand, to disguise their existence. Yes, I am forced to care for both girls and worms, and I am not being so certain which of these is more trouble." Somehow, the manner in which she spoke about running a tavern of prostitutes was so matter of fact that it made for a droll story rather than a lurid one, and Sarah was soon laughing aloud at the tales of drunken palace guards and the subterfuges Athanais must daily work in order to keep the worms secret. "An entire chamber I have, you understand, dedicated to the care of these creatures. So closely was it guarded that stories spread throughout Constantinople of the secrets behind the chamber's closed doors, and my little house became quite the busiest in all of the city, simply because men cannot help but covet what they cannot have! You cannot imagine the stories told of this secret room; and yet all the time, it is trees and eggs behind that door, then worms. I am not certain I would have been believing had I not seen with my own eyes. And this merchant you send me – never do I find such a difficult man, Yosef, and for this I do not forgive you, no, for this man he is the most demanding of all men, and must have this and that for these worms at the most inconvenient times. Ah!" She waved a hand in the air, her eyes shining, her beautiful smile shared equally amongst them. "But enough of this and your worms. They are here safely and we have now our trade, and we escape this Constantinople without dying and this is all we might ask of life, is it not? Yes. So now, we must talk of what is important." Her eyes slid almost imperceptibly over Sarah, but Yosef understood her question.

"Whatever you might say," he said quietly, "my wife will hear. We do not have secrets."

"So." Athanais raised her eyebrows. "But I am thinking there are things I will say that will not be welcome to you," she said to Sarah. "I am hoping you will forgive me." She did not wait for Sarah's consent but went on, speaking directly to Yosef. "The Arabs are gathering their forces. Dahiya is believing this will be the greatest effort they have yet made, and she is sending word to the emperor, Justinian II, asking for help. Justinian, however, is having troubles of his own. Constantinople is uneasy. The aristocrats are not liking his taxes, especially when they are used to build yet another tall building." She rolled her eyes. "Why is it men must always be building such things? But I digress." She waved a hand.

"What of the military?" Yosef asked. "The Karabisianoi? After Sebastopolis, the defeat there, what happened?"

"Ah." Athanais regarded him thoughtfully. "I forget how removed you have been, Yosef. So infuriated was Justinian at Leontios being humiliated at Arabic hands, that upon his return, Justinian imprisoned him as punishment for the defeat. Leontios languishes still in a prison cell."

"Imprisoned?" Yosef stared at her. "But that is extraordinary."

"And yet, it is the truth. Worse, those in the aristocracy who do not like Justinian's taxes begin to mutter about the injustice done to Leontios. Leontios is an aristocrat, one of their own, you understand. There is talk they may rise behind him, if he should leave prison." She went on, speaking at some length of Constantinople politics, Yosef and Ilyan hanging on her every word. It was a while before Yosef realised that Sarah was listening politely, but with little comprehension. "I am sorry." He took her hand and smiled. "This must be confusing to you."

"But it is not to you." Sarah met his eyes, and Yosef saw in hers a glimmer of understanding. "Go on," she said quietly. "It is important, I can tell."

"Well – Dahiya now is riding hard, gathering all the Imazighen she might, training her Riders harder than ever before." Athanais turned grave eyes to Ilyan. "She will call on you, Ilyan. Sooner than you may think." Her eyes shifted to Yosef. "And she bids me ask if you, Yosef, or Theo, may have standing in the Spanish court. If Dahiya is to defeat the Arabs, it may take more than even Septem and her desert Riders, especially if Justinian does not send the Karabisianoi soon."

Feeling Sarah tense beside him, Yosef inwardly winced. Of all the news Athanais could have brought, to Sarah, he knew, this could only seem like betrayal.

"The Spanish court?" His wife's face was aghast. "Do you mean that Dahiya seeks to ally with Spania? To ask Egica for help?" Yosef reached for her hand, but Sarah's fingers lay limp beneath his own, and all colour had fled her face as she watched Athanais.

"If Spania is not wishing to become the latest jewel in the caliph's crown, then, yes, it is perhaps being time they, also, offered forces to defeat him." Athanais met Sarah's question with steadiness but no hint of apology. "This is the news Dahiya is sending Ilyan: it will take more than her army this time, if the Arabs are to be stopped."

Sarah's shocked silence spoke volumes. Hastily, Yosef said, "The Spanish nobility do not believe the Arabs a threat." He met Ilyan's eyes as he spoke. "Egica has never believed in the Arab threat."

"What is this, he believes, or does not?" Athanais looked between them, frowning. "Does one believe the sea exists, or not? Is this king a fool?"

"Unfortunately, yes," said Ilyan dryly. "He is."

"Which is why he must be overturned." It was Sarah who spoke, her voice trembling with conviction. "At his most recent council, Egica passed laws against our people," she said, turning to Athanais. "Harsh laws. Prohibiting us from trade, forcing us to convert, brutally, if necessary. The country is already divided. We plan to launch an uprising to take back the south and hold it against him. With Ilyan's help, of course." She smiled at Ilyan, but the count, Yosef noted, did not smile back.

"A rebellion?" Athanais looked between Yosef and Sarah, frowning. "I am thinking there was already a rebellion in Spania when last I saw you? Was this not why Theo sailed for Spania – to save his bride from this rebellion?"

"Illiberis was lost," Yosef said flatly. "The rebellion failed, though Theo and Lælia survived the aftermath. They are together, on Theo's lands on the eastern coast."

"The coast." Athanais nodded. "This is good news for Dahiya, to have Theudemir there. Does he command dromons, men?"

"I believe the king has put him, with Laurentius, in charge of assembling a fleet, yes."

"This is good news indeed." Athanais turned to Ilyan and would have gone on, but Sarah interrupted.

"It is not good," she said. She was very pale, high points of colour in her cheeks, and her voice trembled with tension. "Lælia has lost Illiberis, and our people have lost everything. These are not things we will simply forget. We have spent months planning to take back the south. Yosef has explained that outright rebellion may not yet be within our means, and this, whilst hard to hear, our people might be able to understand. We are Jews, after all," she said, unable to keep the bitterness from her tone. "Coin and profit we understand."

"Sarah —" Yosef put out a restraining hand, but Sarah shook it off, her eyes glittering with anger.

"No, Yosef. We may not yet have the means to mount an actual rebellion. But to ask us to use the profits we have risked everything for to forge an alliance with the Spanish Crown?" Her voice shook with emotion. "We have not suffered so much at Oppa's hands, at Egica's, to now be a part, even by association, of an alliance with their cursed rule. Such an act would be the greatest of betrayals, to the Jews of Spania, to —" She bit off the rest of the sentence, but Yosef knew she had been about to say Lælia, and he felt a savage stab of guilt, that it should be Sarah, who barely knew Lælia, who would speak for her now when he, her oldest friend, did not.

But if his years of reading men had taught Yosef anything, it had taught him when to remain silent. And even Sarah's accusing eyes would not shame him into speaking now.

Ilyan's fingers beat an impatient drum roll on his wine cup. His thin limbs were almost preternaturally still. Yosef, who knew Ilyan as well as any man could, knew the warning signs did not bode well. Ilyan, he had learned, for all his diplomacy, could be utterly ruthless when he lost patience.

"For some time now I have considered the Jewish cause in Spania lost." The brutal response took even Yosef by surprise. He received it with the impassivity born of long practice, but despite the fact that he had known this day would come, had even predicted it himself, the part of him that was born of Garnata and Illiberis tasted bitterness and resentment at being so summarily dismissed. "I know perhaps more than you do of Egica's intentions," Ilyan continued. "I have an informant in the Spanish court who sends regular updates." *An informant?* Yosef, examining Ilyan's face, did not think the man lied. Mentally he ran through the faces and households he had done his best to familiarise himself with in his short duration back in Spania. No; there were none in his mind he could envisage as Ilyan's informant. He wondered how on earth the man had planted anyone inside Egica's palace. If Egica himself were not paranoid enough to sniff out a spy, Oppa certainly was. That someone could pass unnoticed by Oppa was an extraordinary testament to Ilyan's skills.

"Egica is fully cognisant of the Jewish plans to rise against him," Ilyan went on. "He is allowing it to unfold, just as he did Sunifred's rebellion. He and his bastard son intend to use the uprising to crush any remaining Jewish influence, or allies, in Spania once and for all. They will use talk of rebellion as an excuse to kill those who do not convert, and take the lands of any lord who might ally with the cause. But their real goal," he nodded to Athanais, "is to discover what it is that we have worked so hard to conceal. This is the reason they allowed Yosef passage from Spania and have allowed the few unrepentant Jews in Spania to continue plotting with the very rare lords who might be prepared to help them. Not because they are ignorant of the plot, but because they hope to identify the last of their enemies in the south, and the details of the mission upon which Yosef was so long engaged." He met Yosef's eyes. "It is time to make it clear to the Jewish exiles here that they will never return to Spania; or at least, not so long as Egica is on the throne. To those still in Spania, you must say that they would do well to leave now, whilst they still can. The uprising, for what it was worth, is finished – if ever it truly began." His bland delivery did nothing to soften the brutality of his words. Yosef could not bear to look at Sarah.

His unpleasant task ended, the past dispensed with, Ilyan leaned forward, his face shifting, from bland mask to gleaming interest. "Our goal now must be to strengthen our ties with Egica, consolidate our position at court." His eyes shifted restlessly, his mind, Yosef knew, already leaping ahead. "The silk trade will be indispensable in that endeavour. It will provide us with coin with which to entice Spania, and leverage at court. We must keep it a secret..." He went on, leaning in to address Athanais. What colour remained in Sarah's face leached away

as he spoke, and Yosef's heart ached for the desolation he saw
in her eyes.

Sarah turned to Yosef.

"You," she said brokenly. "You cannot mean to support
this alliance."

More than anything, Yosef wanted to lie to her. He felt the
silent sympathy in Athanais's eyes, the impatience in Ilyan's,
and he knew he could not. "I do not like it, Sarah," he said
quietly, ignoring Ilyan's tsk of disapproval at such a breach in
diplomacy. "But I understand it. And I would not see our
people die needlessly —"

"Needlessly!" Sarah's voice was rising, anger taking the
place of shock. "What of Illiberis, of those of our people left
in Garnata? Are they all simply to be forgotten, now? Is
Illiberis simply to be left in Oppa's hands?"

"Illiberis!" Ilyan leaned forward, his eyes hard, and Yosef
knew the man had reached the end of his indulgence for the
conversation. "This is the second time today you have invoked
that name, so let me be clear. I have protected the heiress of
Illiberis. Lost dromons to an attack because Oppa coveted
Illiberis. Sent men, and horses, across the sea to defend it —
men and horses needed here, in Africa. So yes," he said, his
piercing eyes on Sarah, "Illiberis can remain in Oppa's hands,
and if the Jews of Garnata are smart, they will flee whilst they
still might. Athanais is right. The best place for Theudemir is
on the coast of Spania, with a fleet of dromons at his
command that might help defend our waters, and his wife
might consider herself extremely fortunate to be there at his
side, and not swinging from a rope for treason. I no longer
have any interest in the domestic affairs of Spania, not unless
they can help me fight against the forces of the caliph. Yosef"
— he turned away from Sarah — "we will not speak of this
Jewish rebellion again."

It was as close as Ilyan's diplomacy would come to an
outright rebuke. Whilst it was not exactly a dismissal, Sarah
did not wait for one. Rising to her feet with a certain dignity

despite the mound of her belly, she nodded politely to both Ilyan and Athanais, the latter watching her with palpable sympathy. "I will leave you to your discussion," Sarah said quietly. "Yosef. Will you take me home?"

As much as part of him wanted to remain in the room, to hear all that Athanais had to say, Yosef found, almost to his surprise, that another part of him shared Sarah's disgust and wanted nothing more than to escape the room. "I hope I will see you again," he said courteously to Athanais, hiding his eyes from Ilyan's sharp gaze.

"Of course. We must speak of these worms of yours." But the beautiful eyes were sad as they moved between Yosef and Sarah. Yosef nodded at Ilyan, who waved him away impatiently, already turning to talk with Athanais. His mercurial mind, Yosef knew, was already moving, planning what strategy he would take; Ilyan, he suspected, would be surprised, possibly even disappointed, to discover that Yosef had qualms about allying with the Spanish Crown, no matter what he had suffered at Oppa's hands. Ilyan did not allow such considerations to enter into his calculations. He made his decisions as a master did facing the Tabula board, disregarding all but what made for the best strategy and outcome.

Before tonight, Yosef had admired that. Now, he found he was not so at ease with it as he might once have been.

They walked down toward the busy port in silence, Yosef terribly aware of all that was unsaid between them. Two alleys from their home, Sarah paused, and Yosef turned to her, waiting.

"Before we came to the palace tonight," Sarah said, her voice surprisingly steady, "you said we might need to *plan for a different future.*"

"I did say that, yes." Yosef eyed her curiously.

"Was this what you meant?" Her eyes shone with hurt. "Did you know Ilyan planned to ally with Spania?"

"No! Sarah, no. I swear it." Yosef was not sure what shocked him more, the calm manner in which she had asked the question, or the fact that she knew so little of his heart to imagine him capable of such betrayal.

"Then what did you mean?" She searched his face. "Please," she said, her voice not as steady as a moment ago. "Tell me what you meant. For at this moment, Yosef, I see little in our future to offer promise."

"Very well." Yosef drew her down onto a nearby stack of crates, ignoring the curious glances of the dockside crowd passing by. He drew a deep breath and took both her hands in his own. "I have never spoken of this to anyone," he said in a low voice. "I think, perhaps, I have been afraid to even so much as think of it, myself." His eyes touched hers, and, when he found nothing there but the calm understanding he had come to treasure, he went on. "Everyone I know is committed to fighting the Arabic army," he said quietly. "Whether those people are political allies, or our friends. Everyone I know seems to believe that the Arabs are a threat that must, at all costs, be defeated."

Sarah's eyes had narrowed slightly, but Yosef couldn't read her thoughts. *It is too late now,* he thought. He took a deep breath and then, for the first time since his return, Yosef cast every last shred of his hard-won secrecy aside and spoke the words of his own heart.

"What if Arabic rule is the best thing for Spania? More importantly, Sarah, what if it is the best thing for the Jews of Spania?" Her eyes flared, her mouth forming a perfect O of surprise. "I spent months in the Arabic court," Yosef said, and now that he had begun speaking, he found the words coming in a passionate rush. "The Arabs do not care for the manner in which a man worships. Christian, Jew, Muslim – so long as they are 'People of the Book', as the Arabs call those of the Abrahamic faith, they are welcomed, paying only a tax for the right to trade. The Arabs have little tolerance for pagans, it is true. But in every country I visited that was under Arabic rule, the Jews thrived, often at the highest levels of power.

"The Arabs value knowledge and learning, Sarah, where

the Christians guard it as the preserve of priests alone and fear to learn anything not sanctioned by their clergy. When I passed time with the caliph, he spoke of founding universities, places of learning where men – and women, for they value the female mind, Sarah, in a way Christians do not – of all nations might come together and exchange ideas, learn from one another. Caliph Abd al Malik bin Marwan values knowledge almost as much as he does coin. And it shows, in the prosperity of his nations, the ease with which his rule has been accepted by so many."

His hands tightened on hers, and when he spoke again, he was quieter, but no less passionate. "You ask me what different future we might plan for," he said. "Sarah – what if we began to plan for a future in an Arabic Spania? One where we might, one day, have a right to rule Garnata as our ancestors once did: as a full partner to Illiberis, independent, and free? To run the silk trade as our own, with no need for Ilyan, or a Christian agent such as Illiberis, or subterfuge? To have a seat in an Arabic government, a say in the politics of our nation equal to any other man, Christian or Muslim?"

Sarah's face had changed as he spoke, surprise turning to fascination and now, finally, to Yosef's relief, to a glittering expression he knew well: excitement.

"Do you truly believe such a thing is possible, Yosef?"

"I believe it is more than possible." He nodded. "I believe, in fact, that it is almost inevitable. You heard Ilyan tonight. Constantinople is ill prepared to launch a serious force against the Arabs, and they have already lost a great many of the pitched battles they have fought against that enemy. They do not have the resources nor the leadership to hold Africa against a determined force." He frowned. "Even if I want to believe that Dahiya can prevail, I do not think even she believes it, long term, though she will fight for Altava to her death, I know. And even Theo, though he might not like to acknowledge it, knows, inside, that there is little chance Spania can stand, if it comes to it."

"We should tell the others of this." Sarah was on her feet, her eyes bright with excitement. "It will help, Yosef, to change their view of you, after tonight —"

"No." Yosef's rejoinder was swift, and decisive. "No, Sarah. There is a reason I have never said these words to any but you. Not even to Theo, who is as a brother to me. And it is the same reason you must swear to me that this stays between you and me, and even then, we should be wary of what we say to one another, especially in front of Arun." Seeing her confusion, he took a deep breath and looked over her head, to the darkness of the distant Spanish coastline. "If I am right," he said slowly, "and an Arabic force marches one day for Spania, every man, woman, and child in their way will raise arms against them. To ally with an Arabic force against our own — no matter how persecuted by 'our own' we might have been — will be considered treason of the very worst kind. A betrayal of Spania herself, and of all those who call it home. Can you imagine Lælia supporting an Arabic invasion? Theo?" He shook his head.

"Then what do we do, Yosef? How do we prepare for this future?" Longing coloured her voice in a way that touched him, deep inside, where only she could reach.

"We build our resources." He heard the strength in his voice and thought, for the first time since leaving Garnata all those years ago, that it was truly his own voice that spoke now. "We create a thriving trade in silk, that we own, and control. We make alliances as far afield as we dare and cultivate every relationship I found on my travels. We do as Ilyan has done — become the centre of all, with an ear in every house, but allied to none." He grasped her shoulders. "We become our own nation, Sarah. And we build a dynasty that no-one, ever, can take away from us. A dynasty of coin and intelligence, a bulwark that will always find us a haven, and never leave us dependent. What do you say, *hachever sheli*? Will you join me?"

Sarah's hands clasped his face, her eyes shining. "I will join you, Yosef ben Arun," she said, her voice shaking with excitement. "We will build that world together. I swear it."

And there, in the shadow of the world from which they had been exiled, amidst the refuse and waste of the disenfranchised, Yosef ben Arun and his wife, Sarah, began to plan a future they dared, against all odds, to imagine.

23

OPPA

NOVEMBER, AD 693

Illiberis, Spania
Granada, Spain

T he messenger arrived at Illiberis just after midday on a cold, clear November day. Wittiza was abed with a cold, and Oppa feared the appeal of isolation was waning amidst the hard winter. The sensuality of a late southern summer had offered all the delights an adolescent might enjoy; but winter held few attractions, and, despite Oppa's generous overtures, he and the princeling had yet to be welcomed by the haughty southern lords.

"What news from Malaca?" he snapped now, without greeting the messenger. "Did the count welcome the gifts I sent?"

"I – I could not say," the messenger stammered, eyes darting about the œca. "My lord was not at home when I arrived, and will not return for many weeks, his men told me –"

"That fat bastard hasn't left his villa in a decade," snapped Oppa. Instantly regretting the outburst, he turned away, hiding his frustration and annoyance from the messenger, breathing deeply to calm himself. The southern lords, he was learning, were notably less easy to bribe than their northern counterparts. One whom Oppa had approached on a trade matter had brutally asked to see documented evidence that the Illiberis latifundium had been officially granted to Oppa. "The agreement between Illiberis and my own latifundium," he had said, his mouth curling in a manner that made Oppa's hand wish for the whip more than he could recall in a long time, "has been in place for decades before my own birth. Until the Lady of Illiberis formally cedes her lands to you, and Egica's eagle insignia replaces the Illiberis serpents on the goods in your warehouses, I will respectfully refrain from breaking faith." Implicit in his response was the same scornful assumption Oppa met from any lord with lands south of the river Bætis: Oppa's occupation of the Illiberis latifundium was of a temporary nature, tolerated only until Lælia of Illiberis, whom they universally accepted as their equal despite the girl being little more than a child, returned.

"I do have some other news that may be of interest, Fráuja." The messenger's tentative interruption was not unwelcome in Oppa's frame of mind.

"Well?" Oppa poured himself a cup of wine without offering one to the messenger and tossed it off in a quick swallow, his dark eyes penetrating. "Out with it, then."

"It is said that a visitor came recently to the court of Ilyan, at Septem. From Constantinople. A Persian woman," he added hastily, as Oppa's mouth began to harden in dismissal. Oppa paused. His eyes narrowed. "A Persian," he repeated slowly.

The man nodded eagerly. "It is said that she is very beautiful. The man who brought the news said he had known her long ago, in Carthage. He said she ran a pleasure house there."

"Indeed." Oppa stroked the cup thoughtfully. "And is that what she does now in Septem? Run a pleasure house?"

"No." The man shook his head decisively. "That is the news I bring, Fráuja. It is said that she carried from Constantinople something of great worth, something most prized by Ilyan and the wealthiest of his Jewish merchants. Already there is an entire house set aside in which the treasure is stored."

"Treasure." Despite his legendary self-control, Oppa felt his heartbeat quicken. "What is this supposed treasure, then?"

The man's eyes shone. "It is whispered, Fráuja," he said, glancing around and lowering his voice, "that the Persian woman brought with her the means to make silk."

* * *

RATHER THAN VISITING HIS BROTHER, as he customarily did of an afternoon, Oppa took a horse and rode into the township of Illiberis, making his way to the church there. The horse was one of his own, from Toletum, a fact that still made his mouth purse with annoyance. The famed Illiberis herd had disappeared as if it had never been, along with the many tribesmen whom Oppa remembered tending them. The mountains around Illiberis were oddly still, the tribesmen, he suspected, gone into hiding in the high passes where none ventured in the winter. It was yet another reminder that Illiberis was not a land like Hispalis, which had been taken over following Sunifred's defeat and, to all intents and purposes, continued much as it once had. Not so Illiberis. This was a secretive land, one of old loyalties and ties so complex and ancient Oppa did not know where to begin in untangling them. Even the accounts, such as they were, of the latifundium were a mystery. Though making perfect sense in theory, they bore no relation to the wealth of the lands or the villa itself, seeming to show no more than an orderly income from barley and flax, olive oil and wine. Oppa knew the truth was hidden somewhere in warehouses and horseflesh. But now, he suspected, it was hidden, too, in a house in Septem, controlled by a Persian lady whom Oppa would stake his life was the same one who had once run a pleasure house in Sebastopolis.

He had thought Athanais dead, in the carnage that followed Sebastopolis, if he had given her much thought at all. *That,* Oppa thought, in a rare moment of self-chastisement, *was a foolish oversight.* He had known the Persian was more than just a whorekeeper; Theo, he recalled, had ever been close to Athanais. His men had frequented her tavern, and it was there Elpis had first been employed. Oppa had thought, however, that she was a gatherer of secrets, as were most in that business. He had not considered she might play a wider role. Now, however, thinking back over the past, Oppa chided himself for not seeing the links. Athanais had been the base to which Yosef had returned, after his journey east. And then she had disappeared.

It was smart, Oppa could not help but admit. No wonder he had been unable to find even the slightest evidence of fruits from Yosef's journey. Yosef had not gone east to retrieve chests of coin. He had gone to find an entire industry, and now, if Oppa's suspicions were correct, he and Ilyan were poised to create that industry just two days aboard a dromon away, in Septem.

Unfortunately, for Oppa, that narrow strip of sea might as well be a chasm. Ilyan, he knew, would never welcome him ashore; and Athanais's allegiance was clearly to Theo, and Yosef.

But, Oppa thought, as he dismounted and tied his horse outside the church, calling for Ulric, he still had a piece he might play in the game. A piece whose value he had, though suspected, perhaps not quite understood until now.

At this very moment there languished, in his father's Toletum dungeons, another Persian: Shukra. A man who, in addition to being exceptionally close to both Laurentius Severianus and Athanagild of Aurariola, had also been friend and protector to both Yosef ben Arun and Theo. One who had close ties to Septem, Ilyan – and the Karabisianoi.

Two Persians, Oppa felt, with such similar ties, at work in countries so far away from their own, could not be a coincidence. Particularly when both seemed so closely enmeshed in the affairs of Laurentius Severianus and the priest Athanagild, both of whom Oppa had long suspected played games of their own. Games he had, given all else he was managing, hitherto only idly investigated – but which he now intended to apply himself to discovering.

"Ulric." He greeted the priest perfunctorily, taking in the man's humble brown robes with distaste. Oppa himself was resplendent in white with gold trim. Ulric might do the work of the Illiberis bishopric, for such matters bored Oppa beyond comprehension, but Oppa never eschewed the finery of his office.

"Father." Ulric kissed the ring on his hand reverently. Oppa forced himself not to wince. The man's touch sickened him, not to mention the visible grime under his fingernails.

"How do you get on," Oppa asked when they were seated inside the monastery behind the church, with a jug of bad wine and even worse cheese on the table between them, "with the neighbouring clergy? What do they say of our tenure here?" At the man's politely bland expression, Oppa pushed a heavy bag of coin across the table between them. "I forgot to give you coin for the new roof," he said, with a smile that did not reach his eyes.

"God will bless you for your piety." The coin disappeared before the bag had settled its weight on the table. Ulric sipped sparingly from his cup and said, "The local priests here are almost as savage as their flock, Father. Few are literate. Most minister a strange mixture of pagan beliefs and the word of Christ, and then there are the converted Jews, most of whom are converted in name only –"

"I did not ask how they pray." Oppa waved an impatient hand. "I am asking how they regard Illiberis, and me as its lord. Do they speak of it?"

Ulric's silence stretched painfully long. When he finally

spoke, his voice was muted and his eyes did not meet Oppa's. "They are uneducated peasants, Fráuja, you must know," he began, and cynically, Oppa noted the dropping of his ecclesiastical address, as if the coin Ulric had just taken came from God himself, rather than Oppa's very ungodly coffers. "And full of superstition and heresy, as I said, which their previous overlords, you understand, were tolerant — even encouraging — of. It takes time to eradicate such beliefs —"

"They think she is coming back, don't they." It was a measure of the shadow cast by the Lady of Illiberis that Oppa did not need to say Lælia's name for Ulric to nod unhappily.

"They do, Fráuja." Ulric twisted a corner of his brown homespun robe nervously. "They meet me sullenly and do not make any pretence of their contempt. More than one has asked to see parchment with the Illiberis mark as proof of my legitimacy. I have shown them the eagle of your house, Fráuja," he added hastily. "But it is not so easily recognised in the south."

Not so easily recognised, Oppa thought bitterly. The mark of the royal family itself, of this king and the next, and still, in the south, it was the serpents and staff of Illiberis they recognised.

Well, it would not do. He had toyed with Theo long enough; it was time to tug the string upon which he dangled with a firmer hand. And in the meantime, there were other avenues of persuasion open to him.

"Perhaps," he said lightly, "the attitudes of the southern lords might alter if they were to learn that there is a new line of trade in which they might be poised to play a key role. One lucrative enough to build great houses to God. Even," he said, holding Ulric's eyes, "the converted Jews. Especially them, in fact, since the trade in question would require their particular skills."

Ulric's eyes flared with interest. "Such conversations may, indeed, aid me in the ministering of God's word."

"Then have those conversations. Use what coin you must to ensure your point is made. I am entrusting you with the stewardship of Illiberis in my absence." Oppa stood abruptly, half smiling at the trepidation on Ulric's face. "Not the latifundium, Ulric; I have men of business to manage such things. No, I refer to spiritual guidance." His smile grew hard. "Sometimes people must see the value in conversion. Once it is pointed out to them, they become more willing to share information. Even the slightest whisper, Ulric, in a seemingly distant port, might be of interest. I would ensure you have priests in every tavern, doing God's work in conversion, and that those converts are themselves put to work. Do you understand?" He pulled out another bag of coin, just as weighty as the first, and placed it on the table between them. "Of course, such work is expensive. Should you require more, my man in Illiberis will hear your requests."

"Of course." Ulric bowed his head, his dull eyes glowing. "God is generous indeed."

Oppa strode into the sunlight, his mind made up.

It was time for him and his brother to make a triumphant return to Toletum in preparation for his coronation, and for him to have some conversations of his own – with a certain Persian prisoner, and with those who were familiar with Laurentius Severianus. There were games afoot Oppa had missed, and he did not intend to remain ignorant of them for a day longer than necessary.

24

THEO

NOVEMBER, AD 693

Aurariola, Spania
Orihuela, Spain

Theo had forgotten how bitter the coastal winds could be, not to mention the dreary showers of rain they brought. He entered the atrium to find Lælia pacing restlessly across the small garden at the centre of the tiled space. Parchment and ink lay upon a nearby writing stand that was customarily found in the study. Jadis was prowling the edges of the garden opposite her mistress, silent and restless. The cat's eyes rested briefly on Theo as he entered, and she came to a standstill. "Nice Jadis," said Theo, approaching her warily. Her eyes narrowed as he came close. "Good Jadis." He lowered a cautious hand to the golden head. "Beautiful, wise Queen Jadis, ruler of my home and all within it – how does today find your majesty?" Having deigned, throughout this soliloquy, to permit Theo to scratch her head, Jadis clearly decided she had conceded enough and, with a swish of her long tail, leaped through the window and was gone, into the rain.

"I fear Silas will ever be first in her heart over me," Theo said dryly, coming over to Lælia.

"I should not envy him, if I were you. She has taken to bringing him dead rats to demonstrate her devotion." She kissed him, but her touch was perfunctory, her eyes far away. They were expecting a party of guests the next day, including her aunt Riccilo, and Theo had left her that morning engaged in a frenzy of organisation that seemed abruptly to have stopped.

"Do I dare ask what I have interrupted?" Theo asked warily. He was never too sure, lately, what mood he would encounter on his arrival home. There was Lælia the Wife, a persona that as far as Theo could tell had, in the lack of any real domestic role model, been cobbled together from some vague notion of what constituted the Roman ideal, her own experiences at court, and the lurid depictions of bath house walls. In that particular mood, Theo would find himself met by artfully arranged hair, eyes lined with kohl, and skin scented with rose and jasmine; an elaborately set table, and carefully prepared meal; and a night of wondrous seduction. All of which would make the hardest of men smile. Except that in Lælia's case, such careful preparations could be derailed by one careless remark regarding matters of the latifundium, gossip from the capital, or rumours from the port, at which point her carefully cultivated efforts at dutiful, humble femininity would be exploded in a torrent of questions, speculation, and astute analysis. Since Theo found this infinitely more interesting than downcast lashes and seductive smiles, it bothered him not at all. Lælia, however, would inevitably wind up disheartened at failing to maintain the ideal she had set for herself, which led in turn to the second persona: Lælia the Lady of Aurariola. This one, Theo knew, his entire household had come to dread, for it generally involved a determined overhauling of every aspect of the villa, from menu to cleaning. In this mood, no detail was too small, no issue too minor, to escape Lælia's scrutiny, and her enthusiastic examination of everything from riding leathers to linens had been known to test even Tosius's slavish devotion.

These bouts of manic activity generally then led to her current mood, one that set every nerve in Theo's body on defensive edge but that he knew, in some inner part of himself, was the most authentic of them all: Lælia of Illiberis. In this mood, Lælia would try and discard a thousand different plans for the retaking of Illiberis, mulling over who might help and how this strategy or that might play out. Though never directly consulting Theo, she would muse aloud, casting him sideways glances as if to gauge his reaction. Theo, unsure what role, if any, he was expected to play in these deliberations, and terrified either of betraying himself or of upsetting the fragile balance of their home, maintained a courteous, diplomatic silence throughout these soliloquys. Despite his own deception, and the dark, corrosive knowledge that any effort could only be in vain, Theo had discovered, over time, that he infinitely preferred to see her thus occupied than in any of her other adopted roles. Mostly, he was honest enough to admit, because even planning open war against the Crown was better than the persona Theo feared most of all: Lælia the Absent.

In this mood, the woman he loved, the girl he had fallen in love with, and the mother of his coming child, disappeared. In her place came a silent, pale wraith, who for hours at a time would disappear across the misty fields, alone, on foot, and even, on one notable occasion, amidst a wild thunderstorm. Lælia the Absent was cold and remote as a distant shore, gone into the place deep inside herself that nobody, not even he, could penetrate. That mood could last for days, and when it did, the entire household felt shrouded in grey, every member of it tiptoeing the corridors in silent concern, none game to say what they all feared − that this time, she might not come back.

It was this mood that generally triggered the return of Lælia the Wife, and Theo knew it was because every time she

lost herself, Lælia made a savage promise to be all she thought
a wife should be, to put aside her own dreams and ambitions
and try to immerse herself in the world in which she found
herself. Theo knew he should encourage this. After his conversation in Oppa's brothel, he more than anyone else knew how
remote were their chances of ever regaining Illiberis. And if
any doubt had been left to him, the terse wording of the
formal request he had received only days before had removed
it. Oppa had not minced words: the public concession would
be made soon, or he would make their own agreement public.
But Theo could not so much as consider that now. Not so
close to the birth of their child.

The documents were carefully hidden, from even Silas and
Leofric's eyes. Even the thought of them turned Theo's gut.

Oppa, he thought grimly, could damned well wait.

All he felt, when he saw Lælia twisting herself inside and
out to become something she was never meant to be, was
deep, sickening shame that he should ever have allowed her to
be thus reduced. Even his fury at Oppa was secondary, for
Theo knew, no matter who else he might blame, that the fault
for his wife's agony lay squarely at his own door. All he could
do was stave off the coming catastrophe as long as he could.
He knew, in the depths of his soul, that it would not be long.

So, grateful for now to find her occupied in the one
manner that he knew was true to her soul, he forced a smile
and walked over to the desk. "What manner of conquest do
you plan today, wife of mine?"

"I am writing to Yosef."

"Oh?" Theo's heart skipped a beat, and he kept his face
carefully averted.

"Yes." Lælia moved restlessly across the room. "We should
have had word from him, by now. Regarding the rebellion. It
has been six months since he left Spania. Surely, he must have
made plans by now? It seems odd, indeed, that he has not sent
word of them."

"You know as well as I that Egica and Oppa are watching

the sea routes. Especially now that so many Jews appear to be escaping to Septem rather than convert."

"But that's just it." Theo turned to find Lælia frowning. "If so many are leaving, they must know something we do not. Do you think they are about to attack, Theo, and have not told us for fear of discovery?"

"I suppose it is possible." Theo tried to keep his voice even, but Lælia made an impatient noise. "Which means you think it is not possible at all." She gave him a wry smile. "You are too easy to read, husband."

Thank God, Theo thought grimly, *that is not true.*

"I shall write to him, anyway. And entrust the letter to Tosius. He will ensure it goes with one of the Jewish dromons and reaches Yosef's hands. Once I know more, I can begin to plan."

She said this last in a slightly challenging tone, her eyes resting on his face.

"There is another possibility," she said slowly, still watching him.

"Oh?" Theo strove to keep an even expression.

"The Arab army."

Theo could not hide his sudden sharpening of interest. "What of it?"

"If the Arabic forces are strengthening, Ilyan and Dahiya will be focused on their advance."

"And how," said Theo, forcing a light tone, "does this represent a possibility?"

"Because if the Arabs are coming," she answered swiftly, "a strong Illiberis is even more important than ever. After all, was that not the goal of your and Yosef's mission, from the beginning?"

"It was." Theo's heartbeat had slowed, to a dull, heavy thud.

"Oppa," Lælia went on, watching him closely, "saw the Arabs, too. He knows what we will face, if they reach Spania."

Theo did not answer that. He didn't trust himself to.

"Theo." She stepped closer to him. "Perhaps – if he knew Spania was under threat –"

"We don't know that." Aware his voice was uncharacteristically harsh, Theo softened it deliberately as he went on. "Athanagild and Laurentius will arrive tomorrow," he said. "Along with Egilona, Riccilo, and Roderic. No doubt they will bring more news. At the moment, this is all speculation. Even if you are right, we can't make decisions on a hunch, Lælia."

Lælia's eyes didn't waver from his face. "And neither can we avoid making decisions forever," she said quietly. "At some point, Theo, we will have to speak of Illiberis. Of what is to be done."

Theo drew a deep breath, trying not to think of the leather roll in which lay both the cursed document with his signature, and now, the new documents from Oppa. "I am not certain there is anything I can say that will help, Lælia."

"Egica said that papers would be drawn up. Formal documents of transfer." She paused, clearly waiting for him to speak. When he didn't, she continued, her tone quiet but dignified. "If such documents have arrived, Theo, I should have been told. Despite our marriage, I am still heiress to Illiberis and own more than half the land in my own right." Every word was like a hammer blow upon Theo's conscience. "Do not think to spare me by hiding such matters, Theo."

"If such papers did arrive, are you telling me you would sign them, Lælia?" His voice was harsh in the still air, and he did not look at her; he couldn't. "Consider formally conceding Illiberis – to Oppa?"

There was a long pause, in which, it seemed to Theo, even the rain was suspended in the air about them. Finally, Lælia said softly, "I do not yet know what I will do when I am faced with those papers, Theo. I know only that when it comes to the future of Illiberis, I must do what is right for the people upon it, no matter who may be hurt by my actions, or what you might think of me for them." Her cheeks flushed with a strange, hectic colour, but she held his eyes steadily as she said,

"I may now be only your wife, but such responsibilities are still mine to bear. I do not expect you to carry them for me." There was an edge of defiant pride to the way she said the words that did not escape Theo, and it hurt him, somewhere deep inside.

"Of course." He knew that if ever there was a time to tell her of what lay between him and Oppa, now was that time. But the mountain of her belly drew his eyes every time he would speak, stilling his tongue. He saw again the dread spectre of her walking barefoot across the fields, in the rain, her eyes sad and distant. The image sent a shudder of fear through him. *As long as she has hope,* he thought, *she is still herself. But if I take that from her — so close to the birth of our child — will I lose them both? Will I lose all that I fought to return to?*

He felt a sudden, unwelcome stab of anger that, after they had endured so much, they could not simply enjoy this: peace, the impending birth of their child.

"There is no shame in the life you lead here, Lælia." His voice was harder than he had expected, and he winced inside at the flare of shock in her eyes, the way she took a step backward, recoiling as if he had hit her. He took a half step forward, his hand out. "I didn't mean — that wasn't what I meant to say…"

But her face was already closing over, her eyes hardening against him, and when she spoke, her voice was brittle as ice. "No shame in handing over my lands to the man who tortured you? In betraying those who trusted me to save them? No shame in being spared from execution, only because the king looks favourably upon my husband?"

"Lælia." Theo tried to calm his voice. "That is not what I meant, and you know it."

"You do not need to spare me your true opinion, Theo." She flung the words at him with real hurt, and anger. "You have not so much as spoken the name Illiberis until today, when you ask only if I am willing to concede it. You have never believed me capable of even negotiating on my own behalf, let alone making a plan and alliances to regain it.

"If I so much as broach the topic of Illiberis you go somewhere I cannot follow, or disappear for days with your men." Her face was uncharacteristically flushed, her breathing uneven, and the topaz eyes on Theo's own were dull with an emotion he did not immediately recognise. "You returned to me from halfway across the world." Her voice broke slightly, and Theo had to force himself not to wince as he recognised the emotion for what it was: humiliation. "But there are days when I think a half of you remained there, on a battlefield somewhere, perhaps still fighting Oppa himself, for though you never speak of what transpired between you during those years, his is the only name that seems to break through that mask you wear."

The words that he wanted to say rose from Theo's belly in a hot bile that stuck in his throat. Memories that he kept locked fiercely within raced across his mind, like horses bolting from a locked stable: Oppa, standing over him with a whip, screaming at the boy he had been; Leofric, standing on a Sebastopolis hill, saying: *I have never betrayed the men beside whom I fight*; and Yosef, standing before him, face dripping contempt: *Do you think she will rest quietly as lady of your lands, content for you to rule whilst she bears your children, embroidering cloth when you ride to battle?*

All the things he wanted to say spun amidst those memories, the years of secrecy and shadows choking the words before they could so much as find form. They stared at one another across the atrium for a long, silent moment, the rain a soft grey mist around them. Finally, when he did not speak, Lælia turned and walked quietly away.

* * *

THEO'S BROTHER and uncle arrived at midmorning the following day, at the head of a party that included Egilona,

Riccilo, and Roderic. A bright coastal sun had burned off the rain and mist, leaving Aurariola the sparkling, brilliant jewel colours of Theo's memory. He stood on the portico and watched Athanagild and Laurentius ride through the gates and along the long rising drive, then he came down off the steps to greet them as they approached.

"Brother." Theo thought, as he stepped into Athanagild's lean embrace, that amidst the shifting realities of his current existence, he had never felt so grateful for his brother's cool, calm presence. "Laurentius." He gripped his uncle's arm, noting the tense jaw and dark shadows under his eyes. He thought immediately of Shukra's imprisonment. That could be the only cause for Laurentius's misery. Again, he wondered why his brother and uncle allowed Shukra to languish in Egica's dungeon. He made up his mind to ask about it whilst they were here. "The dromons from Hispalis?" he asked instead.

"Almost here," said Laurentius brusquely. "I sailed with them until yesterday."

"Brother!" Egilona prettily accepted Leofric's gruff help from her horse, bestowing upon the burly Slav a smile of such blazing warmth that even Leofric's customary gloom seemed momentarily dispelled. Leofric barked orders at the servants, showing an entirely uncharacteristic interest in how Egilona's baggage was handled. Silas, helping down Egilona's quiet, unobtrusive lady's maid, shook his head, grinning at Theo.

"Sister." Theo embraced Egilona then greeted Riccilo, who had been helped from her horse by Roderic. The boy had grown, Theo noted, and his expression was more grave than the eager lad he had met in Toletum. Then again, Theo thought darkly, he imagined that being forced to put one's father's eyes out with a hot poker might have something of a sobering effect.

"Where is Lælia?" Athanagild looked around expectantly.

"Here, brother." They all turned to find Lælia in the portico, and Theo's heart twisted to see the joy in her eyes as she held out her hands to Athanagild, and his brother's answering smile, his seemingly ever-present watchfulness completely disappearing as he moved toward her. "I do not move so rapidly, these days," she said, as he embraced her. Not by the merest flicker did she betray any of the tension between them, but Theo felt it, in the odd coolness of her hand in his, the way she did not quite meet his eyes, and it hurt.

"Aunt." Lælia greeted Riccilo and Roderic gracefully, but her smile when she took Egilona's hands was filled with genuine warmth. "Sister," she said. "Welcome home."

"It is a long time since I have thought of it as such; but I thank you, sister." Egilona's pretty smile was as much a mask, Theo thought, with a pang, as his or Athanagild's had ever been.

As they moved inside, Theo could not help but be struck by Riccilo's thin, hard appearance. Any hopes he might have had that Riccilo might be the companion to dispel the grey clouds lurking in his wife's soul were dashed before they even entered the œca. Riccilo was not even a shadow of her former self. Fretful and fearful, she glanced about her as if expecting at any moment to see an enemy force ride through the gates, constantly checking to see that Roderic was nearby, pulling her shawl more tightly about her as if she were perpetually cold. Her tension had an almost instant effect upon Lælia, who, Theo suspected, interpreted Riccilo's demeanour as a direct criticism of her inadequacies as a hostess, and had become withdrawn and defensive within minutes of her aunt's chilly greeting.

"Riccilo," said Egilona, bestowing upon the older woman the blazing smile that seemed to thaw even the coldest room, "shall we take my sister upstairs where we can all recline in peace? I may not carry your burden," she went on, linking her arm through Lælia's companionably, "but after so many days on horseback, I would welcome cushions almost as much, I suspect, as you." Nodding at Theo and casting him the ghost of a wink, Egilona led Lælia and Riccilo upstairs, her maid following like a shadow.

"How is Wittiza?" Theo asked Roderic as he led Laurentius and Athanagild into the library. "I am surprised he let you out of his sight." His words, though light, were not without a sting, and Athanagild shot him a warning look. Theo mentally chastised himself. *I must not betray my hatred.*

"Wittiza is in Illiberis. With Oppa." Roderic didn't seem to notice Theo's hands momentarily pause in the act of pouring wine, or the tension that entered the room at the words *Illiberis* and *Oppa.* Roderic had never so much as visited Illiberis, Theo remembered. He knew Oppa only as a hero of the recent wars, a compatriot of Theo's. And by comparison with what the boy himself had recently endured, the loss of the Illiberis latifundium probably seemed insignificant. "He sent word that he will visit Corduba on his way home, however. And Pelayo is coming to meet us," Roderic went on, with a return of his seemingly irrepressible sunny nature. Theo smiled at him and allowed the boy to chatter on with news of the Toletum court, and of people Theo barely recalled and cared for even less. After a time, they dispersed to allow the newcomers to get settled. Theo, climbing the stairs, heard the sound of feminine voices coming from his bedchamber and stealthily moved away again, grateful that Lælia finally had other women in whom she could confide.

It was evening when they all gathered for the first time since the party had arrived. Lælia entered the œca dressed in a gown of russet wool, her carefully arranged mass of curls hinting at Egilona's hand. Her appearance was clearly elegant enough for Riccilo to eschew her normal criticism of Jadis's lean, silent presence at her mistress's side, to Theo's relief.

Despite their heated conversation about Illiberis the previous day, and the enormity of late pregnancy, Lælia seemed energised, in good spirits. Theo released a breath he hadn't realised he had been holding. He had not comprehended, until then, how afraid he had been that Riccilo's pinched tension might have triggered a return of her hard, glittering anger – or, far worse, the grey, silent depression.

But she seemed, in appearance at least, as much herself as she had ever been. Watching her under cover of the others' chatter, he searched, as he did every time he looked at her unnoticed, for any sign that might betray her inner turmoil, any indication that she had discovered his deception. As ever, he found himself unsure if he was relieved or sorry that she seemed as able as he himself to camouflage her thoughts and emotions. It was only when he looked away that he found Athanagild watching him with disquieting scrutiny. Theo coloured, dropping his eyes. He had forgotten how perceptive his brother was.

They took their seats on the stiff wooden chairs that surrounded the table, a style of eating that mirrored the Toletum custom but was undeniably different to the more relaxed atmosphere of Illiberis, where Theo recalled they still lounged on cushioned benches. Everything, tonight, seemed to exist in counterpoint to Illiberis.

Seated at the opposite end of the table from Theo, between Riccilo and Egilona, Lælia pretended to ignore Riccilo's barbed questions, focusing instead on Egilona, with whom she talked easily. Only her occasional restless shifting betrayed her bodily discomfort and indicated how close to her time she was. Jadis lay at her feet beneath the table, returning Riccilo's disapproval with blank disinterest. Never had Theo found himself liking the animal more. He gave Jadis the ghost of a wink, and he would almost have sworn the cat returned it.

Silas and Leofric also formed part of the dinner gathering, and between them and Laurentius, Roderic sat wide eyed and fascinated by tales of war.

"Are the rumours true?" Roderic was asking Silas now. "Are the Karabisianoi sailing for Africa again? Will we see the fleet here, do you think?"

"Why?" Reaching for his wine cup, Leofric tossed it off and refilled it, his face already rather red. "Are you thinking to take the oar yourself, boy? You wish to be like the *schnecke*, here? I must tell you, he did not always swing his sword so well." Tilting his head toward Theo, Leofric tapped his nose good humouredly. "It was taking the African and me some time to teach him how not to die, you understand." He raised his cup to Silas, who gave a low laugh and raised his own cup in return.

"Is the boy right?" Silas asked, turning to Laurentius. "Is the fleet headed for Africa?"

"It would seem inevitable that it should, given the movements of the Arab army. But nothing is certain." Laurentius's answer was given in his characteristic cool, aristocratic tone, but his eyes were shuttered, Theo thought. Laurentius turned the wine cup slowly on the table in front of him, his eyes flickering briefly to Theo. "If the news I have from Septem is correct, the Arabs are marching in force."

"What numbers?" Silas asked, at the same time as Leofric said, "News from whom?"

"A great force, by all accounts." Laurentius met Theo's eyes. "And the news came from a reliable source." Fierce interest gripped Theo, the urge to know what was happening in the wider world beyond Spania's borders, to be the one receiving such messages. Who had sent them? Apsimar?

Seeing Lælia's eyes narrow with sharp interest, Silas's and Leofric's burning with questions, and Riccilo's mouth tightening to a thin, hard line, Theo realised they were in danger of tipping the evening into a discussion of people and events far beyond what was suitable for a family meal, and hastily he changed the subject. "War and politics," he said lightly, "are subjects best saved for taverns. Tell me, Roderic — is Egica planning a midwinter festival again this year, in Toletum? Will you and your friends attend?"

But his efforts to change the conversation were abruptly halted by Lælia. "Women," she said quietly, "do not tend to frequent taverns. And although I do not wish to speak for all at the table, I, certainly, would be more interested in hearing the news from Septem than about the midwinter festival." She did not look at Theo as she spoke, but he felt her rebuke like a barb in his side, and he noticed Athanagild watching them both closely.

"I would be happy to tell you what I can," said Laurentius, smiling at her, "but, truly, there is little to tell. I hope to learn more soon. It has been difficult, since —" His voice cut off with an almost audible snap, leaving Shukra's name hanging unspoken in the air. "Well," he said, forcing a smile that did not reach his eyes, "I do not have the same access to information I once did."

In the uncomfortable silence that followed, Theo was aware of Athanagild's pale, strained face. Laurentius took an uncharacteristically deep swallow of wine. He did not, Theo noticed, so much as look at Athanagild, and for the first time, he sensed real tension between the two, in Athanagild's fiercely clenched fingers and Laurentius's grim jaw. The subject of Shukra, Theo thought, was clearly still a matter of dispute between them, though the reasons for it were as mysterious as ever.

"I heard" – Egilona's light voice dissipated the atmosphere like sun breaking through clouds – "that there is to be a great festival in Toletum to celebrate Wittiza's return. Is that not exciting?" And as quickly as a passing storm, the atmosphere was once again light with easy topics. By the time they broke for bed, a pleasant evening had passed; but Theo, undressing wearily in his bedchamber later, felt shaken by the unspoken tensions.

"Who was the source Laurentius referred to?" Lælia spoke from behind him. It was perhaps the first direct words they had exchanged since their argument the previous day, and Theo seized upon it gratefully.

"I don't know who it is." Theo turned on the bed and met her eyes honestly. "I thought it might be Apsimar, but I'm not certain why Laurentius would have news from him that I do not. I hope he will tell me more during the visit."

"Why did you close down the conversation?" Lælia shook her head, her tone quiet and tired. "Do you think I don't understand such matters, Theo?"

"No!" Rising from the bed, Theo came around to stand in front of her, holding her hands. "You understand such matters better than most men I know. But Riccilo has just lost her husband, Roderic a father, as surely as if Theodofred had been killed. Egilona has ears that are too sharp for her own good, and Silas and Leofric are soldiers who will happily talk blood and war all night. I did not wish the evening to descend into a quagmire in which civil conversation might be lost. And I'm not sure if you noticed or not, but the topic of Shukra is not one that sits easily between Athanagild and Laurentius."

"You're not sure if I noticed or not?" Was it his imagination, or was her laugh uncharacteristically harsh? "You have no idea what I notice, Theo. Perhaps I simply think it is time people talked openly, rather than keeping things hidden."

Theo's heart seemed to stop, then resume again, thudding slowly. "Lælia – I am sorry –"

Lælia gestured impatiently. "I am not speaking of our words yesterday, but of what you are not telling me now. It is winter, Theo. Nobody wages war during winter. Which means that the Jewish rebellion will not rise this year, nor until at least next summer. That is why you changed the subject, is it not? You've had news from Septem. You just don't want to tell me."

"No." Theo felt a visceral surge of relief. In this, at least, he could be honest. "I have not had any word from Septem, Lælia. I swear it to you. The moment I do, I will share it with you."

She searched his face and then a moment later, her stiff features cracked open, and she swayed forward, into his embrace. "I'm sorry, Theo," she whispered against his chest. "I know you will. I know. And I know there are things you can't speak of. I understand it, even if I don't like it. I do not wish to make the fate of Illiberis your burden, nor your fault. It's just – sometimes – I feel like I'm lost, like I'm drowning…"

"I know," Theo murmured against her hair, holding her fiercely against him, "I know, Lælia. It doesn't matter. It's fine, it's all going to be fine…"

But he knew, even as he continued to whisper words of comfort and hold her against him in their bed, that he was lying; and that nothing, really, was ever going to be fine again.

* * *

THE FOLLOWING days fell into a comfortable pattern. The dromons sailed into the port, absorbing the attention of Theo, Laurentius, Silas, and Leofric. Roderic trailed them like an eager puppy, relishing being amongst men of war. Athanagild accompanied them, often watching from the sidelines with a half smile of amusement. It was so like when they had been boys together, Theo thought with a bittersweet ache, when they had practised swordplay in the courtyard before heading to the port. He and Alaric had once trained just as Roderic did now, in this same courtyard, watched by Athanagild, book in hand.

He glanced up. Through the arched corridor he could see Egilona and Riccilo, sitting with Lælia in the sun on the terrace that looked out toward the distant ocean, Jadis basking peacefully on the stone before them. He could not hear their discussion. Lælia seemed content enough, he told himself. She seemed to like Egilona's company. Egilona's maid leaned forward to draw a shawl over Lælia's shoulders. The girl was very attentive, Theo thought approvingly. She seemed to take particular care of Lælia and, notably, his wife seemed to actually enjoy the maid's care, which was, in itself, a novelty, Theo thought, smiling to himself. At a sharp cry, he turned back to the swordplay, his smile growing as he saw Roderic on the ground.

Theo was enjoying the company more than he liked to

319

admit. Having his brother and Laurentius there, Silas and Leofric at his side, gave him a sense of purpose he sometimes felt had been missing from the moment he had left the fleet. He had heard Laurentius's news, which had not, in fact, come from Apsimar as he had assumed but rather from one of Athanagild's clerical contacts in Rome. Leontios was still imprisoned; the warring factions in Constantinople grew more volatile. "You haven't heard from Apsimar either, have you?" Laurentius said later that morning, as they rode toward the port.

"No." Theo shook his head gloomily. "Nor from Yosef." The latter was more surprising than the former; he had expected to hear from Yosef by now, had in fact sent several letters, without receiving any response. The silence was concerning.

"You should be contacting Apsimar." It was Leofric who spoke. "If war is coming, we should be knowing it."

"He is right, *wenkai*." Silas's thoughtful voice came from his other side. "No matter what happens here, if war is coming, we must be ready."

"Apsimar will be in touch when he has something to say." Theo's voice was uncharacteristically curt. He did not like to admit that they were right, but that he was also dreading hearing from Apsimar. He could not leave Aurariola, not now, when Lælia would give birth any day. Not when things between them seemed so fragile, as if at any moment all he had come home for could be taken from him, lost in the grey coastal mists.

"Well, I will not sit on my arse forever, *schnecke*." Leofric's rebuke had none of his customary sardonic humour. "Not if there is a war to fight. Either we fix this fleet of yours, or we find Apsimar's. If the Arabs are coming, I will not stand here on the cliffs and watch them sail into harbour without so much as raising a sword to stop them."

"Nor I," said Roderic, his eyes shining. "We should get more men. I will talk to Wittiza – he will support us –"

Theo, rolling his eyes at Silas over the boy's head, left them to deal with Roderic's rather boastful chatter, spurring his horse ahead, to where Athanagild rode, out front and slightly away from the others. "You are quiet, brother," he said as he reined his horse in alongside Athanagild.

"I have little to offer in discussions of war." Athanagild spoke quietly, without meeting Theo's eyes. They rode in silence for a time. Theo had begun to relax into his own thoughts when Athanagild's words jolted him unpleasantly back to the present. "What is wrong with Lælia?"

"Lælia is with child." Theo heard the defensive note in his voice but was powerless to stop it.

"It is more than that, and you know it. I have never seen her so − brittle, nor you watch her so closely, as if at any moment, she might break."

"She has lost her home, Athanagild. And she is about to give birth. If that is not enough to make her quieter than usual −"

"I knew her when you were thought dead. When she learned of Giscila murdering her parents. When she thought she would have to marry Oppa." Athanagild's sharp words cut like knives. "I have never seen her like this. Even that cat of hers looks strained. There is something very wrong, Theo. And I do not believe you don't see that."

"What do you want me to say, Athanagild?" Theo's voice was harsh. "The only thing that could possibly help is the one thing I cannot give her. I can't see a way to win Illiberis back, not now, at least."

"Have you told her that?" The question came hard, and fast, and hit Theo like a gut punch, almost knocking the air from him. When he did not immediately answer, Athanagild went on, his voice low, but commanding nonetheless. "In all the time I have known her, Lælia has never ceased fighting for what is hers. She fought for you, Theo. Long after everyone, even Alaric and I, believed you dead." The stark admission hurt Theo more than he liked to admit. "Since our arrival,"

Athanagild went on, "I have heard her ask a hundred questions. Of Laurentius, me, Egilona. Even of Roderic. Gathering information, trying to get a picture of how matters lie in Toletum, and in Septem. And every time she does, do you know what else I see, Theo?"

Theo stared woodenly ahead but made no answer.

"She looks at you," said Athanagild quietly. "And she waits for you to ask the next question. To give her some indication – any – that you are interested in helping her find a way to regain her home, or at least in discussing it. But you never do, Theo. You change the subject as quickly as you can. You avoid so much as any mention of the name Illiberis, let alone any discussion of what is happening there. Have you ever even asked about the foals?"

Theo's head snapped around at that. Athanagild nodded, his eyes hard. "She mentioned them, to me, only yesterday. It is the time of year they should be brought down to the lowlands, she said, lest they be caught in the snows. And her voice when she said it, Theo..." He broke off, shaking his head.

"Do you think I don't know that voice?" Theo's every muscle was taut. "That damned voice is the reason I don't speak of Illiberis in her presence. You think you know her heartbreak, Athanagild? You don't have to witness it across the table every day, knowing you are the reason for it." He choked on the words and stopped, aware, as Athanagild's eyes scrutinised him, that he had said too much.

"How are you responsible for it, Theo? Lælia told me it was her decision to deal with Oppa. But you know I have never truly believed that."

"I should never have even suggested it." Theo sidestepped the question. "It doesn't matter," he muttered, looking away from Athanagild's sharp eyes. "It's done, now."

"Whatever your part," said Athanagild slowly, "if you now regret it, then tell her so. Admit whatever your part in this is, and then tell her that Illiberis might be lost for now, but that when, or if, the time comes to get it back, you will help her do so. Give her something to hold on to, Theo, before she drowns."

Theo looked out over the fields, trying to find the words. "I cannot give Lælia back Illiberis. I know all the ideas she has to regain it are no more than wild dreams, but to acknowledge that will destroy her. You are telling me to offer her lies as solace, and that, I cannot do." *More lies*, he thought bitterly, but did not say. "She is pregnant, Athanagild, due any day now to give birth to our child." He shifted restlessly. "And all the while, the fleet is busy fighting the Arab army —"

"Where you want to be." Athanagild finished the sentence for him.

"I didn't say that."

"You didn't have to." Athanagild's smile was twisted with pain. "You and Laurentius — you are too much the same. He, too, is missing part of himself every day he is not with those damned boats, out at sea."

Theo was as grateful for the change in subject as he was surprised by Athanagild's response. It was, he thought, a curiously intimate way for his brother to speak of their uncle; but then, he thought, he knew they had been close companions for many years now, just as he was with Silas and Leofric. "Is that what pains Laurentius, then? That he is not fighting? Or is it that Shukra is captive still?"

Athanagild's face hardened. "He received a letter recently. Recalling him to Toletum, to prepare for Wittiza's coronation. It was couched as a request, for his scholarly advice at council — but the letter also mentioned, seemingly casually, that the time has come for punishment to be administered to Shukra." His eyes glittered. "The messenger said it is rumoured that Shukra is to be castrated."

Theo blanched.

"Given the condition of Egica's dungeon, it is a death sentence."

Theo's mind was racing. "Have you discovered what it is

that Oppa wants? Why it is that he still holds Shukra and forces Laurentius's return?"

Athanagild's eyes gleamed a hard, metallic shade of gold. "You seem very sure this is a plot of Oppa's, Theo. And yet the letter came from the seniores, not Egica or his son. Oppa is far away. In Illiberis, no less. Nobody has heard a word from him."

"Trust me," Theo muttered. "I know the shape of Oppa's hands, and such a request bears their imprint. It is Oppa behind that letter, and I guarantee that he wants something." He gave his brother a hard look. "Is there anything that Shukra might know," he said, "that could be used as a weapon against you and Laurentius?" When he was met with a stare as impenetrable as his own, Theo shook his head, turning away. "If there is," he said harshly, "be certain that there are no depths to which Oppa will not sink, no depravity he will not employ, to discover it, and use it to gain whatever it is he seeks. If you do not yet know what that is, you will learn of it sooner or later – or I will," he added bitterly.

"Why you?" Athanagild looked at him directly. "What is it, this game between the two of you?" A charged silence was broken by Athanagild saying quietly, "I wish you might trust me, Theo."

Theo turned to his brother, looking directly into the watchful, cautious eyes. "Trust goes two ways, Athanagild. And given your silence to my question, it is clear there are secrets you do not share with me."

Athanagild let out a harsh bark of laughter, but he gave no answer, and after a time, Theo gave up expecting one, and they rode in silence.

* * *

It was several nights later when they all sat down to meat again. Lælia was particularly restless. "It will be any time now," Riccilo had told Theo in an undertone earlier that day. "The babe has dropped."

"Should you be going down to meat?" Theo had asked Lælia as they dressed in their bedchamber. "Perhaps you should be resting."

"I am not an invalid, Theo." Lælia's eyes had flashed dangerously. "Other women fight battles whilst pregnant. I'm sure I can manage a little meat." Theo did not ask who she meant by *other women*. Nor did he argue. Lælia in this mood was dangerously unpredictable. "Safia," she said, in a markedly softer tone, and Theo turned to see Egilona's lady's maid at the door. "Would you help me with my hair?"

Jadis had entered with Safia, stalking haughtily past Theo, and the maid shot him an understanding smile. Leaving them to it with something like relief, Theo had gone downstairs. When Lælia had appeared a short time later, she had been calmer, even smiling at him, but Theo could sense a restless energy beneath the surface that he imagined was what Riccilo had described. Now he looked at his wife across the table, her eyes glittering with a strange, golden light in the flickering flame of the candle, and thought she had never looked so beautiful.

"Have you had word from Yosef?" Athanagild's question was as unexpected as it was disruptive. "You mentioned you had written to him, more than once." He addressed it to Lælia, his words falling across the table like a shadow, drawing the rest of the conversation to a tense silence.

"I don't think —" began Theo, just as Laurentius said, "Athanagild —"

"No." Lælia's voice cut across them all. A strange smile played on her face, her eyes glittering even more feverishly as they met Athanagild's. "Neither Theo nor I have heard anything from Yosef since he returned to join the uprising in Septem."

"Uprising?" Egilona's face was uncharacteristically troubled as she looked between Lælia and her brother. "What do you mean – uprising?"

"I thought you would have heard," Lælia said, "being so intimate with the Toletum court, as you are. There is a Jewish rebellion gathering in Septem. They seek Ilyan's support for their cause."

"A rebellion?" Riccilo had paled. Instinctively she drew closer to Roderic, and her voice shook when she said, "They are insane. Nobody would be mad enough, surely, to even think such a thing."

"But you did not expect the Jews of Spania to simply accept the rulings of the Sixteenth Council, Aunt?" Now there was an almost taunting note in Lælia's voice. "Egica's priests would see the end of Judaism in Spania. It is not realistic, especially not in places such as Illiberis."

"Illiberis is no longer your concern." Riccilo's words rapped out like stones on glass, and Theo winced. The table was not only silent now. It was tense, waiting for the explosion Theo felt certain was about to erupt.

"Lælia," he said placatingly, reaching out a hand over the table. Jadis emerged from beneath the table, growling a low warning.

"No." Lælia snatched her hand away before he could reach it, her eyes still on Riccilo. There was an animation in her face that had been absent for months, a curious light Theo could not ever recall having ever seen in her eyes. Glancing at Athanagild, seeing the knowing expression on his brother's face, he suspected it was the very light Athanagild had hoped to provoke. He was making a point. *But at what cost?* Theo thought, seeing the way Lælia was staring at Riccilo.

"You are a coward, Riccilo," Lælia said scornfully. Riccilo gasped. "Your husband is maimed, and so you simply gave up. That is not the woman Acantha raised you to be. It is not how we women of Illiberis are." Jadis paced behind her chair, her eyes darting between Lælia and Riccilo.

"And where is Acantha now?" Riccilo's lips were bloodless,

her hands trembling. "I am sick and tired of hearing about Illiberis, Lælia, about what you have lost. My husband is barely a shadow of the man he once was. He sits alone in our villa in Corduba barely able to speak. He will never see his son again, never sign his name to a parchment, let alone lead men in battle. We are fortunate to have a home left to us at all. And you sit here, on lands your husband miraculously kept despite his family's treachery, despite the fact that you yourself fought a damned battle against Egica's own forces, and you want to tell me what I should be? How any of us should be?" She pushed back her chair and stood, her face pale with fury. "You are a spoiled child, Lælia. You always were, you, and that damnable wild cat." She cast Jadis a resentful glance that became slightly fearful when Jadis bared her teeth and growled back at her. "That animal should have been killed long ago. Paulus and Acantha indulged you instead of raising you to be what you should be."

"And what is that, exactly?" Lælia shot the words at her aunt with all the accuracy of her arrows. "A wife, Riccilo? A mother? A lady in name only, on lands not my own?"

"That's enough, Lælia." Theo heard the anger in his voice, but he no longer cared. "This is no place for this discussion."

"Is it not, brother?" Athanagild's voice was curiously inso-lent. "Where else should we have it, but amongst friends, and family?"

"Theo." Egilona's strained voice stopped the conversation, all eyes turning to her. "Please." She almost choked on the word. "Please tell me you are not planning to join this upris-ing. Jewish rebellion. Whatever it is. Tell me you won't risk everything, again. You can't be so foolish, Theo. Look at what happened. To our father – Alaric – to *Mother*." Her voice broke on the last word, and Theo felt something inside him crumble. Reaching out to cover her hand with his own, he said, "I will never see you endangered like that, Egilona. Please don't fear."

"But you will." Egilona's hand lay cold and flat in his. "If you support a rebellion, even in name, you will endanger us all. Do you not see that?" Impossibly trapped, Theo looked up to find Lælia watching him, her eyes burning with all that had lain unsaid between them for so long.

"Yes, Theo," she said softly. "These are the choices we face. They are not easy, and they have implications. If we fight against the Crown, we place all at this table in danger. I do not wish that, any more, I think, than you. But I can at least speak of it. You do not so much as even acknowledge such issues exist. We do not talk of Illiberis at all." She shook her head impatiently, and Theo realised, with horror, that it was unshed tears he could see glittering in her eyes.

Pushing back her chair, Lælia stood abruptly. "And whilst you might well be tired of hearing about war, Aunt," she said, glaring at Riccilo, "you had best accustom yourself to it. Because I can promise you this." Although she had begun speaking to her aunt, Lælia's eyes shifted to rest upon Theo, and he knew her words, now, were for him. "I will never stop talking about Illiberis," she said in a low, fierce tone. "Nor fighting to have it restored to me, whether with sword or pen. It is my heart and soul as much as any seated at this table, and I will cleave to it with the same loyalty. And now, if you will excuse me, I seem to have lost my appetite." She turned, but as she did, her face twisted, and for the first time since she had begun speaking, the hard, glittering light in her eyes disappeared. Her mouth opened in shock, and her eyes flew to Theo's. She said his name once – "*Theo*" – and then her body appeared almost to buckle.

Theo reached her just in time to prevent her falling to the floor. Riccilo's eyes met his from the other side of her niece's body.

"The baby is coming," she said grimly.

25

LÆLIA
NOVEMBER, AD 693

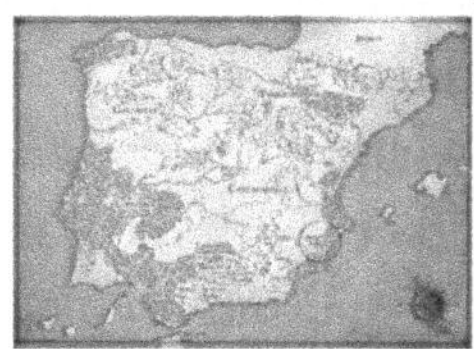

Aurariola, Spania
Orihuela, Spain

Every pain sent Lælia further inward. She was aware of her bedchamber, of Riccilo murmuring encouragement, the midwife Theo had sent for entering the room. She heard herself answer the woman's questions and lie quietly as competent hands felt within her. She heard the woman's reassurance that all was as it should be, but even that did not penetrate the strange fog that had fallen over her consciousness. The only time she spoke was when Riccilo made to order Jadis from the room.

"No," she said, her voice hoarse and unfamiliar to her ears. "Leave her with me." Jadis had retreated to a corner of the room where she lay, her eyes fixed on Lælia, her presence a silent comfort.

Lælia's voice disappeared after that. She retreated into the comforting familiarity of silence, to the place where she lived inside herself, seeing and feeling things she could not share and that people would not believe even if she did.

"Breathe," ordered the midwife, and Lælia did, drawing breath deep into her body and closing her eyes. The pain seized her in a fierce, white blaze, and she felt herself fall inward, toward the caves. She reached for them eagerly, feeling a surge of gratitude that it was now, as she bore a child for Illiberis, that the place of her ancestors should appear to her.

"Do not push. Not yet," said the midwife from somewhere distant, as the pain came again.

"You are doing well, Lælia," said Riccilo reassuringly. "Breathe deeply. It will help with the pain."

A part of Lælia obeyed, breathing through the long pain of the contraction, but another part of her turned further inward, willing the vision to return. She stood in the Valley of the Horse, the entrance to the caves yawning dark before her. She stepped inside, felt the darkness settle about her in a comforting mantle.

She was aware of the women talking over her head, holding her hand as the pains came, but they seemed far away. There was only her and the force ripping through her body, the breaths she took like a small vessel atop the raging sea of pain. She clung to the rhythm of her breath as the other part of her looked beyond the sea, to the distant cave walls.

Further in she went, past the strange rock formations that hung from the earthen walls, past the long, opaque striations upon which, long ago, Acantha had once played the bones whilst Lælia dreamed of Theo.

And now, she thought, some part of her conscious mind joining her in the surging confusion of pain, the bedchamber, and her vision, *now I have my wish. Theo is alive. He came home, to me. He loves me, and tonight his child will be born.* The thoughts travelled through her like a room through which she walked, just something she saw, rather than felt.

She turned her head and opened her eyes, seeing Riccilo look down at her anxiously. "Open the window," Lælia said, surprised at the hoarse rasp of her voice. "I need fresh air."

"It isn't wise to open the window during childbirth," said Riccilo hesitantly. "All manner of ills might enter the body —"

"Open it!" Lælia hoisted herself up on one elbow, holding her aunt's eyes. "I cannot breathe." Her chest felt tight and closed, and Lælia had never longed more for the high, clear air of Illiberis. Shooting the midwife a worried glance, Riccilo went to do her bidding. The wooden shutters were thrown open. Lælia slumped back down on the birthing straw and drew a deep, eager breath; then she tasted the thick coastal air, the salt on her tongue, rather than the sharp mountain tang, and felt unexpected tears prick her eyes. "I am not supposed to be here," she whispered. From the corner, Jadis growled softly, a low, pained noise that hurt Lælia's chest.

"What did you say?" Riccilo bent down to hear her.

"I'm not supposed to be here." Tired tears that cooled as soon as they left her eyes leaked down the sides of her face. "I don't belong here," she whispered, closing her eyes against Riccilo's worried scrutiny. "I should be home."

Then the pain seized her, a violent, urgent rush that felt different from before. "Now, you push!" said the midwife from somewhere beyond. "The baby is coming."

"Push, Lælia! You will give Theo a child before dawn." Riccilo's voice, excited and encouraging, came from even further away than before. Lælia was slipping into the darkness, the room fading from view…

* * *

Lælia and Theo were deep within the caves, children once again, standing before the wall of pictures. A strange song came from behind her, a humming that was both reassurance and life.

"Drink," she heard the boy Theo say. "You must drink."

She felt the cool water on her lips, the metallic taste of the caves sliding down her throat. The last of the oil lamp lit the shapes on the walls of the cave. "Look," said Theo behind her. "Look at the pictures."

Lælia's eyes ran over the shapes on the wall. She was a child and yet she saw with an adult's eyes; she knew the significance of what she looked at, but Theo was just a child, and she couldn't explain it to him. He was humming the song still, behind her, and it tugged at Lælia's heart, made her feel both comforted and achingly alone. She felt the love she had for him combine with the aeons of the past held within the caves, and then, from a far distance, she heard the odd, hollow sound of Acantha playing the bones.

"Acantha!" She turned to listen in the darkness and began to move toward the sound.

"No!" Theo's childish voice was high and clear. "Stay with me, Lælia! Don't leave…"

But Lælia was already withdrawing, moving into the darkness, toward the sound of the bones. Toward Acantha.

The caves closed around her with their profound silence, cutting off any sound except that of the bones playing their muffled, resonant tone, and Lælia drifted through the darkness toward it. She seemed to feel rather than hear the vibrations, as if the sound trembled deep inside her body. It came closer and closer, racking her whole form until it was almost unbearable, filling every cell, and then suddenly she was standing before the tall, opaque growths that stretched from cave floor to roof, upon which the bones beat their primal rhythm.

Acantha was facing away from her. Lælia wanted her grandmother to turn, wanted to fall into her embrace, but the woman's form was not solid but amorphous, unable to be touched. As Lælia hovered in the still air, agonisingly close, her grandmother's leg appeared amidst the misty darkness, a strange mark on her inner thigh suddenly vivid: two vertical lines, joined by another that ran on the horizontal between them.

She heard a voice that was not solely Acantha's, but rather an intermingling of her grandmother and Dahiya's deep, commanding tones: "When the walls fall, so will Spania." Was it Spania, or Africa? The words seemed one and the same in Lælia's mind, and in the distance she saw hard dust plains and tall, thick stone walls, heard the sound of men screaming.

"Lælia!" She heard the boy Theo calling her again, with a high, piercing voice, filled with anxiety. "Lælia! You must come back!"

She reached for Acantha, but her grandmother was gone, whisked away like smoke into the darkness, and she felt a tearing pain of loss as the caves began to slip away.

"Lælia!"

She felt herself drawn reluctantly back, travelling through the earthen tunnels toward the boy's voice. But now the caves changed shape, were no longer the ochre stone covered in black from generations of fires, but a glowing, incandescent light, the strange, otherworldly gleam of limestone, and as she moved she found herself not in the cavern of her infancy, but on the ledge in the caves of Aurariola, looking over the large, still pool at the centre. Theo stood below, but it was no longer the boy Theo, who had once given her water and kept her alive. This was Theo the man, who had shared her bed and to whom she had given her body, the man she had longed for and whom she still loved, with a deep, passionate ache that no time or place could ever truly touch.

Lælia tried to call out, but her voice was silenced, and she could only watch from the ledge as one shape turned into two. A small boy appeared at Theo's side, his white hair gleaming with the same brilliant light as his father's. Lælia was seized by a fierce, gripping pain that seemed to consume her, contracting every muscle in her body. Again she tried to scream, to call Theo to help, but though she opened her mouth no sound would come out.

As she watched, Theo leaned toward the boy. His arm was outstretched, pointing at the wall before them, and as Lælia followed its direction she saw that upon the limestone walls pictures had appeared, just as they were drawn in the place of pictures in her own caves.

Except that these were not pictures she knew.

There was a man, with his spear raised. A man facing a horde of other men. Just men, and their spears, fighting upon the craggy cliffs above a sea of dromons.

There was no horse, no animal at all.

Lælia shrieked, an unearthly, shattering scream of pain and loneliness, and the two figures in the cave turned toward her; but they were no longer Theo and their son, and she was no longer in the cave…

* * *

"Thank all the gods!" Riccilo was bent over the straw, her face pinched with worry. "I thought we had lost you. You must push, now, Lælia. Do you hear me? You are almost there."

And Lælia bore down, feeling the raging sea within her break and, with a final, agonising pain, the child leave her body, even as she heard the midwife's shout of triumph. From the corner of her eye, Lælia saw Jadis leap silently through the window, disappearing into the darkness beyond.

At the end of the straw bed, the midwife rose, smiling. "You have a son, my lady," she said proudly, holding the small, squirming body in her arms.

Lælia held out her hands, her heart twisting with love and wonder as the small figure reached blindly for her. "His name is Geila," she said, tears blurring his tiny features. "He will be a warrior, just as his ancestors were before him."

The memory of Theo standing before her in the atrium flashed across her mind; she thought his expression that day, after she had asked if he had received word about Illiberis, would be seared on her brain forever. "Consider formally conceding Illiberis?" he had asked her. "To *Oppa*?" The emphasis had been barely there, but the contempt in his eyes was something that would haunt her forever. Never had she seen such open hatred in his face, and when she had, Lælia had realised, finally, what such a concession truly meant to Theo. No matter what he might have said to her, no matter even if the original deal had been of his suggestion, Theo was a warrior. He would never, she knew, relinquish his own lands to an enemy. That was why he had told her there was "no shame" in being a wife, and a mother; it was why he did not press her for solutions.

Theo believed she had given up long ago. Perhaps, that she had given up the day she saw him standing before her with a sword in his hand, ready to make her a wife.

And to her deep shame, Lælia knew, deep inside herself, that in a way he was right. She *had* failed Illiberis; she *had* given up, no matter what she had shouted at the table over meat. For no matter how hard she had tried, no matter the myriad scenarios she had turned over in her mind, Lælia could not see how Illiberis could possibly be held.

Geila would be a warrior, it was true. But not because of her. And not for Illiberis.

Lælia felt suddenly tired, and weak. Her arm came up, covering her eyes from Riccilo's visible joy. "Tell Theo that Aurariola has a son," she said, her voice oddly flat and hard in the foetid air of the bedchamber. "A son for Spania, who will fight at his side." She raised her arm to find Riccilo frowning down at her.

"What did you see, Lælia?" Riccilo's touch on her arm was uncharacteristically gentle. "In the darkness of childbirth?"

Lælia met her aunt's eyes. "I saw our son." Her voice was thin, tired. "Standing at his father's side. Here – in the caves of Aurariola."

She held Riccilo's eyes, and something of the shame she felt must have been in her own, for her aunt's sharp features softened. "He may stand at his father's side, Lælia," she said quietly, "but he will always be your son. Remember that."

But Lælia had turned away, absorbing herself instead in the undeniable wonder of the small figure in her arms, the wide blue eyes that stared up at her. "Fetch Theo," she said, her voice catching. "Tell him to come and meet his son." She felt Riccilo move away from the straw and permitted the midwife to help her up, ordering the servants to remove the straw, shifting Lælia to the bed and swaddling the small figure tightly so that by the time the door opened hesitantly, Lælia was propped up in bed, the baby wrapped and warm against her.

"Theo," she said, reaching out her hand as he entered the room cautiously, his face lit with a combination of joy and terror. "Come. Meet your son – Geila."

* * *

THE NIGHT WAS LATE, and the villa quiet, when the baby stirred, and Theo, still fully clothed on the bed beside her where he had fallen asleep, woke with it, his face taut with concern.

"Shhh." Lælia smiled at Theo over the infant's head. "Your son is hungry, that is all." Guiding Geila to the breast, she looked up to find Theo watching her in the soft glow of the oil lamp, his eyes shadowed and cautious.

"He is your son, too," Theo said quietly. "Not only mine, Lælia." Reaching out a wondering hand, he caressed the top of the baby's head. "And he does not have to be named Geila. We could name him after Paulus, if you wish."

"No." Lælia felt something inside her clench, and the baby, seeming to sense her tension, began to cry feebly. She held him close, kissing the soft down on his head and rocking him against her. "He is Geila," she said, meeting Theo's eyes steadily. "He is your son – a child of Aurariola, of this land."

"He is also a child of Illiberis. Of your blood, and your land."

Lælia felt a faint shiver go through her tired body, shame and sadness intermingled. "No." Her voice was resigned. "He is of this place, Theo. Of *your* land. Geila is a son of Aurariola, of Spania, as were his ancestors. He will always be at your side, Theo. I saw it."

"You saw it?" Theo was frowning now, his eyes searching her face. "What do you mean, you saw it?"

"I saw it just as I did you, long ago, in the caves. Just as I saw in my dream that I was with child." She shrugged. "I saw it, and I know it to be true. All children are born of a place, belong to a place, whether they are born in that place or find it later. Your son is born of this place. He belongs to it as surely as I do Illiberis." *Or did,* she thought sadly but did not say. She did not wish to ruin this moment with her own failings.

"And what of me, Lælia?" Theo watched her with dark, unreadable eyes. "Where do I belong?"

Lælia's heart seized in her chest, so full of feeling it hurt. Gathering Geila close, she reached with her other hand to Theo, grasping his fingers in her own, relishing the hard, calloused strength of his skin against hers, the glow of their fede rings side by side. "You belong to me," she said fiercely. "No matter where we go, Theo, no matter what happens – you belong to me, and I to you. It has always been thus, and so it will always be."

With the hand that was free, Theo reached up and covered his heart, his eyes never leaving hers. "Promise," he said roughly, and Lælia, hearing the uncertainty and fear beneath the word, twisted inside again. She nodded, gripping his fingers tightly.

"Promise."

They lay like that through the night, holding their newborn son between them, until dawn glowed blood red on the ocean horizon.

* * *

A KNOCK CAME on her door late the following day, when she was resting with the babe, Jadis watchful on the floor beside her. "Who is it?" she called sleepily. Jadis came to her feet, growling softly, then, recognising the newcomer, dropped down to her belly again. The door pushed fully open to reveal Tosius, looking uncharacteristically nervous as he hovered just beyond the entrance. "Come inside, Tosius," said Lælia, smiling to herself. "My son is anxious to meet you." Stepping cautiously through the doorway, Tosius approached the bedside slowly, his eyes locked on the tiny figure resting in Lælia's arms. "A son," he said, one hand reaching out tentatively to touch the soft down on the baby's head.

"His name is Geila," said Lælia.

"Geila." Tosius nodded. "This is a good name."

"You can hold him." Lifting the infant, Lælia offered him to Tosius, who took the small figure into his arms with a look

337

of mingled terror and wonder, staring at the small features as if he had never seen a baby before, though Lælia knew well he had seen half a dozen of his own children born, and countless grandchildren. "He is his father's son," said Tosius quietly. "A good man, this one will be, *dauhter*."

"Yes." Lælia took back the small bundle, looking in wonder again at the small miracle of her and Theo's child. "He is a son of Aurariola, Tosius. I saw it in the caves." Tosius nodded his head as if this proclamation was the most natural thing in the world. Lælia swallowed hard. When she spoke again, it was in the language of the tribes, and her voice was rough. "He will never be of Illiberis."

"Not all things are known, *dauhter*." Tosius's voice was gentle.

Lælia shook her head briefly. "I know this." Tosius inclined his head but did not answer. "The tribes will not know him." Tears Lælia had not known were there spilled on to her cheeks. "He will not know the drums at the moon." A distant image of Paulus's tall, austere figure passed through her mind like a shadow. "He will not know —" Her voice choked off.

"*Dauhter*." Tosius sat on the bed, his slight figure barely making a dent on the coverlet. One gnarled hand covered her own. "All children know their ancestors," he said quietly. "They walk with us, whether at our side or in spirit. Your son will never be alone, *dauhter*. And he has warriors on both sides of his line who will hold his hands upon a sword, his hands upon the reins. Do not fear your world lost to him. He will find it, in time, and in his own way."

Lælia could only nod, her tears falling silently upon the head of her newborn son. Finally she fell asleep, and she did not feel it when Tosius gently removed his hand from hers and moved away.

26

YOSEF

FEBRUARY, AD 694

Septem, Mauretania
Ceuta, Morocco

"She is beautiful, *hachever sheli*." Yosef stroked his newborn daughter's head, smiling down at his wife as he lifted Arun's small figure up onto the bed. "Will you say welcome to your sister, Arun?"

The little boy touched the downy head tentatively. "What is she called?"

"Tikya." Yosef and Sarah exchanged a smile as they said the name together. The name meant *hope*, in their language. "Do you like it?" Sarah asked, taking Arun's hand in her own.

"Tikya." The boy tried the word out on his tongue. "I like it."

"Well, that is good." Yosef gathered the boy close. "Because it is your job, now and forever, to love her and care for her. That is what family does, Arun. Tikya will always be your sister. She will always look to you for help and guidance, and you will always protect her, and help her." The boy looked up at him with wide, solemn eyes.

"I will, *Abba*," he said seriously. "I promise."

"Good." Yosef kissed his head and deposited him on the floor. "Now you can run and tell all your friends your new sister's name – and that they, too, had better care for her always. Particularly the boys!" he called after his son's rapidly disappearing back. Sarah gave a gurgle of laughter. "Your daughter is barely a day old, and already you are warning off potential husbands? I had not envisaged you an ogre of a father, Yosef."

"You have no idea." Yosef kissed her head. "It is a strange thing, a man seeing his daughter for the first time. Both terrifying and exhilarating in equal parts." He smiled at her self-consciously.

"I know." She pressed his hand understandingly. "I felt the same way when first I held Arun. It was his presence, I think, that made me so fierce in my fight for Garnata. I wanted to give him the world, and protect him from it, at the same time."

"Yes." Yosef nodded. "It is that, exactly." They lay in silence for a while, the sounds of the street beyond drifting through the wrought-iron window on the chill winter air, carrying with it the familiar scents of spices and cooking, animals and wine. Septem was, to Yosef, an odd amalgam of all the places he had travelled, each culture seeming to find its way to a pot or wine flask in the teeming port city. The grapes that grew on the plains to the south came from as far afield as Persia, the dried apricots in the market from Anatolia. He liked it here, in the confluence of lives he had lived elsewhere. He felt liberated in a way he had not during his days back in Spania.

Spania. He frowned. It was only when Sarah spoke that he realised he had tensed, too. "Have you written to Theo, yet? Or Lælia?"

He pressed her shoulder gratefully, amazed as ever at her ability to read him so easily, even now, drowsy in the wake of childbirth.

"No." He met her eyes and shook his head. "Athanais tells me she has sent a messenger. But I cannot find the words, particularly for Lælia."

"You must tell them something, Yosef. It is not fair to remain silent after so long."

Yosef was quiet, a question he had pondered for some time turning over in his mind. Sarah pressed his hand. "What is it?"

"Oppa is blackmailing Theo." He said it bluntly, for he did not know another way to say it.

Sarah's eyes widened. "Blackmailing him? With what?"

Briefly Yosef told her of the parchment and the manner in which Oppa had secured Theo's signature on it. "I do not know if Theo has told Lælia, by now," Yosef said. "But somehow, I doubt it. I know he is bitterly ashamed of it – and terrified of what it might do to her to learn the truth, particularly now, when they are expecting a child. Or perhaps have even had it," he said, frowning as he made rapid calculations.

"It is all the more reason you must contact them." Sarah's face wore a concentrated expression. "Perhaps even go to Spania yourself, Yosef. See them. See them both." She shook her head. "Poor Lælia. How will it be, between them, when she learns the truth?"

"I do not dare imagine. But, Sarah" – Yosef pulled back, staring at her – "Spania will be dangerous."

Her mouth curved in a knowing smile. "Oh, Yosef," she murmured. "And you loathe danger so very much, my love, do you not?"

For a moment he froze, unsure how to react; then, seeing the mischief in her eyes, he burst into a peal of unabashed laughter, joined by his wife. "Oh, Sarah," he said, wiping his eyes and pulling her close. "You see that, then?"

"See it?" She rolled her eyes. "Do you think I don't know you slip into the tavern docks, and lurk in the corners, picking up the intelligence Ilyan normally pays children coin to acquire? Or notice you training with your strange movements, in the early hours of the morning, when you think I sleep?"

His smile faded, and he looked into her eyes with concern. "Does it frighten you, when I do that?"

"No, Yosef." Her smile was sweet, warm, and touched his heart. "I knew when you came back that you had been away a long time, in places inside yourself and without, that I will never know. It is part of the reason I love you so very much. I know you will always seek the dark corners, the secret places, always need to know that which other men do not see. It is a strength, Yosef. One I admire." She plucked playfully at his sleeve. "So long as your clandestine duties do not lead you to the beds of other women, that is. You may visit the pleasure houses, by all means. But if I so much as hear a whisper that you have paid coin in them…" Then they were laughing again, and Yosef, holding his wife and daughter close, felt the same wonder he did every day, that this was his life now.

Which brought him back to the present.

"If I go to Spania," he said, lowering his voice, "what story do I tell Theo, and Lælia, of our plans?" It sent a delicious thrill through him, to speak thus to his wife, of the future that was their secret alone. They had, since Athanais's arrival, succeeded in distancing themselves from the remnants of the Jewish rebellion, a fact that had placed a certain tension between them and the other Jews of Garnata who had taken refuge in Septem. Yosef regretted it, but he could not deny it had freed his time to focus on other matters, too.

"Speak to them of silk." Sarah's answer came immediately. This had been another surprise for Yosef: his wife's quick mind, the ready instincts he was learning every day to trust almost as much as he did his own. It was a revelation, one he was still adjusting to. "That much has not changed, our need for agents in Spania to manage sales for us. Aurariola is a better location for that than Illiberis, as we have already spoken of." They had talked of little else for months. "Of the rebellion, we need say little, I think. Lælia and Theo will know, after Athanais's message, that it is coming to nothing." She frowned. "And perhaps, whilst you are there, you might warn the Jews of Garnata that they must stand down. If what Ilyan says is true, Egica waits only for them to strike in order to crush them brutally. I would not see more suffer for a dream that can never be." She shivered, and Yosef drew her close.

"You cannot tell them of the future we envisage," she said quietly, against his chest. "Of an Arabic Spania. As you told me, they would never forgive it. But you can prepare them, perhaps, to see other options. Lælia especially."

"If Theo has not told her the truth of the parchment," Yosef said, "I cannot break his faith, Sarah. It would be the very worst of betrayals."

"No." She was quiet for a time. "But perhaps you can bring her enough information to make her own choices, Yosef." She looked up at him and touched his cheek with her hand. "It was giving me choices that saved us," she said quietly. "Had you not found the bravery to tell me the truth, Yosef, I do not know if we would be here, together, on this bed today. Somehow, Theo must find a way to do the same with Lælia. No matter what it costs him."

Yosef kissed her again. "I will go in the spring."

They sat together in silence for a long time, neither needing to say anything at all.

27

LÆLIA

FEBRUARY, AD 694

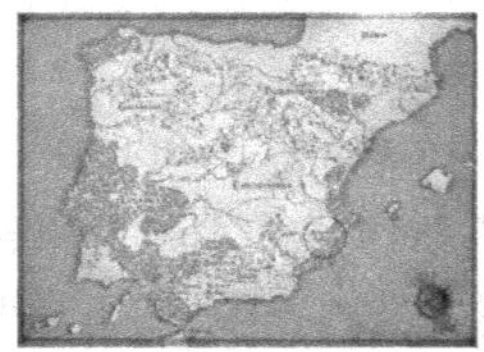

Aurariola, Spania
Orihuela, Spain

"Geila!" Theo swept his son high into the hard morning sunlight, smiling as the infant gurgled with delight. Geila's hands clutched at the horse's mane as Theo rested the plump little figure on the pommel of his saddle. "He will be big enough for his own pony soon enough."

"Tosius, I believe, already feels that moment is overdue." Lælia's hand rested on Theo's thigh, and he covered it with one of his own. She felt the familiar thrill of pleasure she did every time she saw him with their child, a private joy that had seemed to cocoon them both in the two months since his birth, holding the outside world, and her own inner turmoil, somewhat at bay.

"Fráuja." Lælia followed Theo's eyes to find a port labourer.

"What is it?" Theo asked.

"You are needed at the port. A dispute over a shipment."

Lælia was watching the man closely from beneath the horse's neck, so she saw the warning flash in the man's eyes when Theo might have asked something more. She felt a sickening stab, like pressing upon an old bruise. *Oppa has sent his demands, then. Or Yosef word. Either way, there is news.*

It was almost a relief.

"Ah," Theo said, nodding as if he were familiar with the issue. "I thought that merchant might prove to be a problem." Smiling at Lælia over Geila's head, he said, "I am sorry. I will return in time to share meat at nightfall."

Lælia's eyes shifted between the messenger and Theo. She waited for Theo to say something, acknowledge that here was news, at last. But he didn't, instead simply holding Geila out toward her with a smile, though his eyes were shadowed.

She knew he was trying to spare her, to prepare himself for what lay ahead. What must it be like, she wondered, after all this time, for Theo to face public humiliation at Oppa's hands? It hurt to know that her own failings were the reason for it; and yet still, she did not know what she could have done. She buried her face in Geila's head, breathing in his sweet scent, trying to drown out her own sense of inadequacy.

The infant kicked his little legs, reaching for the horse and crying out in indignation at having his favourite plaything removed. "Here," said Leofric gruffly, wheeling his horse to stand in front of Lælia. "Give him to me, or we will none of us have peace." But despite his grim tone there was a curious softness in his eyes, and his large, calloused hands were remarkably gentle as he tucked the squirming figure securely under one arm, muttering away to Geila in Slavic. "Yes, I know, little man," he grumbled as Tosius began chattering anxiously at his side. "I am perfectly able to manage both horse and child without your damned fussing." Lælia smiled despite herself. A not-so-silent war had waged between Leofric and Tosius since the day of Geila's birth, both men seeming to believe they knew what was best for the infant. More attentive – and unlikely – nursemaids Lælia could not have imagined.

Their only other competition for Geila's affections was Athanagild, but he was currently to be found down the coast in the port of Cartago Nova, where there was an important monastery that had been founded by Laurentius's family, many decades ago. Laurentius had ridden for Toletum around the time of Geila's birth. It had not escaped Lælia's notice that Athanagild had lingered unusually long in Aurariola.

"Ah, if the men of the fleet could see you now, *wenkai*." Silas's dark eyes flashed with amusement. "The mighty Slav of legend, a willing nursemaid." As he spoke, Silas rested one large hand unconsciously on Jadis's head. The cat twisted in ecstasy under his touch, purring happily as she clung to Silas's leg. The big man's dark eyes met Lælia's in a quiet, reassuring smile that touched her as much as did Silas's bond with Jadis. She trusted Silas, in a deep, quiet place inside herself that few people had ever really touched.

"I will return before dusk." Leaning from his saddle, Theo kissed her and was gone, Silas at his side. Lælia watched them go, until their figures were lost over the crest.

She fed Geila, then put him down for a nap. Riccilo had left soon after the birth, her presence pleasurable for neither of them. Egilona, though, had stayed, and her maid, Safia, with her. It was Safia who had slipped Lælia the news, just before Geila's birth, that Ilyan had, temporarily at least, withdrawn his support for the rebellion. They had found little chance, though, to speak since the birth. Egilona was sharp eyed, and Safia's role at court was, Lælia well knew, too important to be compromised. Nonetheless, now that her body had begun to recover from the trials of birth, so had Lælia's natural energy begun to stir. She was impatient for news. Impatient for action.

"You seem deep in thought, sister." Egilona folded herself down on the rug beside Lælia and smiled. "I hope you do not find our continued presence here a burden."

"Quite the opposite," said Lælia honestly, smiling. "Geila adores you, and I am grateful for the company."

"I imagine it must be difficult, after having been mistress of Illiberis so long, to find yourself in Aurariola. I have never been mistress of my own home and so find it hard, perhaps, to imagine what it must be like." Her words, though intended kindly, stung, and Lælia had to swallow hard to stop the resentful words on her lips from coming forth.

"I am sorry." Egilona's smile faded. "I did not mean to vex you."

Lælia shot her a rueful smile. "I know that." She was taking a deep breath, casting about for a change in topic, when Egilona said, "Safia tells me that you spent time across the sea. At Ilyan's court."

Lælia nodded. "I did." She gave Egilona a curious look, wondering exactly how much the maid had confessed to her mistress. "How does Safia know of such things?"

Egilona shrugged. "Her mother was a courtesan. Safia still has contacts from her mother's world. They hear many things." She gave Lælia a small smile. "As indelicate as it may be, I encourage her to maintain the contacts."

Lælia's smile widened. "A very intelligent move, I should think." When Egilona did not say any more, Lælia offered a branch of her own. "Perhaps Safia might also have heard of a woman across the seas called Dahiya, or Al Kahinat?"

Egilona nodded, her face oddly shuttered. "I have heard stories of her." She glanced at Lælia with an expression the other could not quite read. "Is it true that you spent time with her, deep in the sands of the desert?"

"Yes." Lælia felt an odd power in saying it, as if even verbally recalling those days loaned her a hint of the strength she had once known as her own, and which had felt, ever since leaving Illiberis, as if it belonged to another life. "I rode with Dahiya for many months and learned much at her side. She commands an entire army – *Riders*, as they are known in Africa. They are the most experienced fighters, on both horse and camel, that I have ever seen."

Egilona stared at her. "An army," she said. Her smile had faded. "And you rode with them? At their side?"

"Yes." Lælia's eyes narrowed. "I imagine it must seem indelicate, to you," she said, trying to stifle her impatience. "But for me, who was raised to the bow and sword, it was exhilarating."

"You miss it." Egilona's voice was flat.

"I miss having a purpose." Lælia could not quell the bitterness in her tone. "I am not made as you are," she said, attempting to soften her voice, "or as my aunt Riccilo is. My battlefield was never found in the games at court. I do not possess the skills, nor desire, to play upon that board." She smiled in reminiscence. "Dahiya once told me" – she deliberately softened her tone – "that if we wish to truly play a part in the game of life, we must make the game our own, not wait for a role to be given to us."

"And you feel that there, you played a role?"

Lælia swallowed hard, feeling unwelcome tears block her throat. "Yes," she whispered. "I did." Geila stirred and began to cry fretfully. She picked him up and held the small body against her own, inhaling the fresh newborn scent, welcoming his comforting heat, hiding her face in his swaddling.

Eventually, Egilona stood up. Touching Lælia's shoulder without speaking, she walked from the room.

* * *

STILL RESTLESS, after lunch when Theo still had not returned, Lælia left Geila in the dual care of Leofric and Tosius and, on the pretext of gathering herbs, walked away from the villa, down to a small stream edged by flowers that always brought Acantha to her mind. Long-dormant thoughts were stirring in her mind, things she had ceased to think of in the all-consuming days following Geila's birth. The recollection of Dahiya's words, her own reaction to Egilona's questions, had fired something in her soul. Suddenly she wondered how it was that so long had passed without her trying to formulate a plan to take back her home. *Perhaps it is not yet too late,* she thought, feeling a surge of her old strength. *Perhaps I may save Theo yet from Oppa's triumph.*

So deep in thought was she that she did not see the slender figure emerge from the mist until Safia stood directly before her, a finger over her lips to silence Lælia's involuntary cry of surprise. Tilting her head, she indicated a path away from the stream and through the field, and Lælia followed her to a fold in the limestone rocks from where they could see in every direction but were sheltered from sight. The air here smelled old and still, thick with salt and barley.

"I had news from my father." Safia did not waste time on greetings. "I have been trying to find an opportunity to speak with you for days, but my mistress, you might have noticed, is very observant."

"Egilona still does not know of your origins, she told me. She believes your knowledge comes from courtesans, apparently."

"For now, that is best. The day might come, perhaps, when I can tell her, but not yet. She thinks me Riccilo's servant, raised in Corduba, and trusts me implicitly. It is better this way. Egilona protects her position at court fiercely. Should she know of my origins, or this discussion, our association, I would be gone from her company instantly, if not denounced to Egica himself." Her words were brutally matter of fact. Lælia shivered at the thought of the inherent danger with which the girl lived, the constant threat of exposure.

"Do not fear for me," Safia said quietly. "I drank intrigue from my mother's breast. It is what I was raised to, what I understand. Which is why I will only risk meeting you infrequently, and far from curious eyes, as I said when first I arrived here." That had been a brief whisper in Lælia's ear, under the pretext of wrapping a shawl about her shoulders. Geila had been born soon after, putting a temporary end to such opportunities. When Lælia nodded, Safia went on, "I know you have been waiting to hear from Yosef, or my father, regarding the rebellion. Before I leave here I would tell you what I know." She met Lælia's eyes steadily. "Some of what I tell you is not because my father asked it of me; in fact, I suspect he may not approve. But I was with you when you negotiated with Giscila. I saw you at court. And in some things, I might still make my own judgements as to what I say, and to whom." There was a curious lack of emotion in her voice; Lælia could not help thinking of Ilyan's mercurial manner, his detached assessment of facts. Safia was his daughter, in more ways than one.

"The Arabs are preparing for a new assault on Africa, and we believe they will target Carthage." Safia spoke quietly and rapidly. "Dahiya is assembling her forces. Soon she will need more help than even my father might provide. He knows this." She glanced sideways, her expression wary. "Ilyan is preparing to ask the Spanish king for assistance. For this reason, it is well that your husband has moved the fleet here, close to his own lands."

Lælia tried and failed to keep her expression blank. "Does Theo know of this?"

"I believe he may be learning of it, even now. I think the same ship that brought news to me perhaps brings it also to him. There is a woman – Athanais. She is Persian, a friend of one you know here, Shukra. She has known Theo a long time, has been a conduit for communication between him and the Greek commander, Apsimar. She ran a – house – in Sebastopolis, where Theo and his men would go."

"Athanais." Lælia's mind raced. "Theo told me of her. That she was a good friend to him, a good ally." *She was also the one who introduced him to Elpis,* she thought, not without a stab of anger.

"Yes, she was all that." Safia's tone was slightly impatient. "But she is also much more. It is she to whom Yosef entrusted the secrets of silk he brought back from the east. She in turn took them to Constantinople, though I do not know anything of that, only that both my father and Yosef have been waiting anxiously for her return – and recently, she arrived in Septem. She is renowned, you understand, not only in Septem, for her ability to move from one place to another unnoticed. There are those who call her witch."

Lælia thought of Shukra, his ability to slip from one place to another unseen. "Yes," she said. "I can imagine."

"I believe she will get a message to Theo. He trusts Athanais, you understand." Lælia felt the world around her tilt slightly, as if the ground itself had shifted. *Theo trusts Athanais. Does he trust me, in the same way?* Although she said none of this, Safia nodded, as if hearing her unspoken thoughts. "Ilyan, my father, places much trust in Athanais also, for she has the ear not only of Dahiya, but of Apsimar, and others in Constantinople. So when Athanais told my father that he must now court the Spanish king's favour, my father listened." Her almond-shaped eyes, deep brown and unreadable, held Lælia's. "Ilyan will no longer give his support to the Jewish rebellion. Nor will Dahiya. Their full attention now is upon the Arab force coming over the sands – and what they might do to stop it. Your battle to win back Illiberis is no longer of interest to Ilyan."

For a moment Lælia was shocked into silence, the brutal end to her hopes, though not entirely unexpected, still stunning in its finality. "But all we have worked for," she whispered, "all Yosef and Theo did to ensure the production of silk could go ahead – all of that was negotiated by Illiberis with Septem. That we might ally with the Jewish merchants, create a strong industry, a wealthy foundation for trade that will benefit us all, and build an even stronger alliance against the Arabic forces coming from the east. What has changed?"

"What has changed is twofold." Safia's response was swift and unapologetic. "Sunifred's rebellion happened too early; and the Arabs are come sooner than any of us anticipated. My father no longer has the time to build an alliance that might overthrow the Crown, then wait for a new regime to bed down. He must work with what he has, now, and that, whether we like it or not, means working with Egica. If what Athanais says is true, Dahiya will need your husband's fleet, sooner rather than later. And for that, she needs Egica's goodwill." Safia held her eyes. "And that means Theo needs Egica's goodwill, also. He cannot both ask Egica to send the fleet to Ilyan's aid, and at the same time fight him for the return of Illiberis, Lælia. Not now." She met Lælia's eyes steadily. "Perhaps not ever."

"You do not know that." Lælia barely managed to get the words out. "You cannot be certain of Theo's mind. He hates Oppa. Perhaps he might use his power at court —"

She could hear the desperation in her own voice, even as Safia interrupted her. "I know nothing of that." The bland brown eyes stared back at Lælia. "But I do know my father's mind. I do not tell you this to make trouble." She glanced over her shoulder at where the mist had begun to settle over the late afternoon fields. "I tell you because I believe you have the right to know. Your plans of relying on my father's help to regain your home are in vain, Lælia. Illiberis is lost to you. For now, at least." Pulling her hood up over her face, she said, "And I must go. Egilona will soon look for me."

"Wait." Lælia reached out to grasp her arm, unwilling to relinquish the one link to knowledge she had. "Do you think Theo already knew of this, before today?"

Safia looked back briefly, the rising sun lighting her eyes. "No, Lælia. If I only had it today, then I cannot imagine he had it earlier. But I do think he has suspected."

"And Yosef?" Lælia found it hard to say the name. "What do you know of his thoughts, Safia?"

"Of Yosef I have no word." There was a faint frown on Safia's face. "I do not know his mind, Lælia, other than to say I do not believe he would support the Jewish cause without my father's backing." Turning away, she said over her shoulder as she went, "Do not seek me out, Lælia. I have told you all I will." Then she was gone, a shadow in the barley.

Lælia remained still for a long time. She leaned against the cold limestone, barely conscious of the sharp edges creasing her skin through the linen. The sun sank and still she stood in the cold shadow of the rock, Safia's words rebounding on the echo chamber of her heart like stones falling into a ravine. The demise of the rebellion was nothing that she had not, somewhere deep inside, suspected; but the rest of it, the plans Ilyan had to ally with Egica – *with Oppa!* – those were something else, entirely.

She felt as if a part of her soul had been cut away, set adrift. The part that had stayed blind, had taken refuge in Theo and Geila and the shelter their life provided, that part was no longer hers. It was like a life that belonged to someone else, to a dream, or an illusion, from which Lælia felt as if she had just woken. The woman who had given birth to a son, had cut herbs in a villa garden and sat to meat with her husband – that woman had been sheared away from her, *Lælia*, from the woman who stood now in the dank darkness of limestone rock, thinking of what she must do next.

That woman might accept the loss of her home and follow her husband's lead, contenting herself with being his companion and support, managing his domestic affairs as he played his role in Spania's fate.

But she, Lælia of Illiberis? She, who had shot a bow before she could walk, learned to fight from horseback amongst Dahiya's famed Riders, learned to track a shadow in a storm with unerring accuracy – was that Lælia ready to accept her fate with not so much as a murmur?

No.

The answer came to Lælia as surely as the sun falling behind the still fields of barley.

A boundary within her soul she had not known existed had shown itself, and Lælia knew, with a terrible certainty, that it was a boundary that nothing on this earth, not even fear or love, could make her cross.

Dahiya's words came to her through the gloaming like a

wraith from the past: *If you belong to Illiberis in the way you say you do, then your war is not for Spania, Lælia. It is for Illiberis — and it is a war that belongs to you alone.*

The sun was gone, and the mist fully fallen, when Lælia finally peeled herself away from the rock and strode back to the villa, strength returning to her with every step she took.

28

THEO
FEBRUARY, AD 694

Aurariola, Spania
Orihuela, Spain

Theo rode back to Aurariola at noon the day after the messenger had fetched him to the port, his mind still churning with the news yesterday had brought, news that had left him so shaken he had sent a message back to the villa that he was delayed at the port, and not to expect him until today. He knew it had been cowardice; but equally, he felt that even his practised mask could not conceal his inner turmoil from Lælia's disquieting eyes.

For the hundredth time, he relived the meeting with the wine merchant from the previous day.

"You have a letter for me?"

"Letters are dangerous." The man accepted the flask Theo passed him and drank sparingly, his dark eyes looking out over the bay. "Much better it is to be speaking what must be said, for spoken words cannot be found by other men."

Theo found himself smiling at the familiar, sing-song cadence. "Athanais sent you."

"This person, yes, I am knowing."

"She reached Septem, then?"

"She is there still."

"What news, then, from Septem?"

"Ah." The man turned dark, meditative eyes to him. "The words I bring are not from *Septem*, Theudemir of Aurariola. They are from this person who is your friend, you understand? This is different to *news from Septem*."

"Very well." Theo inclined his head, unable to hide his amusement. "Speak these words, then."

"These words," said the man, "say first, this: '*Khosh amadid*, friend.'"

The greeting had taken Theo back, to a dark cove many years ago, the impossible choice Athanais had been witness to, when he had been forced to decide between returning to Lælia or sailing forth on an uncertain mission to aid Yosef. They took him back to the small building in Sebastopolis where Theo had first taken Elpis, in a rush of pain, loneliness, and desire. They took him back to the day Yosef had finally found Theo in Sebastopolis, and Athanais, reaching out her hands, had offered him that same greeting. Theo felt an unexpected lump in his throat. It was, he thought, so like Athanais to send a greeting that meant *welcome*, despite being across the sea, in Septem.

The man, seeing emotion chasing across Theo's face, nodded slightly. "It is good, that you understand this. Very well. I will speak now her words to you." He had lowered his head and begun to speak, his voice taking on Athanais's tones so eloquently it was almost as if it were her speaking.

"'I am happy to know you are returned to your bride, and to hear you have a son. Ahura Mazda smiles at your good fortune.

"'I am pleased also that you have retained your family lands on the coast. This will serve well, for the time is come, Theo, for us to build the force we once spoke of.

"'I understand you have favour at court. You must build

upon that. Make of Egica an ally, a friend. Take your time, be smart, and play your role at court well, as you once did in Sebastopolis. Befriend those in power. Power now lies in alliance with your king, not rebellion against him. It is best for all we plan if you remain in Aurariola and relinquish all efforts to regain your wife's lands. The Jews of Garnata, exiled here in Septem, continue to agitate for rebellion, and there are some, here and in Spania, who may still support them. Should they so much as attempt such a foolish scheme you must be nowhere near it, Theo. You are too valuable to be wasted in such an endeavour. I say this only because Yosef has told me that your wife is very attached to her home, and that Oppa now lives in it. I know this must be for you, and her, as salt in a wound. But that battle is lost. To take up arms against Oppa, or your king, will undo all that we need of you at court. I know, too, that you have fought that particular shadow too many times to be drawn by his games. Do not let those lessons be wasted now, Theo. Oppa is still dangerous. Do not be his puppet.

""The fleet is more important now than ever. If you have not already done so, see it is moved to your own coastal port and is under your control. It may be needed sooner than you think, and dromons are no use unmanned, or on the other side of the country. Apsimar sends word that the Arabic forces advance. Dahiya will soon need the help of the Karabisianoi, and of any force the Spanish Crown may be able to offer, your dromons included. We no longer have time to wait for a new regime but must work with the one we have. If you have influence at the court there, you must wield it, Theo. We are already putting in place the business we have all worked for. We will soon have the coin to make of your fleet a true force. Apsimar says that it is time to position yourself there in such a way that when your help is called upon, the king will listen to you.

"And now I have said too much. It is rare that a messenger passes the port whom I trust as I do this one, and so I send these words that you might know Apsimar's will directly and begin to put his plans into place. Ilyan, no doubt, will send word of his own in time, and I will send more when it is safe to do so. But you and I are old friends, and I would have you know the truth from my own mouth, that you might know that you are not alone, Theo, in these decisions you must make.

"'Please send my warmest greetings to your wife. I look forward to meeting her, and your son.

"'*Khodâ hâfez, aziz-am.* May God protect you.'"

* * *

Even now, recalling those words, Theo was grateful for the salt on the wind upon which he might blame the sudden moisture in his eyes. He became aware of Silas riding to his side.

"Go on, then." He turned away abruptly, clearing his throat. "Ask what you will."

"I will not ask, *wenkai*." Silas's voice was deep and uncharacteristically sober. "The wine you drank last night spoke loudly enough for us both. Your news is your own."

"Ah, but that is exactly it, Silas. The messenger was very clear that he did not bring news." Theo's effort to keep his voice light faded by the end of his sentence. "He brought a greeting," he said, rather more grimly. "From Athanais."

"This name is one I am glad to hear." Silas's grin stretched wide across his face. "I would imagine she has news no other in this world might bring, *wenkai*."

"She does. It seems the Arabs advance. Dahiya might soon be at war." Silas tilted his head but did not speak. "So Apsimar believes, at any rate," Theo went on, and despite all his own misgivings, he felt excitement seize him, the surge of men and war that had been his world for so long beckoning like a siren song from across the ocean. "He sends word that I should consolidate my position at court. Ensure my standing with the king, and build up the fleet, so

358

that when Apsimar might send word, we are in a position to answer."

Theo did not mention the fact that Athanais had known of his son, news Theo could not imagine how she had come by. He tucked that away to consider later, at his leisure.

Theo and Silas rode in silence for a time, the words hanging in the air between them. When they crested the slope that led down to the fields upon which the villa lay, Silas drew rein and turned to Theo. The sky was pale blue through the coastal sea haze, whilst in front of them a low mist settled over the barley fields. "And what news from Yosef? Ilyan?" Silas's eyes searched Theo's face.

Heat prickled Theo's skin. "That is what I meant," he said quietly, "when I said there was no news. The message was from Athanais, not from Yosef, or Ilyan."

"But still she gave you news," Silas pushed. "She did not send a man simply to send Apsimar's greetings, *wenkai*."

Theo drew a deep breath. The air had lost what heat the sun gave the day, and the cold seared his lungs, salty and hard. "She told me to remain on my own lands. To forget Illiberis, and any talk of rebellion." He made an impatient noise. "She told me nothing you and I did not already suspect, Silas."

"Then the game has changed." Silas's voice was weary, and he passed a hand over his face. "If the Arabs are coming there will be war and enough, *wenkai*, to keep any man busy." He cast a sideways glance at Theo. "There is no longer room for divided loyalties. You of all men know what happens when men put their own interests above those of war."

"Of course I know." Theo's words were hard as stone, but Silas did not flinch.

"You must speak to your wife, *wenkai*," he went on remorselessly. "Before it is too late and she no longer wishes to hear you."

Theo remained still, staring down the road to where the villa lay grey and silent amid the mist. A lone bird of prey wheeled overhead, its low cry like a cautionary tale on the wind. "I know that," he said slowly. "But what is it I am to say, Silas? What am I supposed to tell Lælia — that the whore-keeper who once sold Elpis's body to me sends her greetings, and tells me not only that I cannot fight for Illiberis, but that I must now ally with the same man Lælia herself risked every-thing to defy?" *Not to mention,* he thought, though he left it unsaid, *that even if she disagrees with that decision, it is too late, because I have already signed her rights to it away.* "How, exactly," he said aloud, trying to drown out the ever-present voice in his mind, "do you imagine such news will be received?"

Silas leaned forward on the pommel of his saddle, his eyes glowing mahogany as the last of the sun's rays lit them from the side. "I would rather imagine that conversation," he said quietly, "than one where she hears such news from elsewhere, and learns you knew of it all along." He frowned. "Do you think the failure of the rebellion will be such a surprise to her, then? Surely it has been foreshadowed?"

"It isn't the end of the Jewish rebellion that concerns me, Silas." The words rasped in Theo's throat. "It's the alliance with Egica — and Oppa." He forced himself to meet the other man's eyes. "You did not see her, back in Toletum —" He broke off abruptly. Saw her face the night they had faced Elpis at court. Heard her low, fierce voice as he had every day since: *We have come too far, endured too much, to let Oppa's games rule our lives for a moment more.* And after that, when he had asked if she might consider signing the papers: *I may now be only your wife, but such responsibilities are still mine to bear.*

Illiberis was hers. Heart, and soul.

I care for you, and Illiberis. All else is smoke.

"This is what Oppa wants." He barely choked the words out. "What he has been trying to achieve from the moment I put my name to that damned parchment, back in Sebastopo-lis. Losing Illiberis to him is one thing, and hard though it is, Lælia has borne it with more strength than most women could. But to openly ally with him, Silas? I cannot imagine what she will say to that. And yet still, I cannot keep this, at least, from her." He shook his head, his mouth tightening. "But if she refuses, there will be no choice but truth." *And that,* he thought, *will end us.* It was an inescapable truth there was no need to state aloud.

"I do not have the answers for you, *wenkai.*" Silas's large hand gripped Theo's shoulder, tugging him back to the present. "But I will say this: I have grown to love your wife as a sister. We did what we had to do to keep her safe, and the child, too. But now is the time for honesty, or as much as you might be able to give. Neither of you are children. Such lies are not honourable between a man and his wife."

"Good thoughts, good words, good deeds," murmured Theo. He cast Silas a grim look. "Sometimes I wish I'd never so much as heard that damned phrase."

"Ha!" Silas gave a sudden, welcome rumble of laughter as he turned his horse down the hill. "That is the thing about wisdom, *wenkai.* All men, once in possession of it, wish they might have remained in blessed ignorance."

* * *

If Theo had dreaded what welcome might meet him upon his return, nothing could have surprised him more than to find Lælia, Geila strapped efficiently to her back in a manner no self-respecting Gothic lady would ever deign to do, hand poised over the writing stand in the study, eyes sparkling with an excitement that was neither feverish nor false, but the girl of his heart, the woman he loved.

"Theo!" She looked up at him with such open enthusiasm that his heart caught. "I am glad you are home —"

"Lælia." He crossed the room swiftly and grasped her hands, all trace of hesitation fleeing his mind in the sudden knowledge of the right thing to do. "Forgive me for my late return. I have news. I should have returned at once to give it to you, and for that, I am sorry. I needed a night to clear my own mind." He smiled ruefully and rubbed a hand over his face. "Or muddle it, more like. Either way, I am sorry I am late."

Lælia did not step away, nor flinch from his eyes. She smiled and nodded. "Thank you for saying that, Theo. Now tell me this news."

As closely as he could recall, Theo relayed all the messenger had told him, holding nothing back. The only thing he did not speak of was that damned parchment. All else had come after their return to Toletum, were matters he knew they could face together. But that one, long-ago betrayal, Theo did not know how to speak of. All he knew was that now, when there was so much else to impart that was hard to hear, that one betrayal he could spare her.

Lælia listened, her eyes never leaving his face. To his surprise, she barely reacted to his words, her eyes never losing their lively gleam. If anything, as he went on, the warmth in them grew ever greater. He could not help but think, all the time that he spoke, that he could not recall the last time he had seen such life in them. It warmed his heart, made him believe that perhaps, even now, they might find a way through the quagmire of lies and deceit that had brought them to here.

"And that is all I know," he finished, drawing her down onto the lecta beside him and watching as she untied Geila and put the sleeping baby on the floor, where he slept on peacefully. "I know the thought of allying with Egica is the worst possible news I could bring. I am more sorry than you know, Lælia. I wish it were different."

"I know." Reaching up, she touched his face, her own full of love. "I want to thank you, Theo. For speaking openly to me of this, and treating me as your equal, as you always have. I wish you to know I value that, above all things." Again he was stunned at how calmly she received the news. "I know you do not wish this, and that you, too, are caught in a web. But if I am honest, such news is not entirely unexpected." Theo raised his eyebrows, doing his best to conceal how taken aback he was, and she smiled wryly. "You never seemed to truly believe in the rebellion. Yosef, neither. But if I had been honest, with myself as well as you, nor did I. Not really. And no matter how much I long for Illiberis, I could not bear to see Egilona endangered, or Athanagild." She took a breath, as if steadying herself to say the next words. "I, too, have spent some time clearing my head, this past day." Her eyes, when they rose to his, were solemn and as open as he could recall seeing since the first time the wary shield had fallen over them. "Illiberis," she said slowly, "has not yet been formally ceded to Oppa." Holding up a hand as if to stem an imagined protest, she said, "I know he has taken possession of it, and that following my grandfather's treason, Illiberis lies in the king's gift. Even so, there is no formal agreement yet in place – and if I know the southern lords, they will not have met Oppa with any kindness. He has inherited a latifundium already stripped of its greatest asset – the herd – and with none left there who know the secrets of breeding that Illiberis is renowned for. If Oppa has not already realised the weighted dice with which he plays, he will soon enough."

Theo did not interrupt her, but he felt the danger of the precipice on which they were poised. He could do nothing but wait, to see what conclusion she reached. "If your news is correct," she went on, "soon enough, you must make an ally of Egica." Her mouth twisted. "Again," she said, "though unwelcome, such news is hardly unexpected. If you are to head his fleet, you can hardly be at odds with the man; and there is no doubt that for Ilyan, as well as Spania, the best place for you is at the head of that fleet. But I believe such an alliance might, after all, offer us an opportunity." Her eyes shone, and Theo forced himself to meet them, even despite his growing dread. "Egilona and Athanagild are here, with us," she said. "Not in Toletum, where they might at any moment be seized. The dromons of the fleet, too, are here. And the news you have today, of Ilyan's desire for an alliance, I would wager is news that Egica does not yet have. Nor does he know of the silk industry Ilyan is about to see created. That is a secret from which we might still profit, Theo.

"Oppa may have forced you to make alliance with him, in order for him to speak for you at court; but what is stopping us from going back to him now, with an offer of our own? We both know he craves power, above all things. Offer him a part of the silk trade – in exchange for returning Illiberis to us. Offer to create a bulwark in the south that is loyal to him, one that can hold Spania against any invaders that might come. You, here in Aurariola with the fleet; and I, in Illiberis, with the herd, training a thiufa of our own Riders." Her eyes glowed. "Oppa may frame it at court as a strategic decision, and name you as count, leaving me out of it altogether. And he does not need to know it is I who will train the Illiberis thiufa," she said, almost mischievously. "He can believe it is you. You can send as many men to form a guard about me as you choose, Theo, and I will accept them all. But let us use this opportunity. Perhaps he cannot openly grant us Illiberis, not yet, not so soon after the public confiscation of it. But if he can take that other prize, the one he has craved for so long, the whole reason he attacked the fleet originally – Theo, if he has control over the coin from silk, is it not possible that he might, just might, listen to us?"

Geila gave a sharp cry, and Theo welcomed the respite as Lælia bent to the child and offered him her breast, turning her back to Theo as she did. He realised that she was granting him this time to consider her words, giving him the same consideration she thought he had shown her, and guilt gnawed at him.

The worst of it was, there was sense in what she said. And she was right in saying that here in Aurariola, Athanagild and Egilona could both be kept safe, even sent across the seas, if it came to it. Under any other circumstances, with any other man, Theo knew she would be right.

The problem was that Theo knew Oppa would never agree to it.

Oppa's voice, silky and insidious, passed through his mind: *I expect to be Spania's future, Theudemir. And to do that, I need you as an ally. One that I might count upon...*

Oppa did not crave coin alone. He wanted power. He always had. And power, to Oppa, meant two things: control, and revenge.

Control over every aspect of their lives; and revenge for every humiliation, both real and imagined, he had suffered at both his and Lælia's hands. One way or another, Oppa intended that parchment to destroy him and Lælia. And Theo knew, perhaps with more clarity than ever before, that there was no deal that could be made that would avoid that outcome.

He considered his next words carefully, and when Lælia had handed Geila to Tosius, closed the door, and turned back to him, he was ready.

"It is a good plan, Lælia. Well thought out, and with good merit."

"But?" The glimmer of a smile hovered at her mouth. "I know you, Theo. Tell me."

"Oppa gains nothing by returning Illiberis to you." Theo felt his own heart skip a beat as he said it, and it took all his self-control to maintain an even tone. "All you describe can be achieved with the latifundium in his name. You are right, that there is no formal agreement yet granting Oppa Illiberis." He thought the words might choke in his throat. "But he will ask for it, soon enough. And when he does, the southern lords will bow, or be named traitors themselves. Egica will never agree to handing it back, publicly or not. Particularly after he learns that Ilyan not only seeks alliance but is willing to pay handsomely for it. He defeated the south. He would be foolish indeed to begin showing favour to the same family that led an army north to face him at Toletum." He shook his head slowly. "No matter what we might offer, Lælia, I cannot see why Egica or Oppa would listen to such a plea. Even if we managed to convince Oppa of it now, the moment he learns of the silk industry, he will renege without a thought."

Particularly when Oppa already has an agreement in writing. One he might pull out at any time, no matter what he agrees to. One that would only have more power if he knew we were having this discussion, and that the parchment was still a secret between us.

"Perhaps you are right in your arguments, Theo." She was frowning out of the window, into the mist, unaware of the emotions on his face. "I know that above all else, you wish to protect me from disappointment. But Illiberis is mine, Theo. My responsibility. I will not hide from it any longer, nor flinch from your arguments. And in matters pertaining to Illiberis, I am better informed, perhaps, than you.

"I know that Ilyan loathes Oppa. And so long as the southern lords have not seen me stand before them in court and admit defeat, so long as Oppa does not have documents in his hand saying Illiberis is his, I know they will not bow.

"We must try, Theo." Behind her back Theo blanched, but he did not speak, and she went on, unheeding of his thoughts. "Would you at least agree to write to Ilyan, and Yosef, with my proposal? I will do so if you do not," she said, a hint of steel in her voice, "but it is better, I think, from you. Perhaps the same messenger who brought word to us might also take a message back." There was no mistaking the challenge in her voice. Lælia, Theo knew, was no longer asking. In some ways it was a relief. "And," she went on, not waiting for his response, "might we take Athanagild into our confidence, and ask him to consult Laurentius?"

That comment made Theo think, again, of the tension between Athanagild and Laurentius. Some of his doubt must have shown, for Lælia put her hand on his arm. "Do not worry for Laurentius and Athanagild," she said, a small smile he could not quite read lurking in her eyes. "I have known them both in the time you did not. They play so many games of politics that at times it is all consuming, particularly since Shukra's conviction. But they will listen to this. I know they will. And if, after we tell our friends, they still believe my plan cannot work, then we will leave it, Theo." She gave him a twisted smile then turned away again, looking out of the window as she said, as if to herself, "For now, at least. Until I think of a new scheme to win back my home again."

Tell her!

The urge for honesty seized Theo, leaving him almost weak. If ever there had been a moment, that moment was now, when she was as strong as she had ever been, fired with plans, trying to make a future path for them both. He opened his mouth, already reaching for the words. *It is time,* he thought, feeling a rising thrill of fear and excitement. *It is time, at last, for the truth. No matter where it leads.*

Then she turned from the window, a shadow in her face that sent a chill through him, temporarily staying his tongue. "Of all the things I feared, when you were gone," she said quietly, "it was that Oppa would find a way to corrupt you, Theo. Destroy that place inside you that belongs to you and me. I always knew he would take Illiberis if he could. The miracle is that he did not find a way to use you to gain it. Once, I could not have imagined suggesting an alliance with him, no matter the reason. But now?" Her mouth twisted as she moved into his arms. They closed around her, but never had Theo felt more wooden and remote. "I have seen him on the ground, Theo, at the end of my sword. I could have ended his life. You could have. Somewhere inside himself, Oppa knows that. And no matter if he sleeps in my grandfather's bed" – her eyes gleamed dangerously – "some part of him knows that he lives only because we both allow him to do so. That thought has been all that has sustained me, over these months. That every night he sleeps in Illiberis, Oppa knows it is not because he won it, but because you and I allow him to." The love on her face twisted the knife more deeply in Theo's heart than anything else ever could have. "You and I, Theo," she murmured, her lips against his ear. "We have always been stronger than him, whether you were at sea as his slave, or I was standing in court facing him down. He has never beaten us. And it is that, more than any other reason, that makes me believe we can ally with him now. Oppa fears us both, Theo. He always has."

And just as quickly as that, his moment of truth was gone into the mist, to the same private hell in which he had hidden it for so long now it seemed to have created a locked room inside his very soul.

"I will soon be forced to ride to Toletum for this damned coronation of Wittiza's," he said, keeping his voice steady with an effort. "I shall speak to Laurentius then, if Athanagild does not before." She nodded, satisfied.

He stood and took her in his arms, feeling his darkest secret retreat, the door guarding it lock fast once more.

29

LAURENTIUS

FEBRUARY, AD 694

Toletum, Spania
Toledo, Spain

As he had every day since his return to Toletum, Laurentius Severianus passed by the entrance to the palace dungeons on his way home from the council chamber. It required him to take a longer route, through a part of Toletum he might not customarily frequent at dusk, but he walked it with a soldier's caution, and with his cloak hiding his face.

The truth was that Laurentius had returned to Toletum for one reason, and one only: to rescue Shukra from those damned dungeons, even if it meant losing his own life to do so.

Now his pace slowed unconsciously, his eyes searching, as they did every evening, for the small details that mattered. The guards' routine he knew; as he did every step, stone, and grate. Still, he had not yet found the way in. But he must. And soon.

Despite the whispers that Shukra was soon to be castrated, Laurentius had heard no further news at all. He was not even certain where those whispers had come from; his usual sources, even those loyal to Athanagild who knew it was safe to report to him, seemed less forthcoming than usual. In fact, Toletum itself, Laurentius reflected grimly as he walked, seemed held in a strange hush in the months preceding Wittiza's coronation. Particularly now, Laurentius thought, after he had received word from Septem.

He had not yet had the opportunity to share it with Theo or Athanagild. Such matters were too delicate to be put in a letter. News had come to him from a woman, dressed in the gaudy finery of a courtesan, her eyes blacklined with kohl. She was waiting in the tavern where Laurentius occasionally drank, more for public image than any other reason, and also because those who sought him knew he could be found there. The woman had passed a few moments at his table before her cloak had parted to reveal the pendant at her neck: the image of an eagle and the rising sun. The symbol, Laurentius knew after his many years with Shukra, of the followers of Zoroaster. He had immediately laid down his coin on the table where men saw it, and she had pocketed it, also openly, so that when they left together they drew no more than knowing smiles and the occasional wink.

It was from the woman that Laurentius learned of Athanais's arrival – and of the success of Yosef's mission, at last. She told Laurentius only that much: that Athanais had come, and with her, *the treasure from the east.* There was no more, and she left soon after saying that much. Laurentius thought he should feel more at the news, that this thing they had all worked so hard to achieve, the making of silk, would now be possible. But in his heart, he wondered how much it truly mattered, now; and even more, he wondered if he cared.

No matter what promises Shukra had extracted from him, Laurentius had realised, during his time in Aurariola, that to stay true to them would break something in his own soul that could not be put back together. Worse, and far harder to bear, was the knowledge that Shukra's ongoing suffering was doing the same, and worse, to Athanagild. Laurentius had not loved Athanagild so much only to now watch the man who had finally brought light into his own heart slowly crumble from guilt and shame, piece by piece. He had not told Athanagild of his plans. Laurentius intended to facilitate the rescue alone – and then run with Shukra.

He knew Athanagild would never agree. Or, worse, that he would insist on running with them. But to do so, Laurentius thought grimly, would spell the end of all Athanagild had fought and suffered to achieve. His role in the Church, gone; his family once more condemned for sins not their fault; his brother, recently returned, lost again. And Athanagild himself, an exile, wandering foreign shores? Laurentius and Shukra were men of war. And there was, always, a war. But Athanagild was a priest, and there was little place in a dromon for priests. No; when they ran, he and Shukra, they would run alone. And perhaps, if he were very lucky, Laurentius thought, ignoring the stabbing pain in his chest, he and Athanagild might yet meet again, one day.

There was an odd movement in the shadows of a nearby alley, and Laurentius, with the soldier's instincts that had never quite left him even in the years since he ceased his role in the Karabisianoi, swung around, hand on the hilt of the spatha he wore, even now, at his side. His eyes narrowed, studying the alley thoughtfully for a long moment before he turned and continued on his way. It was not the first time recently he had felt eyes watching him. He had been a warrior too long to dismiss his concerns as weak-minded paranoia. He was being followed, but by whom, and for what purpose, he had yet to discover. He was grateful, though ashamed to admit it, that Athanagild was still in Aurariola. Their relationship was already a labyrinth of subterfuge and tension to which he had no desire to add the further complication of extra cautionary measures.

He glanced around once more as he opened the heavy door that guarded his family domus from the Toletum street.

Dating from Roman times, it was far grander than most of the newer dwellings, standing three levels high, with an atrium at the centre, and surrounded by a peaceful walled garden that offered a rare sanctuary from Toletum's hustle. It felt empty and cold in Athanagild's absence, however, and as he did countless times a day, Laurentius found his thoughts returning to their tense exchanges in the days preceding his departure from Illiberis.

He knew it was wrong to blame Athanagild for Shukra's imprisonment. And in truth, he did not; it was to himself his anger was really directed. He thought, not for the first time, that he would a thousand times over prefer to be facing death himself than watching Shukra do so on his behalf. Then, as it inevitably did, the thought followed that it would not be him alone facing knife or noose, but him and Athanagild. At even the thought of Athanagild subjected to such horrors, his heart seized with dread so terrible his entire body revolted. That in turn led to the equally sickening realisation that he had, in effect, sacrificed his friend for his lover, even if the choice had been Shukra's rather than his; and that led, increasingly, to the wine jug in his library, in which of late his only solace was to be found.

He was about to reach for that familiar friend when he found himself suddenly thrust, face first, against the wall, the wine jug bleeding its contents onto the floor, and a voice whispering in his ear: "Someone wishes to speak with you."

Despite a lifetime of fighting, or indeed perhaps because of it, Laurentius knew when it was wise to struggle, and when wise to submit. The cords binding his hands, he could tell, were expertly tied, and the men sent to fetch him were no strangers to their work. He would not easily escape, and ironically, his own scrupulous measures to ensure his privacy had come back to haunt him: there were no servants in the house after dark, and, he knew, nobody would come for an unexpected visit, nor hear him cry out.

He resigned himself to whatever was to come and allowed

the men to push him into the rear salon and into a chair, where they blindfolded and gagged him.

He was then left alone, during which time he tested every knot and binding, knowing before he did that it was futile. His mind ran with military detachment through all he had noted about the men, but he was certain he did not know the voices. They were hired muscle, he suspected, though by whom he was unsure.

Presently he became aware of men approaching. He heard a familiar voice and felt his heart leap, then tighten with fear as he wondered why he was hearing that voice here, and now.

"It is entirely uncivilised that you would be expecting me to call upon an old friend without first so much as washing my face. For your dungeons, you must be knowing, are filthy; my beard has not enjoyed the blade's touch in months. I am not a Goth, you understand, with your love of long hair and beards, though I confess I do have a liking for the jewels some of your nobles weave in their braids…"

Laurentius felt a fierce surge of unlikely hope. "Does he ever shut up?" groaned one of the men presumably holding Shukra captive, and Laurentius found himself grinning around his gag with a savage humour he had not felt in what seemed like a lifetime. "I swear he has not ceased talking since the moment we took him from the cell."

"He will stop soon enough," said another voice, "just as soon as he feels the lick of the bastard's whip."

Oppa. Laurentius felt a queer thrill run down his spine. He should have guessed.

"Ah." He heard Shukra being forced into a chair opposite. "And so it is the company of the bastard we are to enjoy, this evening? Well. Honoured though I am —" but the rest of his words were muffled as his mouth, too, was bound.

Silence fell again, in which all Laurentius longed to say pulsed the air about him and choked his chest with so much emotion he was almost glad of the blindfold and gag. He could feel Shukra's presence and knew, even if they might not be able to speak, an unimaginable comfort in just having his old friend close by after so long.

"An extraordinary sight."

Laurentius stiffened; it was a measure of Oppa's skill, he thought, that he had not even sensed the man's arrival. "To see two such legendary soldiers, bound and gagged as common criminals." He tore the blindfold from Laurentius's face with enough force that the fabric seared his skin; Laurentius forced himself not to wince. He opened his eyes to find himself staring directly at Shukra, still blindfolded, only four paces opposite him. The Persian, always lithe, was now painfully thin, his clothes no more than rags, his beard two fists lower than his chin. Nonetheless, his skin was remarkably free of grime, and Laurentius, knowing well his friend's fastidious regard for cleanliness, imagined he had fashioned some kind of brush from his clothes. His face bore the signs of a recent beating, though, and Laurentius winced at the dark bruises on his torso revealed by the torn shirt.

Oppa stepped between them, blocking Shukra from view. His eyes were dark, his smile insidious. "Your friend, it seems, speaks much, but says little." He touched the whip at his side. "I had thought to employ this upon him, but my guards tell me that physical pain has little effect. I have known such men before." He shrugged. "In such circumstances, I find emotional pressure to be more... effective." He took a leisurely sip of wine, filled the cup, and held it out to Laurentius. "Would you like a drink? I believe you have been partaking rather more liberally than you are known to do. I had always understood your habits to be rather more abstemious. You have quite the reputation for scholarly devotion." When Laurentius didn't react, Oppa withdrew the cup, drank again, and smiled. "So devoted, I understand, that you have spent much of these past years sharing your wide knowledge of ecclesiastical texts with a promising young priest." Leaning forward, he flicked the gag out of

Laurentius's mouth, tearing the skin at the edges so they bled.

Holding his eyes, Laurentius said quietly, "You take a chance, Oppa, holding a man in his own home, against his will. What is it you hope to gain?"

Oppa smiled silkily. "I am a man of God, Laurentius. A scholar, come to study your famous library. That is what you do, when Athanagild comes to visit, is it not?"

Ice trickled down Laurentius's spine. He kept his eyes trained on Oppa, refusing to so much as search behind him for a glimpse of Shukra. "You see," went on Oppa conversationally, "recently, after I pondered your Persian friend's recent crimes, I asked some questions of my mother and her ladies. I discovered that in years past, Shukra had been often seen in my mother's brothel. He was a frequent visitor and a favourite amongst the ladies, for he paid well, drank liberally, and, if whispers are to be believed, knew a variety of interesting tricks that left a smile upon even their jaded faces. But never once, in all that time, do any recall Shukra requesting a man for his pleasures." When Laurentius did not speak, Oppa stepped closer. "Interestingly," he murmured, his eyes gleaming, "your face, also, was well remembered. It seems you often accompanied your Persian friend to such places. You also paid liberally, for wine – and even, sometimes, for a lady with whom to pass your time. Always older ladies, those nearing the end of their days on the floor, who might struggle to bring in good coin. Those ladies you would take for hours at a time and pay handsomely for. None of them, however, ever spoke of what transpired behind the closed door. You maintained a good air of mystery, Laurentius, one that did nothing to dispel your rather enigmatic reputation. Perhaps, people thought, you had a darkness in your soul, from so many years abroad. Of course, being the boon companion of such a well-known seducer as Shukra was enough to dispel any other, darker whispers. But do you know what I find interesting, Laurentius?" The handle of the whip came up and stroked his cheek with a slow, insidious touch that so vividly brought to mind the runnels on Theo's face that Laurentius's stomach churned. "I find it interesting indeed that since your friend's imprisonment, you have not so much as been glimpsed entering any of the city's pleasure houses. Not even, I note, my own, which as I am sure you are aware, is perhaps the most famous in all of Spania – and beyond, I believe."

"Perhaps," said Laurentius steadily, "I do not choose to place my coin in the pocket of a man who attacked, enslaved, and tortured his own countryman. A member of my own family, no less."

"Ah." Oppa's eyes shone with an ugly light. "But Theudemir and I, you must understand, have quite settled our differences. In fact, these days, we find ourselves... quite in accord, you might say."

"You might say it." Laurentius's eyes narrowed. "I doubt, somehow, that Theo would say the same."

"But that is where you are wrong." Oppa's smile had vanished. "Theo does say it. And when I convey to him what I know about you and his brother, be assured that he will continue to say it – loudly, and publicly, for as long as I wish him to." Stepping back, he turned to face Shukra. Laurentius twisted uncomfortably against his bonds, seeking an escape, his hands itching to take Oppa's neck and twist it until every last dark piece of life faded from those hated eyes. It had, he realised grimly, been a long time since he had felt the killing urge with such fierce passion. But it was there still, just beneath his carefully cultivated exterior, the deadly instinct that had seen him rise through the Karabisianoi with lethal efficiency. Laurentius might well play the part of a scholar, but beneath the sophisticated veneer lay a certain ruthless savagery, the same raw passion that erupted when he touched Athanagild's pale, lean body. Both memories twisted in him now, threatening to erupt publicly in a manner Laurentius had ensured had not occurred once in a decade or more.

"There." Oppa stepped back, and Laurentius found himself, finally, face to face with his oldest friend.

Shukra's face, though haggard and thin, his mouth cracked and bleeding at the edges, his eyes bloodshot, retained even now an attitude of light disdain as he eyed Oppa with an insouciant smile. "Laurentius," he said, though he did not look at his friend. "It is ever a pleasure, *aziz-am*, though I fear after our last conversation that my company brings you no joy."

It was a warning, one that Laurentius, after their many years together, read as clearly as a flag signal.

"This man is a traitor and a sodomite and is no longer any friend of mine." Despite his internal agony, Laurentius spat the words contemptuously. His eyes shifted to Oppa, who was watching the exchange with an amused expression. "Why do you waste my time with this creature?"

Oppa clapped slowly, in mock applause. "A very convincing performance, my friends. But given that we are alone, I think we might safely drop the charade. Our Persian, here, is most definitely a traitor, if a foreigner with no true allegiance to any but his friend can be called such; but a sodomite, I think we might all acknowledge, he is most surely not, no matter how certain our good archbishop might be of his bestial nature, and how readily he confessed to his sins when accused. Which led me to wonder." He tilted his head to one side. "Why would a man so well trained in the art of war and stealth not fight his way out of capture and flee immediately across the seas? I gave such a question much thought. Particularly recently, when it came to my notice that another Persian, a woman I know to be, in her own way, almost as formidable as you" – he nodded at Shukra – "arrived in the port of Septem. Athanais also, coincidentally, enjoys a close relationship with Theudemir of Aurariola – and with Yosef ben Arun. Such a close relationship, it seems, that she was entrusted with the care of their greatest treasure, the fruits of Yosef ben Arun's mysterious voyage to the east."

Laurentius's heart caught in his chest and seemed to stop

beating altogether. In the complete silence following these words, the slow tapping of Oppa's forefinger on a nearby table was clearly audible. "This discovery," he went on, "gave me pause. The production of silk, no less." He shook his head slowly, his dark eyes never leaving Laurentius's face. "An ambitious plan. One requiring the co-operation of so many. Such a grand scheme led me to look a little more closely into the tangled web of relationships that surrounds my new home of Illiberis. To see alliances where perhaps I had not, previously. And such discoveries led me to look deeper into those alliances." His smile darkened. "I found myself renewing my acquaintances at the Toletum monastery, and making some new ones. The archbishop Felix's new clerk, for example, has a penchant for dice. It was not difficult to – persuade him – to raise the topic of Athanagild of Aurariola with his superior. And there is no point," he raised a remonstrative finger, "in telling me he is your nephew, Laurentius, for I am well aware, having made something of a study of the complex ties binding the Spanish nobility, that despite your always referring to him as family, there is no shared blood between Athanagild and yourself. No doubt your patronage and claiming him as family has assisted his meteoric rise in the Church. Though you must, I fear, suffer some pangs of guilt that you helped him become the unfortunate favourite of the previous archbishop Sisebut, who then corrupted him with the crime of sodomy. According to Archbishop Felix – an admirably pious man! – Athanagild was not only corrupted by Sisebut, but also by your little Persian friend here. Shukra, according to Felix, not only demanded sexual favours, but also forced the boy to spy for him. A difficult burden for a young man indeed, no?" Oppa's voice was smooth and foully suggestive as an oil slick on water. "But by all accounts, Athanagild seems to have recovered remarkably well from his trials. So well, in fact, there are those amongst his contemporaries who suspect that he did not find Sisebut's advances unwelcome, at all. In fact, the clerk tells me he seems to recall him actually encouraging the archbishop's darker instincts."

Laurentius felt a savage rush of fury. Oddly, Shukra's nearness loaned him a calm born of their long years fighting at each other's side, and he maintained his bland expression under Oppa's dark scrutiny.

Just.

Another part of him, hidden inside, was building a slow, red rage, one he knew would only find solace at the sight of Oppa's lifeless staring eyes, and in the knowledge that his death had been painful.

"Would you like to know what I think, Laurentius?"

"I have no doubt you will tell me." He was proud of the faint scorn in his voice, though by Oppa's flat, dark eyes, his tone did nothing to fool the other.

"I think Athanagild seduced Sisebut quite deliberately. I think he passed information to Shukra, here, perhaps with your blessing, perhaps without; and I think he did it all because he wished, above all, to serve you. I think those secrets helped build alliances that Yosef ben Arun's mission abroad was intended to fund. And I think that Shukra – your oldest friend, Laurentius – sacrificed himself so that the Church's eyes remained conveniently trained upon him, thus ensuring they did not see the rotten secret at its very core."

His words were no less lethal for being delivered in a flat, emotionless tone. Not by the faintest twitch did Laurentius betray the dread curdling his gut. He had spent a lifetime preparing for the moment when he must maintain this lie, and he would not break now, no matter the fury and fear churning within.

"*Aziz-am,*" came Shukra's light voice from behind Oppa. "I am thinking you have been living so often in the shadows that you no longer see the light. And I fear you accord me rather more credit than I am deserving, if you think I would sacrifice my cock, or, perhaps more pertinently, my personal comforts, to protect a priest. Particularly one who serves a

God in whom I do not, I fear, have any faith at all, for what manner of God is it, I ask you, who requires His acolytes to eschew bathing for dirt in His honour?" Shukra's mouth twisted in polite distaste. *As if,* Laurentius thought, his heart twisting painfully, *he were clad in the finest silks rather than filthy rags.*

Oppa waved him away with an impatient gesture. "Enough of these games. I will speak plainly. Although I now wear the robes of a priest, do not forget I have lived many years amongst your contemporaries, and I have learned the impatience men of the sword have for the intricacies of language."

"But there, my friend, you are quite mistaken," interrupted Shukra lightly, his eyes dancing with a familiar, dangerous light Laurentius knew well. "I assure you there is nothing I enjoy more than the dance of words, and it saddens me – *ne*, as you Goths would crudely say, it *insults* me – that you would think your meaning needs further elaboration. Shall I reassure you by explaining, *aziz-am*, what I think you are, albeit clumsily, attempting to convey to my former friend and I?" Without waiting for Oppa to react, Shukra continued smoothly: "You accuse me of being a shameless libertine, yet one who, according to you, shuns the pleasure of male company, which shows only that you know nothing of how a successful debaucher conducts his affairs. Then you speak of another Persian woman, whom you seem to feel must be associated with me simply by virtue of her birth country." He shrugged. "It is, I grant you, a reasonable assumption, but hardly, you will concede, the basis for a conspiracy, no? And then finally, though I note you dance around this subject with a delicacy that betrays your Spanish upbringing – such prim attitudes, this God of yours has! – you imply that Laurentius, here, who, I might add, has an almost depressingly pious turn of mind, is secretly a raging sodomite capable of corrupting not only a young priest, but one whom he considers as family. A young priest, I should add, who was not only corrupted by Sisebut, but then seduced by me, a sin for which I cannot feel shame – but then, I am Persian." He shrugged off his imagined sins with perfect insouciance. "I might remind you," he added, "that Athanagild himself freely confessed all the above to his own archbishop, no small thing in this very Christian nation of Spania, and did not spare even me in his desire to purge himself, which has sadly resulted in both my own very unwelcome imprisonment, and the loss of my friendship with Laurentius, here." He tilted his head up at Oppa. "Have I covered it all? Oh, wait: you also think that despite all the above, Laurentius and I somehow have maintained an elaborate plot involving an exiled Jew, Ilyan of Septem, and the making of silk, a practice all know to be an arcane mystery contained beneath the emperor's palace in Constantinople."

Laurentius had seen Shukra's wordplay unnerve a hundred enemies, or at least drive them to frustrated distraction. But he knew that in this case, his frivolous denials came too late, to one who had moved the pieces on the board. Oppa was not just any enemy, and he was not, even slightly, distracted, simply waiting out Shukra's speech and then smiling coldly.

"Enough of this." He looked between the two of them. "I shall tell you what I require, and then show you what will happen if you do not agree to it." He turned to Laurentius. "My first request is a simple one." He put a finger on one hand down. "You and Theudemir are already preparing to train the fleet. I will supply coin and give you men to man it. You will build Spania's fleet into a force to be reckoned with, one every bit as fighting ready as the Karabisianoi you both revere so much."

Laurentius forced his face to remain blank, but his mind was racing. "I had thought," he said calmly, "that the Crown had already decreed as much?"

"It is not the Crown, as you call it, that is issuing this particular command."

"Ah." Laurentius arched an imperious eyebrow. "I see. Are

we to expect a regime change, then, so soon after our recent rebellion?"

If he had hoped to unsettle Oppa, however, he was disappointed; the other man merely smiled. "Nothing so crude, Laurentius, I assure you. But all men die, you understand, and my father is not a young man. My brother, however, is rather *too* young. There may be those amongst our seniores who see in such circumstances an opportunity. I seek merely to ensure they do not find common ground, particularly with those in command of such powerful instruments as the nation's fleet."

"In this future you are imagining," Shukra interjected, "it is you, we are to be assuming, who shall offer counsel to the new king?"

"If I were you," Oppa said coldly, "I would not assume anything past this particular moment – for unless your friend here agrees to offer his public support when the time comes, you will not live to see the outcome."

He turned back to Laurentius, his eyes contemptuous. "I do not know precisely what sick proclivities you hide, and nor do I need to; but given that your friend seems ready to lose his own life rather than confess to what occurred in that bathhouse, I think we might both agree that the secrets you keep are likely to destroy more than just reputations, should they be known." He shrugged. "I understand secrets, Laurentius. I have no reason to tell yours. In fact, it serves me better to keep them, for once exposed, neither you nor Athanagild can perform the function I require of you, and thus you lose what value you have to me. Your friend, here, however, is another matter entirely. Him I will see publicly cut, and left to bleed out his life on the filthy floor of a dungeon." This time, his smile chilled Laurentius to the bone. "Do not insult me with the pretence you are no longer friends; if your many early visits had not given you away, your nightly walks past his dungeon certainly do. I would suggest, the next time you plan to break into my father's cells, that you employ more stealthy methods.

"We both know the only reason he did not flee Spania the night he was caught in that bathhouse was so his presence in this very cell would protect your secrets. So long as you do as I ask, both he, and the secrets he guards, will remain safe. I will even ensure he is kept in a more comfortable prison."

His words were stark and relentless. Laurentius, feeling hope leach away with each accusation, tried to derive some comfort from the hard glint in Shukra's eyes. The two of them had, over the years, endured worse threats. He must use this moment to discover exactly what Oppa wanted.

"Is that all?" he asked politely, despite the sickening fear within. "You wish to secure mine, and Athanagild's, allegiance, and support for your brother's claim?"

"I will also be the sole means by which silk reaches Spanish shores." Oppa's answer was flat and matter of fact. "You will inform Yosef ben Arun, and Ilyan, that if their newly created product does not pass through my hands, my father will be told that the Jewish rebellion in Septem grows dangerous, and the very fragile alliance that currently exists between Spania and Septem will be broken. You will impress upon them the importance of trade with me, in such a way that they see it is in their best interests."

"They will never believe that." Laurentius kept his voice calm with an effort.

"You will ensure they will," Oppa said softly, "if you wish Athanagild to maintain his position in the Church, your sinful relationship to remain hidden − and your friend to remain alive. And I am not unreasonable." His smile did not remotely reach his eyes. "If matters are settled as I wish them to be, it is within my power to see your friend is eventually freed, Laurentius."

"Let me clarify this." Laurentius met his eyes steadily and kept his tone light and even. "To gain support for your plans you threaten me with the public exposure of a supposed secret relationship, for which you have no evidence at all, and to kill, or castrate, a man for whom I have nothing but contempt. If I comply, you offer me the release of that same corrupt, traitorous man." He frowned pointedly. "They told me," he said politely, "that you were a master of intrigue, Oppa. Sadly I see no evidence of such skills here, today."

Oppa's smile did not slip. "I have long learned the value of playing the pieces already on the board," he said softly, "rather than sweeping it clean and beginning the game anew. You, Athanagild, and Theudemir of Aurariola are valuable pieces. Ones I would prefer to work with, rather than against." His smile faded. "Valuable, yes. But make no mistake, Laurentius: not irreplaceable, by any means."

"They are, however," said Laurentius politely, "pieces that have already bested you in battle, and who you fear may yet rise against you."

"Ah." Oppa's smile returned, and this time, Laurentius saw with alarm, it reached the dark eyes. "But as I mentioned earlier, Theo and I have a certain... understanding, these days."

"That understanding, I am thinking," interrupted Shukra, "must not be quite so secure as you might wish, given your somewhat clumsy efforts here, today, no?" He shook his head in mock reproach. "You do not have what we might call the player's face, in my country, *aziz-am*." He shrugged impatiently, which, given his bindings, was an impressive feat. "You have brought us here to play a game of shadows and threats, *aziz-am*, but I do not see that you hold the pieces to match your strategy." He nodded at Laurentius. "My old friend here," he said softly, not looking at Laurentius, "may play the part of scholar well, but I fought beside him for many years, and I know him for the ruthless strategist he is. Even if he could forgive my seduction of his nephew – and no matter what you say of blood this, and family that," he said contemptuously, "the children of Aurariola make no such distinction, I assure you – still Laurentius would not stand between your sword and my cock, or any other part of my body. If anything, he would help you swing the blade, for though he has waited long for his revenge, his visits have left me in no doubt that he intends to take it, in far worse ways than even you might dream up." His dispassionate delivery had the desired effect; Oppa's eyes narrowed slightly, and Laurentius saw the first hint of doubt steal into their dark depths.

Oppa, he realised, was not entirely certain of his claims. Even now.

"Even if we shared the bond of brothers we once did," Shukra continued, "still Laurentius would not do your bidding in such matters merely to save my life. He knows better than to make foolish decisions from emotion."

Laurentius heard the words as the warning they were intended, and with it, he felt the burden of their implication.

Never had a burden felt heavier upon his heart.

"Perhaps." Oppa's eyes flashed dangerously. "We shall see. For now, however" – he turned to Laurentius, dismissing Shukra – "our interests are the same. We wish to protect Spania's shores, do we not? I am offering you the means to do your part, Laurentius. All the rest of this" – he waved an airy hand meant, Laurentius thought, to encompass all the dark threats he had just issued – "is no more, really, than texture to the fabric of our discussion. What must matter to us all is protecting Spania. And the best way to achieve that is with a rich alliance with Septem, and a silk trade that provides the coin to fund our defence." Leaning down to meet Laurentius's eyes, he said softly, "Is it not for this very reason that you have gone to such efforts these past years, Laurentius Severianus? Would it not be a great shame if, after all that endeavour, your efforts were to be lost – and all those who have worked so hard on your behalf disgraced, exiled, or, even worse, executed? I should think carefully on your next actions, Laurentius. Whether you wish to confess it or not, I hold the futures of all those you love in one hand. If you doubt me, I suggest you ask Theudemir yourself if he intends to help his bride win back her home."

He stepped back. "I would like to see all my chosen pieces

play the parts I have set for them, Laurentius. But if you think I am not more than capable of throwing the board aside entirely, then you have not been paying attention, my friend."

Giving Laurentius a final, grim smile, he turned away and called for the guards. Laurentius did not dare look at Shukra for fear they were still watched. As the blindfold slipped over his eyes once more, he felt as if he were falling, into a dark mire from which he had no idea how he might extract himself.

ı

30

LÆLIA
MARCH–MAY, AD 694

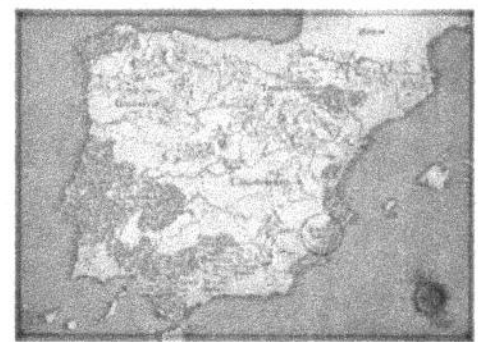

Aurariola, Spania
Orihuela, Spain

Lælia was in the library, seated by the arched window staring out at the soft rain that had begun to fall, when she heard the clatter of Theo's arrival in the outer atrium. Then came his long strides along the corridor, his shout to the servants, and when he pushed open the door, she was already standing to greet him, with a smile.

"I heard that a messenger came for you." She tried to keep the hope from her voice. "Is there news from Toletum?"

"Nothing welcome, I fear." Theo kissed her. "Wittiza's coronation date has been set for July. I must ride to Toletum for it. You will not be expected, of course," he added hastily, "so soon after being with child. But I cannot avoid it."

"It will give you a chance to speak with Laurentius, and Athanagild, at least. I will not pretend, after all we said to Athanagild, that I am not disappointed that he still chose to leave for the capital. And now Egilona, too, will go." Standing abruptly, Lælia moved restlessly across the room, her arms pulling the shawl closer around her. She could not seem to grow warm, in this place, no matter how many layers of wool she covered herself with. The damp was a different type of cold to Illiberis's hard bite, an encroaching ghost that seemed to infiltrate her very bones, making her irritable and weak. She moved to the fire and faced it. "Once Egilona leaves," she said, not for the first time, "we can no longer keep her safe."

"And bidding her stay will only alarm her, as we have previously talked of." When she didn't answer, Theo went on: "If you stand any closer to those flames you will be smoke yourself."

She heard Theo's efforts at levity but did not turn to meet his humour with a smile, saying instead, "Why do you think Athanagild has not answered your letters? And Yosef − still there is no word from him. I do not understand it." She shook her head, staring moodily at the flames. "Perhaps I should go to Toletum myself −"

"No." She turned, surprised, to find Theo standing barely a few feet from her, his face quite pale, drawn, and shadowed. "I am sorry," he muttered. "That was unfair of me, Lælia. I am being unfair. But here, I know you to be safe, surrounded by my men, the port close by. Whereas in Toletum…" He broke off, his voice clearly failing him, and Lælia's heart clenched with love and sympathy.

"It is I who am being unfair." She moved into his embrace. "When the truth is that I can't bear the thought of being apart from you for so long. Even the thought leaves me colder than this damned winter." He caught her close and laughed, slightly shakily, against her head, and she held him fiercely so she could feel the beat of his heart, strong and vital, against her own. She knew there was pain, shadows in his soul that he hid from her still, just as she did not share all that tortured her own nights with him. It was their private, unspoken agreement, that they loved each other in the place beyond the shadows. They were both caught in a trap of fate's making, as they had always been, and despite her determination to keep hope alive, on damp, cold nights such as these, Lælia felt it draining away from her, taking with it the blazing fire of purpose that had sustained her through the darkest nights of Theo's long absence and then been so recently rekindled. Aurariola's grey mists felt as if they were seeping into her very soul, slowly suffocating the brilliant light of the Illiberis mountains that so recently had seemed tantalisingly within her grasp. Illiberis itself seemed to be fading into those mists, like a mythical land, as distant from her reality as if it were wound about in enchantment.

Theo did not speak, but his hands twined in her hair were tense and strong, his body rigid with unspoken emotion, and they stood for a long time like that, in the silence that Lælia found still was her last refuge against an increasingly dark world.

When finally Theo stepped back, his eyes were the deep moss of a still pond, caverns in his face. "Lælia," he said, his voice catching. "I do not know Athanagild's thoughts, nor Laurentius's. But if our plans should not work, if we must consider other options, there are… things… we should discuss…" The words died in his throat as he looked at her, strangled by emotions she couldn't read. She felt his tension, his reluctance to voice what he clearly knew would change their world, forever.

Fear gripped her like the cold mist beyond the window, stealing in to eclipse the last of the warmth that Theo's love and Geila's birth had brought to her heart. Suddenly, uncharacteristically, Lælia felt exhausted by the prospect of whatever those changes would bring and overwhelmed by what he might say.

"Shh." She put a finger on his lips. His face darkened, his eyes hardening with a resolve she knew within was born from conscience. She felt a strange tenderness, not unlike that she felt when Geila reached for her blindly in his sleep. "There will be time," she said softly. "I know you fear that none of our plans can work. But I also trust you, Theo. I know there is nothing you do that is not done from love. So for now, at least, I think perhaps you need me more than I need your words." She drew close to him, feeling her heart soften further at the conflict in his face. "And I," she said quietly, "I need you, too, Theo. I am cold. Inside…" Her voice trailed off, words inadequate to describe the emptiness she felt, and he pulled her against him as if his bulk could somehow warm her through. "I know," he murmured against her hair, and somehow, Lælia knew that he did. "I know that cold. It gets into your bones, makes you feel that you will never be warm again, that you are alone in a place no man or woman can touch."

She nodded wordlessly against his shoulder, aching for the comfort of his skin on hers. The fire of resolve that had been sparked by Safia's news had burned out, taking with it the desire for action that had smouldered since the day she rode north from Illiberis and leaving in the ashes a cold presentiment of what lay ahead, if her fragile plans were dashed. If hope was extinguished completely, Lælia felt, it could never be rekindled again. She found herself uncharacteristically unwilling to so much as mention Illiberis, nor discuss the possibility of public concession. She pressed herself against Theo's tall, hard strength, longing for him with every fibre of her being.

Holding her close, he whispered, "I am taking you to bed."

Lælia had no thought of refusing.

Night had fallen when finally they joined the others for meat, Theo eating with one hand in Lælia's, and his arm around his delighted son. Lælia felt the darkness and cold, temporarily at least, recede in the blaze of this, the love she had for so long thought lost to her. She looked around the table, at Leofric and Silas joking with Theo, doing tricks with a coin to amuse Geila. At Egilona, picking daintily at her meat, watching the interactions at the table carefully, as if she stored each exchange in a private chamber for later reference.

At Safia, who ate quietly with the other servants at another table, her dark eyes watching everything.

Beneath the table, Jadis stirred, her lean body vibrating with a warning that only Lælia could feel.

HALF A MOON HAD PASSED, and spring finally arrived, when Egilona sought Lælia out in the garden, where she was cutting herbs, Jadis at her side.

"There are servants who can do that for you." Egilona's smile was slightly puzzled.

Lælia smiled to herself. Egilona's upbringing, almost entirely in the cloistered surroundings of the royal court, had not included the more humble aspects of daily living. Having always been acutely aware of her precarious position, Egilona was not at all arrogant or pretentious; but neither had she ever tied her own lacings, nor dressed her own hair.

"The servants do not know what I need." Lælia straightened up, brushing the remnants of the herbs from her dress. "There are other plants I would like, but I shall have to roam further for those. They do not grow in tame gardens such as these."

"Tame gardens." Egilona smiled as she picked Geila up from the blanket upon which he was kicking his legs, cuddling him close. "You say that as if there is something wrong with gardens that are tended." The boy clutched at her hair, squealing in delight as he caught a fistful of gleaming white curls in his little fist. He was a good-natured, easy baby, and the servants often told Lælia how fortunate she was. The next one, they said, would likely not be so simple.

"Every environment has its uses." Lælia pushed away the familiar feeling of dread she had whenever she thought of having another baby. "Domestic gardens are good for cooking, creating perfumes and soaps, and some medicines. But there are other things that require plants from the wild that grow to nature's rhythm, blooming at a particular time."

"By other things," said Egilona, watching her closely, "you mean the place you ride to, by the stream? With the rocks?"

"Yes." Lælia met her eyes steadily. "It is an old place of worship. I go there to lay an offering on the new and full moons. It is the way I honour my grandmother, who is no longer with us." She did not mention it was also the place where Safia had once found her, and where she regularly waited, thus far in vain, for the girl to come again.

"I think I recall Athanagild mentioning Acantha." Egilona frowned. "Your grandmother lived in an abbey, did she not? Would she not disapprove of you laying a pagan offering to her?"

Lælia could not bite back her smile. "Acantha did live in an abbey, it is true. But though an iron cross marked the entrance, the women inside worshipped at rather different altars." Looking down at the herbs in her basket, Lælia felt a pang of longing for Acantha's stern, strong presence. "It was she who taught me all I know of herb lore. I feel her closest when I am in the glade by the stream."

"I do not remember my mother." Lælia looked up in surprise. Egilona was not given to personal revelation. The younger girl smiled at her, though dark clouds chased over the piercing summer blue of her eyes. "I can recall her touch, the smell of her skin. But I cannot see her face. Not clearly. And I know she whispered words to me when I was taken from her, but I do not recall those, either." She spoke quietly, in a matter-of-fact tone. "I should remember more; I was not a baby when she died, as Theo was when his mother was taken. Queen Liuvgoto told me it is not unusual, for children to forget such things, when the manner of the death is violent. She herself does not recall some things from her own childhood."

"Queen Liuvgoto?" Lælia looked at her curiously. "You

must be very close to the old queen, for her to speak of such things?"

"I spend what time with her that I may." Egilona's eyes were slightly opaque, just as Theo's became when he wished to conceal his inner world. It was slightly unsettling to see the same habit in his sister's young eyes. "The queen's own daughter, you understand, is quite befuddled. She was weak minded to begin with and has only grown worse since Wittiza went to live at the palace. Cixilo does not understand power," she said, with a sudden surge of strength in her voice, blue eyes flashing.

"But Liuvgoto does." Lælia busied herself with the herbs, watching Egilona from the corner of her eye.

"Liuvgoto knows more about this kingdom and those who wield power in it than any other person living." The statement was flat and hard, and, Lælia thought, immensely revealing. "There is no better person to teach me what I need to know to survive at court." She met Lælia's eyes directly. "I know you wish me to stay here. You and Theo, though you think yourselves subtle, are not at all. You think that so long as I am here, you might keep me safe – or, perhaps, you think to make me a piece in a game of your own."

Lælia was shocked into silence, and before she could think of the words to respond, Egilona went on: "You ride to your sacred groves and lay offerings to pagan gods that have been prohibited by our Church. You wait for messages from foreign friends, who, perhaps, plot to overthrow our king." She waved a dismissive hand. "I do not say this to threaten you, just as I do not tell you of my friendship with Queen Liuvgoto to impress you. I am trying to make you understand something important, something that I think I must make clear before I ride with my brother for Toletum." Lælia waited, watching her. "I intend to make Wittiza my husband," Egilona said. Her words held neither boast nor bravado, just simple determination. "I wish to be safe. For my children to be safe. And more than that – I wish to wield power. Have dominion over my own fate. I will not be left behind in this villa" – and now a note of bitterness entered her voice – "defenceless, playing a role in someone else's game. I will not be pierced with a sword with no more ceremony than a fatted goose, as my mother was."

She placed Geila carefully back down on the blanket and straightened up. "I do not judge you for the path you have chosen. For wanting Illiberis returned to you, being determined to fight for it. Nor will I ever stand against you, for you are my sister, and I love you." She met Lælia's eyes directly. "But I will never be used as a pawn, especially in anything that might endanger Wittiza's rise to power. If you – or my brother – involve yourselves in such schemes, I will distance myself from you. I do not say this as a threat, nor in anger. But I cannot ride from here without saying it, or keep from begging you this." For the first time her composure cracked slightly, her face pale and pinched. "My family has lost so much," she said in a low voice. "And now, by some miracle, my brother has won it back. If it were only Aurariola, Egica could take it, and be damned. But it is Theo. My brother. You. Geila." She glanced at the small boy on the blanket, who was watching her with wide blue eyes so very like her own it was uncanny. "I do not want to lose you so soon." She held Lælia's eyes for a moment, then, as two servants came toward them, whirled away. "You are so curious, sister," she called gaily over her shoulder, "cutting herbs when there are servants to do so for you! I shall be fascinated to see what perfumes you make."

And in an elegant turn of sage wool she was gone, leaving Lælia staring after her.

* * *

As the day neared for Theo's departure to Toletum, Lælia found herself going over and over Egilona's words. She had wanted to reassure her, to say that she would not bring war to their door again, for if she understood anything at all, it was what they had all lost, in the last rebellion. No matter her desire to regain Illiberis, her deep frustration at how slowly the time without it seemed to pass, she entirely understood Egilona's fears. She thought they were the same ones Theo, too, secretly held. She recalled the day Theo had begun to speak to her. Was it that he had meant to say? She had thought he planned to speak of concession. But did he still believe, even after their conversations, that she would risk all their lives by joining a rebellion that was doomed to failure?

Despite her longing for her home, she felt a faint edge of resentment at the thought they might both consider her so naïve, and selfish. Instinct, perhaps sharpened after Egilona's terse warning, whispered that perhaps she should not have so quickly deterred Theo from speaking his fears. Whatever shadows he hid, she thought, chastising herself, she should hear with equanimity before he left.

But despite her efforts to open that conversation again, whatever weakness had overcome him that day was not repeated. The closer he came to leaving, the more withdrawn he became. Lælia had the impression that he was bracing for battle, going inward to prepare himself for what he might meet in the capital. But he did not share his worries with her, and despite not blaming him for his shadows, Lælia could not quite forgive him for not sharing them with her, either. Hurt, she retreated into herself. She would let her actions speak for themselves, she told herself, and tried to ignore the disquieting feeling that there was more to his silence than even her own suspicions guessed at.

The night before he was due to leave, she turned to him in the midnight silence, reaching for him with her body, in search of the connection she could no longer find with words. He caught her with a savagery that took her breath away, and for a time, they lost themselves in the place that had always existed between them, the otherworldly bond that had joined them in flesh and soul, and across time and place. It was like falling into a welcome darkness, and briefly, as pleasure took her, Lælia felt herself to be in the caves back at Illiberis, wrapped in the cocoon of their shared destiny. They fell asleep entwined in each other, but when Lælia awoke on the morning of their departure, the bed was empty.

She gathered with Silas and Leofric in the courtyard to bid the party farewell. Neither was bitter about being left behind; they disliked the bustle of Toletum almost as much as Lælia did.

"I will return as soon as I might." Theo moved forward to embrace her, and despite her fears that his return would bring an end to all her hopes, or perhaps because of those fears, Lælia found herself reaching for him with an odd ferocity, as if her body could say what her words could not. When they finally parted, Leofric was chortling nearby, and Theo's eyes were glittering with a hard, painful light. "I will miss you," he said roughly. "Every moment."

"And I you." Lælia held his face between her hands. "I will never do anything to betray you," she said, hardly knowing where the words came from until her eyes slid to Egilona. She saw an answering flash in the sapphire depths. "No matter what, Theo, I will protect you, and Geila. I will make sure no harm ever comes to your family." There was the faintest nod of blonde curls. Lælia's eyes returned to Theo to find him searching her face, his eyes shadowed with all that lay between them.

Theo's mouth tightened into a hard line. His hand rested briefly on Geila's head as his eyes held hers for a long, final moment. "I love you." Abruptly, before she could respond, he turned and mounted his horse; then he rode from the villa, without turning back again. Lælia watched them go, Geila squirming in her arms, uncomfortably aware that Theo had not so much as recognised her vow of loyalty – let alone returned it.

31

YOSEF

JUNE, AD 694

Garnata, Spania
Granada, Spain

"I know it is not the news you wish to hear." Staring around the Garnata room at the tight, hostile expressions, Yosef stifled a sigh of exhaustion. It was perhaps the twentieth time he had held the same conversation, faced the same accusations, of betrayal and weakness. "But mounting open rebellion now would be fatal. Ilyan will not support it, and we do not have the resources to mount it alone."

"As well for you to say." The speaker was the rotund wife of the baker Yosef recalled from long ago. She was no longer so round, and her face, once merrily plump, was now pinched with fear. "You are safe in Septem whilst we are here, forced to convert or die, and even then, treated as little more than criminals."

"We are working the Illiberis fields as little more than slaves." Another man took up her argument, his face red from a day of labour; his hands, clearly more accustomed to a pen than a scythe, were swollen and scratched. "As converts, they cannot enslave us; but they cannot kill us, either. Or not officially." His tone was grim. "And now you come here, and tell us there is no hope of reprieve?"

"You can still leave." Yosef met his eyes steadily. "I can see you safely through the mountains, and onto a dromon to Septem. There, you are free to trade. Free to live as you might."

"And I told you the last time we spoke of this that I cannot leave," interrupted the first woman. "Garnata is my home. We must believe that we will prevail, in time, with or without Ilyan. And Illiberis can still rise again."

There was a murmur of agreement to this. Yosef looked around the room. "You seem very optimistic," he said, his voice politely enquiring.

"Oppa left before the first shoots rose above the ground," said one of the men scornfully. "The Illiberis herd is still in the mountains. The southern lords do not acknowledge him. It is said he is gone to Toletum, and that there he will be forced to relinquish Illiberis, back to the Lady." There were nods and knowing smiles to this.

"The Lady of Illiberis will fight for us," said another. "Illiberis has always cared for Garnata."

Yosef felt a sudden surge of irritation at the man's words. "And that is what you are fighting for?" he said, unable to keep the scorn from his tone. "A more benign overlord?"

Looking at the affronted faces, realising he had gone too far, he took a deep breath and tried again. "I do not think Lælia will regain Illiberis," he said. "But perhaps that can work to our advantage."

"Oh?" The woman folded her arms and glared at him. "And how is that?"

"I do bring some good news." Yosef smiled. "The silk trade you were promised is even now beginning." Finally, the mutinous expressions showed some signs of thawing. "In just a few months," he went on, "we will be ready to weave cloth."

"What does it matter," said the man with the scratched hands, eyeing Yosef belligerently, "if we are not permitted to trade in it?"

"Again." Yosef met his eyes steadily. "I would encourage you to join us, in Septem, where Ilyan allows us to trade freely, taking only a tax as payment. But where we once must have paid Illiberis to be our agent in these matters, from Septem we may trade the cloth directly, charging what we will for it, rather than being forced to compromise our profits to acquire an agent."

The assembled faces frowned and exchanged surreptitious looks. "But that would mean relinquishing the cream of the trade," one pointed out. "The profit is made in the margin between cloth and customer, not cloth and agent."

"Not," said Yosef, smiling, "if one is the only purveyor of such cloth. Which, to all intents and purposes, we will be, my friends." He spread his hands. "Many of you in this room were raised to weave cloth. Now, in Septem, you can once again create your own houses. Your own cloth. And sell it at whatever price you set."

"Such business takes time to establish." The woman glared at him. "Time and money. They would be exiles, with neither."

"I will provide the raw silk." Yosef answered her directly. "I will advance all who wish to begin manufacturing cloth the means to do so. I will provide training, and introductions to buyers." The baker's wife folded her arms belligerently, but he saw hope dawn in the eyes of others. "I will give you a new life," he said quietly. "If you let me."

"AND WHAT DID THEY SAY?" Lælia balanced Geila on her knee, her eyes shining as she listened to Yosef's story. He had left out the part about Illiberis in his recounting of the tale.

"Some began to pack immediately." He lifted a shoulder, smiling at her. "But there are others who will not leave." His smile faded. "I fear, despite their hopes, that they will find their options increasingly limited."

"I, too." Yosef looked at her in surprise. Lælia's mouth twisted ruefully. "We have all had to face unwelcome truths, these past years," she said quietly. "Athanagild was recently here for some time. From all he said, the Church grows more intolerant of unconverted Jews, not less. He anticipates that the next council will see the harshest laws yet imposed upon your people. There will always be sympathetic lords, of course, as I am, and my grandfather before me was, in Illiberis." Her speaking in the present tense did not pass Yosef unnoticed. "But there is only so much we might do. As you say, the freedoms Septem offers are better – and far less dangerous." She shook her head and looked at Yosef with a concern that touched him. "You should not be here," she said. "It is no less dangerous for you, Yosef."

"I had to come. Besides, as Sarah frequently reminds me, I rather like a touch of danger." He smiled ruefully at Lælia then stood and strode restlessly to the open window, where he looked out over the barley, rippling gold in the sunlight.

"Yosef." He did not turn when she said his name. He knew, by the tentative note in her voice, what she was going to ask, and he could not bring himself to face it. Not for the first time, Yosef cursed his lack of foresight in arriving at Aurariola without first discovering Theo's whereabouts. "You did not send word. It has been more than a year, and nothing. Not so much as word of your daughter's birth."

"I did not know what to say." Yosef leaned against the wrought-iron lattice. "That I watched, from a distance, as Oppa's men rode into Illiberis? That I returned from Spania to discover Ilyan had no intention of supporting rebellion, and no further interest in supporting your bid for Illiberis?" His tone was bitter with self-recrimination. He took a deep breath and forced himself to turn, to face what their lies had wrought, his and Theo's.

"But did you ever, truly, believe in the talk of rebellion?"

There was a curious opacity to Lælia's eyes, a shadow lurking behind them he could not quite make out.

"Didn't you?" Yosef countered.

"No." Lælia shook her head slowly, holding his eyes. "Not really. Not after the fever of holding Illiberis against Oppa's army had faded. I turned it over and over in my mind, but I could not see a way clear to mount another rebellion." She frowned and said, as if speaking to herself, "I keep imagining what Dahiya might say, if she were here."

"You could have no better mental counsel than hers, in such matters." Yosef gave her the ghost of a smile, but Lælia did not seem to notice.

"Then I received word," she went on, "that Ilyan had no intention of supporting a rebellion. That he wished Theo to forge an alliance with Egica, rather than rise against him."

I received word. Yosef frowned. The message Athanais sent, he knew, had gone to Theo. "Theo told you, then," he said, watching her carefully; and it was only his long years of diplomacy, he knew, combined with a childhood spent observing Lælia's moods, that made him notice the hesitation that was just a moment too long, the slight shift of the golden eyes, the way in which that lethal-looking cat of hers stirred uneasily, as she said, "Yes. Yes, Theo told me." She met his eyes and if he had been uncertain before, her next words confirmed his suspicions. "Theo had word from Athanais. She told him that the Arabs are said to be launching a force on Carthage, and that Dahiya will likely soon need help. He relayed all she said to me."

Except, Yosef knew, it was not Athanais who had spoken to Ilyan of Carthage. That had been a conversation between Ilyan and Dahiya, one for which Yosef himself had been in the room. To his knowledge, Carthage as the Arabic goal was no more than Dahiya's own speculation. Athanais might have spoken of the Arab threat, and of forging an alliance with Egica, though even that terminology was not hers. No, Yosef thought rapidly. Somehow, Lælia had received a message of her own. If not from Dahiya herself, then from someone close to Ilyan. He had a sudden recollection of Ilyan speaking of a source at the heart of the Spanish court. Whoever it was, he thought, their allegiance was also to Lælia.

The thought was more disquieting than he might have imagined.

"You are shocked," Lælia said, watching him, and Yosef realised that if he knew her well, she, too, knew him.

"Perhaps a little, yes." He gave her a small smile. "I do not think I could have imagined the day when you would speak of losing Illiberis with such equanimity."

"I have not lost Illiberis." Her answer came hard and fast, and with a savagery that took Yosef by surprise. Her smile was quite gone, and her eyes flashed a dangerous, hard gold that Yosef knew well. The cat at her feet growled, a low, feral rumble that set Yosef's teeth on edge. "Even now, Theo and I are endeavouring to win it back."

Yosef had to force himself not to visibly blanch. *Theo still has not told her, then.* Perhaps because of the recent under-standing he and Sarah had reached, the golden warmth in his soul at the knowledge they lived a shared destiny, he felt even more acutely the pain of the separation that lie must have wrought in the marriage between his oldest friends. And now, seeing the fierce light in Lælia's eyes, the uncompromising set to her jaw, he thought he could see why Theo had kept his silence.

No matter if the rebellion lived or died, Lælia had not ceased fighting for Illiberis. She never would.

"I see," he said carefully. "And how do you envisage this being achieved?"

She rose as abruptly as he had, stalked across the room, then turned and came back. "I have not yet formally conceded Illiberis to Oppa," she began, and Yosef was reminded of the arguments he had heard back in Garnata. "Until I do, you and I both know that no matter what is decreed in Toletum, the southern lords will never accept his rule there.

"The herd is gone, high in the mountains where he cannot follow. Until it is Oppa's eagle branded on their flesh, the horses of Illiberis are mine – and all the south knows it. Ilyan wants a force in Spania," she went on, her words coming ever faster. "A fleet, which your coin will help Theo build. But what if we can build a land force, as well? An army to defend Spania's shores? Illiberis would be the perfect place to do that – and I could do it."

"Lælia." Yosef looked at her meditatively. "You are not a fool. Theo certainly is not. You cannot believe Oppa would ever agree to this."

"He might," she returned, her eyes flashing. "If there was enough profit in it."

Yosef stared at her. "You mean," he said flatly, "if you used the coin from the silk trade to buy him off."

"Not buy him off." Lælia frowned. "I know you loathe Oppa, Yosef. So do we all. But was it not Ilyan himself who ordered Theo to court favour with the Crown? Oppa *is* the Crown, Yosef, whether we like it or not. At least this way, we might get something for ourselves from dealing with him."

Yosef had forced himself to accept that Ilyan would use part of his profits from the silk trade to subsidise an alliance with the Spanish Crown. He had been able to reconcile that in his mind simply because it was once removed: the Jews of Septem paid taxes, and Ilyan would do with those taxes what he would. But Lælia's was a more immediate, personal insult, a suggestion that he direct his personal capital, the profits of what as yet was only a planned shared enterprise between them, to Oppa's purse.

He thought of the pain he had lived with, all this time, at deceiving Lælia. Of the risks he had taken to return to her, here in a land where he was considered exile and traitor, to honour their childhood friendship by bringing her the truth. And yet, it seemed, he had misjudged the balance of that friendship. It had, Yosef realised, never been one of equals. He was a Jew from Garnata; she was the Lady of Illiberis. The silk trade for which he had risked everything, endured deprivations she could never in her wildest dreams imagine, she considered her right to trade – and to Oppa, no less.

An old, visceral fury stirred somewhere deep inside Yosef, corrosive and ugly, goading him to speak where diplomacy demanded silence. But diplomacy belonged to the adult Yosef, the man who had walked through a hundred nations and learned to become none of them. The fury belonged to the boy who had grown up in the mountains and valleys of Illiberis, his only true friend the girl he had sacrificed his own honour to protect – and who now betrayed him without so much as a word of apology.

"Something for ourselves?" Yosef's voice shook with rage as he repeated her words. "Even if Oppa was fool enough to agree to such a thing – which, if Theo was too nice to tell you, he most certainly is not – who would benefit from such an agreement, Lælia? Are you so naïve you believe that your mere presence in Illiberis would suddenly liberate the Jews there, make their existence any less precarious? Do you think they would trade with impunity, simply by virtue of your rule? Would the king's priests cease torturing them to convert, or forcibly removing their children from their parents?" Yosef tried and failed to get his temper under control, his voice dripping with scorn. "All those years we lived in the same place," he spat, "we lived two different lives, you and I. You were Lælia of Illiberis. Born to rule, heiress to the greatest estate in the south. Whilst I was Yosef ben Arun." His mouth twisted. "Son," he said bitterly, "of a family as old and venerable as your own. Born of the Illiberis valley just as you were, Lælia – but dispossessed, as all those of my blood have been, of the land we once culti-vated and ruled as lords ourselves." His hand cut the air in a frustrated gesture, palm up. "Have you ever wondered what country Spania might have been, had those of my faith been allowed to thrive with impunity? Of the art, and culture, that might even now live here, as it does upon so many other foreign shores?" He would have gone on but he knew, with a sudden rush of sad exhaustion, that his emotion was spent. He shook his head, swallowing on the painful lump in his chest, already ashamed of losing control in such a way.

Lælia was staring at him, her face blank with shock. "Yosef," she whispered, "I am sorry —"

"As am I." He cut her short, reaching for the cloak that hung on a chair back. "More than you know, Lælia. But not sorry enough to refrain from sharing a secret of my own, before I go. A secret that is not mine to tell, perhaps; but it seems to be the custom, now, to give away what does not belong to us."

He saw the words hit her with the precision of the stones he had once cast at Oppa across a wooded glade, and though he did not delight in the marks they left, nor did he mourn them.

"No matter what Theo has told you," he said, his voice now utterly cold, with no trace of his earlier emotion, "he will never make that deal with Oppa. He may make a deal, yes, it is true, for Theo is no stranger to dealing with Oppa. But if you think he will make an agreement that will give you back Illiberis, Lælia, you are much mistaken." He drew the cloak around his shoulders and tied it with slow, deliberate movements, his eyes not leaving hers. "The last deal Theo made with Oppa was not here, in Corduba, Lælia. It was back in Sebastopolis. And it required Theo to sign his name to a contract." He saw the shadows begin to enter the gold of her eyes, the dawning awareness of what was to come, and went on, his words falling remorselessly into the stillness between them. "The contract bound Theo to silence over Oppa's actions abroad," he said. "The attack on the fleet; his treachery with the Arab forces. In exchange for his silence, Oppa would speak for him at court. For him, Lælia." His mouth curved in a hard smile. "But to speak for you, also, there was a price."

"Illiberis." The word was barely a whisper.

Yosef nodded slowly. "Illiberis. In exchange for Aurariola."

"But he fought Oppa —"

"Yes, he did." Yosef met her eyes uncompromisingly. "But he never got that parchment back, Lælia. And Oppa has wielded it over his head ever since." He did not flinch from the stark horror he saw in her face. "And I," he said, unable to hide his fury, "did all I could to shield you from that betrayal. Compromised my own honour out of fear for your life, to save you from what you might do if you learned of his treachery." He stepped closer, staring her down, her eyes locked on his own. "Because," he said with lethal softness, "I thought to myself: how could Lælia, a person of such honourable character, ever forgive Theo for so recklessly trading away the one thing for which she had risked everything — as if it were his very own?"

He watched her face as he spoke, though he found little satisfaction from the shame he saw there. Turning abruptly, he made for the door. "If Theo is dealing with Oppa now, in Toletum," he said scornfully over his shoulder, "he is not dealing with any hope of winning your home back, Lælia. He is dealing to survive — and it is you who will pay the price." In the fading afternoon light, the customary fierce topaz gleam in her eyes had dulled, as if slowly subsumed by the heavy, suffocating sea mist. "Remember this feeling," Yosef said softly, meeting the devastation in her eyes with his own, "the next time you would so easily gamble with something that is not yours."

He paused just long enough to see the mist consume the last glimmer of hope. Then Yosef closed the door behind him.

He stepped out into the night, away from his past, and toward a future of his own creation.

32

THEO

JULY–AUGUST, AD 694

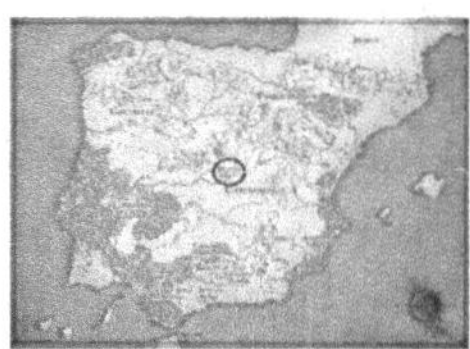

Toletum, Spania
Toledo, Spain

Theo stood in the dim light of the Basilica of Peter and Paul, fists tightly clenched, every muscle in his body rigid with tension. He was glad Silas and Leofric had not come with him to this farce of a coronation, and he was equally relieved Riccilo had offered him the usage of Theodofred's domus in their absence, negating the need for him to face either Athanagild or Laurentius. There had been many times in Theo's life when he had thought himself at breaking point. But never had the stakes felt so high.

His eyes bored a path through the chattering crowd of nobility to the dark, lean figure who stood on the side of the altar, a small smile playing on the angular features. Oppa had ridden out from the capital to accompany Wittiza's party into Toletum only one day before the much-lauded ceremony of co-rulership between Egica and his son. Wittiza had spent much of the summer months languishing in Corduba and "touring", as the palace seniores would have it, the surrounding latifundia. Theo, obedient to Athanais's instructions, had spent enough time in the tedious frivolity of their company to be aware of Oppa's absence, which had left him uneasy. He knew Oppa's ostentatious arrival at his brother's side, as the bacchanal approached Toletum, had been no accident. Oppa had spared no expense to make Wittiza's return nothing less than a triumphal march. He had sent men ahead to every township along the road with meat and wine, so that Wittiza's procession toward the capital had taken on all the pomp and celebration of a returning hero, rather than the controversial crowning of a plump boy with no more right to rule than the accident of his birth. By the time they rode through the horseshoe gate that marked the entrance to Toletum, the winding road to the palace was lined with cheering onlookers, all bought and paid for by Oppa. But it was not, Theo knew, for Wittiza's benefit Oppa had staged such an elaborate theatre; it was so all might see who rode at Wittiza's side. Now Oppa, clad in the white robes of a bishop, stood beside Archbishop Felix to give the Church's blessing to his brother's rule. *Why,* Theo thought bitterly, *be the one to carry the burden of the crown — when he can so easily instead be the power by which that crown was bestowed?*

"They say," murmured a nobleman nearby to his wife, "that Princeps Oppa resisted the urging of his fellows to contest Wittiza's position and instead asked for a bishopric. He wishes to ensure the Church remains loyal to the Crown, after the recent rebellion."

"All kings should hope for such a son, and brother," replied his wife admiringly. "Which bishopric will the king grant him, do you think?"

"Hispalis is the obvious choice. It is the most powerful, next to Toletum itself."

Theo turned away in disgust, not trusting himself to hear any more. As the clerk announced the entry of the king and his son, Theo slipped through the crowd until he was at the very rear. In the shadows he leaned against the final column before the rectangular apse, folded his arms, and waited for the farce to be over.

* * *

AN HOUR LATER, after florid speeches and pompous pretension by clergy and nobility alike, the crowd came one by one to kneel before their newly appointed co-ruler. Theo's feet felt heavy as the slow procession neared the king and his son, seated beneath the votive crown. Egica, he thought, looked older than he recalled from even a year ago. There was something petulant in the once hard mouth, a fractious air in the impatient way he dismissed each of the noblemen. More than once, he turned to the silent, lean figure of his illegitimate son, beckoning Oppa forward to ask a question or murmur an aside. If any in the assembly had been in any final doubt as to who held the reins of power in Toletum, the dynamic on display in the dim light of the basilica dispelled it.

Theo knelt before Wittiza, his heartbeat heavy and slow with tension as he avoided Oppa's eye and made his pledge in a low, clear voice. He half expected Egica or Oppa to make some additional request, force a scene to humiliate him, but the moment passed unmarked, other than a surprisingly warm smile from Egica, due, perhaps, to Theo's daily presence at court and an ongoing obsequy that had turned his stomach but seemingly achieved the desired result. Theo's reward was seeing his own relief mirrored in Egilona's beautiful face in the corner of the room, where she sat with the other ladies of the court.

He strode from the church into the welcome light of day, gulping deep breaths of air, feeling as if he had narrowly escaped a grim fate. He did not know what he had expected, only that he had not anticipated coming so close to Oppa and emerging unscathed. Part of him did not trust the moment, and he felt an instinctive urge to leave the city as quickly as possible, return to his wife and child before they were somehow taken from him. Then he thought of Athanais's instructions and tasted a bitter intermingling of resentment and self-loathing. Here he was, at home at last, playing an even worse double game than he ever had in Sebastopolis. Perhaps more upsetting, Theo knew a certain thrill in being amongst the cut and thrust of the political machine once more, even if he loathed his current place in it.

He must go now to ingratiate himself with the seniores, whilst also finding a way to speak to Laurentius and Athanagild of Lælia's plans. For even if he knew, in his heart, the smoke dream her plan was, still he could not bring himself to break his word that he would at least broach it. It was surprising, he thought, that neither man had so far approached him, given that both he and Lælia had already spoken to Athanagild of her idea. In fact, given the tone of that conversation, he had been surprised when Athanagild had chosen to return to Toletum. His brother and Laurentius had been noticeably absent from all but the most pressing matters at court.

He moved sideways off the road to avoid a cart, onto the hard beaten ground that marked the old Roman circus. The very ground, he thought bitterly, upon which his father had so recently lost his life. It was this final thought that hardened his resolve. He would track down Athanagild and Laurentius tonight, he decided. Tell them of Lælia's idea and hear their thoughts. There would be time enough for him to ingratiate himself at court. For now, what mattered was Lælia, and Geila. Her face, which for so many years had been no more than a wished-for mirage, passed before his eyes. He heard once more the odd fierceness in her voice when she said, *I will never do anything to betray you.* Theo's fists clenched, his whole body seizing with the same queer pain he had felt every time he had recalled those words on the long road from Aurariola to here. That she should say such a thing, when it was he who had betrayed her, had been betraying her all along... "Tyr!" Lashing out in involuntary frustration,

Theo drove his fist into the remnant of a crumbling stone wall.

"Hardly the deity to which you should be appealing, having so recently left God's own house." Theo did not need to turn to know to whom the silky, knowing tone belonged.

"I believe congratulations are in order," he said tersely. "On your soon-to-be-announced rise in the Church. Hispalis, is it?" Forcing his features under control, he turned slowly to find Oppa lounging against a chestnut tree, idly shredding a leaf with long-fingered delicacy.

"There is little point in being bishop of Illiberis." Oppa smiled coldly. "The taxes, you understand, have suffered a significant decline in recent years."

"Perhaps if you did not impose such severe restrictions upon the Jews of Garnata, you might find it a more lucrative office."

"Ah." Oppa's tone was sardonic. "But as you know, Theo, an unrepentant Jew is an insult to God, and any coin taken from him is tainted by sin."

"I do not recall you being so fastidious about sin." Folding his arms, Theo glared at Oppa. "What do you want, Oppa?"

Oppa let the skeleton of the leaf flutter to the ground and brushed his hands together to rid them of any detritus. "I see you are in no mood for idle conversation. Coincidentally, I find myself equally disinterested in prevarication, so I will come to the point."

Tense as a whipcord, Theo waited but did not speak.

"You have had in your possession for some time now," Oppa said, "parchment requiring your wife's hand. My patience has its limits, Theo. The next council will be held in October, and the southern lords will be informed that their presence in Toletum is not optional. You and your wife will also attend — and there give your public support to me, as the new Count of Illiberis."

"And?" Theo stared at Oppa with hard eyes.

"Whispers already reach Toletum," Oppa said quietly, "of

a new trade in silk. None know from where it comes. In particular, none yet know that it is not a line of trade from Constantinople – but an entire industry, barely a day's voyage across the sea."

He knows. Knowing what he did of Oppa's networks, it wasn't entirely a surprise, but Theo still felt a prickling unease, his mind racing in search of the best course to take.

"Your friend, Yosef, it seems, did indeed bring back a treasure from his journeying, albeit belatedly. A clever ruse indeed, to entrust his secrets to Athanais; one I confess I did not see. However, those secrets are out now." Oppa smiled coldly. "And the man who brings silk to Spania, Theo – that man will become, overnight almost, one of the nation's richest.

"The nobles of Spania will throw coin at the man who facilitates this trade. Dressmakers will order months in advance. The first cloth will be a prize men will be prepared to pay their last coin to own, to demonstrate their standing at court. The demand for silk, Theo, is insatiable." His eyes gleamed. "I will see to it that every ecclesiastical vestment uses it. The fashion, in my father's court, will be for silk, in every shade and manifestation. And you, Theo, will ensure that I am the agency through whom that coin will travel."

He stepped closer, the heavy musk oil he wore wafting over Theo. But despite his revulsion, Theo's mind was working. There was an opportunity here, one that would shortcut all the tedious work he faced at the council, and perhaps, achieve even more.

With the discipline of long practice, Theo schooled his ravaged face into a mask of indifference and turned blank eyes toward Oppa. "Why is it," he said lightly, "that you think I would not welcome such a proposition?"

He had the satisfaction of seeing Oppa's brow crease in confusion.

"For once," Theo went on, "not only does it seem our interests align, Oppa, but it is I who have a proposition for you. I had planned to have other discussions before broaching it, but it seems you have pre-empted me." Oppa watched him, dark eyed and silent. "The silk trade was our objective, yes. In this, you are correct. But our reasons were not merely pecuniary, as yours seem to be." Theo's mouth curled. "My objective, and that of my uncle before me, has always been to establish a force equipped to defend Spania's shores. A fleet at sea; an army on land. The silk trade was our way of ensuring coin that would achieve that end."

Oppa's eyes narrowed sharply. "After first funding a rebellion that would overturn my father's rule, in alliance with Ilyan of Septem."

"Perhaps." Theo did not attempt to deny it. "But that chance died with Sunifred's stupidity. Now our — and Ilyan's — only objective is the force itself, regardless of who sits on the throne." He lifted a shoulder. "You have already told me you plan to fund the fleet. This industry will give us both the means to do exactly that."

Oppa's eyes narrowed. "I think, Theudemir, that you miss the point. I do not wish for alliances. As I have said before, I prefer —"

"Control." Theo finished his sentence coolly. "Which you will still have. The taxes Ilyan collects from the trade in silk will be sent as his gift to the Spanish Crown, the basis for a new alliance to combat the coming Arab threat. It will be up to you to ensure that coin is used to put men in those dromons, Oppa."

"I do not care for taxes." Oppa dismissed him with a wave. "Official coin is of little use —"

"I am not finished." Theo cut him off again.

Oppa folded his arms and watched him, waiting. Theo's heart slowed to a heavy, thick beat. *Careful.*

"It is possible," he said, "for me to grant the first of your requests and ensure the first, and then the finest, of the cloth is available exclusively through you."

"Did I not just inform you that is what you would do?"

Oppa lifted a disdainful eyebrow. "If you thought it a request, Theo, you are much mistaken."

"It is Yosef who controls the production. And Yosef will never trade directly with you. Not even at my request."

Oppa's eyes glittered dangerously. "Yosef, I believe, has a wife. And children. I do not make requests, Theo, as you should know."

"Ilyan despises you." Theo met his eyes. A vision of Sarah's sobbing, battered body crossed his mind with sharp detail, and he had to clench his fists tightly to keep from reaching for his spatha. "Yosef would die, taking the secrets of silk with him, if you so much as touched a hair on his wife's head. If I did not kill you before that."

Oppa tilted his head in acknowledgement. "Then what exactly is it that you propose?"

"Yosef will not know it is with you he trades." Theo ignored the stab of his own conscience.

"And how, exactly, do you envisage working such a deception?"

"By trading through Illiberis, as his family and my wife's once agreed." When Oppa didn't speak, Theo took it as a signal to continue. "Give Illiberis back to Lælia. Tell your father your ecclesiastical duties are too arduous. Tell him you have tasked me to create a southern force under your command. Tell him I am your puppet – whatever you need to say." Theo drew a deep, steadying breath. "See it back in Lælia's hands, and she will sign any agreement you wish giving you control over the silk trade in Spania. Your brother will have our public support for his claim, and the southern lords will follow where Illiberis leads. Not only that – they will give you a land army to defend the southern coast alongside the fleet. An army" – he stepped closer – "that is loyal to the Crown and dependent upon it for coin. Just as the fleet, under my command, will be."

There was a long moment of pause, in which Theo felt the

dangerous light of hope steal into his heart. *Perhaps,* he thought, *we may yet survive this, Lælia and I.*

Then Oppa smiled, and the tremulous hope dissipated, its gleaming promise sucked back into the foetid Toletum air.

"I will never relinquish Illiberis, Theo. As for empowering a woman, and the daughter of a traitor, at that, to create an army?" He pushed away from the wall and stepped back from Theo, shaking his head and smiling contemptuously. "This, Theo, is a dream I can only presume came from your wife's mouth, for I cannot believe a man of your experience would ever have truly considered it. No." He tilted his head and the cold, black eyes met Theo's. "Control, Theo, not alliances. You forget that my father is still king, and your father is still a traitor. I might wish for your support in my brother's claim – but do not make the mistake of thinking I need it, Theo. Aurariola can be gone in an instant – and your sister given to whatever lord I choose."

Every word was like prison doors closing on the last cells of hope Theo held. He forced himself to meet Oppa's eyes without flinching as the man went on. "Your Jewish friend still requires a Spanish partner. Of course he intends it to be you – who else would he trust but the man who protected his journey all this time? You know well my ability for stealth, Theo, and nor am I ungenerous. None will know you trade on my behalf, and I will ensure you take a good portion of the coin. You might even use it for this land army of which you speak." He shrugged. "Armies are expensive, of course, but the choice is yours." He smiled coldly.

"The parchment." Theo could barely get the words out.

"Will remain with me." Oppa's eyes glittered. "Though I promise you, as I ever have, that no man will know of it so long as you and I remain in agreement. Some secrets are best kept in safe hands, Theo. Think of the parchment as the binding agent of our... association."

"And my sister?"

"Ah. On that, I think we might find some agreement at

last. Your sister is becoming quite the lady of the court. She, I think, should remain exactly where she is, for now, at least. And so long as you and I remain in agreement, Theo, you have no need to worry for her safety.”

“In other words,” said Theo tightly, “she remains your hostage.”

“Such an ugly word.” Oppa examined a nail with care, holding it out before him so the sun gleamed from the pale skin of his hand. “I prefer to think of her as a guest.”

It was only by the barest thread that Theo maintained control.

“One more thing.” Oppa’s face was hard. “Your uncle has not proven as compliant as I might wish. I would like to be sure of his voice on the council, when the time comes for my brother to take his rightful place.”

Laurentius? Theo strove to keep an even countenance. A sudden image of Shukra’s face crossed his mind. “You still hold my uncle’s friend in your dungeons,” he said slowly. “I would speak to Laurentius on your behalf, if he was released in exchange.”

“Your uncle’s friend.” Oppa repeated the words slowly, a small smile playing about his mouth. “Odd that you would refer to him as such. Laurentius, you understand, is quite adamant that the man is a sodomite and traitor, and most definitely no friend of his.”

Theo’s mouth twisted with distaste, but he did not answer. Oppa looked at him quizzically. “Do you truly not know, Theo? Or do you choose not to see?”

Theo ignored the bait. There would be time to ponder whatever dark meaning lay behind Oppa’s latest game. For now, he needed to go, before he lost the last thread of control he possessed.

“Then I will see you at my father’s council, Theo.” Nodding courteously, a small, unpleasant smile on his mouth, Oppa turned and walked away.

Theo stood in the middle of the road and watched him go,

his eyes staring unseeing into the middle distance long after the hated figure had disappeared.

Theo did not go to see his brother, or Laurentius.

He turned toward the river, and the oblivion of a wine jug.

* * *

THEO WENT to a tavern on the outskirts of the city, one frequented by soldiers and criminals alike, the kind of tavern he had avoided throughout all his years abroad and had all but prohibited his own men from attending. He downed his own weight in ale and then ordered a jug of wine.

Good thoughts. Good words. Good deeds.

Theo found himself mentally repeating the words every time he raised the cup, the mantra pounding through his head with merciless repetition. Each phrase conjured up images that turned his guts to water and his blood to ice: Lælia's devastation at being forced into submission at court; his sister's face across the court schooled into the calculating mask he had begun to loathe; Yosef's horror when he learned Theo had traded the fruits of his journey with the one man he had sworn to kill.

Good thoughts. Theo tossed off a cup of wine, trying to kill every thought left in his rotten soul. *Good words.* He tossed off another, hoping it might drown his treacherous tongue. *Good deeds.* He looked at his hands and saw, as if from a distance, only blood upon them.

A part of him, Theo realised, had known how this would end. The same part of him, perhaps, that had signed the parchment back in Sebastopolis. The part that had kept that parchment secret from Lælia for so long. The part of him that had heard Athanais's message and understood it with cold, military logic.

That part of him, Theo understood, with stark, foul clarity, had for years, now, placed duty to Spania ruthlessly above all else.

Friendship. Loyalty.

Even love.

Ultimately, Theo knew, he had always faced a choice, between what his heart wanted, and what he felt duty bound to do. Perhaps, if he were truly honest, he had faced that choice even before he met Lælia. Their very marriage had been agreed not to save Illiberis but Spania itself. Yosef's mission, Theo's service in the fleet – all of it had been born from that one purpose: to save Spania, prepare it for the wars to come.

He drank again. Gestured curtly for more wine.

If he had fallen in love with Lælia more deeply than he could ever imagine, if Yosef had become a brother in all but name – still, Theo thought wearily, he had always chosen Spania first. And the wars he had fought had only deepened his commitment to that duty by showing him the enemy his country would one day face first-hand.

But that duty, he saw now, had been at war, almost as long as he could remember, with the part of him that loved Lælia. When he had chosen to follow the fleet instead of returning to her; when he had signed the parchment; when he had let Oppa live.

In a war, one side had to win. Theo realised that although he had fooled himself that he could fight to a truce, he had, all the while, been fighting for duty. And now it was love that would pay the price.

Whether he told Lælia of the parchment or not, Theo knew either way that she would never truly recover from the loss of Illiberis. In his hubris, he had overlooked the one truth that mattered: Lælia, too, had a duty. One that she had been born to just as much as he had to the dream of Spania. Only hers, he realised too late, was no intellectual ideology. Hers was an allegiance of blood and earth, bred into her with every breath, imprinted upon her heart. Illiberis was not just Lælia's heritage, as Spania was his.

It was her soul.

He had traded her soul, Theo saw with stark, horrible clarity, as if it were no more than currency. As if his duty to Spania were somehow a loftier ideal than the very real stuff of her bond to her homeland. And in doing so, he had traded away both his own moral core, and their future happiness.

And now his last chance of regaining Illiberis for her, of at least in some way righting his terrible wrong, was lost – and no matter what he did now, Theo knew, with it would be lost both the soul of the woman he loved, and the future he had dared dream of.

He had emptied more than half of a third jug when a burly man in the uniform of the king's own thiufa knocked into him in passing, upturning his cup. "Excuse me, friend." The soldier clapped Theo on the shoulder with a paw of a size to rival Leofric's. "No harm meant." Theo looked down meditatively at the meaty hand, then at the wine running in red rivulets onto the stone below.

"And yet," he said slowly, feeling the anger in him coiling to a burning point, "harm has been done. And now, it is too late to undo it." As the man's face turned from bleary, good-natured drunkenness to startled awareness, Theo rose from his stool in a vicious turn, the full force of his body slamming into the unwary soldier. Men jumped back in surprise and eyed warily the tall, fierce man with savage scars and eyes of green fire. Roaring with fury, Theo knocked the burly soldier to the ground and then turned to face the man's fellows, a dark smile on his face and his fists balled. He wanted only the mindless rage of the fight, the blunt pain of fist and muscle. "Come on!" he roared at them. "Come!"

"Get out of his way!" snarled an older man from the side of the tavern. "That's a killing look, I tell you."

Men were already scrambling over one another to make for the door, casting nervous glances over their shoulders as Theo's fist knocked first one man, then a second and third, clean to the floor. He was about to toss another man against the wall when a lithe arm slid about his neck. Theo felt a sharp pain in his kidney, then the sudden descent of darkness as breath began to leave his body. "That is more than enough," said a cool voice in his ear. "You can come with me, now." The last thing Theo saw, before he slid into blissful darkness, was a fist driving into his face.

* * *

HE WOKE with a pounding head and rolled over, only to find himself toppling onto a cool tiled floor, still fully dressed in his clothes from the night before. Opening one eye, he found himself staring at the unexpected sight of a bookstand, upon which lay an open codex with leather covering and rich, heavy pages. Theo took this in at the same time he realised that the floor upon which he had landed was inlaid with a complex mosaic, and the air itself was scented with frankincense. This was no tavern floor. Nor was it Theodofred's domus. He lay still for a moment, partly because his head throbbed with such savagery it made him faint to move, and partly because he was trying to recall what series of disasters had landed him here. His lip was split, he realised, wincing as he touched it, and one eye was so swollen that he couldn't open it. He had spoken with Oppa; that conversation needed no effort at all to recollect, for it was burned into his brain like the brand on a horse. He had gone to that tavern by the river and drunk − a lot. Then there had been a man, he remembered, and the man had knocked over his wine, an injury that had seemed simply too great to bear… Theo winced as he recalled the punch he had thrown. He frowned. He could remember a strong grip − someone behind him…

"But what was he doing there?" A voice drifting from another room stopped his mental recollections. He knew that voice, but he couldn't quite place it…

"He was drunk, Athanagild. And furious, by the look of him."

Iesu Xristus. Theo sat up so abruptly he had to bite his

damaged lip when he hit his head on the underside of the lecta. He knew this study. And those voices. He was in the villa of Laurentius Severianus – and his brother was here, too. Theo stifled a groan. This morning of all mornings, this was all he needed.

"Theo has never been a drunk. Alaric, now he was an expert, at both drinking and tavern brawls. But I don't think I've ever seen Theo even approaching drunk, let alone starting a fight."

"Well, there is a first time for all things, I expect, Athanagild." There was an uncharacteristically grim tension to Laurentius's voice that caused Theo to still, listening closely. "I imagine whatever caused him to drink in secret is the same reason he did not see fit to tell either of us he was in Toletum."

"I knew he was here. I saw him at the basilica yesterday." Now it was Athanagild's voice that was unfamiliar, with a sombre note that made Theo even more alert.

"You knew he was here? And you didn't think to mention this to me?"

"I didn't exactly have the opportunity, Laurentius. As far as I recall, we've exchanged barely two sentences for months now. I am not even certain where you spend your nights. God knows it isn't here, or at least not when I have come to visit. Which speaks to the point – how did you even know Theo was in that damned tavern?"

"I heard it at the barracks." Laurentius's voice was careful, Theo thought, and slightly defensive. The hairs on his neck began to rise with a dawning awareness.

"At the barracks." Athanagild's tone was flat and hard. "What possible business could have kept you at the barracks, so late in the evening? Or do I not wish to know the answer to that question?"

"How dare you ask me that!" There was a sudden rustle of movement, the sound of a body hitting a wall hard, and Theo shot to his feet involuntarily, upsetting a small side table as he did so. Abruptly, all sound in the other room ceased; a moment later, Laurentius strode into the room, his face as austere as ever, only a curiously dark light in his eyes betraying the emotion Theo had overheard a moment earlier. "Good morning." Laurentius handed him a jug of water. "I imagine you will need this, and more." He gave Theo the ghost of a smile and turned away, busying himself in the corner of the room with every pretence at nonchalance. Theo gulped the water gratefully, watching the stiff back of the older man, wondering what, exactly, he should say, if anything, of what he had overheard. Laurentius's next words decided his course.

"When did you awaken?" It was not the question, so much, but the careful, deliberate manner in which Laurentius asked it that set Theo's nerves alight. He swallowed another mouthful of water and said, with all the casual confusion he could muster, "When I rolled over and knocked the table to the floor. I do apologise for finding myself on your lecta, Laurentius."

"No matter." Laurentius faced him, his own expression smooth and imperturbable as ever. "You got yourself in quite a state last night. Fortunate for you that your face is not one that goes unremarked. Word travels quickly of such a face — particularly when it belongs to a man with your name, drinking in a tavern such as that."

"Yes." Theo winced as he felt the bruise beneath his eye. "Perhaps it wasn't wise. But did you have to blacken my eye, Laurentius?"

The older man gave him a ghost of a smile. "It seemed called for, under the circumstances."

"Perhaps you are right." Theo passed a hand over his face. "I need a wash, and a shave."

"Of course. I will have the servants bring you water and a change of clothes. I will show you to a room — I'm afraid that in your state last night, navigating stairs seemed unwise."

"Ha." Theo laughed mirthlessly and walked toward the door, where he paused. "I thought I might visit Athanagild today," he said carefully. "I'm afraid I was in no mood, yesterday, to wait for him after the ceremony, or visit the monastery. Do you know where I might find him?"

There was a short pause, then Laurentius said, equally carefully, "I can send word to him to meet you here, if you wish. I imagine he can be here when you are finished bathing, if I send a messenger now." *Oh, I imagine he can,* thought Theo grimly, *given that from what I heard, the messenger need only ascend the steps to your own bedchamber.*

But he said only, "Thank you, Laurentius. I shall see you both then." He left his uncle in the study, his mind whirling as he climbed the stairs.

Later, as they ate together in the internal courtyard of Laurentius's villa, he watched his brother and uncle. Unbidden, he recalled Athanagild's words long ago, when Yosef, assuming they were blood brothers, had commented that Athanagild reminded him of Laurentius. *I am not related to Laurentius,* Athanagild had said. His brother's face had flamed, Theo remembered, and he had thought nothing of it, for Athanagild was inherently shy and given to raging colour when embarrassed. Now, though, he saw that moment through another lens, and as he watched the careful way in which the two behaved, from the distance at which they sat to the manner in which they avoided catching the other's eye, he became increasingly certain his suspicions were correct.

He answered their questions mechanically, hiding his thoughts behind the mask he had long ago perfected, making courteous conversation about his new son and Toletum politics with every appearance of indifference, whilst beneath the exterior calm his mind whirled, Oppa's words spinning through his mind taking on a dark significance: *Do you truly not know, Theo? Or do you choose not to see?*

At first he was furious, almost physically restraining himself from throwing Laurentius up against a wall and demanding what kind of man could call himself a soldier whilst availing himself of the body of a boy ten years his junior.

But then, as the conversation deepened into a more complex discussion regarding the revisions made to the great *Lex Visigothorum* by King Erwig, Egica's predecessor, and their implications for the Jews of Spain, Theo sat back and watched as the two men grew animated, throwing ecclesiastical and scholarly references across the table with increasing fervour to support their arguments, until Laurentius lay back against the cushions of his lecta, laughing, his eyes for a moment softened from their customary stern grey. "Your brother," he said, smiling at Theo, "is a difficult man to outmanoeuvre in argument. He would, I believe, be a match for Isidore of Hispalis himself."

"If I am a match for Isidore's memory, you have certainly inherited his obstinacy," countered Athanagild, returning the smile with a brief blaze of warmth Theo had so rarely seen on his brother's face that it warmed him somewhere deep inside. "What think you, Theo?" Athanagild went on, turning dancing, momentarily unguarded eyes to his brother. "Might Laurentius not have been better served arguing with priests than with Arabs on the end of a sword?"

"Do you know," said Theo slowly, his eyes moving between the two men, "I believe that both of you are exactly as God himself chose to make you." Then, to disguise the sudden surge of emotion he felt, he turned to the servant standing nearby. "Given that this is a soldier's house," he said, lightening his tone, "surely you have something stronger than water to drink? Our father" – he winked at Athanagild – "always swore that only watered wine could cure a man of the evils from the night before." When they began talking again, it was of inconsequential matters, but Theo, noticing the two men sitting slightly closer than they had before, felt a curious warmth inside.

* * *

IT WAS mid-afternoon when Theo left the villa.

He had avoided answering any of his brother's or Laurentius's questions and they, undoubtedly cautious of their own business, had not pushed him. Theo could not bring himself to speak of what had taken place between him and Oppa. If he had looked into the darkness of his own soul last night, the light of day had brought a return of his strategic mind, and the inkling of a plan. He thought he knew the game that must be played, but before he acted, he must know the whole; and for that, he needed Shukra.

Now he hesitated at the gate that led to the dungeons and drew a deep breath. This had to be done, had to be faced.

Mastering himself, he nodded grimly at the guard and went down into the darkness.

He paused as his eyes adjusted to the gloom, wincing at the stench of raw sewage, unwashed humans, and worse. He walked past huddled figures that were no more than bone and rags, chained to the walls. Shukra, he had learned from the guard, had his own cell, a privilege paid for by an anonymous donor – *Oppa*, Theo thought grimly – at an increasingly high price, given Shukra's lethal ability to cause serious harm to any unwary guard who strayed too close. He passed the last of the rows of misery and went down further, past several empty cells. He was just thinking that he must have missed Shukra when the soft, familiar accents reached him through the silent gloom.

"Theudemir of Aurariola. An odd, and unexpected, pleasure, indeed, *aziz-am*."

"Shukra." Theo gripped the bars and peered into the oddly clean, well-swept small space. Shukra sat against the rear wall, his hands, contrary to what Laurentius had told Theo, chained to the wall.

"You must forgive my lack of courtesy in greeting you." Shukra's voice was as light and amused as if they had met in a grand hall, over meat. "The guards, it seems, have recently grown tired of our games."

"Not the guards," said Theo grimly. "I'd lay every coin in my purse those chains are Oppa's doing."

"Ah. You have met with our old friend, then, I take it?" Theo nodded. "And so now he thinks to bring the game to conclusion." Shukra tilted his head to one side and smiled gently at Theo. "And he chains me to remind you of his power."

"Why are you here, Shukra?" Theo had intended to take his time with his questions, try a more tactful route. But the sight of the lithe Persian in chains had jolted him more than he had expected. Shukra, Theo knew, possessed not only extraordinary courage and skill, but also unwavering loyalty and kindness. His years in the Karabisianoi, and his long friendship with Athanais, had served only to increase Theo's respect for the man who had once helped Yosef escape from Spania and had served as guide and counsel to his younger self. Seeing him now for the first time after so long took Theo back to the boy he had been all those years ago, when they had ridden together from Aurariola down to Illiberis, to meet Lælia for the first time. *I know my duty,* Theo had said to Shukra on that ride. Shukra's response was etched upon his mind, as if it had been drawn in stone: *It is a strange thing, duty…*

"Why?" Theo asked again when Shukra did not immediately answer. "Is it because of my brother – and Laurentius? Because of what lies between them?"

"Ah." There was a certain weariness in Shukra's voice, a resigned understanding, that was as much confirmation of his suspicions as Theo needed.

"Oppa knows, doesn't he." It was a statement, not a question.

Shukra inclined his head once. "Our friend is almost as adept in the gathering of whispers as I myself. Sadly, Theo, yes, Oppa is aware of that of which you speak – though as yet, I suspect, he does not have the evidence of it he might like."

"Why?" Theo's voice broke on the word this time. "Why

do you languish here? How can they let you take the blame for a crime that is not yours?"

"Because it is my wish. And even in chains, you will find I can be remarkably stubborn in my wishes." When Theo did not speak, Shukra went on, in a slightly less flippant tone. "Do not think me innocent, Theo. And of all things, do not think what lies between Athanagild and Laurentius a crime, for to do so is to take something beautiful and make of it something dark."

"I do not despise them for... what they are." Theo met Shukra's eyes through the gloom. "I have been a soldier a long time, Shukra. You and I both know such things are more common than men might speak of." He frowned. "But that doesn't explain to me how it is that you are in here, and not them − nor how they can allow it."

"*Aziz-am.*" Shukra's fists clenched impotently inside the chains. "There are secrets that are not mine to tell. Know only that in his own way, your brother fought a war, Theo. A dangerous war − one of unimaginable personal sacrifice. He fought it alone, with me his only confessor, and I, to my eternal shame, allowed him to fight it, alone and in darkness. When I saw the opportunity to in some way atone to Ahura Mazda for that crime, I did so." He lifted his shoulders slightly. "He and Laurentius do not *allow* me to languish here, Theo. I insist upon it." His mouth tightened. "And besides − I had the immense satisfaction of hearing the death screams of the evil creature I went to murder that night. There are not many times I approve of torture, you understand, *aziz-am*. But the painful death of the good Archbishop Sisebut was so satisfying to me that I confess I bribed the guards for a jug of wine to drink whilst I listened to him scream. If ever a man was taken by the darkness of Ahriman, it was that demon in white robes."

Theo stared at Shukra, as shocked by the bitterness of his words as he was by their implication. "He corrupted Athanag-ild," he said slowly. "That archbishop. Didn't he? And

Athanagild tolerated it, in order to rise in the Church and pass information. To whom?" He frowned, thinking, then almost groaned aloud as he realised. "To Laurentius," he breathed. "Athanagild did all this because of how he felt about Laurentius."

"Not only that," Shukra said quietly. "Your brother has as much sense of duty as you – or Alaric – ever did. He did what he did because he saw evil and could not allow it to triumph."

Duty, thought Theo dully. *The evils we have all committed in the name of that damned word.*

"Alaric," he said aloud. "Did he know of this? What Athanagild was – enduring?"

"Not at first, no. By the end, yes, I am thinking he knew. But by then Alaric had made sacrifices of his own and ceased to judge, I think, those of others. He and your brother were men of war both, bonded as any soldiers might be. Alaric knew your brother fought what battles he could with the tools he had."

"Tyr." Theo pushed away from the bars impatiently and strode a few paces, then back again, unable to stand still. That all this had happened, the suffering of both his brothers, whilst he was so far away; the thought of Athanagild, the shy, lean figure his brother had been when Theo sailed, being subjected to such abuse – "Tyr!" he spat again, shaking the bars in frustration.

"It is no more than what your brother must feel when he sees those markings on your face." Theo looked up to find Shukra watching him. "And by the lines on your brow, and the chains I wear, I am thinking that Oppa is not finished with you yet, Theo, no? Still he forces you to dance, to play the part he has set for you. Now it is my turn to ask you questions, Theudemir of Aurariola, and I will ask that you answer them truthfully." When Theo did not respond, just stared at him grimly, Shukra smiled faintly. "Ah, your brother Alaric would give me much the same look, you know, when I would have such conversations with him. Athanagild, too. Not to mention your uncle Laurentius. But I digress." Fixing Theo with an uncomfortably perceptive eye, Shukra said, "What is it that Oppa wants from you, Theo? And what has he promised you?"

Never before had Theo felt such an overwhelming urge to unburden himself, to lay the whole before Shukra. But to do so, he knew, would be to place the other man in an impossible position. There was nothing in Oppa's demands that he could not think through on his own – and he was too old to hand his troubles over, especially to a man in chains facing imminent death. Theo despised himself for even imagining such a thing.

"There is nothing Oppa threatens that I cannot manage." Theo forced his face into the mask he had perfected during years of slavery and war. "He plays a game, yes. But it was I who chose to play it with him, long ago, and I who must bear the consequences of the outcome." As he spoke, he was aware of thoughts stirring, distant threads at the back of his mind. "You mentioned Alaric," he said, frowning. "In the end it was he, if I understand it, who led the bulk of Sunifred's forces, was it not?"

"It was." Shukra nodded, watching him with a faint smile. "And more than led them. Many of them yet hold their lands because Alaric sent them home soon after Sunifred reached Toletum, when he knew it could not stand. There are many lords in the south who owe him their lives. And, as I have learned since I came to this land, the south does not forget such debts."

Theo gripped the bars, his heart thudding, staring at Shukra. "All this time," he said slowly, "I have been playing by Oppa's rules. Rules that were set between us the night he pulled me from the sea and I found myself under his whip. I have been fighting the chains in which he holds me ever since."

"And now," Shukra said softly, "you begin to see that chains exist only in a man's mind, Theo."

"*Ja.*" Theo's mind was racing, hitherto unseen possibilities coming together with the rapidity that had made him Apsimar's star pupil. "Oppa has controlled every play on the board between us. But I believe there may yet be pieces he has underestimated." Theo felt a smile like a stranger on his mouth. "And other pieces," he said, nodding into the cell, "that he must learn to play without."

Shukra's eyes narrowed. "I would ask that you do not factor me into your decisions, *aziz-am*. I did not make the choices I have only to become another piece in Oppa's games. You will not be making decisions because you wish to see me spared. And do not think to save Laurentius, either. Both he and I have learned long ago how to box shadows such as the one Oppa casts. Trust us, Theo, to do what is right. For us, and for Athanagild."

"Once," said Theo, smiling slightly, "long ago, you and I spoke of duty, Shukra. Do you recall that conversation?"

Shukra made an impatient sound. "I recall talking with a boy who was about to face both marriage and war. That was a different conversation, *aziz-am*."

"Ah, but it is not. Not really." Theo's smile twisted painfully. "I am still facing both marriage and war, Shukra. And I believe your advice still stands. You told me, *Duty is nothing but words, unless it is coming from the place in a man where he knows his thoughts, his words, and his deeds match.*" Shukra made an impatient noise, but Theo went on: "Good thoughts. Good words. Good deeds. You told me that, Shukra. And after you, Athanais told me the same thing. And yet despite all that advice, every day since I left the shores of Sebastopolis, I have thought, done, and said many things I know have not been good. I have done things in the name of duty that have diverged from that place inside where we know what good is. And in doing so, I have destroyed all that duty was meant to preserve.

"I will not live that way anymore, Shukra. I cannot. Even if it means I lose all I once told myself I was fighting for."

Shukra met his eyes across the room. After a long

moment, he nodded once. "Then may Ahura Mazda be with you, *aziz-am*," he said softly. "For the One sees your heart and knows what is true, for every man. May this be true for you."

Theo stepped back from the bars, feeling an almost heady lightness to his body, the lifting of a weight he had almost ceased to notice he was carrying. "I will see you soon, Shukra," he said, pounding the bars a last time with one hand. "I will see you soon."

33

LÆLIA
AUGUST, AD 694

Aurariola, Spania
Orihuela, Spain

L*etter to Lælia, in Aurariola, from Rekiberga, in Tarraconensis*

My sister,

I received your letter this morning. Be assured it had not been opened. Your messenger rode hard and is clearly loyal to you. He waited until I was alone in the courtyard and was not seen. I will send this reply with him tomorrow.

Your letter was more welcome than you can know, and I cannot thank you enough for thinking of me. Whilst we may never be family in name now, you will forever be the sister of my heart.

I am glad to hear that Geila is well. I, too, have delivered my husband a child, a daughter, though I confess I cannot feel the joy that such a gift should bring. The truth is that with a child I am now irrevocably trapped, bound to Ataulfo forever. There are many who would be grateful to be in such a position. Ataulfo has high standing at court, and our lands are rich and extensive. I am mistress of a villa barely smaller than the one in which I was raised.

But a cage is a prison whether it is made of gold or stone, and I am no less trapped here than I ever was as the daughter of Sunifred. I do not love Ataulfo; I never can. My heart died in Illiberis, with Alaric, whom I would have followed anywhere, to exile and beyond. I wish now that I had simply kept riding that day, into an unknown future, and met what the road may have brought.

You, I think, would have done that. You have a strength and fire that few women possess, the skill to survive on such a road. Women such as I are raised to needlework and weaving, not the sword and bow as you were.

I do not write this because I am bitter, Lælia. I write it because I hear between the words in your letter a question, a shadow you do not voice. Perhaps I imagine it, hear only my own discontent echoed back to me. But I was there, that day, in Illiberis. I saw you command a battle. I saw men bow to you in respect and fight to the death in your name.

I cannot imagine the same person who did all of that, now content to relinquish the land she fought so hard to keep. I cannot imagine the girl who once publicly defied both the Church and the Crown now cowering before both. And most of all, Lælia, and perhaps unfairly, I cannot imagine the girl I knew without any other role to play apart from that of wife and mother.

Perhaps you find my words harsh. And perhaps they are no more than a reflection of my own situation, for God alone knows that I would rather be dead than living this pale half-life. But perhaps, too, living such a life grants me a certain freedom to speak my mind. I have nothing left to lose, Lælia. The rebellion took everything from me. I am left now to live out my years as the wife of a stranger, raising his children to be loyal subjects to a king I despise. I look at my daughter, Lælia, and I see for her only the same road walked by most women — one from her father's house to that of the husband chosen for her. A life of servitude and suffering that is sold to every girl as a dream, but which in reality is the cage I spoke of earlier, no matter how grand a cage it be.

But you are different, Lælia. You have a chance the rest of us do not.

LÆLIA FOLDED the parchment for the hundredth time and slipped it back inside her dress. She stood at the window staring unseeing at the shorn fields, their stubble dead and hard under the August sun. Jadis was gone. The cat spent much of her time, now, prowling the coastal plains. When she entered the house she looked at her mistress warily, and she slept alone. Jadis had grown thin with her roaming and did not easily submit to caresses, even from Silas.

As if summoned by the thought, Silas's deep voice gently broke the silence.

"Your son grows tired of Leofric and Tosius's company."

"My son should grow used to the company of men." She did not attempt to hide the bitterness in her tone. "Men are the world to which he was born."

"There is a time for boys to become men." Still she did not turn. "When they are old enough to sit on a horse unaided, to hold a sword alone. Not," Silas said, "when they are yet to sit up without assistance."

"What is your point, Silas?" She turned abruptly from the window. Despite the heat of the day, she pulled the shawl close about shoulders that had, in the weeks since Yosef's departure, grown painfully sharp. "Did you come here to lecture me on my failings as a mother?"

"I came because I fear that if someone does not soon speak, Geila may not have a mother at all." Silas met her brittle anger with a steadiness and calm that Lælia found a harder reproach than any scold might have been. "You are thin, Lady."

"I am not your lady." Her answer was hard and fast. "And the fat on my bones is no business of yours, Silas." Lælia knew her words were unjust, childish. But Silas was Theo's man. Part of the world he had hidden from her. Part of the lie.

She turned abruptly back to the window, not trusting herself to speak.

"You are angry." Silas's voice had not altered in timbre. Lælia gave a harsh laugh in response but said nothing.

"Your friend," Silas said. "Yosef. He said things that upset you."

"He told me the truth." Lælia's voice was harsh to her own ears. "No more."

"Ah. Truth." There was something in his voice that made Lælia turn. She found Silas leaning against the wall, arms folded, his eyes dark. "Truth, in my experience, is a strange thing."

"Truth," said Lælia slowly, holding his eyes, "is the one thing that is not at all strange. It is the simplest of all things. It is lies that are hard." Her mouth twisted. "And yet my husband, it seems, does not find them so; and nor do his companions, who live under our roof and hold my son in their arms."

She did not move her eyes from his. "You knew," she said softly, not a question so much as a statement. "You all knew

Theo had dealt with Oppa. And none of you thought you could tell me the truth. Why? Because I am a woman, too feeble to understand the truth?"

Silas met her eyes without flinching, his face impassive.

"Well?" Now that Lælia had begun, she found she could not stop. "Have you nothing to say, Silas?"

"Did Theo ever tell you of the storm during which we met?" The question was the last one she expected.

"What does it matter?" Folding her arms, Lælia eyed Silas with hostility.

"I was close to death." Silas went on without asking permission. "I had carried another boy through the storm at sea for many hours when Theo helped us both onto his raft. Leofric was unconscious. Sometime in the night, the boy I carried slipped from this world. A whole life, gone, just like that. Then it was just Leofric, Theo, and I. We all of us thought we would die. Throughout the entire time we floated in that storm, I do not think that Theo once let go of the amulet you had given him. And, by some miracle, we did not die." He met her eyes gravely. "Later, when we became slaves and Theo was whipped every day, long past the time when most men would have gladly slipped into the darkness and let it take them, still he did not die. Still he held the amulet. And even when Oppa tore his skin to shreds and told him he could make it stop if only he relinquished you, still Theo would smile and say to him: 'Lælia is mine.'"

Despite herself, Lælia could not help but listen. Theo had never spoken of either ordeal, other than in the most broad terms. To hear it laid out in such graphic detail was both shocking and fascinating.

"Before every battle we fought. After them. Every morning he woke, before he lay down to sleep, and at night when he dreamed, Theo held that amulet in his hand and whispered your name on his lips. You were his prayer, his mantra, and the lodestar that drew him home." Silas's eyes were oddly magnetic, his voice both soothing and remorseless in the pictures his words drew. "That also made you Oppa's greatest weapon against him. One he tried, repeatedly, to wield. When finally he succeeded, it was because Theo thought it was the only way to save your life – and even so, I do not think Theo will ever forgive himself."

"And yet still, none of you thought to own it." Lælia's words sounded harsh to her own ears. "Including Theo."

Silas's mouth twisted. "In all those years, it was not only Theo your memory saved," he said gently. "His will to return to you kept us all alive. You became not only Theo's lodestar Lælia. You became our mascot. A home to men who have long been without one. When finally we found you, miraculously whole, it was not only Theo who could not bear losing you again." He shook his head. "Perhaps we were wrong. But can you honestly say, if you had known Illiberis lost from the start, that you would not have ridden immediately south to defend it?"

"Perhaps." Lælia did not hesitate in her answer. "But it should have been my choice to do so, or not."

"It would not have been a choice." Silas's tone was kind but resolute. "You would have ridden, and Theo would have had no choice but to ride with you."

"And instead, he chose lies, and a role at court. A place in Spania's future."

"He chose life for you both."

"No, Silas." Lælia looked at him steadily. "He chose a life for him. The life he chose for me is just another form of death." She had the satisfaction of seeing Silas visibly recoil. He raised a hand toward her, then slowly let it drop. Whatever words hovered on his lips were swallowed again as a dark, painful realisation shadowed his eyes. There was a short silence in which they stared at one another, then Silas bowed his head in silent acknowledgement, as they both absorbed the dull truth of her words.

Then, in an odd slip of light, the room and the fields beyond it slipped away, and suddenly Lælia was back in the sands beneath the desert sun, Dahiya's hard words falling upon her like arrows:

"You have won nothing... Proven nothing. You are the same girl you were when Theo left, still waiting for him to return, for your dream life to begin. You live beneath your grandfather's roof. Soon you will live beneath your husband's..."

So immediate was the vision that she was startled when Silas spoke again. His voice was subdued, no longer the authoritative counsel of earlier. "What is it that you see, in your mind, now?"

"I see Dahiya," Lælia said slowly. "I hear the words she once spoke to me."

Silas watched her soberly. "Is this the first time she has called you?"

"No." She stared out of the window, remembering. "Once before – on the birthing bed, when Geila was born. I saw her in my mind." She frowned. "Dahiya – and Acantha, my grandmother."

"And did they speak to you?"

"Yes." She touched her thigh, remembering the scar she had seen on Acantha's, long ago. "They said that when the walls fall, so will Africa." She frowned. "Or Spania. I could not tell." Realising how she sounded, she coloured and turned away. "I know such visions are not uncommon on the birthing bed."

"Mother of Geila." She looked at him sharply, and Silas's mouth twisted, but not in derision. "This is how we call women, in my country," he said quietly. "As the daughter of this man, or the mother of that one. We do not call them as you do here, Lady of this place or that. My people do not name themselves for soil. They take their names from those of their blood."

"They name their women for the men who helped make them, or those the women birthed." Lælia laughed mirthlessly. "It is not so different from here, Silas. I am no more Lady of Aurariola than I was of Illiberis. There, I was the granddaughter of a man. Here, I am the wife of another, and the mother of his heir." She shrugged. "That is what I am. That is what all women, in this time, are forced to be." Yosef's face, tight and furious, crossed her mind with the stab of pain that grew no less no matter how many times she remembered their conversation. "And perhaps," she said softly, swinging away to hide her face, "I never deserved to call myself Lady of that soil at all."

"And perhaps," said Silas quietly, "Theo's choices have saved you from being bound to that soil." Lælia turned back sharply to find his dark eyes watching her with an expression she could not quite read.

"What do you mean, Silas?"

He paused, and when he spoke again, his voice was particularly slow, and an odd light glowed somewhere behind his eyes.

"We are all held by the manner of our birth, and those of our blood, Mother of Geila. From them we are made and to them we return. Whatever we do in our time on earth we do as part of the blood to which we were born, and that which we ourselves create. We can no more ignore such ties as we can control the soil upon which we are born – or upon which we fight." He stopped speaking abruptly, almost as if he had said too much; Lælia found herself staring at him, thoughts spiralling through her mind, disconnected and impossible as they were exhilarating. Something inside Lælia shifted, like the sands moving in the midnight winds, to be reformed anew the next morning. One moment she was Lælia, Lady of Aurariola and the wife of a Spanish nobleman, trapped and impotent. And in the next, a part of her she had thought gone forever awoke once more, spiralling up through her body like a serpent coming to life, thrilling her every sense with the memory of who she had once been.

She heard Dahiya's voice echo inside her: *Even as you disdain the chatter of the women, you are preparing for the life they lead, not the one I do. You came here wrapped in the protection of the legacy you were born to and the one to which you are now betrothed. And if you think any man such as Theo will stand by and watch his wife, the mother of his children, lead men to war, you are deluded.*

Lælia realised she was gripping the wrought iron of the window covering, so hard her knuckles were white. Her heartbeat was no longer slow and dull but rapid, fired with an energy she had thought lost. Then she remembered Silas. She turned slowly to face him. His eyes widened then retracted, sadness entering them. As if regretting what he had just said, Silas pushed himself away from the wall and strode toward the door.

"Silas." He stopped but did not turn around. "Can you send Tosius to me?"

He nodded slowly, still without turning. "Yes, Mother of Geila," he said slowly. "I can." He did not ask further questions but left her standing by the window, her mind turning rapidly so that when Tosius came to the door, she was still in the same position as when Silas had left her.

"You sent for me, *dauhter?*"

"Yes." Lælia met the little man's eyes, switching to the chatter of the tribes. "Do you think you can find your way to the men of the desert, to Zdan, and Dahiya?"

Tosius nodded impassively. "This I can do, *dauhter.*"

"You will give Dahiya a message and get her answer to me as quickly as you might."

Tosius nodded. "What would you have me say?"

Lælia took a deep breath. It seemed to her that, as she did, the coastal haze slipped away and the golden sunlight entered her like a fine, bright shard of clarity. She saw the words on Rekiberga's letter tucked inside her dress: *You have a chance the rest of us do not. Options I never will have. Places you might run to, and people who might welcome you…*

"Tell her," she said, "that Lælia, granddaughter of Acantha, sends her greetings." She looked sharply at Tosius. "Not the Lady of Illiberis," she said. "You understand, Tosius?"

The tribesman nodded impassively. "This I understand."
He met her eyes. "And your message, *dauhter*?"

"Tell Dahiya that I ask if I might come to her." Lælia held
his eyes. "Tell her my bow belongs to her – if she will
accept it."

Tosius nodded briefly. He turned to go.

"Tosius." He stopped and turned back. "You have nothing
to ask of me?" she said, curious despite herself.

Tosius glanced away. His eyes returned to her, then
dropped. "I belong here," Tosius said, staring at the ground.
"There are places you will go that I cannot follow."

Lælia's heart twisted painfully. "I know that, Tosius."

He nodded. "I will return as soon as I might." He slipped
through the door and left his mistress staring out of the
window, her heart in turmoil.

34

LAURENTIUS

AUGUST, AD 694

Toletum, Spania
Toledo, Spain

"Theo." Laurentius looked up in surprise at the tall figure filling his library door. "I had thought you already gone to Aurariola. If you seek your brother," he went on, "Athanagild is not here —"

"I do not." Theo's voice was not curt, but neither was it friendly. "I came to speak with you, Laurentius."

"Oh?" Turning his back on the pretext of pouring himself wine, Laurentius took a deep breath in an effort to compose himself. He had a feeling that he might need more than breath, or indeed wine, to face what lay ahead. He had thought, after the morning that Theo woke from his drunken stupor, and in the days following it, that the three of them had come to some kind of understanding, albeit unspoken, regarding his and Athanagild's affairs. So fragile was that understanding that it had remained unspoken even between Athanagild and himself. *And perhaps,* Laurentius thought grimly, *I was a fool to believe any understanding existed at all.*

"I think it is time you told me," Theo said quietly, "what game Oppa plays with you." Laurentius's hand froze halfway to his mouth. He swung around so abruptly the wine slopped over the side of the cup. He placed it on the table, his hand shaking slightly as he did.

"That," he said slowly, trying to buy himself some time, "was not the question I was anticipating."

"No." Theo strode across the room and poured himself a cup of wine, then turned back to him. "But it is one I cannot ask my brother, since I believe both you and Shukra have kept certain matters from him."

Laurentius took a slow sip of wine, his eyes not leaving Theo's. "Go on."

"I believe," Theo said, "that Oppa has been playing the same game with us all. His usual tricks, shadows, and darkness." He paused, holding Laurentius's eyes. "Secrets."

"I assure you, Theo." Laurentius kept his tone even. "Neither Shukra nor I are strangers to the manner of game Oppa conducts. We know how to dance around such shadows." He smiled bitterly. "We have been doing it longer than either of us cares to remember."

"I have no doubt." Theo took another drink. "But it is not only you two with whom he plays. It is with my brother. My sister. My wife." His mouth tightened. "With me, Laurentius."

"Ah." Laurentius nodded slowly. "Illiberis." When Theo raised his eyebrows, Laurentius smiled grimly. "Even had Oppa not informed me of that himself, Athanagild and I already suspected. What does he have, Theo? A contract? A signature?"

"Both." The answer was hard and unforgiving, and Laurentius had to force himself not to wince at the pain behind it.

"How long," he said quietly, "have you carried this burden, Theo? Since the battle at Illiberis – or longer?"

"Longer." When Laurentius did not speak, Theo went on: "It was in Sebastopolis."

"And Lælia does not know."

"No." Theo sounded tired. "But she will. As soon as I get home." He paused, then continued: "But I am not here to lay that burden at your door, Laurentius. I am here to ask you to share your own."

It was not that he did not wish to speak, Laurentius found, but rather that he did not trust himself to. There was a gentleness in Theo's voice, a weariness, that was both disarming and touching.

"Shall I, perhaps, tell you his game, instead?" Theo gave him a small smile. "One of us, after all, must say it aloud.

"Oppa knows the nature of the relationship between you and my brother. He may have direct evidence of it, although, knowing your caution as I do, I doubt it. Whether he does or not, however, is not the point. He will contrive to expose you if you do not do as he pleases. He knows that Shukra wore the public face of guilt to draw eyes away from you and Athanagild." At that, Laurentius could not disguise his involuntary shudder, the excruciating shame he felt every time he so much as contemplated Shukra in that dark cell, covering for sins he himself had committed. "And now," Theo said quietly, "Oppa orders you to do three things: see that I sign Illiberis over to him. He asks that you ensure coin from the trade of silk flows into his pockets. And, above all, he instructs you to take command of the fleet by my side. At which stage he will, of course, begin to direct you as to how that fleet will conduct itself – and for which cause."

"You almost have it all." Laurentius's voice sounded old to his ears, rasping like a key in an unused lock. "If coin from the silk trade does not find its way to him, he will instruct his father that there is a rebellion brewing in Septem and see that Egica ends all alliance with Ilyan." Abruptly he turned, crossing the room and staring out of the window at the growing darkness. "But as I have already told you," he said quietly, "Shukra and I have managed such shadows before. We will find a way to manage Oppa, too."

"What if I told you I have already found a way?"

Laurentius swung around to find Theo half smiling, the arctic eyes glittering with a dangerous light that Laurentius, who had led many men to war, knew well. "Go on," he said tersely.

"No matter what Oppa says, he holds only two pieces of the game: that parchment, and Shukra in his dungeons." When Laurentius would have spoken, Theo held up his hand. "Yes, he threatens other things. To expose you and my brother. To end the alliance with Ilyan. To make my sister a whore and you an outcast. There is no end, it would seem, to Oppa's threats. I have heard them, Laurentius, in differing variations, a hundred times over the past years. Every time darker, more dangerous. Every time seeming poised to take everything from me. But here is the truth." He stepped forward, his face hard with excitement and anger. Gripping a chair back hard enough to turn his fingers white, he rocked it for emphasis as he spoke. "The parchment and Shukra are the only two weapons he actually holds. Neutralise those, Laurentius, and he is fundamentally disarmed."

"What, exactly, do you propose?"

"Oppa himself once said of that parchment that it has value only so long as it is a secret I wish kept." His fists clenched briefly. "And that particular secret," he said, "is no longer one I wish kept. When I leave Toletum I will ride to Aurariola and do what I should have done the moment I returned to Spania: tell Lælia about that document." A spasm of pain crossed his face. "It is too late to lessen the damage I have done," he said quietly, "but I can, at least, ensure no more is done by it. That leaves only Shukra." He gave Laurentius a hard smile. "And I do not think you have fought so many wars, Uncle, to find breaking into a dungeon so much of a challenge."

Laurentius stared at him, his heart beginning to thud with excitement. "I had the same thought," he said slowly, "long ago. At first I did not execute it at Shukra's explicit request.

Then I thought I might find another way. But since the day he took me captive…" He broke off, shaking his head. "Even before, perhaps, I confess, I have thought of nothing else."

Theo nodded. He stepped around the chair, came close to Laurentius at the window. "I know Oppa," he said, "in a way none of you can. We are… joined, in a way. It is the reason he has so often sought to bind me, and the reason I have so often allowed myself to be bound. Sometimes, what we believe to be the truth, in our own soul, becomes the truth by which we live, even when it has long ceased to be true at all." He gave Laurentius a twisted smile. "That little philosophy did not, for once, come from anyone else. I found it, believe it or not, in the depths of Shukra's dungeon, just recently. But once I saw it, I could not unsee it; and with it came a clear view of our escape from this mess.

"Oppa's power lies not in what he will do, but what he threatens to do. I have seen Oppa at his worst." His face hardened briefly, one hand unconsciously touching the whorls on his face. "His whip on my face; his abuse of young women; his betrayal of allies and alliance with enemies. I have seen all these things, over the years, and they have created a shadow in my soul that Oppa has used ever since, with good effect: the fear that I will see that darkness unleashed again, upon those I love. It is a shadow that finds men's guilt and shame, Laurentius, and makes of them weapons with which we torture ourselves."

"But weapons they are, nonetheless," said Laurentius quietly.

"No, they aren't," Theo said, with a certainty that took Laurentius slightly aback. "Not anymore. Not here, in Spania, where Oppa has returned with the aim of making it his own. I know his goal, Laurentius. Not the immediate goals; his long-term plan. Oppa wants Spania. He told me as much. But the irony is that here, nothing can be gained without alliances – and Oppa needs us all if he is to have those. Without us, each of us, Laurentius, he is one more step away from his goal.

"Oppa will not expose you. He will not destroy Athanag-ild's reputation. And he will not make of my sister a whore." Theo shrugged. "Oppa needs us, Laurentius. His threats are empty vessels."

Laurentius folded his arms sceptically. "That is a big gamble, Theo. And the stakes are too high."

"Think about it." Theo tapped the lattice with an impatient finger. "Oppa is cultivating Wittiza as his creature. Egilona is not only Wittiza's favourite, but the darling of the king, also. Athanagild is a favourite of Archbishop Felix and, unless I misunderstand the ways in which a man of his young years might advance so rapidly in such an institution, holds enough secrets about the bishops of Spania to undo the entire Church, should he so wish. Oppa may be a master of secrets, but Athanagild is of the Church in a way Oppa never will be. They protected him once. They will do so again, should they need to.

"And you, Laurentius, hold one of the most esteemed names in all Spania. Men look at you and see, in your villa and your library, the authority of the old Roman elite. You were supposedly neutral during the recent rebellion. Bishop and soldier alike listen when you speak, and Oppa knows it. If he wants the council to support his claims when the time comes, he needs your voice. And it is you who has been the official diplomatic tie with Ilyan." He strode restlessly across the room, then back to the window. "Ilyan loathes Oppa," he said meditatively, looking out at the garden beyond. "Even though he may now be willing to treat with Egica, he will never involve Oppa in his plans, nor entrust him with coin. For all that Oppa talks of exposing us, destroying us, it would serve nothing." He turned back to face Laurentius. "We are the greatest pieces in his game. If he wishes to control Spania, Oppa needs us."

Laurentius felt the jittery excitement course through him. "He needs us, you say." He looked at Theo. "But he doesn't need Shukra."

Theo nodded. "And nor does anyone else. Shukra is a foreigner who was condemned for treason and sodomy. His only value lies in Oppa using him against us."

There was a short silence, in which Laurentius's mind raced. When finally he looked back at Theo, he felt a decade younger. "Thank you, Theo," he said quietly, holding out his hand.

Theo nodded curtly. "Break him out, Laurentius. And leave Oppa to me."

MANY HOURS LATER, when Athanagild slipped through the side door from the garden, Laurentius was still sitting in the darkened study, the wine jug beside him empty.

"I got your message." Athanagild took in the two cups, and the empty jug, without comment. "What is it," he said, in a carefully even tone, "that is so important?"

Liberation, Laurentius thought with detachment, was as intoxicating as any wine. Exhilarating, even. "Athanagild," he said, hearing the odd quaver of excitement in his voice. "Do you recall what you asked me, when you returned to Toletum from Aurariola?"

A shadow crossed the angular features, a wariness that hurt Laurentius deep inside. Coming swiftly to his feet, he crossed the floor in a matter of paces and gripped Athanagild's shoulders, aching to take the lean frame in his arms. "Do you recall?" he asked again.

"Of course I recall." Athanagild's eyes glittered so similarly to the manner in which his brother's had earlier that Laurentius almost smiled. "I asked you why, if Shukra's imprisonment was going to tear you apart anyway, you did not simply rescue him, and set him free."

"And what did I tell you?"

Athanagild's jaw tensed. "That I did not understand what was at stake."

"And then you gave me a black eye that took a fortnight to

fade, and walked out." Grinning, Laurentius released him, walked over to the sideboard, unsealed a new jug of wine, and poured them both a cup.

"I'm glad the memory amuses you," Athanagild said, eyeing him cautiously. "I confess, it is not one of my favourites."

"What I did not tell you then," said Laurentius, his smile fading, "was that barely days before, Oppa had taken me captive. Right here, in fact," he added, looking around meditatively, "in this very room. Tied me to that chair, there" – he pointed – "and Shukra to the other one."

Every last hint of colour drained from Athanagild's face. He drained his cup and wordlessly held it out to be refilled, his eyes not leaving Laurentius's face.

"It is a story barely worth telling." At Athanagild's incredulous expression, Laurentius gave a bark of laughter that sounded uncharacteristically wild, even to his own ears. "Your brother was here, earlier," Laurentius said. "He reminded me of something every soldier learns early in their training. Something that lately, I had forgotten.

"An enemy only has power so long as you choose to believe he can defeat you. In reality, Athanagild, there is always a path to victory. One simply has to be brave, and patient, enough to find it."

Athanagild shook his head impatiently. "What are you trying to say, Laurentius?"

"You and I," Laurentius said slowly, "are going to break Shukra out of prison, Athanagild."

"Break him out," said Athanagild flatly. For a moment Laurentius felt a flash of concern – should he have left Athanagild out of his plans? The man was a priest, after all, not a soldier.

Then Athanagild grinned. It was an expression Laurentius thought he had never seen before on his lover's face, a wicked, lethal smile every bit as deadly as Theo's arctic glare, or Alaric's dark fury. It was the killing face of a son of Suinthila, and it sent a thrill through Laurentius's blood, the answering rush of a brother in arms.

Laurentius took a halting step forward then paused, the tension and uncertainty of the past months still a barrier between them. A moment later, though, it was Athanagild who closed the distance between them, meeting him in a rush of heat that was both sweet and fierce and was more than any words could say. Into the embrace flowed all the loneliness of their estrangement, the longing and unworthiness they had both fought as they each tried, in their own ways, to come to terms with the impossible betrayal of Shukra's imprisonment. Laurentius held Athanagild's face between his hands and stared into the vivid golden eyes in which he had, for so long now, found the only home that had ever mattered to him. Felt the intangible understanding that was the only solace his soul knew, and realised, with a hard, thrilling certainty, that what lay between them was all that mattered, now, and forever. Had he just trusted this feeling, Laurentius knew, they would have come to this place much earlier. Theo had been right in more ways than one: Oppa's only true power lay in Laurentius's own fears, the old, corrosive shame that had haunted some part of him every time he sought refuge in Athanagild's arms, the deep-seated fear that there was something inherently wrong with them both – and that neither of them deserved to feel what they did in these moments.

"I promise you," he said roughly, "that I will never turn away from what lies between us again, Athanagild. I will be worthy of this. Of you."

"I know." Athanagild nodded slowly, the understanding in his eyes an oath greater than any Laurentius had ever taken, to sword or country. "I have always known, Laurentius."

Stepping back, Athanagild gripped his shoulders. "Now," he said, with a return of the lethal smile that stirred every nerve in Laurentius's body, "tell me what we are going to do."

35

THEO

SEPTEMBER, AD 694

Aurariola, Spania
Orihuela, Spain

T he leaves had fallen, and taken the warmth with them, when Theo finally rode through the gates at Aurariola. He found the villa oddly quiet. Geila was in the stables with Tosius, Silas and Leofric with the dromons at the port. Lælia, the servants informed him, was in the library. Taking a deep breath, Theo touched the parchment inside his tunic and pushed open the door.

He found Lælia standing at the window, staring out over the fields. There was a strangely hard set to her mouth, a barely restrained tension in the hands clenched on the lattice screen. Jadis stood at her side, tail low and straight behind her, as still as if she were about to pounce upon an unseen enemy.

"Lælia." He waited, then cleared his throat and said her name again, this time more forcefully. "Lælia."

"Theo." She turned slowly from the window, her eyes glittering with a brittle light. Jadis growled softly. "You have returned." It was not a welcome, but rather a statement of fact, and Theo, wary of the expression in her face, did not try to embrace her.

"*Ja.*" He stepped forward. "And before we speak of other matters, there is something I must tell you."

Reaching inside his tunic, he withdrew the parchment, wrapped in leather, and laid it on the small round table between them. The sun caught it, gleaming off the leather roll. "It is a contract," he said quietly, without prevarication. "Between Oppa and myself. A contract that Oppa also holds, and which bears my name, and my signature." He spoke directly, not embellishing the story, nor trying to excuse it. "Next month, in Toletum, Oppa will require our public concession at court. He will present documents with our signatures to which you and I must attest. But even if we do not, he will present his copy of this contract, with a priest to testify it was I who signed it."

Lælia stared at the parchment but made no move to pick it up. "How long?" she asked simply. "When was it agreed?"

"Before the fall of Sebastopolis." Theo spoke ruthlessly, without apology or explanation. The time was long past, he knew, for either.

"And this contract." Theo could not read what was behind the topaz eyes. "What exactly does it say?" Jadis swung her long tail slowly, staring at him warily.

"It states that as your husband, I grant ownership of my portion of the Illiberis latifundium to Oppa." She did not flinch as he laid it out. "In simple terms, the contract grants Oppa ownership of Illiberis in exchange for Aurariola."

"And in exchange for our lives." Lælia's eyes did not leave his own. "The lives of your family."

Theo inclined his head. "Yes," he said reluctantly. "Those, too. But do not seek to excuse what I did, Lælia —"

"I know why you did what you did, Theo." She cut him off. Theo frowned but fell silent. "But you, I think, do not understand my mind at all." She tilted her head and stared into the distance behind him. "I have had time to think on

that," she said meditatively. "As I have on many other things."
Theo wanted to speak, but there was something in her
demeanour that stilled his tongue.

"I accepted your silence," she said. "From the moment
you came home and would not speak of Oppa, except for the
broad strokes of what happened between you. You told me of
Apsimar, and the battles you fought. The men who stood at
your side, or with whom you held an oar in slavery. But you
never spoke to me of what lies between you and Oppa; and I
accepted that. Worse, I took it as my own cue. I told myself
that you stayed silent so your suffering might not influence the
decisions I made about Illiberis. When you did not seek to
advise me, nor counsel me on a course of action, I chose to
believe it was because you respected my right to determine my
own fate, and that of my homeland." Her eyes, distant and
oddly emotionless, shifted back to his. "I was ashamed," she
said flatly, "of my weakness in seeking your direction. So
certain was I in the nobility of your character that I mistook
your restraint for respect, and your actions for love."

Every word was like a hammer blow. To stand and receive
them without flinching was, Theo thought bitterly, the very
least he could do now.

"Dahiya once told me, you know, that I was protected by
my family legacy, and by our betrothal." Her voice was curiously detached, rather than furious or accusing. "I thought
then that her words were unduly harsh. But in recent times I
have seen their truth. Known she was right. I accepted what
you told me because I have been raised to believe that men
will look after me, protect me. I did not allow myself to
consider the possibility that you might act out of interests
other than my own. No." She held up a hand as Theo began
to speak. "I do not blame you for so doing, Theo. I know
Oppa must have manipulated you into signing that document.
I know, too, that you signed it believing that doing so was your
only option to save me, and your family. And I do not doubt
you have regretted it almost every day since." The fierce pride

in her voice silenced Theo. Jadis paced between them, turning first this way, then that. "I, too," she said slowly, "have learned a little, of late, about regret."

"Silas told me," Theo said cautiously, "that Yosef had been here."

"Yes." Just that one word, again. Curiously formal, and utterly without emotion. "Yosef came to see me. But he is no longer our friend, Theo; or certainly not mine, at least. It was he who told me about your agreement with Oppa."

Theo blanched. "Yosef told you about it?"

"It was said in anger." Her mouth twisted with a sudden pain. "I said earlier that I assumed the nobility of your character." The words hurt as much the second time as they had the first, though Theo faced them without flinching. "But Yosef made me see that my own character is equally flawed." She met his eyes, the stark desolation in hers striking Theo at his core. "I thought to trade all Yosef has worked for to achieve my own ambitions. Not only trade it – but to Oppa, no less. The one man whom Yosef has every right not only to hate, but to wish dead. I considered his future to be synonymous with my own, when the reality, as he clearly pointed out, is that we have never been equals, he and I. I am the Lady of Illiberis. Yosef is a Jew from Garnata. He journeyed to the very edge of the Circle of Lands for a prize that I thought to trade as my own." Her eyes drove into Theo's own. "So yes, Theo. I know something of playing pieces I have no right to."

"Yosef." Theo's voice, rough and uneven, sounded like it belonged to someone else. "How was it left between you?"

Lælia passed him again. "Yosef plays his own game now," she said quietly. "I am not sure that he cares what happens to the Spania we know." Her eyes flashed with a sudden, hard light. "I am not sure I do, either."

She focused on him again. "The parchment." Her voice was resigned. "Is that all of it?"

Theo cleared his throat. "No."

"Tell me the whole."

Theo inclined his head. "Shukra," he said. "If I do not own the contract, Oppa has threatened to kill him."

Lælia nodded. Her eyes narrowed. "But that is not all, is it?"

"No, it is not." Theo glanced sideways out of the window, steeling himself to betray his brother. "He also threatened to tell the court that Athanagild was not corrupted by Archbishop Sisebut but instead went to him willingly." His mouth twisted with contempt. "He threatened to tell everyone about what Athanagild and Laurentius are to each other." He met her eyes. "Why did you not speak of it to me, Lælia? I know you understood the truth between them."

"It was not my secret to tell." She shrugged, her eyes glittering with that same strange light he could not read, something that made Theo terribly afraid inside. It was as if she had gone somewhere far away, somewhere he could not follow. He felt it as if someone had sheared away part of his soul. "But this secret," she said, her voice brittle with pride, "the contract – this secret was not yours, Theo. It belonged to me, as well. You have lied to me from the moment of your return."

Theo tasted bitter regret. All he could do was nod wordlessly. Bracing himself for a barrage, he was surprised when she abruptly changed the subject.

"What will happen now? Can Oppa still hurt you?"

You, Theo thought. *Not us.* Theo shook his head abruptly. "The next council will be held several weeks from now. It is there we must sign his papers. But the moment it is over, Shukra will be gone from those dungeons, and from Spania. Then, Oppa's last weapon will be gone."

Lælia nodded, almost, Theo thought with increasing fear, with disinterest. "Disarm him. That is a good plan, Theo." She half smiled. "One I am certain Athanagild and Laurentius welcomed."

"They did." Theo tried to return her smile. "My brother, it seems, has an almost unhealthy talent for diabolical plans."

"Yes." She looked away from him. "We all had much time to learn war in our own way, Theo."

Before Theo could ask what she meant, Lælia went on, the expression she turned to him almost disdainful. "Regardless of what is written upon any parchment," she said, "Illiberis belongs to the women who are born upon it. I will not see it transferred in a court by a man whose only claim to it is a childhood betrothal." Her words cut Theo as effectively as any sword edge could. "I will come to Toletum with you," she went on. "It is I who will stand in court, and I who will grant Oppa ownership of Illiberis. This much you owe me, Theudemir of Aurariola, and you will not deny me the right to do it."

"Of course not." Theo shook his head in bewilderment. "But I had not thought you would wish to be part of such a humiliation. It is my mistake, my sin against you. I should be the one to carry it."

"I would have traded Yosef's soul to save Illiberis, all the while telling myself I did it to save his life. That is my sin, one for which there may never be atonement." Her voice cracked like winter ice, exposing the turbulent waters beneath. "But nor can I absolve you of yours, Theo. And I will not allow you to give away twice what was never yours to trade.

"Illiberis is mine." Her eyes flashed dangerously, her voice regaining its strength, and Jadis growled low in her throat, staring at Theo with savage, accusing eyes. "I, and I alone, shall hand it to Oppa. You will stand beside me at court, and no man shall know I give it by coercion, rather than by my own decision. Do you understand me, Theo?"

He could only nod. *Here it is,* he thought dully. The destruction his misguided actions had caused.

"Then I shall prepare to leave." Lælia turned from him, not so much as having touched the leather roll on the table. "And we will ride to Toletum as soon as we might."

"Lælia." She paused at the door but did not turn to him. "What of – us?" Theo's voice was low and pained.

"You are my husband, Theo. Geila is our son. These are things that cannot be changed." She stopped abruptly, and for a moment, Theo thought she would say something else. But she did not, and a moment later, without once looking back, she left the room. Theo stared after her, wondering what had just taken place – and what it meant.

36

LÆLIA
OCTOBER, AD 694

Toletum, Spania
Toledo, Spain

Lælia stood in her bedchamber in Riccilo and Theodofred's domus, staring out at the morning sun glinting from the cobblestones, crystalline and sharp on the crisp air of the coming winter. From the upper level of her bedchamber she could see the nobility, dressed in their finest, making their way up to the gleaming palace on the hill. She watched them impassively, feeling nothing. Jadis's head turned swiftly to the door, though the cat did not move from her side.

"Tosius." Lælia spoke without turning around. "You are returned sooner than I anticipated." The little tribesman slipped into the room and closed the door. Lælia turned. "Were you seen? Did you find her?"

Tosius made a dismissive noise that was intended to convey both his disgust that she should ask such a question, and confirmation that he had succeeded. "The Riders were close to Septem. I was barely a day ashore before I found

458

them." Tosius gave her a slightly injured look, as if he had looked forward to rather more of a challenge.

"And?" Lælia stared past him, her mouth a grim line.

Tosius's eyes darkened. "The desert queen says she will remain in Septem for a full moon. If you wish to come, you must arrive before then – and nobody must know."

Lælia gave him a half smile that did not reach her eyes. "That is why I sent you." She looked at him briefly. "You will make the arrangements I ask for."

He nodded and listened impassively as she gave her orders. "Everything is already in place," she ended. "I need only that you ensure it is done as I wish."

Tosius nodded, but he didn't leave. Lælia frowned. "What is it?"

"*Dauhter.*" Tosius cleared his throat. "Geila – your son –"

"We will not speak of my son." Her words were harsh even to her own ears, and looking down, Lælia realised she was gripping the back of a carved wooden chair hard enough to impress marks into her palms. She drew a deep breath. "The white mare," she said quietly.

Tosius nodded slowly, his eyes dark and solemn. "I will send word to the tribes."

"Good." Nodding decisively, Lælia stepped away from the chair and gestured to the door. "Tell my husband I will join him downstairs." Turning away from the window, she looked around the room one last time.

She waited until she heard the bustle of movement in the atrium below, then she opened the door and descended the steps slowly. One by one Silas, Leofric, and Theo turned to watch her, and gradually their chatter fell silent. A shaft of hard winter sunlight fell across the atrium, catching the ruby eyes of the serpent torc she wore about her neck. It was Riccilo's, rather than the sapphire torc Lælia had been left by her mother. She had sent word to Riccilo asking that she might use it, and instead of offering a loan, Riccilo had given it to her. *Take it,* her aunt had written. *I no longer wish to be reminded of all we have lost.* Beneath it, hanging slightly lower and in the place where she should have worn a cross, lay the bone carving of the Illiberis brand, two serpents entwined about the staff of Hermes.

Her hair was piled high on her head in a mass of snaking curls. Rather than being covered with a wimple, as was the custom for married women, she wore her hair bare. Wended through the curls was a silver chain, from which hung the ruby that Dahiya had once given Acantha. It fell to the centre of Lælia's forehead in a fiery splash of red that matched perfectly the crimson wool of her gown. Just as Athanais's had been upon her arrival, Lælia's gown was cut daringly low, exposing far more of her cleavage than any Gothic noblewoman would deem seemly.

Lælia would face the Toletum court as the Lady of Illiberis, and as her ancestors would have expected.

She saw Theo's eyes narrow, but rather than harden in disapproval, his mouth twisted in a slight smile. "I remember that dress," he murmured as she took the last step toward him. "You wore it in your father's œca on the day you pretended to sign our contract of betrothal."

"Pretended?" Leofric raised his eyebrows and gave a great bark of laughter. "Your wife, it seems, has more intelligence even than I had first thought." He adjusted Geila in his arms, batting the small body away affectionately as Geila clutched at his beard. Briefly, Lælia rested one hand on her son's head, feeling the downy softness of his hair, the sturdy pudginess of his arm as her hand trailed down the little form. "You will take care of him, Leofric," she said, keeping her voice steady with an effort.

"We plan to go to the market. See the watersellers." Leofric grinned. "Your son, I suspect, will torture them all."

Lælia touched her lips swiftly to the small head and turned away quickly. She nodded at Theo, who watched her with the same shadowed wariness that had lain between them ever

since their conversation about Illiberis. "Then let us go," she
said.

* * *

LÆLIA WONDERED, as they entered through the tall wooden
doors into the marble-tiled council chamber, why she had ever
found the palace daunting. It smelled of unwashed bodies and
tension. The men muttering in small huddles by the walls
looked bloated with drink and good food, their eyes hard and
beady as they darted around, searching for other men of influence to whom they might affix themselves. The women gossiped
behind their hands, tittering in scandalised horror as Lælia
passed by and they took in her provocative garb. The bishops
clustered together by the dais glared at her, their faces dark and
forbidding. Lælia stared back at them implacably. Let them look.
None would dare interrupt today's proceedings over something
so unimportant as a pagan symbol. They had come to see the
might of Illiberis cowed, formally surrendered to the Crown.
The formal contracts had already been signed, would be delivered after the ceremony. Today was no more than theatre. Lælia
intended to stage a show they would not easily forget.

They came to stand beside Rekiberga and her husband.
Rekiberga met Lælia's eyes and nodded slightly, touching the
necklace at her throat. It was the coin of Geila, a coin once
worn by Alaric, and confirmation Rekiberga had received
Lælia's letter. Lælia nodded back then turned to the dais.

She stood quietly at Theo's side as the other business was
conducted – a betrothal here, the distribution of a rebel estate
there. Even more than a year after the Sixteenth Council of
Toletum in which much of the business of the rebellion had
been decided, there were claims still to be settled, lands still in
dispute. Egica sat in a large carved chair on the dais, Wittiza
at his right as these minor matters were settled. There were no
crowns in sight; those hung in the Basilica of Peter and Paul

461

and were not on display here. This was a matter of politics, not the Church. The Church had, after all, already blessed Egica and his son's co-rulership.

"Theudemir of Aurariola." As the clerk called her husband's name, the low murmur of voices fell silent. Theo, however, did not step forward. He inclined his head to the dais and spoke in a low, clear voice: "In the matter before the council today, it is my wife, Lælia of Illiberis, who will speak." There was a low murmur at this. Theo glanced sideways, but seeing Lælia's face, he offered no further comment.

She stepped forward.

"*Reiks*." She inclined her head to Egica but did not address him by name, and nor did she wait for him to answer when she went on, eliciting gasps from the assembled nobles. "The lands of Illiberis have been held by the women of my family since before the Romans came. Though by Gothic law it is my husband's signature that lies upon this contract, by the laws to which I was raised, only a woman can grant ownership of Illiberis lands." The faces of the clergy grew darker and the expressions of the nobility more scandalised. Lælia ignored them all. She was looking at Oppa, not Egica. He had waited too long for this moment, she knew, to allow it to be disturbed by the outraged propriety of the nobility. Sure enough, when Egica's face grew grim and forbidding and he looked as though he would object, Oppa stepped forward and murmured something in his father's ear that cause the man to subside, albeit reluctantly.

"Oppa Egicason." Lælia spoke in a high, clear voice that rang though the suddenly hushed council chamber. "I am the daughter of Callista of Illiberis, granddaughter of Acantha of Illiberis. I am the sole heir to the lands to which you lay claim, and I speak not only for the portion in my name, but the portion too that is granted by Gothic law to my husband, Theudemir of Aurariola. I have affixed my own signature to the contract you agreed with him." She held up the faded, worn parchment so the signature could be clearly seen. "I come before you today," she said steadily, "to grant you title to the Illiberis latifundium." She stepped forward, approaching the dais without waiting for permission, and did not kneel when she came close to the thrones there. She held out the rolled parchment to Oppa. He stared down at her with dark, wary eyes, and between them lay the ghost of the last time they had faced one another in a place such as this, when Lælia had contrived to humiliate him. Her mouth twisted slightly. "I do not come here to play games, Oppa Egicason," she said softly, still proffering the parchment. "You have guaranteed the safety and position of my husband, Theudemir of Aurariola. Of his sister, Egilona of Aurariola." She nodded at where Egilona, pale faced with tension, stood between Roderic and Pelayo at the side of the dais. "You have attested to the innocence of Athanagild of Aurariola, after his sufferings at the hands of a corrupt member of your own order, and guaranteed to offer him your guidance and protection. Do you freely attest to all of these things?"

Archbishop Felix stepped forward, red faced and furious. "I will hear no more of this!" he rasped. "It is not for any woman, and particularly one clad indecently and daring to wear the symbols of paganism in a house of God, to question the word or intention of a man of God, as Oppa is. You will cease your questions and relinquish your title without further incident or suffer the wrath of your king – and of God himself." The crowd murmured uneasily, and Egica, stony faced, frowned at his bastard son. Oppa, meeting his father's eyes, shook his head briefly, then stepped forward. One hand touched Felix's shoulder gently, and the bishop, glancing at him, moved stiffly aside, clearly furious.

Lælia did not move, her eyes never leaving Oppa's face.

"You offer Illiberis to me." Oppa's voice was low, but it carried clearly through the council. "With your own hand, and of your own free will, you cede your family latifundium to my hand?" There was the barest hint of incredulity in his words, as if now that it was taking place, he could not quite believe that it was happening. At the rear of the hall, the southern lords stood stony faced, glaring at the dais.

"I cede to you the title to Illiberis, yes."

Oppa's brows lowered, and he looked at her closely. "*The title to Illiberis.* Is this some trick of words, my lady? For I warn you, this contract is drawn up in the presence of men of God. It cannot be reversed, nor gainsaid. Once ceded, Illiberis is mine, as all in this council will attest."

The murmur grew louder, men nodding in agreement. Lælia waited until the chatter eased.

"I cede you the title to Illiberis," she said again, "for such things may be traded by men. Words upon paper speak of coin, of things made from stone and wood. But Illiberis is not coin, Oppa Egicason. It is not stone, nor wood. Not a villa or fields of grain or even a herd of horses.

"Illiberis is the earth upon which I was born, the caves in which I met my ancestors. It is paths you will never know, and songs you will never sing. Illiberis lives in my heart and my veins, and I in the very soil upon which your feet will now tread." She drew herself up and looked around the dais, meeting the eyes of the assembled clergy one by one, passing over both Egica and his son with disdain. "I grant you title to Illiberis, Oppa Egicason," she said, her voice ringing off the marble tiles. "But ownership of my land, you will never have, for that will forever belong to me and the daughters of my blood, who are born to a legacy no man can ever carry." Bowing her head, she held the title out again with both hands, and when Oppa did not take it, she let the leather-wrapped cylinder simply drop to the ground. It landed with a soft, flat sound, nonetheless clearly discernible in the hushed chamber. "Take it," she said coldly. "It is yours."

Then, not waiting for a dismissal, she turned and walked from the chamber. The nobles parted for her as she went, stepping aside, and this time none murmured behind their hands but simply watched in horrified fascination, waiting for the inevitable command for her to halt.

But it did not come.

Lælia heard a commotion on the dais behind her, but she did not turn, and she heard Oppa's sharp command to stand down. Whatever fate may have befallen her, Lælia knew, would have been quelled by Oppa's fear of what Theo might be compelled to say. It was only as she reached the doorway that chaos erupted behind her, the council bursting into excited, scandalised chatter.

She continued to walk without pause, down the hill and into Riccilo's domus, which was dark and silent, the servants and Geila gone to watch the spectacles at the market. She had been inside barely an hour when she heard Theo's familiar tread on the stairs.

"Where are you going?" His voice was wary, and he did not approach her as she stood beside the bed. The crimson gown lay upon the coverlet. Set neatly upon it were the silver torc and carved bone pendant. She was clad in a plain woollen gown, her hair bound in a long plait.

"Tonight I will stay with Rekiberga." She turned to face him. "She is miserable after the birth of her child, and I wish to bring her what comfort I may whilst she is in the capital."

"And after that?" Theo stared at her, his eyes hard and brilliant as a high mountain lake. "Where will you go after that, Lælia?" When she did not answer, his eyes travelled down to her throat, where the coin of Geila rested upon a leather cord, the lone adornment she wore. "You wear my grandfather's coin," he said roughly. "The coin I sent you long ago, from Barca."

"I have never taken it off." Lælia stepped forward, touching his face with one hand, her eyes searching his. "I will never take it off, Theo. Not ever. It is part of my soul – as are you."

His hand covered her own, and for a long moment they stared at each other.

"But the other part," he said hoarsely, "I gave away. I know what I did, Lælia. Never think I do not."

"You did what you thought was your duty." Her heart twisted painfully. "But your duty gave away the part of me that you never had a right to, Theo. And unlike when I waited for you, this time there is no hope it will be returned. You committed me to half a life."

"Is it enough?" Desperation made his voice ragged. "Can we not make it enough, Lælia?"

They stared at one another in the dim light, shadows drawing close. Words rose in her throat only to die there. Accusations, and declarations. Words, she knew with tired certainty, that could neither heal, nor hurt, any more than those already spoken.

The words did not exist, Lælia knew, to fix what was broken between them.

"Rekiberga is expecting me," she whispered, the words catching in her throat. "Let me go, Theo."

His eyes were hollow caverns, his face a pale mask. She left him there, standing in their bedchamber, staring into the space where only a moment ago she had been.

* * *

The night was black and starless, smoke from the feast fires covering the sky. Toletum was celebrating, as it always did at the opening of the political season.

None noticed the two cloaked figures riding down a narrow alley that led to the bridge over the river. There were many visitors to Toletum who chose to leave after dark, and without being seen. The two were clad in the skin cloaks favoured by the tribes, and they wore humble clothes. Perhaps the only notable features were the horses they rode; those were of undeniable quality. Then again, many of the tribes came to Toletum to trade in horseflesh. There was nothing particularly unusual to see. Those who might have been alert to such things did not mark the couple's passing, and by midnight they were through the olive groves on the edge of Toletum and into

466

the hidden pathways of forest and mountain known only to the tribes.

Lælia rode behind Tosius, wrapped in her cloak, her face, twisted with grief at leaving behind all those she loved, well hidden in swathes of cloth.

Lælia's hand stole down to her belly, as it had a hundred times in the past month, since first she had felt the child's presence inside her. "Take note, my daughter," she whispered under her breath. "Feel the earth beneath the horse's hooves as we cover it, for this is your land. Your home. And one day, I swear it to you, we will come back to it.

"But not yet, my daughter.

"Not yet."

37

LAURENTIUS

NOVEMBER, AD 694

Toletum, Spania
Toledo, Spain

The night was late, and despite the king's council having ended a week before, many of the nobles had yet to leave. Toletum was still abuzz with men and drink. Laurentius looked around the court blearily. To any casual observer he seemed, as all the others in the chamber by that late hour, insensible with drink.

Oppa was at the high table, between his father and Wittiza. Two of the northern lords hovered nearby, hoping for a chance to speak. Egilona sat on Egica's other side, smiling sweetly up at the king, her maid waiting attentively behind her chair. Roderic leaned around her, craning his neck to gain her attention, whilst Pelayo lounged in the chair next to him, grinning. Laurentius stared at the high table, his red-rimmed eyes bitter with resentment and humiliation. Oppa's eyes passed over him, then returned. A sly, insidious smile stretched across Oppa's mouth; he raised a cup in an ironic salute. His amusement deepened when Laurentius made to return the gesture but instead clumsily sloshed wine across the table, garnering disapproving scowls and pointed reprimands from several of the nobles close by. Oppa's eyes moved pointedly to rest on Athanagild, pale and wan at the edge of the room, clustered with Archbishop Felix. Athanagild met Oppa's eyes, flamed with colour, and dropped his eyes with every attitude of one entirely cowed. Oppa smirked as he looked deliberately between the two.

It took another hour before the interminable evening began to wind down, and Oppa, clearly deciding the action had moved to the more interesting entertainment of his brothel, slipped from the room.

Unnoticed by any at the table, most of whom were, by now, as insensible as Laurentius had feigned being himself, Laurentius slipped from the room. Across the tables, Athanagild was engaged in a deep debate with a priest from the monastery, oiled by substantial quantities of wine.

Oppa was some distance ahead of Laurentius, flanked on either side by guards. Laurentius remained in the shadows.

Close to the brothel, two palace guards ran down the street, calling to Oppa, who came to a halt and turned in annoyance. "What is it?"

"Two men," said one of them, puffing. "Rebels from the northern border. They tried to overpower the guards at the dungeon. You told us to tell you if anyone tried anything –"

"Where are they now?"

"Chained up, Fráuja." One of the guards grinned. "And sorry they ever tried it."

"And the guards themselves?"

One of the men shrugged. "Beaten up pretty badly."

"See that they are replaced immediately. Wounded guards are careless."

"Yes, Fráuja."

"And keep the northerners in chains. I will attend to them myself, tomorrow." He shook his head. "I thought we killed the traitors from the north."

"Most of them, Fráuja. There are a few still alive, on the order of your brother Wittiza. Friends of Pelayo, I understand."

Oppa's eyes flashed with annoyance, but he did not speak, just nodded curtly and continued on his way.

Laurentius followed him through the silent streets until Oppa entered the low door by the river. Laurentius waited a full hour, at which time a group of the southern lords approached, passing a wine jug between them and joking loudly.

"We will keep him entertained until past dawn," muttered one of them as they passed Laurentius's hiding place. "Oppa believes we are finally falling at his feet."

Laurentius grinned. "I owe you one."

"No." The man met his eyes, all trace of drunkenness gone. "My son was on the fleet that bastard sank. It is I who owe you a debt." Nodding, he rapped sharply on the door and cried out drunkenly to be admitted. A moment later, the door opened and the men were gone.

Laurentius slipped back through the shadows to a bathhouse on the edge of town. The brothel at the front of it was long deserted, but the scent of rose and almond still lingered in the cold walls. He opened the door from the street and slipped inside to wait.

He sat on the bench that lined the walls, stared into the darkness, and thought of all the times Athanagild must have sat in this same room, whispering information to Shukra, risking his life that Laurentius might have the slightest advantage. His heart twisted at the thought of his old friend sitting on this same bench, forced to hear the whispers he knew came at such a high price.

For what? Laurentius thought tiredly. *All of it, for a rebellion that failed.* All their carefully laid plans, he and Ilyan, Paulus, and Arun. And what had they achieved? Yosef was exiled and, according to Theo, estranged from Lælia. Lælia herself had lost Illiberis, the key to the bulwark he had once envisaged making of the south. And all of Suinthila's children were, in some way or another, held captive by the very man they had dared to believe they might unseat.

No, Laurentius thought, as he lit an oil lamp, the Spania he had come home to was gone, and the Spania he had planned to create was more distant than ever. Nothing had eventuated as he had hoped. All he could wish now was that this one, terrible wrong could be righted. Beyond that, Laurentius thought, he cared little.

"*Aziz-am.*"

Laurentius stiffened, almost afraid to let himself feel hope as the door opened and a slim figure slipped inside. "I had thought," Shukra said dryly, putting back his hood so his face was visible in the low light, "that your choice of meeting places might have more taste than mine."

"And I thought," Laurentius said, struggling to keep his voice steady, "that you would be more comfortable in close proximity to a whorehouse."

"Ah." Shukra lifted a thin shoulder, the ghost of a smile flitting across the wasted hollows of his face. "My cock, you must understand, is still learning it is to remain attached to my body. It may take a while before it is fit for much else." There was a pause, during which both men stared at one another; then Laurentius caught his friend in a hard, wordless embrace, and for a long moment, that was how they stood, the two old brothers in arms.

Finally Shukra pounded his back and stepped backward. "Almost a full hour I am out of that stinking dungeon," he said amiably, "and you are yet to offer me wine. Do you have brain, man, or simply no heart?"

"Cretin." Laurentius passed him a flask and nodded at a large pail of water close by. "Water and soap, too. Even a whore would not touch you as you are now." He nodded ironically at their surroundings. "And it is a bathhouse, after all."

"You are not, it seems, entirely useless, *aziz-am.*" Shukra stripped and began washing. "It was not a terrible plan. The new guards were yours, I imagine?"

"A gift from our southern friends."

"Ah. Then releasing the northern prisoners was an especially nice touch."

"Thank you." Laurentius inclined his head sardonically. "I am glad the manner of your escape meets with your approval."

"I must ask, though." Shukra kept his face averted. "Was I unclear, in my instructions? Your friends did not give me a deal of time to argue, you understand, but I had thought we were agreed that I would remain where I was."

Laurentius shrugged. "I changed my mind."

"Hm." Shukra shot him a curious look. "I am not entirely unhappy, you understand. The guards were not such good company, and I did crave wine." He took a mouthful and screwed up his face in distaste. "Although Spania still, it seems, cannot make it to my taste."

"Then it is well," said Laurentius, smiling, "that you will be drinking wine in Septem from now on."

"Well indeed." Shukra finished pulling on a fresh tunic and drank deeply again. He eyed Laurentius. "And you, *aziz-am?*"

"I will stay." Laurentius met his eyes with a half smile.

"Ah." Shukra nodded gently. "I am glad."

"Are you?" Laurentius laughed bitterly. "I wonder, sometimes, what is the point. But Athanagild would never be happy if we left. And there is Theo, and Lælia..." His voice broke off.

Shukra looked at him narrowly. "What of Yosef?"

There was a long silence. "I fear," said Laurentius quietly, "that Yosef might, for a time at least, be lost to us."

There was a low noise beyond the door, and Laurentius stood. "I wish I could tell you more," he said, "but we have no time. There is a tribesman outside the door with a horse for you, and Sexi is many days' ride. Go swiftly, and stay in the shadows."

Shukra rolled his eyes. "And now," he said, with an exaggerated swirl of his cloak, "you presume to tell me how to remain in shadows. You! Whom I taught all he knows!" Shaking his head in mock despair, he pulled the cloak over his head and was instantly a bent, wizened old man.

Laurentius shook his head admiringly. "Magician," he murmured, his heart twisting.

"Perhaps." Shukra's voice was dry beneath his cloak. "But even this magician, *aziz-am*, cannot conjure wine, so I am hoping you have packed a large flask for the ride."

He reached out and gripped Laurentius's arm firmly, his eyes momentarily flashing from beneath the hood.

"I owe you my life."

Laurentius returned the grip. "As I owe you mine, many times over."

"Then we will drink wine together again, *aziz-am*." Opening the door and looking carefully either way before swinging himself onto the waiting horse, Shukra cast him a last glance. "Until the next cup."

"Until the next cup."

Laurentius watched them until the two horses were taken by the shadows.

Then he returned to his family villa, where he lay awake until dawn came, bringing with it another day of lies, subterfuge, and danger.

And friendship, Laurentius thought as he rose from his bed with a surge of purpose. He saw Shukra's hooded figure and then, in a flash of heat, Athanagild's fierce eyes.

And love, he thought, hope surging in his heart as he strode toward the palace gates.

Love, friendship, and duty.

What more, he wondered, could any man ask of his life, than to understand what those things meant — and fight for them?

"Good thoughts," he murmured, smiling to himself. "Good words. Good deeds."

The gates to the palace opened at his command, and Laurentius Severianus, soldier, statesman, and spy, entered, schooling his face into bland lines with the discipline of long practice.

THEO
NOVEMBER, AD 694

Toletum, Spania
Toledo, Spain

Theo —

I have left Toletum. By the time you read this, I will have left Spania.

I do not intend to wage war for Illiberis. I will do nothing that will jeopardise your life, nor that of our family, for I consider Egilona, Athanagild, and Laurentius as much my family as you and Geila. I cannot, however, remain in Spania and play the part that has been made for me. This is not my life, and I am not that woman. I never was. You asked me if that life is not enough; I tell you now that it would only ever, for me, be another form of death.

I am gone to Septem and then, gods willing, to Dahiya. I do not know what fate will bring me. I know only where I must go now.

Geila will stay with you. He is born of Aurariola, and to Aurariola he will always belong. I have sent a tribesman to bring Pallas, the white mare, to Aurariola. She is a gift to our son, a part of me he might keep, should you allow it.

Her twin, Ares, the black stallion, I take with me to Africa, where he will learn war as you once did. Like this, I will always have a piece of you with me. The twin foals we once brought into the world have always kept us bound one to the other, just as the amulet and coin have kept our promise alive. I can no longer wear the amulet of Illiberis. I gave away my right to bear it, and this my ancestors saw. Until the day a woman of my blood walks Illiberis land once again and calls it home, I will not wear the amulet, for I do not deserve to. The coin of Geila, however — *this I will wear forever, for it binds me to you, Theo, as does the black colt, and that bond is not one I can break even if I wished to.*

I do not leave you, Theo. I do not leave our son.

I leave a life I cannot lead.

Your wife,

Lælia

THEO FOLDED the letter for the hundredth time and placed it back in his tunic, his hands clenching and unclenching the wrought-iron bars over the window.

He knew he should have left the city by now. If he was honest, he had known from the moment Lælia left the domus for Rekiberga's that he should leave, should simply sweep Lælia onto his horse, bind her if he must, and take them all back to Aurariola. But he had not.

Instead he had sat by the window all that first night, watching the smoke swirl into the city sky so the stars were obscured, listening to the raucous sounds of men drinking in the streets. He had sat with Geila sleeping in his arms, and he had waited.

In the early morning hours he had roused a servant, sending the man to the domus of Rekiberga and Ataulfo. The servant had returned with the news that the household, including Lælia, was abed and not to be disturbed. Despite his own misgivings, Theo had been reluctant to cause any further scandal by sending another messenger. Servants in Toletum gossiped even more than the nobility at court. He would not humiliate Lælia by giving them cause.

When he had not heard anything by sunset the following day, he went to the domus himself. It was closed up, Rekiberga and Ataulfo having left for their lands in the north, according to a disdainful servant. No, he told Theo. Lælia had not been amongst those in the party.

It was no more than Theo had, somewhere inside himself, already known.

But something within him had still hoped she would come back. That she had gone, as she often did, to ride alone in the wild places. He had hoped – even though he had known, deep down, that it was futile – that she would return.

And so he had waited, and stalled, and told himself he should not worry. He had refused all visitors, kept even Silas and Leofric at bay. He had done this even after he had heard word that the king had convened another of his interminable, damned councils, due to be held this very day. Barely any notice had been given and only a few bishops would attend – Oppa amongst them. Perhaps it had been his awareness of Oppa's proximity that had jolted him from his stupor. Perhaps it was the cold winter winds stealing through the windows.

Either way, he had woken this morning, still fully clothed, from a fitful hour of snatched sleep to find a rolled parchment on the pillow beside him, and an open window where the stealthy messenger had slipped in and out of the room in a way only those of the tribes could manage. He had unrolled the parchment slowly, already knowing what it would contain, but unwilling to believe it even after he had read it a hundred times.

"It is time we left this place, *wenkai*."

Theo started at Silas's low voice from the doorway; he hadn't even noticed the big man approaching. "Where is Geila?" he asked without turning around.

"Your *son* is in the stables with Leofric."

Theo flinched at the subtle rebuke. "I will go to him." He turned away from the window. "I should not have left him alone so long."

"It is not your son that concerns me." Silas stepped into his path, blocking the doorway. "What is in that letter you read over and over, *wenkai*?" He folded his arms, staring directly at Theo. A moment later, the sound of a heavy tread came up the stairs. Leofric entered, Geila gurgling in his arms. Theo's hand rested briefly on his son's head. The boy reached for him with pudgy arms, and Theo, his heart twisting, took the small body and held him against his chest. He must be both mother and father, now; he must be all that Geila needed. "Leofric," he said quietly. "Send for my brother, and Laurentius, and ask them to join us at meat. I will address all of you at once."

The two men looked at Theo, then at one another, then went silently to do as he had asked.

The afternoon was quiet and cold when Athanagild and Laurentius arrived, joining Theo, Silas, and Leofric at the low table set amid old Roman-style lectas. Geila was sleeping peacefully on a cushion at Theo's side. Athanagild, seeing the small figure curled up by Theo, frowned slightly. Theo ignored his unspoken question.

"It seems that Shukra is gone." He nodded at Laurentius, who grinned back.

"It does seem that way, yes," Athanagild said, his eyes gleaming wickedly.

"I am glad," said Theo quietly.

"Where is Lælia?" Athanagild glanced around. "She, too, will enjoy this story, I think."

Theo took his time before finally answering the question. "I believe," he said slowly, "that it is likely Shukra would be better placed to answer that question than I." He looked around at the expectant faces. "By now, Lælia will be with Ilyan, in Septem."

"Septem." Athanagild looked at Theo blankly. "Lælia has gone to Septem? Why? To join the rebellion there?" His face tightened. "After what I heard at the council today, there will be no rebellion left to join. It is done, Theo. Egica used the whispers of rebellion to impose the harshest strictures yet upon the Jews of Spania at his council. Any who have not yet converted will almost certainly be executed, if they do not flee before they are caught. And I had thought Ilyan had more sense —"

"Lælia does not ride to the rebellion." Theo cut him off. "We both knew there was no chance for it to succeed, even before this council of Egica's was announced." Theo's heart twisted again. He cleared his throat and forced his voice under control as he brought out the parchment, though he didn't unfold it. "Lælia left Toletum the night after she ceded Illiberis in court. She has gone to Ilyan, and from there, if she can, to join Dahiya and her forces." Ignoring the startled expressions and Laurentius's sharp intake of breath, Theo went on, "I do not expect her back."

Athanagild leaned forward, staring at Theo, his hands clasped between his knees. "This is all you intend to say, Theo? How long have you known of this?"

"Days. Since the day in court." Theo shrugged. "I had hoped my suspicions unfounded, until I received a letter from Lælia this morning. I believe it was sent from the port, at Sexi. Wherever it came from, I know she is gone from Spania's shores. I can feel it," he said, unsure whether he was speaking to himself or to the room. "Inside. I know she is gone. I think I knew all along, in my heart."

In the short, uncomfortable silence that greeted these words, Theo turned to Silas. "You will ride from here tomorrow," he said, "if you are willing. You will join Lælia in Africa, and stay at her side. Be the sword at her back, as you have been mine all these years."

Silas nodded gravely. "This, I will do, with pride, *wenkai*. It is right that I should do so." Theo saw his own shame mirrored in the other man's eyes, and he understood that Silas, too, must live with his regrets. "I will protect her life with my own." Silas put his hand over his heart. "You have my word."

Theo tried and failed to smile. "I thank you."

"Wait." Leofric looked between Silas and Theo in blank astonishment. "You will just let your woman ride from you, like this? The mother of your own son, *schnecke*? You do not so much as saddle your horse to bring her back?" When nobody spoke, he made a snort of disgust. "Are you man, Theo, or willow stick?"

Theo opened his mouth to answer, but he was interrupted by Athanagild. There were high spots of colour in his cheeks and gold gleamed hard in his hazel eyes. "Was it because of us?" Leaning across the table, he gripped Theo's arm, shame and fury warring in his eyes. "Tell me you did not trade Illiberis to protect us –"

"This was not your fault." Theo cut him off, frowning at Leofric to stop the question writ on the other man's face. "And nor is it Lælia's." He drew a deep breath. "It was just as you had already guessed," he said, looking at Athanagild, "and as you rightly warned me, though I was too blinded by hubris to see it. In Sebastopolis, I signed a contract with Oppa – ceding Illiberis in exchange for Aurariola, and for my life."

Leofric snorted. "Not just your life, *shnecke*. No." He held up a hand when Theo began to object. "I will not sit here and listen to you take the blame for this, as always you do.

"Theo put his name to that parchment because he was told Lælia's life, and the lives of his family, depended upon him doing so. He believed the rebellion lost, his father and brother condemned as traitors, Illiberis already taken – and, on top of that, he believed his own men had betrayed him." When Theo made an impatient sound, Leofric again held up his hand, glaring around the table at Athanagild and Laurentius. "You here, in Spania, you are thinking you know of war. But you do not. Not of what it was like in Sebastopolis, where all men have secrets and those secrets mean the death of thousands. Even then, amid all that, he thought to save you, not himself. He signed that parchment knowing it would mean losing Lælia either way – if he did not, she would be forced to marry against her will; if he did, she would blame him for giving up her family land. And still he did it, because this *schnecke*, it is what he does, the right thing, no matter the cost." He cleared his throat, colouring, clearly embarrassed at the emotion in his voice. "You will not be blaming him for this," he muttered. "And your wife, *schnecke*, forgive me, but she also should not be blaming you for this."

A short silence greeted this uncharacteristically long speech.

"And so she left?" Athanagild could not keep the edge from his voice. "Despite knowing the reasons, still Lælia left you – and her son?"

"Do not blame her." Theo rose suddenly, unable to sit still, and stalked across the room, his eyes on his sleeping son. "She did not blame me. She understood – she always understood." He could not hide the bitterness in his tone. "You were right, long ago, Athanagild, in your warnings to me. I gave away the thing I had no right to. The fault is mine, no matter what Leofric says. No," he said, as Leofric began to protest, "it is true. Both you and Silas warned me not to deal with Oppa. The mistake was mine, one I have regretted every day since my hand signed that parchment."

"But it did save her." They all turned to Laurentius, whose voice was gravelly, his eyes dark cavernous holes, the carefree grin of earlier gone. "Even if she is not here, your sacrifice saved her life. Perhaps it might not be the one she dreamed of, but yet she is free to live it as she chooses, rather than as Oppa's pawn at court – or dead on the gallows. Whether she sees it or not, your name on that parchment saved us all, Theo, the fleet included. And after your public concession of Illiberis, you have the king's trust, as well." He looked at Theo with wary respect. "You have sacrificed everything for this," he said quietly. "For Spania."

"For Spania!" Athanagild spat the words viciously. "And what is Spania, anymore, this damnable idea that has killed our fathers and brothers? It has taken your wife, Theo. What else will you give? Your son?"

Theo put his hands on his hips, his head sinking down as he shook it. He felt tired, to the bone. When he looked back up, they were all watching him. "My son must make his own choices, when the time comes," he said quietly. "Until that time, I must be both mother and father to him, as his mother entrusted me to be. For that," he said, turning to Leofric, "I would be honoured if you would remain here, by my side. I need your help to train the fleet – and my son needs you to be with him when I am not and, perhaps, even when I am. I know it is much to ask, when you and Silas have fought side by side for many years. But ask it I will, though I shall understand if you wish to ride instead with him."

Leofric had paled whilst he spoke, and for a moment, Theo thought he would refuse. Then the Slav's hard black eyes moved over to the cushions where Geila lay, and they softened. "Pah!" he said, waving his hand at Silas. "This one, I have taught him all I know. If he cannot protect a woman after all I have done, then he is not a man." He met Silas's eyes. It was not a long look, but when Silas reached out his arm, Leofric took it, hard and briefly, then nodded. "I will stay," he said decisively. "The *schnecke* needs me more, I am thinking, than even you."

Theo found he could not speak. He had not, he realised, known what he would do if the Slav had not agreed.

"But what will she do?" Athanagild was still tense. "Lælia? Where is it that she will go? Does she hope to win back Illiberis?"

"I am not sure that even she herself knows what her future plans will be." Theo met his brother's eyes and found his mouth twisting into a rictus smile. "She knows only that she cannot stay here," he said softly. "The life my choices created for us is, to Lælia, no more than a living death. It is my eternal shame that I did not understand that. And no matter how I might hate it, or how much I might want to mount my horse and force her back, at sword point if need be, I know that I cannot." He looked around the table. "Lælia is no ordinary woman," he said, and his voice found an odd strength. "She never was. And the promises we made are not easily broken. Forcing her back here, however, would be the one sure way to break them forever. I will not do that. I will raise our son as she entrusted me to do, and I will raise him to honour his mother." Geila woke at that, crying aloud, and Theo bent down to pick him up. "For she is the bravest woman I know," he said softly, staring into his son's eyes. "And I have to believe, even if she can never forgive what I have done, that she will, one day, find her way back to me. To us."

They sat in the room until the night was late around them, drinking wine together as men do when they mourn, and before they part.

When morning came, Laurentius and Athanagild left, calmer and more at peace than Theo had seen them since his return. Leofric was asleep, Geila tucked against his chest.

And Silas was gone, riding with the rising sun, to Africa — and Lælia's side.

39

OPPA

MARCH, AD 695

Toletum, Spania
Toledo, Spain

Spring was coming. It was, Oppa had decided, time to leave the city and visit his new latifundium. "The south is particularly beautiful in the spring," he said to Wittiza as they rode. "The last time you visited Illiberis you were a boy, and I was a bishop. Now, you are co-ruler with our father – and I am archbishop of Hispalis. We both deserve a good rest from the offices we carry, do you not agree, brother?"

"I believe you make my office far easier than it would otherwise be." Wittiza shot his older brother a grateful glance. He had grown much over the past year since the ceremony in which he had been declared co-ruler. But though he was taller than before, and his face carried the shadow of a beard, still he was plump, his eyes sunk into pudgy, indecisive features. He resembled his mother, Cixilo, far more than he did Egica, his father. He looked now at Oppa with the familiar expression of gratitude and awe that Oppa found both amusing and mildly

484

repulsive. The boy was so dumb, he sometimes thought, as to be almost considered a simpleton. He truly believed Oppa to be both saviour and mentor. And Egica, rather than suspecting Oppa's motives, as he once would have, seemed almost pathetically content to allow Oppa to lead Wittiza where he may. Oppa had begun to suspect, based on the whispered reports of some of the palace servants, that Egica himself was actually losing his wits. The reports were no more, for now, than whispers, and they would not be any more than that until it suited Oppa for it to be so. But for now, he allowed his father to continue sitting beneath the crown, though he ensured that he, Oppa, was never far distant when he did.

"I am here to serve you, brother. I have told you this before, *ne*?" He shot Wittiza a brief smile.

"Still." Wittiza frowned. "I think you should have more than just the bishopric of Hispalis, and a latifundium in the southern backwaters."

"Ah." Oppa tilted his head in an appearance of humility. "But I was not born to the court as you were, my brother. I dislike ostentation. My place is at your side, serving your reign as I might. Illiberis is more than enough for my needs, as Hispalis is all the clerical responsibility I can manage."

That was no lie. In fact, Oppa had been obliged to confer an indecent sum of money on an entire team of clerics to run Hispalis in his almost permanent absence. His own businesses consumed far more time, and produced far more of worth, than the seat of Hispalis; and besides, he had neither the knowledge nor the interest to manage such an important ecclesiastical position. The Church tolerated his light touch for the twin reasons that he did not interfere with their business and he helped ensure their taxes were paid on time, along with added coin that they might use for their own discretion.

To Oppa's knowledge, none of that coin had yet found its way to church roofs, or the building of monasteries. Several of his priests, however, had managed to build themselves rather impressive dwellings. He wished them well.

"I wish Roderic and Pelayo could be here," said Wittiza wistfully. He glanced behind them, at where a heavily veiled Elpis rode a fine horse, flanked on either side by two of Wittiza's *gardingi*. "I wish they could meet Elpis properly, too."

"It is wise to keep such matters private, brother." Oppa gave him a benevolent smile. "A prince's friends should never know his secrets. And Roderic and Pelayo can, I believe, best serve you by learning the art of war in Count Theudemir's fleet."

"You and he fought together, did you not?" Wittiza turned eyes shining with adoration to Oppa. "On the field at Sebastopolis?"

"Oh, we fought together many times," said Oppa, white teeth gleaming in the hard southern sunlight as he smiled. Had anyone been looking closely, they might have seen an odd light flash in his eyes as he spoke, but then again, it could have been a trick of the sun.

"Roderic said that you set off in the fleet together."

"We were intended to do so, yes. Unfortunately, winter came early that year, and fierce storms raged across the seas. Pirates took advantage, and most of the fleet was lost in one of their attacks, Count Theudemir's dromon amongst them."

"But you saved him." Wittiza's eyes shone.

"Men do not speak of such things, brother." Oppa's smile was mysterious.

"But men at court do. They say you plucked Count Theudemir from the sea, back then, just as you saved him from the battlefield at Sebastopolis. They say that is why his wife gave you her latifundium – even though, I know, she gave it with ill grace." He grimaced. "My friends said it was ill done of her, and done only at her husband's behest. They say that even now the southern lords deny you access to their ports in her name, though they kneel to you at court and say pretty words."

Oppa's mouth tightened. "Such rumours are naught but court gossip, and not worthy of your ears."

"Such things do not matter, anyway, not when you and Count Theudemir work in such accord now, and for the same goal. It is common, men say, for allies to forget their anger when they fight at one another's side. If you and Count Theudemir can do so, in time the southern lords will surely follow." Wittiza's admiration was almost breathless. "I know you will not admit to your heroism, brother, nor speak of your battles. I have heard it is so for many of those who have fought dark wars, that they do not like to tell tales of their exploits. But I wish you to know that I know of them – and admire you for them."

They rode together over the last pass, and Oppa reined in their horses at the top of the descent, looking down at the valley of Illiberis laid out before him.

Though he had taken it in sight of all men, the door to Illiberis's treasures remained, still, stubbornly closed to him. But Oppa was nothing if not a patient man. He would find the key, no matter how long it took, nor the lives he must destroy.

Wittiza, still clearly thinking of their previous conversation, sighed. "I hope that one day I, too, might have deeds to my name of such glory as you."

Oppa reached out and gripped Wittiza's shoulder.

"You will, brother," he said softly. "I shall see to it that you will."

AFTERWORD

Please do leave a review if you enjoyed Spania. It helps so very much.

If you'd like to be an advance reader for future books in the series, please do go to www.paulaconstant.com - you can also download Saharan Queen, the prequel novella for the series for free there when you sign up.

These books are a personal labour of love. I believe the story of the fall of Visigothic Spain, and rise of Arabic al Andalus, has many parallels with today's world.

There are lessons to be taken from the past, if we choose to heed them . . .

ACKNOWLEDGMENTS

Writing historical fiction set so far in the past is challenging on many levels. I'm extraordinarily grateful to all those academics who have so patiently answered my very specific questions on a variety of topics. I'm also utterly indebted to my brilliant editor, Kahina Necaise, who truly knows how to get the best from me and the stories I want to tell. To you, and all the team at the wonderful History Quill editing group, I am forever grateful for your patience, care, and professionalism.

Most of all, thank you to my wonderful advance reader team, who picked up the final (I hope) small errors and took the time to pass them on. I am very fortunate to have such an experienced and professional group reading the book! You're amazing.

ABOUT THE AUTHOR

Between 2004-2007, Paula Constant walked over 12000km through eight countries, including 7000km through the Sahara with her own camels and only local nomads for support. She wrote two books about her journey, Sahara and Slow Journey South, both published by Random House. The Visigoths of Spain series was conceived on that journey. She moved to Granada (Illiberis) in Spain where she lived for several years whilst researching the series. She now lives in Broome, Western Australia, and also writes fantasy romance under the pen name Lucy Holden. If you'd like more free samples, and to stay in touch, go to www.paulaconstant.com, and sign up.